FEAR THE ABYSS

EDITED BY ERIC BEEBE

POST MORTEM PRESS

CINCINNATI

Post Mortem Press Cincinnati, OH

www.postmortem-press.com

FIRST EDITION

Printed in the United States of America

ISBN: 978-0615732510

TABLE OF CONTENTS

Without authors, there would be no Post Mortem Press. This book is dedicated to the brave writers who have joined me aboard this insane roller coaster. We're on to something here, and I have you to ~~blame~~ thank.

INTRODUCTION

ERIC BEEBE

Fear is one of those concepts that is easy to understand, but difficult to describe. Many of the previous Post Mortem Press anthologies have dealt with the concept of fear: the fear of being alone, the fear of death, the fear of losing a loved one, the fear of things that go bump in the night, and so on. Yet more than any one particular topic, the fear of the unknown is likely the most dreaded.

Ironically, the search for knowledge and understanding, what some folks like to call science, tends to create the biggest sense of unknown. We stare into the abyss, hoping to learn, to understand. But the abyss is a cold and uncaring muse.

We risk all when we enter the abyss, usually with little hope of significant payback. The idea behind the Higgs boson particle, known to us lay folks as the "God Particle," suggests the mere act of discovery could end reality as we know it. Of course the idea of a universe-ending scientific discovery is shrugged off by physicists, but that doesn't stop the lesser informed or skeptical among us from being afraid.

In an everyday sense, the abyss is the absolute bottom of an unending unknown. What's more frightening than an unending unknown? I am not sure I can think of anything.

The stories that follow present twenty-two unique visions of the fear of the unknown, in many cases when that fear is associated with science and the quest for knowledge.

Among these pages are stories from authors who have been nominated and won the most prestigious genre fiction awards: Hugo, Nebula, Aurora, Stoker, and many others. Jack Ketchum's *Amid the Walking Wounded,* was part of his Bram Stoker Award™ winning collection, **Peaceable Kingdom**. Harlan Ellison® has won more awards that I can mention, and we still have twenty original stories from numerous award winners and nominees alike. These folks understand fear.

But, rather than read my ramblings, you came here to read some excellent short stories, **Fear the Abyss** will not disappoint. Remember, they're just stories.

CUTTING THE CORD

JOSEPH WILLIAMS

*Joseph Williams has appeared in several Post Mortem Press anthologies alongside New York Times Bestselling authors and Stoker Award winners including Clive Barker, Jonathan Maberry, F. Paul Wilson, and Jack Ketchum. He has released two collections of stories (*Detroit Macabre, Swinging with Stars*) to critical acclaim. His work has also appeared in* The Wayne State University Literary Review, A Fly in Amber, The Western Online, *and* Bewildering Stories. *He also writes freelance articles for* Real Detroit Weekly, *where he has interviewed artists ranging from American Book Award winners to Grammy Award winners. He lives in Michigan with his wife.*

Jeff talks backwards when he's anxious.

One time, he told me there are seventeen thousand different species of centimeter on one cubic bacteria of dust out here. Another time, he told me I'm full of shit.

Actually, he said, "Shit fills you."

I guess it's not really backwards all the time. Just incorrectly processed. He assures me he's not mixed up when I tell him so.

Well, actually, he says, "I am not a mixture." You get the point.

It sounds crazy. It sounds ridiculous.

That's just Jeff.

I think his wires have corroded, or whatever the fuck they used to put his brand together. He's twenty-years old now. They were using a lot of experimental alloys, prosthetics, and processors back then. Regulations are stricter these days.

Anyway, he doesn't like when I touch him, or especially when I tease him about his wife. She's been dead for seven years. Her circuits fried having crazy machine sex, but not with him. He doesn't know who her tango partner was. Hard as the lab coats have tried, androids still don't have DNA, so nothing was revealed in the postmortem.

That's why he started talking backwards, he says. Or, "chronologically misplacing" his words.

See what I mean?

1

I'm on to him now, though. I don't think it's part of his mental breakdown. I think he does it on purpose. He thinks if he talks backward then I'll start thinking it's actually forward. Like I'm just hearing it wrong. I'm hearing it in the past. I'm thinking backward. Like I'm the one who's really going crazy. My wires have corroded or something. Programming is fucked. Synapses no longer firing at optimum levels.

"Fuck you," I tell him. "At least I wasn't made in a factory."

I may as well have been.

That's what I tell myself, not what he says in response. Besides, he'd be agitated after a remark like that, so really he'd say, "Might you have," or something.

What a prick, huh? Well he's all I've got for company right now.

Dirks told me to cut the cord on this whole mess if they weren't back in three days. It's been five, and I already want to slit Jeff's throat. But we haven't cut the cord. We won't until there's no other option.

Jeff and I fight about this every day. He's good at taking orders and I'm good at ignoring them. He says that if Captain Dirks told us to cut the cord after three days, then we should have cut the cord after three days. I tell him it's murder if we don't give them every chance to get back to the shuttle by then. He says, "He won't be happy you disobeyed him."

But the way I figure it, that's contingent on his survival. If he's already dead, it doesn't matter. And if he survives, well, you'd think he'd be grateful that I didn't give up on him, right?

"Wrong," Jeff says.

He left us here because we don't need to breathe, Jeff says. Just because we survived doesn't mean they did. They must have run out of oxygen by now. And if we don't get back to the ship to let somebody know what happened, they'll just send another, and another, and another. All that blood on our hands, Jeff says.

We're in a big storage bin that Jeff converted into an emergency medical facility. It's crude. No windows. No air flow, minimal atmosphere. No gravity. Just two horizontal tubes of light over an eight by six steel table which once held core samples and mining equipment before the big wigs decided to give up on this lifeless rock. Sometimes the lights flicker. But we were built to adapt.

Jeff brought along all the important gear from the ship. Scalpels, IVs, sutures, trauma shears, oxygen masks, gauze, syringes, pain medication, anesthetics, anything the rescue party might need. It looks out of place in this huge metal bin, and it takes up a lot of space. We don't know what sort of shape the Captain will be in if and when he gets back, though, so we have to be prepared for all eventualities. At this point, after five days of exposure, five days' worth of oxygen used up, the chances we'll have anyone to operate on are slim. But if we do, at least we're prepared.

I'm getting close to cutting the cord. I'm close to giving in.

"We have to draw the line somewhere," Jeff says.

"Where?"

I think the better question is *when*.

Jeff talks backwards when he gets anxious. My secret is much worse. I get a-whole-nother personality when I'm overtired.

Overtired, you say? Yeah, it happens to us, too.

Jeff's here because he's got a background in medicine. He's a surgical model.

I'm here because I can see the past.

It's not what I was programmed for, mind you. I'm a masseuse by trade, or was. It's a glitch that wormed its way into my system seven years ago.

Can you guess how?

Can you guess what special talent Jeff's wife used to have?

Besides being a real good lay, of course.

Anyway, they thought it would help for me to come and see if I could pick up on the trail of the lost ship. The last signal they put out, an SOS call, supposedly came from the surface of this moon, but I don't sense anything. The only vision I'm seeing is Jeff walking around his apartment, naked, and it's creeping me the fuck out. They don't make the surgical models attractive. Otherwise, they wouldn't get anything done. They save that for the service industry models, like me. So Jeff isn't much to look at naked, even in the past. It's even worse when I have to see him right there in front of me in this goddamned metal box, knowing a part of me had sex with that flabby stomach, those protruding ribs, that bald head.

These goddamned memories.

Memories can be a venereal disease, you know. Apparently, so can the ability to see the past, as long as the Betty you're bopping fries her circuits mid-coitus.

You get my secret now?

I was the one fucking Jeff's wife when she died. When I don't shut down long enough, she starts poking up in all kinds of weird places inside of me. Part of her consciousness was burned into me when she died. The ghost in the machine, you might say.

Sometimes, I just want to wear a short skirt and paint my nails.

Don't tell Jeff, though. He'd either want to kill me or fuck me, and neither option sounds particularly appealing to this bag of bones and wires.

On the morning of day six, which may as well be the night, Jeff puts it to me straight.

"We have to make the decision today. There's no way they could have lasted this long. They don't have enough air."

"Why didn't you give them the oxygen masks?"

He looks insulted. "Because those are for emergencies."

I say, "What's more of an emergency than running out of air on the surface?"

I'm about to go to school. Jeff doesn't say this, but I was married to him and I know when he's about to condescend.

"Suppose they made it back just before their reserves ran out and I needed to operate on one of them immediately. It would take hours to get back to the ship even if they went straight to the shuttle, and then it would be too late."

I don't like how he's talking about this scenario in the past tense, but maybe that's just because he's anxious. Maybe he's just talking backwards, 'cause I'm looking into the past and all I see is Jeff's pale, hairy ass bobbing up and down the day I (she) made love to him the first time. I don't see Captain Dirks gasping for air while dust swirls around him in the purplish black wind. Maybe that means he's still alive, maybe it just means I'm processing the information wrong.

Memories. Save my soul.

I'm so goddamned tired. I don't know when we'll be able to sleep again.

"Not until we make the decision. You know that."

He must not be agitated. I sure as hell am.

Jeff must realize I'm not in the mood for spirited debate or the guilt of pronouncing a dozen of my closest friends dead, because he goes back to whatever the fuck he's been working on with the medical equipment this whole time. Hooking wires to power packs, unhooking them, hooking them back in. Making crude, leather restraints to hold his unseen and as yet unidentified patient down. Adjusting the two bars of light overhead so they reflect the horrible sterility of death from the dulled steel. It just makes them flicker more.

Like he expects to save someone.

Didn't this asshole just tell me we need to cut the cord today? Cutting the cord means death. Cutting the cord means leaving a brother behind.

"What the hell are you doing?" I ask him.

"Prepping for surgery."

Jeff is a surgical model. I'm not. But I've seen him work enough to notice the anesthetics are still in a container by the door next to the old archaeological equipment. They used to dig here.

"For who?"

Jeff doesn't answer me. His brow is furrowed and he's reading something from a worn datapad. I can't tell at first whether it's because he's trying to sound threatening or if he just doesn't hear me.

But *she* knows. She remembers, therefore, I remember.

Before I can stop her, my hands are around his waist and my dry lips are touching his neck.

Jeff doesn't like when I touch him. He likes it even worse when I impersonate his wife. He thinks I can help it.

"Off the fuck me!" he yells.

I'd laugh if I weren't so scared. I don't like when I'm not in control.

He's agitated. I'm exhausted. That's not a good combination, but one inevitably leads to the other. And so on and so on, always and forever.

"Relax," she says through my mouth. It's really her voice, too. That's the fucked up part. Probably why he gets so goddamned mad when she pops up. "I know how to calm you down."

She's got my lips on his earlobe and my hands on his stomach. I want to die. Jeff wants me to, too. I can actually feel her taking over my thoughts. That's when the shit really hits the fan.

Two things happen at once.

First, Jeff lets me (her) kiss his ear, waits while my calloused, hairy-knuckled man-hands tread the line between his belt buckle and his flab, watches like he's scientifically observing them in their natural habitat. He hesitates, we both know it, and that puts him over the edge. He knows he let me touch him, and that brings up all sorts of uncomfortable questions even if he tries to chalk it up to hearing the seductive voice of his dead wife.

So that's happening.

Jeff was already experiencing some technical problems, as evidenced by his reverse sequential speech patterns and general difficulty with word retrieval. If he were a real person, this would be called a symptom of early onset dementia. He's not, but it all amounts to the same. And I'm thinking to myself, this can't be good.

Second, I get a vision of Captain Dirks and he's gasping for air in the purplish black wind. It's bad. His oxygen is low, and I can tell just by looking at him that the only reason he's alive is he took someone else's tank after they died. But he's not dead yet, at least, and he doesn't look like he's really that close to it. In the same neighborhood, sure, but not on death's doorstep. Not quite.

I'm glad we haven't cut the cord.

Jeff has, only it's a different one. Jeff's short circuiting.

He wheels around so fast and so powerfully that I go sprawling against the empty bins of medical supplies. Something in my back flares with pain. A pinched wire.

Yes, we feel pain. How else do you keep someone in line?

"You!" he screams, jabbing one, sparking index finger in my direction. He's shaking, but not the way you would shake. More like the way the road shakes a mile in front of you on a hot day. A humidity shake. "You!" I don't think he trusts himself to say anything else right now.

I can feel her leaving me, retreating to the safety of my heart and wires. The bitch never had much of a backbone. That's why she never told him about us.

I guess I could have.

"I can't help it, Jeff. I swear."

But it's too late. Jeff has turned into an unintelligible cyclone of rage and sparks. If I could make out any of his jumbled words, I'd tell you. I can't.

They aren't even words anymore. Jeff's so fucked up now that even the letters are backwards. If he wrote them down, I might be able to make sense of them. He doesn't.

"Come on, Jeff. We both just need to relax."

I feel like I'm pleading, but my voice is even. It's always like this when I'm in control again. Nothing really compares to the feeling of being inhabited by someone else's ghost, so I'm all relief when I re-establish myself.

"I didn't mean it," I try to tell him.

But Jeff's got his hands locked around my throat. Even with a reinforced neck, he's crushing my windpipe.

Yes, I have a windpipe. Don't you?

"Bastard!" he shouts.

I'm proud of him for getting that word out. He's really pissed. His wires need tightening.

My heightened anxiety brings her up again, and even though I try to push her back down into my waste compartment, gravity's not what it seems and she just keeps floating up through my throat through the grips of Jeff's strong, bony hands. Tight spaces never bothered her.

"Jeff," she begs. I don't know how she can get her voice through, but she does.

Jeff screams and squeezes even harder. The sound of her voice infuriates him.

The pain is a dusty, purplish black wind and the world is fading. The lights flicker. A single ray reflects into my left eye from the makeshift operating table. I'm drifting. But she's in my head now, in my lips and in my tongue, so another vision hits me like a rocket.

Captain Dirks was three kilometers away two hours ago. He should be here soon, but it's been slow going. There are too many hills. His legs are getting tired. I wish I knew if he'd get here in time to save me, but she only sees the past. I don't understand why fortune teller models are programmed that way, but maybe it's to prevent war. That would make sense, I guess.

Then, she's gone and I'm back in the real world, thinking at least I got a moment away from the pain.

When Jeff drags me to my feet and slams me onto the operating table, I'm just north of consciousness. When he pushes my face against the cold steel and tightens the crude leather restraints on my legs, I'm somewhere south of it. She sees everything in the past, though, and she jumps forward now that I'm too weak to resist.

I can see everything, but there's a two or three second lag between transmissions even in this special circumstance, so I'm reacting to everything too late. Jeff ties my left hand down and I'm resisting it two seconds later. He jabs the scalpel into my stomach, and even though I feel the pain in real time, I don't see it until she shows it to me. She's no help.

I think she's doing it on purpose. Punishing me for being such a great lay that I could fuck a woman like her to death. Literally blow her mind. Wouldn't you want revenge for that?

Are all ghosts so mean-spirited?

Jeff opens me up without anesthesia, without an IV, without pain medication of any kind. That must be a good thing, because the pain is so blinding that I'm wreathed in darkness for a while. He keeps working though, probably muttering something like, "Fuckmother kill. That I'll him." He's off the deep end. Someone cut his cord.

Meanwhile, he's trying to cut mine. I think he's forgotten all about Captain Dirks and the rescue mission. Guys like us aren't supposed to be so unstable, that's why they left us here instead of a couple of real army Joes. It had almost nothing to do with oxygen and food and water, and everything to do with our propensity to ignore the deeper questions of life and death. We still feel pain, though.

Right now, I'm probably feeling more of it than you'd ever feel in ten lifetimes. The curse is that we feel it but sometimes it's so much that our systems are overloaded and we can't react. Can you believe that? Some people work their entire lives to be like that. Not numb, but calm in the face of a knife severing tendons, wires, motors, processors, hearts, and identities.

Jeff's cutting my cord, but not gently. He wants to shut me off but a lobotomy isn't enough.

"Jeff, please," I say, but I'm buried beneath that other consciousness now. He's re-routed my mental processes and I'm wallowing in the pit of my stomach even as it's naked to the world.

But she's come forward, she's stronger than ever, so I know Dirks was at the door to our sanctuary seventeen seconds ago.

What the hell is taking him so long?

And what is Jeff doing with the broom and the archaeological paint brush over by the old mining equipment?

Five seconds ago, he was bending over me with a crazed grin. Three seconds ago, he kissed my dead, open mouth with too much tongue.

And before I know what's happening, she's kissing him back with my hand behind his head.

"My God, Jeff," she says. She's (I'm) starting to cry. "God I've missed you so much."

"Mutual affection," Jeff says.

He helps her to her feet.

And I'm somewhere buried inside all of this.

At least I know that Dirks started opening the door three seconds ago. He's gasping in a purplish black wind, but he's never looked so relieved in his life. Salvation is right around the corner for us.

But something's wrong.

For just a moment as he falls into the makeshift surgical room, I see things through his eyes.

Jeff's sparking all over the place. He's grinning and seizuring as his system starts to fry, but he's still holding her hand and she's got her arm around his waist in the flickering lights.

The blond bristles from the broom cover my head. Jeff's painted my lips red with the blood from the procedure, only his hands were so spastic that it's splattered all over my face. I look like an animal after feeding, or like I just made out with someone's jugular. He's cut off the legs of my paints so that it looks like I'm wearing a short skirt. My stomach is still open, and I'm somewhere down there.

But she's somewhere up in the real world.

Dirks is on the verge of death. He can't believe what he's seeing.

And the new-old couple limps toward him with outstretched arms. She bends over the Captain in my dead body and plants a kiss on his lips.

CUTTING THE CORD

"Welcome home, Captain," she says.

"Homeward death," Jeff says.

I don't know what the fuck that means, but I'm in it for the long haul.

EXTRACTION

JESSICA MCHUGH

Jessica McHugh is an author of speculative fiction that spans the genre from horror and alternate history to epic fantasy. A prolific writer, she has devoted herself to novels, short stories, poetry, and playwriting. She has had twelve books published in four years, including the bestselling Rabbits in the Garden, The Sky: The World *and the gritty coming-of-age thriller,* PINS. *More info on Jessica's speculations and publications can be found at JessicaMcHughBooks.com.*

I can't stop jerking off at work. Even when I don't see Dana Cully. Even when she wears her frumpy out-of-season sweaters that make her breasts look like lumpy potatoes beneath a faded Rudolph face. Even when her glasses are smeared with nose grease and her head appears topped with phallic knots of half-digested hair. Even then, my hand flies to my zipper, tears the dog out of its house, and beats it for howling at such an unappealing piece of flesh. It's not all her fault. I also blame the Zelko, the DeKuyper, and the Listerine. Oh, and myself too. I'm not so deluded as to negate my blame in this. It's my dog that howls, my hand that beats, my stomach that gurgles and erupts in the seconds before I ejaculate, staining another "Potty Poster" with Crème de menthe and Cream de Marvin. As I wipe away the excess, I read the poster and make a mental note: Turn off your monitor before leaving for the night. Do your part to save power, save money, and save the world. Also, there's some cum on your shoe.

A few months ago, I was only slightly queasy before I came. Now, chunks of revulsion and blades of blinding pain precede my spurts. A fiery accordion in my gut squeezes and spreads my organs like they're fine to push every which way. Who cares if my intestines get tangled in my ribcage? Why not interchange lung and liver? On second thought, I don't think I want my liver in charge of important shit. Not even literal shit. Its job is to process alcohol, and it already has enough on its plate.

When I emerge from the men's room, wiping away a string of bile clinging to my chin, Dana is there, wrinkling her bulbous nose. I try to rush past her, but her perfume nets me, slowly reeling me back to her.

"Are you making the buffer this afternoon?" she asks. Her voice sounds coated in clotted milk. It makes me clear my own throat several times in hopes she'll copy me, but she never does.

"That's what Regina said," I reply. "I should probably get that staged."

She smiles, giving me a glimpse of Brown Lightning, her prized molar. The tooth is not dead; rather, it's afflicted with a brown vein that cuts it in two. I can't stand to look at it, but no other part of her is any better.

"If you need help..."

"Yeah, yeah," I say, pulling myself out of her aromatic haze.

My stomach aches so badly, buds of tears burn my eyes, but I don't let them fall. I've never been much of a crier, never saw the point. Besides, what can crying do that a box of wine can't?

I didn't always have that attitude. At least, I don't think so. It's so hard to remember anything before a month ago, before my life became strangled by liquor and inexplicable lust. I think I used to be a good man. I think I used to have a purpose. Trying to remember hurts my brain, though not as badly as the pain currently boiling my stomach. The distended lump there cries out for attention, but the only attention I care to give my belly lives in the bottle hidden under the desk in my office.

"Desk" is actually a misnomer. "Office," too. The truth is I sit in a lab, separated from all of the other employees. I don't mind since it gives me plenty of freedom to drink, but I'm not exactly in Siberia. Dana can find me quite easily, and my boss Regina Bauer always calls to check in and issue my assignments for the day. My assignments are usually the easiest production a manufacturing technician can get, I assume because Regina can tell how hard it is for me to function these days. She's never brought up my drinking, but I can't believe she's oblivious. She's a smart lady, and except for her wrinkles and unfortunate chicken pox scars, quite beautiful. So how come my dick doesn't give the zipper a hard hello when Regina is around? Why Dana? Why does disgust turn to lust at the mere whiff of her perfume?

So maybe I don't take my work seriously. So maybe I'm a full-fledged alcoholic. So maybe this blinding pain in my gut is just the first symptom of a body that's grave-ready. But in exchange for health and harmony, I was allowed to recognize the greatest gift God bestows: that even when liquor is out of reach, this world is constructed from elements that fuck you up. Growing, cooking, crushing, smoking…I want to put Earth up my nose.

That hunger began after my first week of work at BioTech, with one drink—bought by none other than Dana Cully. Until she hippoed up with a glass of liquor, I was content to spend a few hours by myself. It always comforted me before, watching people. I guess I was just one of those weirdoes. Now, I'm a different kind of weirdo. The kind who keeps his ears perked during nightly strolls, listening for kids with severe coughing fits so he'll know which house has good medicine. Nothing makes my heart skip a beat quite like seeing a bottle of Delsym perched on a child's bedside table. Breaking into houses isn't always easy, but I'm fairly quiet for a drunk. I slip in like a snake, coil myself around the bottle and ooze away like some otherworldly creature. In a life with so little to revere, I pride myself on any accomplishment.

I initially refused Dana's drink without a hint of temptation. But then she sat down, flashed me Brown Lightning, and pushed the glass into my hands. Her perfume smelled like childhood. What from childhood? Your guess is as good as mine. All I know is that I wanted her to sit closer. I wanted her on my lap. I wanted her to wriggle and bounce and give me a revolting reason to call out of work the next day.

She repulsed me, but I craved her immeasurably, and the alcohol made it worse. Then, "worse" became the alcohol. After one sip of bourbon, I had to have a full glass. Then a beer. Then some wine. Then a dusty pill I found under the urinal. I asked Dana how quickly other people got hooked on the stuff, but she just brayed and squeezed my thigh. With a cough, I came in my pants. Whether she noticed, I don't know, but she did leave soon after. My pants were so wet I was afraid to stand, so I kept ordering more drinks. Two hundred dollars later, the bartender had to peel me out of the booth and call a cab to drive me home. But I couldn't go home yet. There was no liquor there.

After that night, that was never the case again. At this point, I've only been at BioTech for a month, but things have changed drastically for me in that short time. I started out with a desk surrounded by coworkers. I resuspended DNA primers, even worked with magnetic Dynabeads for an eColi testing kit. I didn't have much experience, but I was a fast learner and Regina liked that kind of gumption. But I was gradually moved away from manufacturing certain products. After my encounter with Dana, my duties focused solely on manufacturing Extraction Buffer, and my workspace was moved to the farthest lab.

Regina calls the lab phone just as I swallow some Zelko.

"Hey, Reg. Good morning," I say, gulping down a bit of bile that jumps up with a belch.

"You're going to make Extraction Buffer today," she says.

Surprise, surprise. "Ten liters?" I ask.

"You got it. Say, how's the temperature in that lab today? Not still too hot, is it?"

"Nah, it's actually pretty chilly." I look at the thermostat. "62 degrees."

"Oh my, that's a little cold, isn't it? I'll have Facilities fix that right away."

"Why bother? They can never find a happy medium. One day, it's freezing. The next day, it's a sauna."

"What, you don't trust me, Harvey?" she asks.

"Of course I do."

"Good. Do you want Dana to help you manufacture the buffer?"

"No!" I adjust my volume with a vodka-laced grunt. "No, thank you. I'll be fine."

"Good. I'll check in later," she says, cutting off the call before I can respond.

In those few minutes, the temperature has dipped to 59 degrees, so I choose to start production on the buffer just to get out of the cold. Before I begin, I make sure to take a sip from the flask I have stashed under the bench. The more I drink, the easier the day slides by. Before I know it, it's time to head home; I just hope I can make it there in one piece. But then I ask myself, "Why?" One piece, two, eight: does it really matter? The vodka tells me it does. I am very, very important, it says. I tell ya, vodka, there are times I've believed you. I just don't remember when they were.

*****

The next morning, I step into an inferno. The temperature of the lab has sailed to nearly 90 degrees, making my vodka taste like rotten milk. Still, it was rotten milk that could get me drunk enough to ignore the heat.

My head thumps terribly. I sit down, awaiting Regina's phone call when the lab door flies open. The blast of AC from the hallway feels good, but the scent it carries makes my stomach twist into a fistfuck of a knot.

"Jeez, it's hot in here!" Dana squeals.

I notice her getting moist. Her armpits, her neck, her fourth chin. Misshapen "U's" appear below her sweaty breasts, and though I don't want to look, I can't tear my eyes away. My dick burns against my zipper, crying out for relief. A hand will do, but it wants something warmer, something wetter.

Dana fans herself with her hoof and coughs up a chuckle, "Wasn't it cold in here yesterday?"

"Sure was," I hiss, digging my elbow into my balls, hoping the pain will soften me.

"You okay, Harv?"

God, the smell of her. What is it? Cookies or roses or Versace FuckJeans, it's amazing. And no, I'm not okay, you mustached hag. I need to beat off. Now.

The phone rings, and I know right away it's Regina.

"Yes, I'm here," I sputter into the phone.

"Oh good. How's the lab today?" she asks sweetly.

"Hot," I reply. Dana giggles, making the Tigger appliqué on her shirt dive down her chest until he's swimming in the pool between sweat-splashed mountains.

My body screams. Hand. Toilet. Flask. Hand. Toilet. Flask. I need to get away.

"That's too bad. I'll have Facilities fix it tomorrow."

My stomach churns, causing a beast of salty bile to claw its way up my throat. Dana's perfume is overpowering, and Regina's insane promises make my blood boil.

"Don't worry, Harv. We'll take care of it," she says. "Oh, and I know you worry about being alone back there, so I have a surprise for you."

"I don't worry about that," I grunt through rising pain.

Dana touches my shoulder. Her scent thickens as if she were spraying me like a cat in heat. I turn to see drops of sweat clinging to her mustache, so thick and imposing, I swear I can smell it. Through her pleasing perfume, one of skunk cabbage and black licorice punches free, causing my aching stomach to lurch. But it's not quite as bad as the ache in my crotch, especially when she licks the droplets away and I imagine her licking my ache with it. The thought makes my testicles feel like iron death.

"Sorry, gotta go," I exclaim, throwing the phone with no care to the cradle and flying from my seat.

I reach the bathroom with my hand already on my dick and vomit searing my tongue. I spit up a stream of brown liquid that appears to steam when it hits the toilet, but I'm too focused on beating away my screaming erection to care.

Dana Cully fills my mind. Her rat-nest hair. Her rotting chomper. The way one of her socks is always lower than the other, revealing a patch of bristly hair she's missed for the last twenty shaves.

I growl as I cum, spattering the toilet seat with something that looks too similar to my vomit to be normal. My stomach feels like a balloon at full capacity—as well as already lacerated latex. I've gone soft, but the pain continues. My dick is coated in brown goo that I try to wipe away with toilet paper, but the cheap stuff sticks to the tip. As I try to peel it off, my eyes well with burning tears.

I run my hands under the cold water and wash away the gummy patches of toilet paper. I cup my hands again, ready to splash water on my face, but my reflection makes me freeze. The water drains between my fingers as I lean in and watch a brown tear roll out of my eye. As it falls, it sears a ravine into my cheek, causing the surrounding flesh to peel back and curl into itself. Another tear falls, but I catch it with my fingertips. The droplet burns through both flesh and nail, giving me a glimpse of brown bone before I run my hand under the faucet. Under the pressure of the stream, the steaming hole in my finger widens before slowly fusing closed. After splashing water on my face, I try to wipe the tears away, but my fingernail catches on a tag of burnt flesh, causing a new rip from cheek to nose. I slap a paper towel over the wound, desperately trying not to cry despite my panic.

After a few steadying breaths, I gently pull back the paper towel. The wound directly below my eye has healed, and as I remove more of the towel, I realize the other wounds have too. Unfortunately, it gives me a bit of resistance at the end. In healing, my face has stitched some of the paper into the wound. It takes a tug, but it finally breaks free, leaning a small piece of towel protruding from my cheek.

My stomach still hurts and it's noticeably distended, but I'm able to leave the bathroom. My only hope is that Dana has vacated the lab, leaving me to cool off with my sweaty vodka. When I enter, Dana isn't there, but five other people are, staring at me like I have a piece of paper sticking out of my cheek—so I suppose their expressions are warranted. Their sleeves are hiked and safety glasses fogged by the 97 degree lab temperature. I immediately parch, but a man with a unibrow stands in the way of my liquor cabinet.

"There's something on your face, fella," he says. I grunt and ask him to move. "No can do. We need all the bench space we can get. We're assembling 6000 primer kits.

Nice "surprise," Regina.

The man's slick arm rubs against me, scraping me with its wiry fur. He apologizes, and I'm about to tell him it's fine when a familiar scent strikes my nostrils. It's Dana—but Dana isn't there. The smell is coming from the bristly man with sweat dripping between the whiteheads along his nose. My stomach tightens as the blood rushes south, making me stiffen with each scented surge. My balls swell and stretch, filling my jeans with aching flesh. I can't tell if the warm fluid rolling down my thigh is blood or semen, but either way, it's not good.

The amount of people in the room doubles, then triples. None of them seems to be doing any real work, just milling around and getting between me and my liquor.

"I just need to get to the cabinet. Just for a second," I say to the group of dripping women now clustered in front of the door, but when they turn, I am pummeled by their scent. More technicians spin to stare at me, blowing sweaty gales of the aroma in my direction. The lab is hazy with the stuff. I'm convinced my dick has split open and is pouring blood down my legs, but when I pull aside my lab coat, I see that the river of blood starts at my belly—at the enormous growth on my belly, more precisely.

"Oh my god, are you okay?" a woman asks. For once, I stiffen from her beauty, not the strange perfume. I would fuck her in a second, but something tells me she wouldn't want the man with a football-sized tumor to stick his dick inside her. The knot looks more like brain than skin, and with each increase of nausea, another vein pops, oozing brown soup down my pants.

People scream at the throbbing mass. I'm afraid, too, but the fear is so much worse when I take in all of the faces: blanched in terror, green in revulsion, their throats burbling with the upward travel of vomit. Against every desire, I start to cry and can't stop. The brown tears burrow through my face, dropping entire panels of skin to the lab floor. I try to dam the flow with my fingers, but the burning liquid causes me to shake my hands in pain, spattering bare arms and faces with molten tears and slivers of soggy skin.

I catch my sloppy reflection in the cabinet and promptly coat the mirror in hot heaves of thick, chocolate vomit. My brain tries to cling to consciousness, to the last few drops of blood that haven't defected to the tumor overcoming my innards, but its grip is weak, and down I go. I could swear my face smashes like a melon when I hit the floor, but I can still smell perfume in the seconds before I black out, so I think my nose is fine.

My nose is not fine. I know it as soon as I wake up. I can't quite see my reflection in the glass of the transfer window, but I see enough to know that my face as I knew it is probably still on the floor in front of my liquor cabinet. What's left wouldn't even make for a passable companion in a peanut butter sandwich.

My vision is fuzzy, but from the chair I'm tied into, I can tell I'm in a lab. I don't recognize it, but there are lots of labs at BioTech I've never seen. As my vision clears, I spot Regina in the entry way, zipping up her sterile suit. I'm surrounded by tanks of Extraction Buffer, each one labeled with my handwriting. What the hell is going on?

"Harvey," Regina says as she enters the lab.

My throat is full of clotted phlegm. I try to cough it up, but it hurts my stomach too badly to clear it. I look down at my belly's new bloody friend and groan. It takes up most of my torso now, but some of the connective tissue has been detached, so it hangs low on my waist.

Before I know what's happening, she's holding a few vials in front of my face and I am pummeled by the familiar smell. The tumor swells, and my erection spews ropey mud.

"What is that smell?" I scream.

"A highly concentrated dose of secretion from—as far as we can tell—the prostate gland of a female Kathonian," she replies.

"A what?"

Regina grabs a pipette aid and sticks a 50mL tip into the nozzle. She pushes the trigger and the pipette hums. She sucks up a heavy dose of Extraction Buffer and advances on me. The tip presses against my face, scraping through the slop as it draws closer to my cornea. She dispenses the buffer into my eye, sending burning liquid throughout my skull. The buffer eats through the meat in the socket, making it easier for Regina to slip in and start digging under my eyeball. The humming and sucking drown out my screams, which continue after the tip pops the eyeball out onto my lap. My jeans sizzle beneath the lump of tissue until she knocks it to the floor, squishes it under her protective boot, and goes to work on the other eye.

Once my eyeballs are gone and the sockets stripped by the buffer, the oozing stops completely. But I can still see Regina. She nods to the other suited technicians in the room and is handed a clean scalpel.

"I am sorry about this, Harv. You were just too obvious," she says.

"About what?"

"You can still see, can't you?"

"...Yes. How?"

"Because your vision isn't like ours, not even when you're impersonating one of us," she replies. "This was your first mission, wasn't it? From what I've seen, your people should spend more time training their spies. This whole 'If I don't remember I'm an alien I'll fit in better with the humans' thing just isn't working well for them."

"What the hell are you talking about?"

Regina pokes my tumor. It has gotten so massive I feel like the tail-end is tickling my uvula.

"Come in," she says into an intercom, and a few seconds later, Dana appears at the door. She dons a protective suit like the others, but hers is transparent, giving me a clear view of her clumsy nudity. My stomach swells in disgust, but when Regina pours a vial's pungent contents over Dana's suit, pain cracks through my crotch. The tumor grows by the second, spurting its fluid across the lab floor.

"You're the first we've tried this on, Harvey. Aggravation always works, but the mix of desire and revulsion is even more successful. I knew what you were the moment you set foot in BioTech. That's why I had Dana follow you after work. To tempt and repulse you—and to weaken you with alcohol," Regina says. "Now we just have to remove the bladder and we can send you on your way. You have no idea how many humans this disgusting growth will help. We've been experimenting with what we call the 'Duplex Bladder' for years, but yours—My God, Harvey—I could cure cancer."

I feel like I'm going to pass out, like my mind is a knot forged from frayed threads. But one shining thought breaks through the tangle of puking and fucking and sounds my desire as clear as a bell.

Alcohol.

God, what I wouldn't give for a drink right now. Just one bottle, one frosted monolith filled with heaven that pours like hellish oil.

"A drink," I whisper as Regina and the techs start to pull the mass out of my belly. "One last drink."

"Don't be so dramatic, Harv. There's plenty of time for that when we're through. Although, I doubt you'll want a drink once you're back in your real form."

I'm tired of questioning every cryptic thing she says, so I scream instead. A technician's scalpel jumps to my throat, pressing my courage as Regina's eyes latch onto my cavernous sockets.

"We have no problem killing you," she says. "The rest of your organs are pretty useless, but I'm sure we could find someone who wants them. We could market them as dog chow, shark chum—Oh, I know. I bet the fellas at Area 51 wouldn't mind a few pounds of your flesh."

I shut up and the scalpels resume their talent, slicing and freeing the tumor from my stomach. It takes one of the techs to hold the brunt of the mass and the other to slowly extract the spongy tail that has snaked through my organs and up my throat. This feeling of being emptied is like none I've ever known. I start to have the same thought about the buzzing pain in my limbs, but when pain turns to pleasure, I realize I have felt it before. When the tumor is gone, my physical form starts to change. Every sensation is suddenly different, yet familiar. My morphing body slides out of its restraints, out of the chair, and onto the floor where my legs can fully unfurl. The tile is cold against each of my forty-eight feet, filling me with chills of memory.

Everything comes back: landing on Earth, my mission to infiltrate BioTech, the warnings to avoid intoxicants. Another warning, too: "Your mind will be hard to hold onto," the Captain had said. "Once you're in human form, you'll forget who you really are, but you will remember when needed."

Regina's right. Our training is subpar. No wonder our turnover is so high. The humans are smarter than us. But Regina was wrong about one thing: I'm back in my real form and I still want a drink.

I scuttle across the floor, winding around the technician's shaking legs. With a few lunges and squeezes, I could crush the life out of them, but killing them wouldn't put the venilist (Duplex Bladder, to them) back in my body. I couldn't care less about that anyway right now. I smell liquor. My liquor. My flask—in Regina's pocket. Planting myself on my back twenty-four legs, I lift up my thin body to beg like a dog.

"Oh, you've got it bad," she laughs. She steps into the vestibule, unzips her suit, and removes my flask from her pocket. She passes it to a tech, who pours it into a weigh boat and sets it in front of me.

I step into the pool of vodka and absorb all I can through my toes. That way, it hits every inch of my cylindrical body. The liquor is nearly gone when Regina reenters the room. My body flushes with intoxication as she bends to my level, too proud of her success to bother with her hood. Something about the way she smiles angers me. She's won, and she knows it. That smug, pockmarked bitch. I can't stand what she did to me: the revulsion, the desire, the addiction. I'm a Kathonian, shardammit. I've had xetarge that makes human pussy looked like potted meat.

I swell again, this time on my own terms. The fear in Regina and the techs is sudden and beautiful, and, once again, I remember my strength.

A breast presses against the lab door, spreading across the glass like putty against a newspaper. Dana is still naked, beating against the pane as I transform into the monster that will destroy them all. But when I catch of glimpse of her gnarled forest of an armpit, I lurch in disgust. A tech pierces my primary gills with a 50mL pipette tip, causing blood to spray from the slits. The humans scream when it hits their suits, but the loudest is Regina, who gets a faceful of the stuff. I'm about to tell her to shut up; my blood isn't poisonous. But the sight of her fingers sliding beneath her skin gives me pause. The blood coagulates on her face, and when she tries to rub it away, the face goes with it, sloughing to the floor with wet slaps. I expect her to be no more than a mess of gooey muscle, and apparently, so does she, because when she uncovers her face and beholds her reflection, she gasps in joy. Her wrinkles are gone, her scars just bad memories. Her face is as smooth as a baby's…but how? To my knowledge, Kathonian blood has never had that effect on human skin.

I step on the weigh boat and the last drop of Zelko is absorbed. Regina stares at me ravenously, as if my blood is her Kathonian perfume. But unlike the perfume's effect on me, my blood doesn't make her want to tear off her clothes. It makes her want to tear me to shreds: thick, profitable shreds.

"It's the alcohol," she whispers. "It changed you. I tell you, Harv, we've done hundreds of tests on the usefulness of your blood and never found a thing. But this!" She looks again at her perfect face. "It's a miracle!"

I notice the techs grabbing glassware with no intention of scientific use. I start to puff up again, raising my defenses, but a burning pinch beside my gills deflates me. I hear Regina say, "Sorry, Harv," as my legs start to shake and crumple beneath my weight.

A graduated cylinder crashes down on me; I find it unnecessary due to the tranquilizer Regina deployed into my bloodsacs.

My body is giving out, but I have energy enough to growl at her, baring my pincers. She jumps back, bumping the lab bench and knocking a vial of the perfume to the floor. The smell is overwhelming, even more than the tranquilizer. If I were still human, my sudden erection probably would've knocked a few other things off the bench, too. But as Regina and the technicians approach with their weapons, I grin for the gift of being a Kathonian again.

My lust hits its peak and, with a screech, I cum harder than ever before. The reproductive darts fire from my laneer ducts, discharging my webbing all over the lab, while the darts themselves penetrate whatever stands nearest.

The scalpel falls first, followed by the graduated cylinders brandished by the techs. By the time my assailants hit the floor, it's covered in shards of glass and wasted genetic material. Not that they care. Even if the hits hadn't been fatal, the darts are poisonous enough to a human in minutes.

A gasp calls my attention to the door where Dana still stands, gawking at me through the glass. Brown Lightning is in clear view, but not for long. Too petrified to move, she weeps as I rip the door off its hinges. When the sense to run finally strikes her, the air flow system won't allow her to open the door to the hall.

It will be tough to escape the building and find my way back to the ship, especially doused in the putrid stink of Dana's blood, but I'll make it. Even though I hate to fly, I'll make it. Even though all it would take is a swig of vodka to calm me, even though the bottle is only a quick scuttle down the hall through the few people still clustered in the lab. Even though I'd strangle them all for just a sniff of the bottle cap and have to deal with the heavy clean up, I'll make it.

Yes, just one drink and I'll make it.

AMID THE WALKING WOUNDED

JACK KETCHUM

Stephen King has called Jack Ketchum the "scariest guy in America," remarking that there's "a dark streak of genius" in Jack's work. Ketchum lives in New York City where he continues to write, articles, reviews, short stories, novels and screenplays. For more information visit: www.thejackketchum.com. "Amid the Walking Wounded" *originally appeared in the Bram Stoker Award™ winning 2003 collection,* Peaceable Kingdom.

It was four in the morning, the Hour of the Wolf he later thought, the hour when statistically most people died who were going to die on any given night and he awakened in the condo guestroom thinking that something had shaken him awake, an earthquake, a tremor--though this was Sarasota not California and besides, he'd been awakened by an earthquake many years ago one night in San Diego and this was somehow not quite the same. The glow outside the bedroom window faded even as he woke so that he couldn't be sure it was not in some way related to his sleep. He was aware of a trickling inside his nose, a thin nasal discharge, unusual because he was a smoker and used to denser emissions. He sniffed it up into his throat and thought it tasted wrong.

The guestroom had its own bathroom just around the corner so he put on his glasses and got up and turned on the light and spit the stuff into the sink and saw that it was blood and as he leaned over the sink it began leaking out his nose in a thin unsteady stream like a faucet badly in need of new washers. He pinched his nose and stood straight, tilted back his head and felt it run down the back of his throat, suddenly heavier now so that it almost choked him, the gag response kicking in and he thought, now what the hell is *this?* So he leaned forward again and took his hand away from his nose and watched it pouring out of him.

He grabbed a hand towel, pressed it under and over his nose and pinched again. *One seriously major fucking bloody nose*, he thought, unaware as yet that he was not alone, that others in town had awakened bleeding from the nose that night though none of them had been taking

25

ibuprofen, eight pills a day for over a month's time trying to fight off some stupid tennis elbow without resorting to a painful shot of cortizone directly into the swollen tendon--unaware too that ibuprofen was not just an anti-inflammatory but a blood-thinner, which was why he was not going to be doing any clotting at the moment.

The towel, pink, was turning red. The pressure wasn't working.

If he put his head up it poured down his throat--he could taste it now, salty, rich and coppery. If he put his head down it poured out his nose. Straight-up, he was an equal-opportunity bleeder, it came out both places.

He couldn't do this alone. He had to wake her. He crossed the hall.

"Ann? Annie?"

There was a streetlight outside her window. Her pale bare back and shoulders told him that she still slept nude.

"Annie. I'm bleeding."

She had always departed sleep like a drunk with one last shot left inside the bottle.

"*Whaaaa?*"

"Bleeding. *Help.*" It was hard to talk with the stuff gliding down his throat and the towel pressed over his face. She rolled over squinting at him, the sheet pulled up to cover her breasts.

"What'd you do to yourself?"

"Nosebleed. Bad." He spoke softly. He didn't want to wake her son David in the next room. There was no point in disturbing the sleep of a fourteen-year-old.

She sat up. "Pinch it."

"I'm pinching it. Won't stop."

He turned and went back to the bathroom so she could get out of bed and put on a robe. He was not allowed to see her naked anymore. He leaned over the sink and took away the towel and watched it slide out of him bright red against the porcelain and swirl down the drain.

"Ice," she said behind him and then saw the extent of what was happening to him and said *jesus* while he pinched his nose and tilted back his head and swallowed and then she said *ice* again. "I'll get some."

He tried blowing out into his closed nostrils the way you did to pop the pressure in your ears in a descending plane and all he succeeded in doing was to fog up his glasses. Huh? He took them off and looked at them. The lenses were clear. He looked in the mirror. There were beads of red at each of his tear-ducts.

He was bleeding from the eyes.

It was the eyes that were fogged, not his goddamn glasses. She came back with ice wrapped in a dishtowel.

"I'm bleeding from the eyes," he told her. "If it's the ebola virus, just shoot me."

"Eyes and nose are connected." She hadn't grown up a nurse's daughter for nothing. "Here."

He took the icepack and arranged it over his nose, tucked the corners of the dishtowel beneath. Within moments the towel was red. The ice felt good but it wasn't helping either.

"Here."

She'd taken some tissues and wrapped them thick around a pair of Q-tips.

"Put these up inside. Then pinch again."

He did as he was told. He liked the way she was rushing to his aid. It was the closest he'd felt to her for quite some time. He managed a goofy smile into her wide dark eyes and worried face. *Ain't this something?* He pinched his nose till it hurt.

The makeshift packs soaked through. He was dripping all over his tee-shirt. She handed him some tissues.

"Jesus, Alan. Should I call 911?"

He nodded. "You better."

*****

The ambulance attendants were both half his age, somewhere in their twenties and the one with the short curly hair suggested placing a penny in the center of his mouth between his teeth and upper lip and then pressing down hard on the lip, a remedy that apparently had worked for his grandmother but which did not do a thing for him and left him with the taste of filthy copper in his mouth, a darker version of the taste of blood. Annie asked if she should go with him and he said no, stay with David, get some sleep, I'll call if I need you. She had to write down their number because at the moment he couldn't for the life of him remember.

Inside the ambulance he began to bleed heavily and the attendant sitting inside across from him couldn't seem to find any tissues nor anything for him to bleed into. Eventually he came up with a long plastic bag that looked like a heavier-grade of Zip-loc which he had to hold open with one hand while dealing with his leaking nose with the other. A small box of tissues was located and placed in his lap. When one wad of tissues filled with blood he would hurriedly shove it into the bag and pull more from the box, his nose held low into the bag to prevent him from bleeding all over his khaki shorts. The attendant did nothing further to help him after finding him the bag and tissues. This was not the way it happened on *ER* or *Chicago Hope.*

The emergency room was reassuringly clean and, at five in the morning, nearly deserted but for him and a skeleton staff. They did not insist he sign in. Instead a chubby nurse's aide stood in front of him with a clipboard taking down the pertinent information, leaving him to deal with his nose, replacing the half-full Zip-loc bag with a succession of pink plastic kidney-shaped vomit bowls but otherwise treating him as though it were ninety-nine per-cent certain he had AIDS.

He didn't mind. As long as the pink plastic bowls kept coming and the tissues were handy.

He was beginning to feel light-headed. He supposed it was loss of blood. He couldn't remember Annie's address though he'd written her from his New York apartment countless times in the past four years since she'd moved away and knew her address--quite literally--by heart. He couldn't remember his social security number, either. The nurse's aide had to dig into his back pocket to get his wallet. The card was in there along with his insurance card. He couldn't do it for her because his hands, now covered with brown dried blood, were occupied trying to stop fresh red blood from flowing.

The ER doctor was also half his age, oriental, handsome and built like a swimmer with wide shoulders and a narrow waist, like the rest of the staff quite friendly and cheerful at this ungodly hour but unlike them seemingly unafraid to touch him even after, having swallowed so much of his own blood, he vomited much of it back into one of the pink plastic bowls. He asked Alan if he was taking any drugs. And that was when he learned about the blood-thinning properties of ibuprofen. He thought that at least he was probably not going to have a heart attack. He supposed it was something.

The doctor used a kind of suction device to suck blood from each of his nostrils into a tube trying to clear them but that didn't work which Alan could have told him, there was far too much to replace it with, so he packed him with what he called pledgets, which looked like a pair of tampons mounted on sticks, shoved them high and deep into the nasal cavities and told him to wait and see if they managed to stop the bleeding.

Miraculously, they did.

Half an hour later they released him. He phoned Annie and she drove him back to the condo and he washed his hands and face and changed his clothes and they each went back to bed.

*****

He woke needing to use the toilet and found that both his shit and piss had turned black. A tiny black droplet clung to his penis. He shook it off. He supposed he'd learned something--a vampire's shit and urine would always be black. He wondered if Anne Rice could find a way to make this glamorous.

*****

The second time he woke he was bleeding again. He squeezed at the pledgets as he'd been told to do should this occur but the bleeding wouldn't stop. He roused Ann and this time she insisted on driving him to the hospital herself, handing him her own newly opened box of Puffs to place in his lap. Upstairs David continued to sleep his heavy adolescent sleep. It was just as well. The boy was only fond of blood in horror movies.

The chubby nurse's aide was gone when he arrived but the pink plastic bowls were there and he used them, sat in the same room he'd left only hours before while his doctor, the swimmer, summoned an Ear Nose and Throat man who arrived shortly after he'd sent Annie back home.

By now he felt weak as a newborn colt, rubber-legged and woozy. It seemed he needed to grow a new pair of hands to juggle his kidney-shaped-pan, eyeglasses, tissues and tissue boxes, all the while holding his nose and spitting, vomiting, dripping and swallowing blood at intervals.

He felt vaguely ridiculous, amused. A bloody nose for chrissake.

What he felt next was pain that lasted quite a while as the ENT man--another healthy Florida specimen, a young Irishman who arrived in pleated shorts and polo shirt --withdrew the pledgets and peered into his nose with a long thin tubular lighted microscope, determined that it was only from the right nostril that he was actually bleeding, and then repacked it with so much stuff that by the time it was finished he felt like a small dog had crawled up and died in there.

A half-inch square accordion-type gauze ribbon coated in Vaseline, four feet of it folded back-to-back compacted tight into itself and pushed in deep. In front of that another tampon-like pledget, this one removable by means of a string. In front of that something called a Foley catheter which inflated like a balloon. Another four feet of folded ribbon. Another pledget.

He had no idea there was so much room inside his face.

The man was hearty but not gentle.

He was given drugs against the pain and possible infection and put into a wheelchair and wheeled into an elevator and settled into a hospital bed for forty-eight hours' observation. Once again a nurse had to find and read his insurance and social security cards. The drugs had kicked in by then and so had the loss of blood. He didn't even know where his wallet was though he suspected it was in its usual place, his back pocket.

The bed next to him was empty. The ward, quiet.

He slept.

*****

He awoke sneezing, coughing blood, a bright stunning spray across the sheets--*it could not get out his nose so instead it was sliding down his throat again, his very heartbeat betraying him, pulsing thin curtains, washes of blood over his pharynx, larynx, down into his trachea.* He gagged and reached for bowl at the table by the bed and vomited violently, blood and bile, something thick in the back of his throat remaining gagging him, something thick and solid like a heavy ball of mucus making him want to puke again so he reached into his mouth to clear it, reached in with thumb and forefinger and grasped it, slippery and sodden, and pulled.

And at first he couldn't understand what it was but it was long, taut, and would not part company with his throat so he pulled again until it was out of his mouth and he could see the thing, and then he couldn't believe what he'd done, that it was even possible to do this thing but he had it between his fingers, he was staring at it covered with slime and blood, nearly a foot and a half of the accordion ribbon packed inside his nose. He'd sneezed it out or coughed it out through his pharynx and now he was holding it like a tiny extra-long tongue and it continued to gag him so he reached for the call-button and pushed and fought the urge to vomit, waiting.

"What in the world have you done?"

It was the pretty nurse, a strong young blonde with a wedding ring, the one who'd admitted him and got him into bed. She looked as though she didn't know whether to be shocked or angry or amused with him.

"Damned if I know," he said around the ribbon. *Aaand ithh eye-o.*

He vomited again. There was a lot of it this time.

"Uh-oh," she said. "I'm going to call your doctor. He may have to cauterize whatever's bleeding up in there. I'll get some scissors meantime, snip that back for you, okay?"

He nodded and then sat there holding the thing. He shook his head. *A goddamn bloody nose.*

*****

It occurred to him much later that an operation followed by a hospital stay under heavy medication combined with heavy loss of blood was a lot like drifting through a thick fetal sea from which you occasionally surfaced to glimpse fuzzy snatches of sky. In his younger days he'd dropped acid while floating in the warm Aegean and there were similarities. He awoke to orderlies serving food and nurses taking his blood pressure and handing him paper cups of medication. None of it grounded him for long. Mostly he slept and dreamed.

He remembered the dreams vividly, huge segments of them crowded spinning inside his head with unaccustomed clarity of detail and feeling-- and then he'd seem to blink and they'd be gone, just like that, his mind occupied solely by the business of healing his ruptured body. Adjusting the new packing to relieve the pressure, swallowing the pill, nibbling the food. Then hurrying back to dream.

There was something ultimately lonely, he thought, about the process of healing. Nobody could really help you. All they could do was be reasonably attentive to your needs. He began to look forward to his momentary visits from the pretty blonde nurse because of all the hospital staff she seemed the wittiest and most cheerful and he liked her Southern accent, but ultimately he was completely alone in this. He'd told Annie not to call for a while after her first phone call woke him, he was fine but he was not up to conversation yet. And that felt lonely too.

When the black man with the haunted eyes appeared in the bed beside him by the window he was not really surprised. He assumed a lot went on in his room that he wasn't aware of. He'd looked over at the window to see if it was day or night because as usual he had no idea, no concept of time whatsoever, and there he was lying flat on his back and covered to the chin, hooked up to some sort of monitor and an elaborate IV device of tubes and wires much different from his own, his face thin to emaciation, drawn and grey in the moonlight, eyes open wide and focused in his direction but, Alan thought, not seeing him, or seeing through him--and this he proved with a smile and a nod into the man's wide unblinking gaze.

Possibly some sort of brain damage, he thought, poor guy, knowing somehow that this man's loneliness far exceeded his own, and moments later forgot him and returned to sleep.

*****

Imagine the seats on a slowly moving Ferris wheel, only the seats are perfectly stable, they don't rock back in forth as the seats on a Ferris wheel do, they remain perfectly steady, and then imagine that they are not seats at all but a set of flat gleaming slabs of thick heavy highly polished glass or metal or even wood, dark, so that it is impossible to tell which--and now imagine that there is no wheel--nothing whatever holding them together but the slow steady measured glide itself and that each is the size and shape of a closet door laid flat, and that there are not only one set but countless sets, intricately moving in and out and past each other, almost but never quite touching, so that you can step up or down or to the side on any of them without ever once losing your footing.

It is like dancing. It gets you nowhere. But it's pleasurable.

That was what he dreamed.

He was alone in the dream for quite a while, until Annie appeared, a younger Annie, looking much the same as she did the day he met her, sitting across from him on the plane from L.A. with her two-year-old son beside her, over a dozen years ago. Her hair was short as it was then as was her skirt and she was stepping toward him in a roundabout way, one step forward and one to the side, drifting over and under him and he wasn't even sure she was aware of his presence, it was as though he were invisible, because she never looked directly at him until she turned and said, *you left us nowhere, you know that?* which was not an accusation but merely a statement of fact and he nodded and began to cry because of course it was true, aside from these infrequent visits and the phone calls and letters he had come unstuck from them somehow, let them fend for themselves alone.

He woke and saw the black man standing in the doorway, peering out into the corridor, turning his head slowly as though searching for someone with those wide empty eyes and he thought for a moment that the man should not be out of bed, not with all those wires and tubes still attached to him reaching all the way across the room past the foot of his own bed but then heard movement to the other side of the darkened room and turned to see the form of a small squat woman who appeared to be adjusting the instruments, doing something to the instruments, a nurse or a nurse's aide he supposed so he guessed it was all right for the man to be there. He looked back at him in the doorway and closed his eyes, trying but failing to find his way back into the dream, wanting to explain to Annie the inexplicable.

It was almost dawn when the arm woke him.

He had all but forgotten about the arm, the inflamed swollen tendon that had started him on ibuprofen and landed him here in the first place. The drugs had masked that pain too. Now the arm jerked him suddenly conscious, jerked hard twice down along his side as though some sort of electric shock had animated it, something beyond his will or perhaps inside his dream, needles of pain from the elbow rising above the constant throbbing wound inside his face.

He guessed more drugs were in order.

He was hurting himself here.

He pressed the call button and waited for the voice on the intercom.

"Yes? What can I do for you?"

"I need a shot or a pill or something."

"Pain?"

"Yes."

"I'll tell your nurse."

They were fast, he gave them that. The pretty blonde nurse was beside him almost instantly, or perhaps despite his pain he'd drifted, he didn't know. She offered him a paper cup with two bright blue pills inside.

"You hurt yourself awake, did you?"

"I guess. Yeah, my arm."

"Your arm?"

"Tennis elbow. Didn't even get to play tennis. Did it in a gym over a month ago."

She shook her head, smiling, while he took the pill and a sip of water. "You're not having a real good holiday, are you?"

"Not really, no."

She patted his shoulder. "You'll sleep for a while now."

When she was gone he lay there waiting for the pain to recede, trying to relax so that he could sleep again. He turned and saw the black man staring at him as before, and saw that the man now nestled in a thicket of tubes and wires, connected to each of his arms, running under the bedcovers to his legs, another perhaps a catheter, two more patched to his collarbones, one running to his nose and the thickest of them into his half-open mouth. Behind him lights on a tall wide panel glowed red and blue in the dark.

*****

By morning it was gone. All of it. Alan was lying on his side so that the empty bed and the empty space behind it and the light spilling in from the window were the first things he noticed.

The next thing was the smell of eggs and bacon. He did his best by the food set in front of him though it was tasteless and none too warm and the toast was hard and dry. He drank his juice and tea. When the nurse came in with his pills--a new nurse, middle-aged, black and heavy-waisted, one he'd never seen--he asked her about the man in the bed beside him.

"Nobody beside you," she said.

"What?"

"You been all alone here. I just came on but first thing I did was check the charts. Always do. Procedure. You're lucky it's summertime, with all the snowbirds gone, or we'd be up to our ears here. You got the place all to yourself."

"That's impossible. I saw this guy three times, twice in the bed and once standing right there in the doorway. He looked terrible. He was hooked up to all kinds of tubes, instruments."

"'Fraid you were dreaming. You take a little pain-killer, you take a little imagination, mix and stir. Happens all the time."

"I'm an appellate lawyer. I don't *have* an imagination."

She smiled. "You were all alone, sir, all night long. I swear."

Some sort of mix-up with the charts, he thought. The man had been there. He wasn't delusional. He knew the difference between dreams and reality. For now the dreams were the more vivid of the two. It was still one way to tell them apart.

Wait till the shift changes, he thought. Ask the other nurse, the blonde. She'd given him a pill last night. The black man had been there. And he was on her watch.

He dreamed and drifted all day long. Some time during the afternoon Annie and David came by to visit and he told David about coughing up the accordion ribbon and what he'd learned about the color of a vampire shit. Teenage kids were into things like that he thought, the grosser the better. That and Annie's cool lips on his forehead were about all he remembered of their visit. He remembered lunch and dinner, though not what he ate. He remembered the doctor coming by and that he no longer wore the shorts and polo shirt as he took his pulse and blood pressure but instead the pro forma white lab coat and trousers. He decided he liked him better the other way.

*****

"Sure," she said. "I remember. You hurt yourself awake."

"You remember the guy in the bed beside me?"

"Who?"

"The black man. I don't know what was wrong with him but he looked pretty bad."

"You know what your doctor's giving you for pain?"

"No."

"It's called hydrocodone, honey. In the dose you're getting, it's as mean as morphine, only it's not addictive. I wouldn't be surprised if you told me you were seeing Elvis in that bed over there, let alone some black fella."

*****

He *hurt himself awake* again that night.

This time he was batting at his aching face--at his nose. He was batting at the culprit, at the source of his misery. As though he wanted to start himself bleeding again.

What was he doing? Why was he doing this?

His dream had been intense and strange. They were alone inside a long grey tube, he and Annie, empty of everything but the two of them and stretching off into some dazzling bright infinity and he was pulling at her clothes, her blouse, her jacket, trying to rouse her and get her to her feet while she crouched in front of him saying nothing, doing nothing, as though his presence beside her meant nothing at all to her one way or another. He felt frightened, adrift, panicked.

He woke in pain batting at his face and reached for the call-button to call his nurse for yet another pill but the black man's big hand stopped him, fingers grasping his wrist. The man was standing by his bedside. The fingers were long and smooth and dry, his grip astonishingly firm.

He looked up into the wide brown eyes that did not seem to focus upon him but instead to look beyond him, into vast distances, and saw the wires and tubes trailing off behind him past the other bed where the squat dark form he realized was no nurse nor nurse's aide hovered over the panel of instruments and a voice inside his head said *no, we're not finished yet, my accident became yours and I'm very much sorry for that but it happens sometimes and for now no interruptions please, we need the facilities, deal with your own pain as I am dealing with mine* and he thought, I'm dreaming, this is crazy, this is the drug but the voice inside said *no, not crazy, only alone in this, alone together here in this room and the nurse cannot see, cannot know, the nurse is not in pain as you and I, you'll only disturb her, you can live with that, can't you* and he nodded yes because suddenly he thought that of course he could. *Good,* the voice said, *a short time, stop hurting yourself and instead of her, dream of me, you've been doing that already but she always gets in,*

36

doesn't she. He nodded again and felt the pressure lessen on his wrist. *Stop hurting yourself. She is not the pain nor are you. Rest. Sleep.*

The man sat back on his own bed and rested, adjusted the wires, smoothed them over his chest. The dark female figure resumed her work at the lighted panel. The man's touch was like a drug. Better. The pain was vanishing. He didn't need the call button. Or perhaps he was just living with the pain, he didn't know. One more night, he thought. One more morning, maybe.

Maybe there were things he could do for her and the boy that he hadn't done, things to make it better. But he needed to let go of that now.

He dreamed of a Ferris wheel. Only there was no wheel. He dreamed of a thousand wheels intersecting.

He stepped down and up and forward and side to side.

A BOX OF CANDY

NELSON W. PYLES

Nelson Pyles currently resides in Pittsburgh PA. He has written numerous short stories and is currently at work on his second novel. His response to the Twilight series, "Where the Apple Shine Won't Reach", appeared in the Post Mortem Press Anthology Mon Coeur Mort.

Frank Ridgeway winced as the ship violently lurched against the crashing waves. He cursed himself for booking a ship across the Atlantic. He had suggested it as a sort of second Honeymoon; a cruise to the Caribbean would be "romantic" he had said to his wife. He cursed himself again for thinking it was a good idea.

*****

He also thought that taking the cruise three months after her death was a good idea too.

He thought about her as he lay sprawled on his cabin bed, always on the verge of throwing up, but never quite able to do it. The storm had been going on for an hour and wasn't getting any better. Sometimes, the lights flickered on and then off. He couldn't even watch the flat screen TV as a distraction because they had opted out of the closed circuit and satellite networking to save money.

"Why get TV on a ship?" Candace had asked, unsmiling. "We'll be having too much *fun*."

He laughed a little, thinking of that conversation when they were booking the trip.

Then, he started to cry.

They'd been married for ten years and although some patches had been rocky (*like the discovery that he would not be able to father any children*) he'd thought it had been a decent marriage. He had watched in growing horror that all of their friends were getting divorced while they just "kept rocking on" as Candace had put it. There wasn't anything wrong in their little world at all.

The three months since her death however had brought the reality a little more into focus.

Candace was a stunningly beautiful woman; honey blonde hair, a very fit figure and ice cold green eyes. She was a confident, brilliant scientist.

Frank was very average in every way; slender, nearly pale in complexion, balding prematurely and slouched a little. Candace had said he was a milquetoast.

And Candace hated him.

Her accidental death at the pharmaceutical research company, though, had just about killed him too or so it felt. The details of the accident were sketchy at best and Frank was considering suing the shit out of them, but the life insurance settlement and the additional financial amount given to him by the company had held him off for the time being.

"It was a freak occurrence," Stephan Bosen, the company's CEO had told him. "As safe as we try to make radiation research, sometimes..." And he just waved his hand dismissively as if to say "*You know what I mean.*"

Frank still didn't know what he meant.

All Frank knew were that the last things he'd said to her were in anger as were the last things she'd said to him. He'd never argued with her before (*as much as he'd wanted to*) but she had always liked to yell at him. He had always been hesitant to argue with her and yes, he knew she pretty much walked all over him, but she was still his wife and that needed to count for something.

And *God*, she was angry that morning. She'd mentioned calling her mother in Ohio and that maybe she was going to move out for a little while.

Maybe for a lot longer.

He tried to block that conversation out, which was easy as the ship lurched to the right. He heard something move in his room and then heard a thud. He pried his head off of his pillow and looked in the direction of the noise. His suitcase has fallen over and spilled out some clothes.

And the box of Candace.

He bolted upright and got out of the bed. The room wobbled and he wobbled with it as he made his way to the suitcase. Dropping to his knees, he picked up the box with Candace's ashes and cradled them like a baby.

He sat on his knees and looked at the little cardboard box. Inside was a sealed plastic bag and in the bag was his wife--all that was left of her; a small pile of ash. He choked a little but didn't start crying again. He was thankful for that at least. He was tempted to open the box, but he didn't want to see her like that again. It was bad enough when he had collected the bag in the first place. He had cried until it hurt and the funeral home had to call a cab to take him home.

The ship rocked again, but the sick feeling had stopped when he held the ashes. He stood up and although the boat still wobbled, he wobbled a little less.

The stateroom was small, but had several places to sit other than the bed. He'd been in the room two days already and had only left for dinner. He decided to take the box over to the little desk in the corner and sit down. He carefully walked over; trying not to fall as the ship still tilted and rested the box near a small clock radio. He pulled out the chair and sat, turning on the little desk lamp.

The radio was off, but he heard a humming sound. The digital number display was flickering. Puzzled, he moved the box away from the radio to see what was wrong with the radio. He picked it up and held it to his ear.

Nothing.

He looked again at the number display and it read 5:34PM and it was not flickering. Shrugging, he put the radio back in its spot. He figured it was just the power as the ship negotiated its way through the storm.

He reached for the box (*of Candace*) and slid it in front of him. Almost instantly, the radio began to buzz again. He looked at the radio and the display again was flickering, although softer than before. Frank frowned at how odd this was and without thinking, he slid the box slowly closer to the radio. The closer the box got, the louder the buzz was and the more the display flickered.

He slid the box away from the radio slowly and the radio adjusted itself once again-quiet and non-flickering.

This was odd, Frank thought, but nothing that unusual either. Most things had some sort of electrical discharge. Candace had taught him that early in their relationship. They were at a carnival, years before getting married--when things were good and happy. She had taken the balloon he had bought for her and rubbed it on her head. Frank had laughed.

"Now, check this out," she said gleefully and held the balloon over her head. Frank laughed harder as her thin brown hair rose up from the static electrical charge. "That's pretty damn wicked, right?"

"No one says wicked, Candy."

"I do," she replied, rubbing the balloon on his head. "All the cool scientist chicks are saying it."

She held the balloon up and Frank's longish black hair had stood up as well. She giggled at the look on his face.

"I only know one scientist chick," he said grinning down at her.

"Yeah, but I am the only one you need to know," she replied and kissed him, letting the balloon go.

If a stupid red balloon could do that, Frank rationalized, then why *not* a box of scientist chick ashes? He chuckled and moved the box back and forth from the radio, hearing it buzz on and off as it neared the radio and then away.

After a few minutes of this, he decided he would leave the room for a while and try to get up to the dining deck. It sounded like the storm was backing off at last and he was feeling a little less nauseated and slightly hungry.

He stood up and left the box on the little desk.

"I'll be back, Candy." He said. He slipped his shoes on and left the room.

When he came back an hour later, the first thing he noticed besides that he'd left the light on, was the buzzing. He closed and locked the door. The storm had indeed ended and the Captain assured the passengers that it would be relatively smooth sailing for the rest of the trip there and possibly on the way back. Frank was half-resigned on catching a plane ride back though, but he decided to wait until he got there.

He walked over to the desk and the buzz coming from the radio was louder. The display of the time was worse. Not only did it flicker, but it was displaying the incorrect time. It read 9:43AM.

The box, however, was on the far side of the desk.

He sat down and picked up the radio. It was buzzing, louder than before, but the box was further away. He put the radio down and slowly slid the box closer to the radio. The buzz increased in volume and the display began to flicker once again, but this time the numbers changed.

The display was churning out random numbers. Sometimes it would seem to count down slowly and then quickly. But it was moving the numbers around in no discernible pattern.

Frank slid the box away from the radio and it calmed down, but it did not stop. The clock went back to reading 9:43AM.

Frank leaned back in the chair and rested his chin in his left hand. Candace used to call it his 'ponder face" and that what he was doing.

Pondering.

He sat like that for a minute and turned the radio on.

There was a screech of electronic noise; static, but somehow worse. It didn't sound like white noise. It sounded almost like a scream and it was nearly deafening. His head began to pound and he shot a hand out to turn the radio off. The scream sound stopped and the buzz returned. He looked at the radio again and saw the volume knob on the side. He turned it all the way down and turned the radio back on again, this time, ready for the sound.

He could still hear the screaming electronic noise, but the volume control lessened it-even though it was all the way down. Slowly, he turned it up to a comfortable level-as comfortable as the screeching sound could be.

He listened carefully to the sound. It really did sound like a scream, but there seemed to be something else behind it.

He looked at the box (*of Candace*) and slid it closer to the radio. As he did so, the scream seemed to change. Not in intensity, but in pitch.

He slid the box right next to the radio. The digital display again jumped to 9:43AM, but the last number kept flickering to the number 4 and then back to 3.

The scream stopped and a voice came out of the radio.

"*Frank?*" the radio asked.

Frank's face went pale and he felt seasick again. His stomach began to swing.

"*Frank, can you hear me?*" the radio asked.

He opened his mouth to speak, but that was absurd. This was not happening. There's no way it could.

"*Frank, its Candy. Can you hear me?*"

Frank's world went black and he slid off of the chair.

When he came to, he found himself half under the desk in the stateroom. His mouth was dry and it felt like he'd eaten a pair of socks. He pushed himself off of the floor. The ship was rocking again, but he felt a little better.

He pulled himself in the chair by the desk and looked.

The box of ashes (*Candy*) was still next to the radio. The radio display still read 9:43 AM and the radio as far as he could tell was still in the on position, but he couldn't hear anything.

Frank sighed and chuckled.

"My wife is a radio," he said aloud. "That's almost funny."
"*I'm not a radio,*" the radio said. "*Frank, I need your help.*"

Frank stared at the radio.

"I don't believe this," he said. "You're dead."

"*I still am.*" The radio with Candace's voice said. "*At least I think I'm dead. I don't really know for sure what I am.*"

Frank began to weep. He was going crazy, he was sure of it. He was talking to the fucking radio now, on a cruise he was taking with a box of his wife.

"I'm talking to myself," Frank said, almost laughing. "Or, I'm talking to the box of ashes with you in it, but it isn't you."

"*Frank, you need to listen,*" Candace's voice returned. "*I know this is hard to accept, but you are hearing my voice and I need your help.*"

Frank looked around the stateroom and as he thought, he was still all alone.

"Where are you?" he asked.

"*I'm not exactly in the room with you,*' his dead wife said. "*You can't see me and I can't see you.*"

"No," Frank said softly and put his head in his hands. "It's not possible."

"*Frank? I don't want to scare you.*"

Frank, still holding his face in his hands laughed.

"I don't know if it's fear or misery, Candy. I really don't." His laugh turned into a sob. "I don't want you to be dead and I don't want to be crazy."

"*I'm dead. And you aren't crazy. You have to help me.*"

Frank considered this for a moment; his dead wife was talking to him through a radio on a cruise ship headed for what was originally a second honeymoon.

"Some second honeymoon, huh?" he said.

Radio Candy laughed.

Frank stood up and walked away from the desk to clear his head a little.

"*Where are you going?*" the voice sounded worried.

"I'm here," he replied. "Just, walking around a little. Trying to let this sink in, you know?"

"*Okay, thought I lost you. I'm so sorry.*"

"Sorry for what?"

"*I don't know,*" Candace said.

"It does put a damper on this trip, but it's not like it's your fault. I was thinking of suing that goddamn company."

"*You won't win*" Candy said. "*It's not their fault. It was mine. I got stupid. Clumsy.*"

Frank looked at the radio and frowned.

"You aren't clumsy or stupid, Candy. You never were."

Candace on the radio sounded like she sighed.

"*I was. More than you know.*"

Frank walked back to the desk and sat down.

"How are you able to talk to me? You're some kind of ghost, right?"

"*Not exactly,*" she said. "*There was an explosion at work. They told you that much I'm sure.*"

"They did,"

"*Well, the explosion didn't just kill me; it irradiated my body in some terrible way near as I can figure. It killed me, but it kept the molecules intact. Alive and aware somehow. Even when I was cremated. It must have been the new isotope generator we had started using. Experimental. My ashes are nearby the radio I guess.*"

Frank looked at the box and put a hand on it.

"You're right next to the radio."

"*I can feel it, that makes sense,*" the voice said. "*Where have you kept the box? I've been hoping you'd put me near something electronic to test my theory.*"

"Theory? You've been a pile of ash for three months."

"*Yes, and I've been just hovering around. It's been awful--hearing you and not being able to say anything. It's like being in hell.*"

Frank was still reeling from this, but it was starting to sink in a little bit more.

"God, I've missed you so much Candy," he said.

"*Then you need to help me, Frankie. You have to free me.*"

"Free you how?"

"*I need you to dump the ashes. You need to separate the ashes and scatter me. I think I can move on if you do that,*"

"Is this another theory?" Frank asked. Although he was getting closer to believing what was happening, he wasn't so sure he wanted it to be over; just hearing her voice made him feel better.

"*It is, but if I was right about the radio, I should be right about this,*"

Frank felt his eyes well up again.

"I don't know that I can do that, baby. I really don't know-"

"*I have to tell you something that may make you change your mind,*" she said.

"What?"

"*I didn't accidentally blow myself up.*"

"I know. Those bastards were careless..."

"*No, Frank. I blew myself up.*"

Frank stared at the radio in disbelief. That didn't make sense.

"Honey, that--"

"*I killed myself.*"

"You're lying," he said. "You were happy. We were happy. You didn't kill yourself."

"*You were happy,*" Candace said. "*You were always happy, Frank. I'm sorry to say that, but you have to know.*"

"You're just saying that to make me dump the ashes," Frank said, but he knew when she was lying. He always did and she wasn't lying now. "Why didn't you say anything?"

"*I tried to, but I couldn't. I knew you'd never divorce me. Not without a fight. I just couldn't...face you after our argument.*"

Frank sat there, looking at the clock. He didn't say anything at all, he just looked. The digital display still read 9:43 and flickered to 44 every few seconds.

Candace had wanted out. And she got out, alright. But that number...what the hell was that all about?

"*Frank?*" Candy asked. "*Are you still walking around?*"

"No, I'm here." He said. "Just pondering I guess."

"*Ponder face,*" she said and gave a small laugh.

Frank wasn't getting something. She couldn't face him about not being happy? She was able to face him about nearly everything else and talked about leaving him. He looked at the clock.

"What happened at 9:43AM, Candy?"

"*What?*"

"The radio your voice is coming through? It's a clock radio. It flickers on and off between 9:43 and 44. What's that all about?"

There was a silence and she responded,

"*I don't really know.*"

"The time of death was 10:32AM, so it's not that. What happened at 9:43?"

Again there was silence.

"*I don't...really know. That's odd.*"

Frank laughed.

She was lying.

"You're a box of ash talking to me through a radio and *that's* odd?" He clapped his hands. "Oh Candace, that's wicked."

"*Frank, are you going to scatter my ashes? Are you going to let me go?*"

"I want to know what happened at 9:43." Frank said.

He stood up from the desk and walked over to the TV. It was a big widescreen television that was mounted on the wall. In all the time he was in the stateroom, turning it on was never an option. He just wanted to cry, mourn and go on. But now...

"I have a theory, Candace." Frank said and pushed the power button on the TV.

"*Frank*?" Candy said through the radio and then a large burst of static shot out.

The TV screen was a bright blue that began to break up as soon as the static sound blared over the radio.

Behind the loud white noise he could hear Candace calling for him. It sounded like she was at the bottom of a well, but slowly on the TV, the screen began to clear up; not enough to where he could see anything clearly, but he could make out something.

"I can almost see you Candy," Frank said and sat the edge of the bed. "Are you there?"

"*What are you doing*?" Her voice was very faint, but he could hear her.

"I turned on the TV." He said. "I have a *theory*."

"*Frank, turn off the TV*," she said, still sounding distant, but getting closer.

"Let's see. Show me the explosion," Frank said, and almost instantly, he got a grainy looking point of view looking image on the screen. It was Candace's lab. It was scattered with microscopes and gloves and computers that all flashed by like a continuous wild camera shot. Occasionally, Frank could see Candace's hands come into view and she was moving frantically across the lab. The quick blackouts that happened must have been her blinking, he thought.

"I'm seeing what you saw that day," Frank said. "This is amazing,"

"*Frank, stop it! Please-you don't want to see this*!"

Frank ignored her and kept watching. He watched Candace walk to a power box filled with fuses and switches. She began to flip random switches and then she ran to a large terminal that had a huge warning sticker above a dial. She grabbed the dial and turned it all the way to the right. She spun around and looked at the power box from across the room. There was a moment and then a blinding explosion. Frank jumped back from where he was sitting and gasped.

He had just watched his wife die from her point of view.

He cried as he heard Candace calling to him.

"*Frank, turn the TV off. Oh God, please...turn that off.*"

Frank let out a big sigh.

"Show me what happened at 9:43," he said.

The TV went to static and then cleared again. It was another point of view from Candace but this time she was typing at a computer. It looked like she was typing an email. Candy looked away from the email and at a picture of her and Frank on her desk. Then she looked at something in front of the picture.

It was a pregnancy test. Frank couldn't make out what brand, but he could see the color pink.

Candace again looked back to the email. She hit the 'send' button and the email sent. Candace looked at the bottom corner of the computer screen and saw the time.

9:43AM

And a split second later, it was 9:44.

Frank turned the TV off.

He sat there.

"*Frank?*"

Frank sat and said nothing.

"*I'm so sorry, Frankie. I don't know what to say.*"

"You couldn't tell me?" he asked. "You could tell me every horrible other thing but that? Who was it?"

"*No one you know,*" the radio said.

"Obviously," Frank said and chuckled. "You cheated on me and then you got pregnant and then killed yourself *and* your unborn child."

Silence.

"How could you?" Frank asked.

"*I'm in hell, Frank. Literally. I'm sorry. You'll never know how sorry I am.*"

Frank laughed.

"What was the email? Was it to him?"

"*Yes,*" Candace said simply. "*He didn't want to pay for an abortion and I wasn't about to tell you. I panicked and told him I was going to kill myself. He wrote back, 'fine.' Can you believe that?*"

Frank just sat there, not saying anything. She sounded so cold. As cold as ever, in fact.

"I'm going to go take a walk, Candy. I'd ask you along, but I don't think the cord to the radio is that long,"

"*Frank, wait!*"

Frank got up and stormed out of the stateroom.

He walked around the entire length of the ship twice, which took longer than he thought it would take. He thought about what had just happened. He had spent three months feeling broken and now, he was broken all over again in a different way.

The question now was what to do.

After an hour, he came back into the room. He didn't hear anything on the radio, but when he slammed the door closed, he heard Candace start to cry.

"*Frank? Oh, baby. Are you back?*"

Frank sat at the desk.

"I'm here, Candy."

"*Are you okay?*"

"Is the baby in there with you?" Frank asked. "I know it wasn't really formed yet I guess, but is it?"

"*Yes*," Candace replied. "*You can't hear her? She screams all the fucking time.*"

Frank remembered the scream when he turned the radio on earlier.

Frank nodded. "I'd always wanted a daughter, you know."

"*I know*," Candace said, sadly. "*But you wouldn't have wanted someone else's baby, would you? You would have thrown me out and--*"

"Bullshit, Candy. Just bullshit." Frank said. "You should have known me better than that,"

"*I do know you better than that,*" Candace shot back. "*You never would have let me go. You would have wanted counseling or some such thing. Truth is I just wasn't in love you, anymore. Sorry, but it's true.*"

"You're sorry," Frank said flatly to no one in particular.

"*Yes I am and I'll never be able to make that up to you. But please. You have to help me! After the explosion, all I have is this baby screaming and nothing else. There's no light, nothing else but her and her damned screaming and I hate it!*"

Frank looked at the radio and cocked his head to one side.

"You hate your own daughter?" He asked. "Candy, that's *your* daughter!"

"*She was an accident!*" Candace nearly screamed and Frank heard, for the first time, the faint sound of a baby. But he also heard something else, in the back of his head.

She really doesn't love you anymore and probably hasn't for a very long time.

Then another thought.

She killed herself and an unborn baby to get away from *you*.

"You really hated me. Didn't you?"

"*Yes!*" She screamed. "*I fucking did and I'm sorry, but I did. For a long time I did. Now, I just want to move on.*"

"Why didn't you just go to your mother's in Ohio?"

"*Just dump my ashes, Frank. Can you just do that one fucking thing for me please?*"

"Candace, I want to know--" Frank started, but Candace, dead or not, still interrupted him.

"*No, we are not picking up from our last fight!*" Candace said. "*Can you just let it go? For the love of God, can't you just let it go?*"

Frank, heartbroken, said nothing.

"*You're pathetic! I figured you'd at least get a little satisfaction out of dumping my ashes into the god damn sea, but you just want to talk and argue. I wanted you to be a man! You never fought back no matter what I threw at you. Do you see why I--*"

He got up and turned off the radio. He grabbed the cord and yanked it out of the wall. He threw the radio hard on the stateroom floor. He picked up the box of ashes, stormed across the room and put it roughly in the suitcase, then put the suitcase in the little closet.

He walked over to the bed and kicked his shoes off. He felt awfully tired and figured he'd try to go to sleep. Tomorrow or the next day (*he couldn't honestly remember*), he'd be in the Caribbean. Frank fell onto the bed, still in his clothes and fell fast asleep.

In the early afternoon two days later, Frank walked off the ship--the *SS Celeste* from Happytime Cruise Lines--in a pair of shorts, a T-shirt, some flip flops and a back pack. The air was warm and smelled like sunscreen and tourists. The sky was a deep blue and there wasn't a cloud in the sky. He put on his sunglasses and looked for the nearest beach.

He found a bar, instead.

After about an hour, he'd managed to have three Pina Coladas. He was directed by a young islander to a small beach about a mile away from the bar. Somewhere where there weren't a lot of people was what he'd wanted and after about 45 minutes of walking, he saw the beach the young man had told him about.

It was perfect.

He walked on the sand about half way to the shore line and took his back pack off. He opened it up and pulled out a very small blue kid's shovel.

Then he pulled out Candace's box of ashes and dropped the back pack.

He dropped to his knees and began to dig a hole. Not a very deep hole, but one just deep enough.

Frank had been tempted to bring a small portable radio so he could hear Candy scream and yell, but he'd decided he'd had enough. He picked up the box and rested it in the hole--it was about two feet deep.

"Bye, Candy," was all he said and covered up the hole. Somewhere in his head, he could almost hear her yelling at him.

He stood up and looked at the small grave. Bending down to grab his bag, Frank stuffed the small blue shovel inside. He turned and walked away. Maybe he'd go back to the bar. The drinks were great and inexpensive.

He thought about Candace one more time and hoped that someone with a radio didn't lay their blanket anywhere near the box.

He smiled.

THAT WHICH DOES NOT KILL YOU
MATT MOORE

Matt Moore is an Aurora Award nominee with short fiction in several print, electronic and audio markets such as On Spec, AE: The Canadian Science Fiction Review, Torn Realities, Cast Macabre *and the* Tesseracts *anthologies. His novelette* Silverman's Game *was published in 2010. When not writing, he is the Communications Director for ChiZine Publications. He can be reached at mattmoorewrites.com.*

When Fynn stepped out of the shadows, duffel bag in hand and surgical apron over her fatigues, Teller's junkie heart quickened. And he hated himself for it—mouth going dry, craving the graceful oblivion she'd deliver.

Teller yanked the gurney to a halt, wheels groaning. Watching up and down the dimly lit basement hallways, he pressed his thumb against the door's scanner, trying to hide the shakes.

"Relax," Fynn commanded. "There's nothing wrong here."

"Right," he replied, craving the bitter taste on his tongue. Hoping anyone who saw them would believe a surgeon had a reason to accompany a corpsman disposing of limbs removed during surgery.

The scanner beeped. The door popped open, releasing the dry, sterile smell into the dank hallway. Teller wheeled in the gurney, piled high with black medical waste bags headed for the incinerator. Not that it was a true incinerator. The name had stuck, but this nasty piece of technology used microwaves to reduce almost anything to ash in moments. If the military could shrink it to something they could mount on exoarmor, the war would be over.

Fynn followed him in and pulled the door shut. The room, empty except for the chute to the incinerator, its controls, and a buzzing overhead light, was barely big enough for the two of them and the gurney. While Fynn snapped on gloves, Teller keyed in the ignition sequence and kept his eyes fixed on the pad.

Didn't mean he didn't hear it. Smell it.

The first time she'd done this, he'd almost passed out. He saw his share of shit working in a forward field hospital, which had started him on the pills, but it was the care she showed that freaked him out. The delicateness, almost love, sorting through the bags, unzipping them, gently examining the limbs that had been cut from soldiers only hours earlier.

"You're jonesing," Fynn said.

Teller hadn't known he'd been shifting from foot to foot, his fingers twitching. "Not too bad. Been eight hours," he lied, adding two hours since he'd last popped a pill.

"Good," she said. Plastic crinkled against the duffel's heavy fiber as she slid a bag in.

What did she do with them? Teller asked himself for the thousandth time. Research, she'd told him once after fucking. He hadn't been paying attention. Hadn't even asked. Something about an abandoned program to keep severed limbs viable. Surgeons could focus on the critical procedures and re-attached amputated limbs hours, even days, later. Need to keep it quiet, she'd said. I don't want the military to know because I want to save lives. They'd use it as a weapon. She'd then sprung out of her cot, naked, sat at the small desk in her quarters and typed into her tablet.

"We're done," Fynn said, wiping bloody gloves on her apron before snapping them off. The room reeked of coppery, congealed blood. She reached into her fatigues pocket and handed him a plastic bottle.

Not wanting to, hating himself, he shook it. Not as full as usual.

"If you can go eight hours," Fynn said, "try for ten. That will last you four days." She hoisted the duffel onto a shoulder and ran a finger down his cheek. "Come by when you're done." She turned and left.

Teller cursed, hands quivering now. When she wanted sex, she wanted him clean. Not that he didn't enjoy it. She wasn't much to look at, but military service gave her a firm body. She didn't even make him wear a condom. I'm a doctor, she'd said, I'll cure anything you have. And getting knocked up? All she'd said was Uncle Marty took care of that when I was 13.

At least after sex she opened up, talked about herself. Like it was pillow talk. Like they were a couple. He hoped she'd let slide some sliver of knowledge he could leverage against her. An officer, a surgeon and his source—she held the cards. Hell, she was in her mid-thirties and he'd just turned 22.

Now she was cutting him back. To help wean him off the pills, he knew. To get clean.

But his junkie heart and junkie brain had control. He needed to know something about her. Even things out. Her taking body parts would be his word against hers if he didn't know what she did with them. Where she took them.

Leaving the gurney, he went into the hall in time to hear the stairway door slam shut. He followed, sprinting up the metal steps, and paused at the main level. Doors led outside and into the hospital hall. Checking outside, he spotted her crossing the gravel road between the main building and a row of DRASH tents. He waited for her to move between tents before crossing the road himself, waiting in the shadows of the next tent over. Beyond the row of tents, flood lights from the main building barely illuminated the few large supply tents and pre-fab sheds in the no-man's land between the main compound and the perimeter fence. Beyond the fence, its outward facing lights showed the brown, hard scrabble countryside. And beyond its illumination, the enemy.

Teller spotted Fynn in the no-man's land. She stopped at the side of a large shed with two roll up doors on its front. Teller had assumed it was part of the motor pool. Fynn undid a lock on a side door and went it.

He'd check it out later. Right now he was jonesing too bad. He moved back to the main building, hoping no one had found the gurney unattended.

*****

By the time he reached his tent, the world had gone deliciously waffling-baffling, topsy-turvy-curvy.

Sex with Fynn had been fine.

Pills were better.

His sleeping tent mates appeared as distorted beasts, their snoring an alien rumbling from reality's deepest depths. Bliss enwrapped him like a soft shroud, leeching away his self-hatred.

And when, some slippery-time later, the world rolled and shivered, he thought it just part of the high. But motion surrounded him, tugged at him. The high's clutches slipped down his skin like warm, slick tentacles. Mind sharper, animal panic stabbed his heart before his brain assembled the flurry of movements and sounds of his tent mates into a cohesive thought: incoming artillery. A concussive blast thudded. Instinct and training had him up, pants on, helmet on, running for the bunker.

Through the tent flaps, visions slapped him—red and orange flames, brown sand, black smoke, blacker sky. Acrid smell of burning tents and spent artillery shells. He flowed among the swarm of people toward the main building's wide, blank north wall. The hard packed ground shifting and rolling beneath him. Bodies pressed close, the stink of sweat and panic. Down the ramp, through the open steel doors, into the bunker's concrete depths. He turned into the room for medical staff. Finding a spot on the hard, cold floor he leaned against a wall that vibrated with each landing shell and every volley fired back.

By now, drones would be up, scanning, relaying enemy artillery locations to their own cannons.

War by proxy, Fynn had called it. For centuries, man fought face-to-face. One man kills another. Now exoarmor hides our faces. But the armor loses a leg, the person loses a leg. We should send machines to kill machines. Or send the soldier home and let the leg keep fighting.

Teller glanced around the room, a flickering overhead lights casting everyone in shadow. Some stood, most sat. A captain did a head count, a corporal in tow. Teller spotted Fynn, hunched over, typing at her tablet. He didn't let his eyes linger. That typing. In the mess hall, the break room, at the infirmary, after fucking.

Letters? Reports? She'd been a researcher in Vancouver before she'd been drafted. She told him how lonely she'd been, how much she'd sacrificed for her career. How she wanted to save life, maintain it, create it. She wanted to have children and it pained her that she never would.

Maybe she was writing about him. The research talk was bullshit. She'd decided to record his junkie life after catching him smuggling pills. He'd been bribing Sallen, an MP whose thumbprint could open any door on the base, for access to the dispensary. Teller had been caught before, but most of the docs had been as fucked up as him by this place. He had connections to feed their secret needs or kinks. A balance. Keep each others' secrets. Colonel Brice didn't have to know anything.

But Fynn had offered to help him get clean. She'd give him pills, but control the dosage and amount. She just wanted to look at whatever he put in the incinerator. Maybe take a few limbs.

What kind of surgeon did that?

Maybe the tablet had the answers.

*****

The infirmary hallways bowed down and up and around, a bubble of right angles.

Still feeling the pills.

Sallen, bought off with some kinky Korean porn, unlocked Fynn's office. With her in surgery, he had no better time. Teller stepped in, the room big enough for a desk, chair and filing cabinet, and Sallen locked the door behind him. The turning tumblers sounded monstrously huge.

Sorting through several tablets scattered on her desk, he found the one she typed on. The one without military markings on its case. He also knew her password from watching her enter it. "Herbert".

Her documents folder held dozens of files, but between the pills and the medical jargon he couldn't make heads or tails of them. The message center was surprisingly empty. He'd thought she'd have friends back home writing her. He opened her sent messages and found it full of messages. Over twenty per day. Mind too affected to do anything but scan and absorb words:

...might not read this... I'm sorry... I can save them... Please write back... new life, like (finally) my own children... I've heard you have a little girl now... let me know you read this... I know you'll make a great Dad... viability of limbs... to feel needed, desired... shelling last night... I know I put my needs before yours... not crazy to want to maintain life...

Some messages had attachments. He opened them, fingers moving fast, swiping through images. The desert, the base, damaged building. Others showed severed limbs, limbs sewn to other limbs with fine silver wire, amalgams of limbs attached to some kind of machine. Then a video—body parts, silver wire spilling from the wounds, twitched and moved. Fingers gripped, ankles and knees flexed as if running. An eyeball perched on the back of a hand pivoted, following a point of light, looking into the camera—

He dropped the tablet. Its clatter, bass-deep from the drugs, made him jump. Had he really just seen—

"What are you doing here?"

Teller turned. Fynn in bloody scrubs, stepping into her office. The door shutting, Teller caught a glimpse of black MP's fatigues in the hall. Sallen. She'd probably paid him off to let her know if anyone tried to get into her office.

"Answer me," she commanded.

Caught. Caught and no way out. Junkie logic gave him two choices: bob and weave, or go straight through. He reached for the tablet to show her the images. But as he reached, his hand looked huge.

High. So fucking high.

Fynn pushed past him and grabbed the tablet. "My messages? You've been reading my fucking message?!" She swiped through some screens. "This is private! Just because we're fucking doesn't mean you get to know everything about me. Yes, I've screwed up relationships. And I'm consulting people about my work. Sometimes they're the same men. Happy now?"

"I'm high, okay?" Teller blurted. "I don't know what I was thinking." Bobbing and weaving. "I couldn't even read the words, you know?" Play to her sympathies. "I was looking for pills. Really? You want to know? I was looking for how I could get more pills."

Something in her posture shifted. Just slightly. Just enough to let him know he'd reached her.

"You've finished the ones I gave you. You didn't trust me to help you."

A statement. Not a question. "I—," he began and let it hang there. Truth was, he still had three pills left. He drew strength from that realization. Two months ago, before he met her, he'd have been through the pills in two days. Now he'd lasted four days and had a few pills left over.

"You don't need my help, it seems."

"I do," he said too quickly, hating the desperation.

"Do what I tell you. Make them last."

"Okay," he replied, hating the word, its shape. The humiliation.

Twelve years old again, his mother telling him how to dress, what summer school courses to take, what friends he could and couldn't play with. He hated it, hated her. And his dad in the den, watching TV, letting her run both their lives.

The drugs hadn't even been to rebel. Just to deaden his anger. He hadn't noticed how pissed his mother had been until she threatened to kick him out. He had one chance: Join the military, like his father and both grandfathers. Do that, and he could have money for college when his tour ended.

Or he could leave and never come back.

At least joining up saved him from the infantry like the draftees. Grunts locked inside exoarmor sent up against old-style tanks and rockets. But even though he didn't see combat, he saw its results. Transport drones dropping off screaming men and women, charred bits of their exoarmor sliced into their skin and muscle, limbs hanging by bits of tendon. Wheeling in casualties, wheeling out parts.

Too much. He'd needed the escape. The pills were a common enough sedative. But one in thirty-five experienced hallucinogenic side-effects. Teller was that lucky one.

Like she could read his mind, Fynn opened a desk drawer, removed something and slid it into his hands. Another pill bottle. But the clicking of the pills against plastic sounded wrong. "Lower dosage," she said. "Make these last five days. Withdrawal might be a bit more acute, but stay with it. This is the hard part. If you make it five days, we can get you off the pills in two more weeks." She moved to the doorway, body language making it clear it was time to get out.

He did.

"I have to get back to surgery," she said, closing and locking the door. "Let me know on your next run to the incinerator." She hurried down the hall toward the hospital section.

Dismissive. In charge. Telling him what to do.

At least she didn't want to fuck.

If he'd just gone to another doctor, told him about the pills, that he wanted to get clean. In too deep, now. If he went to Colonel Brice, told him everything, she'd get a slap on the wrist. An officer. A surgeon. He was a junkie corpsman. The stockade. Or transferred to infantry.

Tongue dry, imagining the bitter pill dissolving on his tongue, reality warping. His junkie mind's automatic reaction to stress.

But he was close to kicking the habit. He'd resisted the tickling need to get high until he couldn't stand it. Each time longer and longer. He'd beat it on his own. He wouldn't need her.

But his junkie mind needed to show her she'd fucked with the wrong guy.

*****

Shelling pulled him up and out of dreamless sleep.

Body well-practiced, he had on his pants, helmet, boots before fully awake. A shirt in hand, he sprinted to the bunker, joining the group funneling for its depths. The night exploded yellow-red, bits of gravel raining down on them.

Fynn would be headed there, too. Hunkered down, waiting it out, tapping into her damn tablet. Then into surgery for those who'd been hit.

Crazy, but this was his shot. He broke off from the group, running between a low, wide supply shed, its corrugated metal sides rattling in the concussions, and the main administrative building. Flattened out on the ground, arms over his head, he fought against digging into his pants pockets. Fynn had been right—they weren't as strong. Only lasted about two hours. But kicked in quicker.

An explosion spit light and heat, gravel peppering against his helmet. Someone screamed: "My leg! My fucking leg!"

On their own, hands dug for the bottle, opened it, and popped a pill into his mouth.

Each concussion lasted longer, deeper. Ancient gods furious he could plumb the depths of their ancient wisdom.

When the sound of men and machines replaced the explosion of shells, he stood, brushed himself off and wandered out into the base's grid work of gravel roads. He moved quickly, purposefully like the soldiers and vehicles around him. They shouted orders and reports about damage and causalities. Fires lit up the compound, sirens sounded, people screamed. He stumbled over a piece of rebar, scorched black, and picked it up.

Suitably high, either his courage stoked or fear deadened, he made his way out toward her shed, hoping he moved like someone with purpose and not a junkie well into his high.

Reaching the shed, he slid the rebar into the lock's clasp, settled one end against the frame and yanked. The lock popped and he opened the door.

An ozone smell and something else—fleshy, meaty—made this stomach roll. Running his hands over the wall, his eyes and ears told him something moved just as he found and flipped the light switch.

Fleshy things skittered and flopped across the floor. A creature of eight arms, joined at the shoulders, moved like a spider, palms slapping as it scampered toward him. Two legs led up to a metal box, a head emerging from its top, strode back and forth. A torso without a head, but arms emerging from both shoulders and hips, marched in a circle. On tables along the walls, more of these things moved among tools, scraps of machinery, vials and beakers, rolls of that fine silver wire.

She'd slipped something into the pills, Teller told himself. Fucking him over. A hallucination, fueled by what he'd seen on her tablet. If what he'd seen on the tablet had even been real—

The door clicked shut. A thing of three legs meeting in a swollen torso wobbled at the door, one of its three arms pressing it closed.

Not realizing he'd wandered into the middle of the room, Teller turned 360, the tables bowing and sagging. A creature of two hands, attached at the wrists, with a single eyeball perched where the hands met, flitted across it.

"Who are you?" something asked.

It was the two legs and head.

"What the fuck?" spilled out of Teller's mouth. "No. Nonononono."

The two legs and head tottered toward him, the arm-spider following. Something in the legs-head monster whirred. "You should not be here." It whirred again. "Mother said so."

"Mother?" Teller backed up toward the door, not sure how he'd deal with the tripod that guarded it.

"Mother." Whirring. "She was Dr. Fynn, but gave us life. That makes her mother." Whirring again. Some kind of fan. That's how it spoke without lungs. "You shouldn't be here without mother's permission. Mother said we must keep her secret. No one can know."

The arm-spider rushed him, six arms propelling it, the front two extended.

How does it see? shot through Teller's mind, taking a step back before the arm-spider was on him. Front arms wrapped behind Teller's knees, the rest pushing forward. Teller went down hard, pain shooting up his tailbone, shocking him out of his high. A second set of arms wrapped around his legs. The two-hand thing climbed down the table. Something he didn't see slapped across the floor. Things of all shades of flesh crawled and slithered.

His eyes fixed on silver threads holding the arms together. He swung a fist down on where they met and felt hard, sharp edges beneath the skin. Its grip weakened for a moment, but a third pair of arms grabbed him, the front pair shifting to reach around his waist. He swung again, loosening its grip, allowing him to roll over, pinning it squirming beneath him. If he could crawl for the door—

A blur of motion. Something small sprang at him. The two-hand thing, headed for his throat. Teller managed to catch it, hands grasping its fingers, and tried to pull them apart. Silver stitches popped, gray-black liquid seeped from where they came loose. The fingers of the things twitched in Teller's, the eyeball shifting back and forth. He angled his hands up, not just pulling but cracking. His eyes fixed on the thick black hairs on the back of one hand, the smooth skin of the other. The two hands came apart with a wet crunch. He threw them as a snake made of finger joints, two feet long, slithered close.

Fynn's voice: "Stop!"

The snake halted, curling into a coil. The arm-spider, still trapped beneath him, ceased squirming. Teller kicked it off.

The head-legs whirred and said, "Mother, we were doing as you—"

"I meant him!" she screamed. "Tell me what you're doing here." The things circled around Fynn as she moved into the room.

"You're insane!" Teller shouted, getting to his feet.

"Answer me! Answer—Oh no!" She sobbed, sinking to her knees and cradling the remains of the two hands Teller had ripped apart. "What did you do?" she wailed.

"You're—" he began, making for the door. Words failed him.

"You're high," she said, laying the hands down gently. Almost lovingly. "Doesn't matter what you think you saw. Who will believe you?" She stood, turning, following Teller out the door and into the cool night. In the doorway, half-lit from the shed's light, she said: "In an hour, Colonel Brice will know you're addicted to pills and suffering hallucinations." Reds and golds danced on the shed's sides from the fires burning across the compound. She turned back. "I'll protect you," he heard her say before the door slammed shut. "I'll make sure no one finds you."

Teller turned for the base, heading for the administrative building at the far end of the compound. She'd tell, he knew. He had to go to Brice first. Tell his side. He jogged a dozen steps, stumbled and vomited into the sand. After the final wretch, he looked back at the shed. Light spilled out around the door's edges. Shadows of things horrible and inhuman moved across a narrow window high on the wall.

He stopped between two tents, cloaked in shadow, spitting bile. How much of a fall would he take for the revenge of exposing Fynn? He'd have to admit to being on pills, stealing them, everything. Even implicate Sallen.

What if Brice didn't punish her, but rewarded her? Those things were recycled soldiers. Warriors. The pills still working, he imagined a battalion of body parts scrambling across the desert toward the enemy. Hands blown off arms, then hands combining into another creature that kept advancing on the enemy.

The adrenaline rush fading, nausea's warm, damp fingers slid around him. His head went light, cold sweat on his scalp. Fuck it. He had to tell. Come clean. Get free of her.

Looking up, the administrative building seemed further way, pulling back down a tunnel. Ears ringing, head light—

—wiping sand off his face. Dawn touched the eastern horizon pink. Pushing himself to his feet, memories of the previous night flashed across his mind. He was clean, he knew. He felt it and, with sunrise at 0530 hours, it meant he'd been out almost six hours. The drugs would be out of his system.

Ahead of him, the base moved as it always did. Soldiers walking at a brisk pace, vehicles roaring from one place to another. Overhead, drones circled, waiting for a pad to drop off wounded.

What had happened?

She must have seen or found out he hadn't been there for the headcount in the bunker. She'd gone looking for him.

Everything else had to be the pills. Pills cut with bad shit to really make him freak out.

Behind him, the shed's lights were off, its door open and banging against the metal wall in the hot desert wind. He moved toward the shed in an arc so he could see in its door from a distance. Yet the doorway remained flat and dark, the sunrise at the wrong angle to illuminate the interior. He moved closer, slowly, finding wheel tracks in the sand leading to the shed door. Narrow, not too deep. A light duty jeep.

Close enough to make out shapes within—all blessedly flat and angled—he approached the doorway. The shapes resolved into tables and crates, but not the elaborate set up of last night. And without the jumble of materials, there was no place for the things to hide.

Had any of it happened? Or had she packed up her gear? But where would she take it? He knew one thing for certain—with the shed empty, he had nothing. She'd played him again, still held all the cards.

Not sure where to go, he moved to the hospital. He had a shift that would have started at 0400 hours. The jones for a pill grated on him. Their promise of sweet oblivion called to him. Needing them to get through another shift. He dug in his pocket, knew the withdrawals he'd faced, and threw the bottle as far as he could.

The duty sergeant gave him an earful. There was a load to go to the incinerator. Teller grabbed the cart and took the elevator to the lower level, wondering if Fynn would be waiting with another bottle.

The elevator doors opened and he wheeled the cart forward. In the shadows, he fought to ignore motion in his peripheral vision. His junkie heart, trying to scare him, make him want that fix. The scampering sounds were rats, the dull slapping sounds the machinery of the place.

Rounding the corner, the door to the incinerator room hung open. Slowly, he wheeled the gurney forward. Two sets of legs lay on the ground, partially obscured by another gurney. One in scrubs, the other an MP's black fatigues. Black medical bags covered the gurney. Most empty, but a few remained zipped shut, their contents twisting and squirming against the black plastic.

Bile rose in Teller's mouth. He backed out into the hall. Sallen and Fynn, something within him concluded. She's gathered those things and bought off Sallen. She was going to destroy her children. In case Teller told. Then find another junkie. Start someplace else.

But they'd rebelled. They were warriors, after all. Killers.

He turned. Shadows moved and slithered. Impossible shapes, like a spider made of eight human arms, hovered in the shadows. Behind him, zippers slid open, flesh slid against plastic.

Teller bolted for the staircase. The flat slapping of eight palms pursued him.

HUMAN CAVERNS
LAWRENCE C. CONNOLLY

Lawrence C. Connolly's books include the novels Veins *(2008) and* Vipers *(2010), which together form the first two books of the* Veins Cycle. Vortex, *the third book in the series, is due in 2013. His collections, which include* Visions *(2009), This Way to Egress *(2010), and* Voices *(2011), collect all of his stories from* Amazing Stories, Cemetery Dance, The Magazine of Fantasy & Science Fiction, Twilight Zone, *and* Year's Best Horror. Voices *was nominated for the Bram Stoker Award™, Superior Achievement in a Fiction Collection. He teaches writing at Sewickley Academy and serves twice a year as one of the residency writers at Seton Hill University's graduate program in Writing Popular Fiction.*

Kevin paused by a frozen creek to check his GPS. He was in deep, miles from the road, surrounded by old growth pines. It was getting late, but there was something about the stillness of the frozen valley, the soft shadows of the trees, and the shimmer of light on the glazed rocks that made him want to savor the place. He snapped some pictures and continued on.

The creek valley was steep, naturally contoured by centuries of flowing water. He climbed out, pausing beside an ancient pine, roots exposed along the brink. He took a long, slow piss against its trunk, then turned and headed south toward an even deeper valley. And it was here that he found the charred remains of a derelict farmhouse, scorched beams standing upright amid drifting snow and ash. It had been recently burned, the smell of char still fresh in the air. He snapped some more pictures. Then he continued east, moving along a flood plain, finally coming to a draw that brought him into sight of a deformed hillside: right angles, stunted trees, tangled weeds. He knew the signs. Years ago, the slope had been mined.

He pushed on, taking pictures as he went, then putting the phone away as he climbed along a series of bench cuts to the crest of yet another valley, deeper than the others. And here, a hundred yards below, stood a dozen buildings: dark, silent, abandoned.

The sky ahead was deep blue, almost purple. Behind him it was black. He took out the phone again, checking his weather stats to verify what his eyes already told him. The sun had set. It was time to go.

He took a wide-angle shot, marked his location on the digital map, then turned and started back, making good time until his sense of solitude was broken by five men approaching through the trees on his left. There were more to his right. One of them carried a shotgun.

They spread out, surrounding him.

He reached for his phone.

"Hold on!" the shotgun man stepped closer. "Just hold up right there." He wore a patchwork of animal hides, fur turned inward for warmth. His hat was a hollowed out raccoon, head facing front, jaws molded into a dead snarl. "Right there." The gun looked heavy, with two iron barrels that became 12-gauge holes as the man took aim at Kevin's head. "You out for a stroll?"

"Yes. I mean...no. Not really."

The man sighted across the barrel. "Which is it?" His accent wasn't local. It came from somewhere to the east. New York, maybe Boston.

Most of the other men carried railroad shovels. One carried a pickax.

"You with the government?" the shotgun man asked.

"No." He was trembling now.

"What then?"

"Nothing...just a blogger. I write about ghost towns, abandoned houses, old places--things like that."

"Why?"

"It's interesting."

"People pay you?"

"No. I just do it. Like a hobby." He looked at the others. "Listen. I don't represent anyone. I'm not with the government. I'm just—"

"Got a name?"

"Kevin."

"Where you from, Kevin?"

"Pittsburgh."

"How'd you get here?"

"Car."

"Who drove?"

"No one."

"It drove itself?"

"No. I drove. It's just me."

"Where's the car?"

Kevin pointed. "The county road. I'm heading back now."

The man considered, then said: "What's in the pack?"

"Not much. Just stuff. A little food. Some water."

"And that?" He pointed to Kevin's hand.

"My phone." Kevin showed him. "I use it to—"

"All right, Kevin. I know what phones do. Now here's what." The man stepped closer, still aiming. "You're going to put everything you're carrying and wearing into that pack of yours. Understand?"

"Why?"

"You're going to mash it in real tight, as much as you can fit. Everything else I want you to just fold up and set on the ground."

"My clothes too?"

"That's right."

Kevin studied the gun. It was a breech loader. *Two shots. Then he reloads. If I run, maybe. . . .*

"I don't have all day, Kevin!"

"I don't understand."

"It's not complicated"

"What do you want?"

"I told you."

"Listen." Kevin slipped the pack from his shoulder. "You can have my stuff. Take my phone. It's got a camera, GPS, Internet—"

"What I want you to do is put it in the pack!"

Kevin fingered the screen. "I'm calling 911."

"And tell them what? Come get you? Even if you have a signal, how long will that take for them to get here? This isn't the city, Kevin." He aimed at the phone. "Truth be told, I wouldn't mind blasting that thing. Give me a reason, and I will." He stepped closer, barely three yards between them now. "In the sack, Kevin. Just do it. Phone, clothes, everything."

"I'll freeze."

"Not if you hurry."

The others stared, and Kevin felt something break inside him, a realization that resisting would just piss them off, make things worse. "All right." He pulled off a glove, felt the wind against his skin. Then he pulled off the other, put them in the pack, unzipped his coat.

The shotgun man turned toward the pickax man. "All right. Get it done."

The pickax man looked young, wispy beard, rash of acne. College age. He paused beside Kevin's pack, lifted the pick, brought it down hard on the frozen ground. *WHUMPH!* Dirt flew, the impact echoing from the trees. Another swing. *WHUMPH!*

"What's he doing?" Kevin asked.

"Digging."

WHUMPH!

"Why?"

WHUMPH! WHUMPH!

"We're waiting, Kevin. And you're wasting time." The gun had two hammers. The man cocked these now, one at a time. In the cold, the leavers popped like cracking joints.

Kevin took off his coat and tried shoving it into the pack. It wouldn't fit. He set it on the ground and unbuttoned his shirt.

By now the pickax man had cut a two-foot trench and was stepping back as the shovel men advanced. They looked to be in their mid-twenties. One had a full beard. The others had maybe a month's growth between them, dark shadows against the lines of their cheeks and jaws. They set about clearing the trench as Kevin removed his boots and socks. The snow bit hard against his soles, but he kept stuffing the pack, straining the seams.

"Can you zip it?"

Kevin tried. The seams popped, but the bag held. Only his coat and boots remained outside.

By now the shovel men had piled the dirt into a berm beside the trench. The thing looked like a miniature grave. Too small for a man . . . unless that man were chopped into sections with a pickax.

"It'll do." The shotgun man turned to one of the diggers. "Trevor. Come on. Let's get this done."

Trevor raised his shovel, then looked at Kevin. "This isn't personal, you know." Trevor's accent was different from the shotgun man's, more Midwest than Boston. "This isn't against you, *per se*." Then Trevor swung the shovel, bringing it down hard against the side of Kevin's pack, knocking it into the trench. A few more swings took care of the coat and boots. Then Trevor and the others set to work putting the dirt back in the hole.

"You got anything else, Kevin?" the shotgun man asked. "Things I can't see? Hearing aid? Implants?"

"No."

"Contact lenses?"

"No!" He was freezing now. "Nothing. What're you going to do?"

The man nodded toward the others, and one of them tossed something at Kevin. It landed, rolling like a severed head. It was a canvas sack.

"Honest clothes," the shotgun man said. "Shoes too. Put them on before you freeze."

The sack had a pair of loop handles tied together to secure the things inside. Kevin fumbled with the knot, shivering as he pulled it apart. Inside he found a wool sweater, flannel shirt, vintage jeans, rawhide belt, leather boots. No underclothes. The pants were wide and long. He cinched the belt and rolled the legs to his ankles. The boots were of a straight-cut pattern, no curves to differentiate right from left. The innersoles were contoured with the impression of another man's toes.

"You need to put that sack on too. Over your head, cover your face."

By now the trench in the ground had been completely filled in, his personal effects buried beneath a mound of earth. If they killed him now, there'd be nothing above ground to prove he'd ever been here.

"The sack, Kevin. Put it on."

"You going to—" His voice cracked. "You going to shoot me?"

"Not unless I have to."

"So why do I need a hood?"

"To keep you from seeing."

"Seeing what?"

"Put it on, Kevin. Now!"

Kevin pulled the sack over his head. Then someone came up behind him, tugged the handles, tied them tight.

"All right. Let's go." A hand took his arm. "Walk with us. Slow and steady."

*****

They moved for what seemed a quarter of an hour. Then the hand tugged hard, making him stop. "There's a stoop here." The voice belonged to Trevor, the one who had told him this whole thing was nothing personal.

Kevin's next step thumped on wood. A moment later the wind fell away. He felt warmer. His footsteps echoed. He was inside. A left turn. Then a right. Then pressure on his shoulder, easing him down. "Just sit still a second. Almost done."

Hands grabbed Kevin's feet, lifted his legs, removed his boots. Then something cold touched his ankle, encircled it, clicked into place. He felt the weight of a chain.

"Like I said, it's nothing personal."

Footsteps receded. When Trevor spoke again, his voice was far off, maybe a dozen feet away: "You can take off the sack now, Kevin."

Kevin tugged the knot, yanking the canvas from his head as the men exited down a dim hallway, leaving him in a wooden room with a high, plastic-covered window.

He was sitting on a pressboard sheet atop rough-hewn legs. A quilt covered the board. That was it. No mattress or pillow. Two buckets sat on the floor beside him, old metal things, dented and empty.

A cast-iron stove burned in the corner, throwing a ruddy glow toward the hall. He got up. The chain dragged behind him, going taut after three steps. He called toward the door. "Hey!"

A knothole popped in the stove, sparks spewing through the grate. There was no other sound, no sense that his captors were still in the building.

"Anybody out there?"

The floor felt cold.

"Can I have those boots back?"

No sound but the crackling fire.

Standing at the limits of the chain, he saw the edge of another room as the far end of the hall. He seemed to be in an old farmhouse, the kind of place he blogged about, but tidied up as if his abductors had been

72

squatting here for a while.

"Hey!"

Still no answer.

He returned to the cot, stood atop it, tried seeing out the window. The plastic sheeting snapped in the wind. He turned an ear to it, listening as something banged in the night, lonely and intermittent: *Whump. Whump-ump. Whump!*

"No!" A voice spoke from behind him. "You can't do that!" A woman had entered from the hall. "You can't see out that window. It's plastic, not glass." She wore a coat over a loose-fitting dress, frayed around the cuffs and collar, hem dark from dragging. She carried a tray. "There's nothing to see anyway." She set the tray on the floor, then stepped back. "Besides, you shouldn't mess with things you don't know."

"You mean the window?"

"I mean things you don't know."

The tray held a covered bowl, wooden spoon, mealy biscuit. There was a cup too, steaming and smelling of rooty tea.

"They found your car," the girl said. She was college age, though her hands looked older. "It was where you said." She backed into the hall, but didn't leave. "You seem honest. That's why they say you can eat." She smiled, revealing the kind of teeth that came from wearing braces. "Go on. It's honest food."

He knelt beside the tray, lifted the lid and smelled the steam. When he looked up again, she was gone.

*****

He carried the tray to the cot and studied the contents of the bowl: cabbage, carrots, turnips, squash. There was meat too--slow boiled pieces that came apart beneath the spoon. And there was other stuff, coarse-cut herbs and leaves. He tasted it: sweet and rich, but with a wildness that must have come from the herbs. He spooned up the pieces, then tipped the bowl to drink the broth. After that, he used the biscuit to wipe up the rest before starting on the tea. It was all good.

When he finished, he set the tray aside and drew his feet under the quilt. He felt warm, relaxed. He closed his eyes, lay back. A bitter taste clung to his throat. Not unpleasant, just strange.

For a while, he slept.

*****

Pain woke him.

He lunged for one of the buckets, hugged it, vomited hard. Everything came up. Then he collapsed, hugging the floor as the pain moved to his lower tract, forcing him to drop his pants and straddle the second bucket. His bowels let loose, venting with a single blast that seemed to go on forever. Then he collapsed again, exhausted, shivering.

The stove glower brighter now, almost molten with heat, but he was cold...chilled to the core. He forced himself back under the quilt. It didn't help. The cold was inside him. He rolled into ball, closed his eyes, convulsed.

And then someone else was in the room. It was the pimple-faced boy who'd worked the pick in the clearing. "You'll be all right." He said it without l's: *Yaw be awright.* Unlike the others, this kid sounded local. He walked to the buckets, peeked inside. "We're simple people." He picked them up, grabbing the handles with gloved hands. "We're not ignorant, though. We know what companies are making now days, interfaces and such, apps and nannies."

Kevin didn't have the strength to ask what the kid was talking about. He just closed his eyes, plunging into icy sleep that broke when he realized someone new was sitting beside him. It was a woman with a three-string dulcimer, sitting in a chair that hadn't been there the last he'd looked. The floor around the chair had been cleaned. A tray of fresh food lay where the buckets had been.

"You had a rough night," she said. "Breakfast will set you right." She had eyes like stones, cold and blind.

"Not hungry," he said. It was barely a whisper.

"But you are." Her hair was gray, pulled back, coiled like rope at the back of her head.

He looked at the food: slice of fruit, cup of steaming milk.

"They call me Mother," she said. "You can call me that too, if you like. If it feels right." Morning sun glowed through the plastic window, forming a nimbus behind her head. "It's not what I am. Just what they call me." Like most of the others, she didn't sound indigenous to the mountains. "I was a teacher once," she said. "College professor, actually. When I left that life, some of my students followed. Since then, others have come, locals mostly...and a few are pilgrims like yourself." She reached for the tray on the floor beside her. Didn't grope for it the way a blind person would, but grabbed it as surely as if she could see. "Take this." She held the tray toward him. "Sit and eat. Fill your terrible hollows."

He sat up, both legs moving freely beneath the quilt. The manacle was gone.

She fingered the dulcimer. "It was never our intention to harm you, only to cleanse you of the terrible things you brought with you. We can't be around them. We've come too far to let such things back into our lives."

"What're you talking about?"

"Why, your phone for one thing. That was the most obvious danger."

"And my clothes?"

"A not-so obvious danger. You might not even be aware of what's being woven into fabrics these days. Even before I left the university, designers were already including magnetics in their weaves, supposedly to help detect knockoffs. But there were other motives." She tuned the dulcimer, plucking softly, working the pegs. "It's the same with processed food and water, which is why we had to clean you out, for our sake as well as your own."

"The kid who took the buckets said something about nannies."

"Yes. Nano transmitters. The components are microscopic, added to drinking water and processed grains. They assemble over time, lodge in the gut."

"And do what?"

"Transmit data. They're used for tracking people. If we hadn't gotten them out of you, the signals would have led the agents right to us."

"What agents?"

"The ones who are looking for us." She spoke as if it were common knowledge. "We've been eluding them for years. They think they ought to be able to find us in these hills, but there's more land here than you'd think by looking at a map. Take a few acres of mountains and valleys, flatten them out, and you've got miles of country. And there are always places to live, houses and towns abandoned by folks wanting to live closer to the grid. We move in, take up residence for a while, then move on."

"But why?"

"Because they're looking for us."

"But why are they looking for you?"

"Because we're off-grid. Can't have that, you see. Not in a world where everyone must be connected and accounted for." She turned toward the tray of food, seeming to stare with unblinking eyes. "You should eat. It'll all seem clearer when you're not so empty."

He sniffed the slice of fruit.

"It's just food this time. Go on. Trust it. Trust me."

He took a bite. It was cool and sweet, nuanced with earthy tones. He took some more.

"There you go."

He tried the milk: warm and silky, with traces of grass and clover.

"Clean food, Kevin. Filling food. Just what a hollow man needs. We'll teach you to eat right if you stay."

He finished the milk. "Stay?"

"Maybe. If you like."

"And if I don't."

"Then you don't. We aren't about kidnapping."

"So I can go?"

She opened her mouth as if to laugh, but only sighed. Then she straightened up again, hands braced against the dulcimer. "You don't see it, do you? What brought you here wasn't a desire to take pictures of some old mining town. You might have thought that was it, but there's more. You're a hollow searcher. I knew it the moment I saw you." She tapped her temple as if to indicate a vision behind her dead eyes. "I saw it and knew. And something else. I knew even then that you'd decide not to stay. Not right away. The pull of the hollow world is too strong."

"Hollow world?"

"The world you came from. A hollow world of hollow people, each one a human hole, drained from years of living on the grid. That's what we fear, Kevin. That hollowness. And although you might not know it yet, it's that same fear that led you to us. The fear of the human abyss, the immeasurable cavern that once held your soul." She moved her hands, sliding one into position on the dulcimer's neck, the other resting on the bridge, perched like a bird claw.

Kevin thought of what she had said about working at a university, about how her students had followed her into the wild. He believed that. There was still something of the academic about her, a quality that reminded him of a poem whose title he couldn't recall.

A damsel with a dulcimer
In a vision once I saw:
It was an Abyssinian maid,
And on her dulcimer she played. . . .

Strange how he remembered the words but not the title. It was like that with so many things these days.

"You've lost your soul, Kevin. That's the sorry truth of it. But we can teach you to grow another. It won't be easy...won't happen at once...but the seed's been planted." She crossed her legs, lifting one moccasined foot from under the hem of her dress. Then she plucked three strings together, sounding a chord. "Part of you thinks I'm crazy. But another part is listening. It's the part that knows you've been empty for too long."

He had finished eating, and now he was sitting, looking toward the open door and the hall beyond. "You said I could leave if I wanted?"

"That's right." She stuck another chord, slightly different from the first--darker, pensive, unresolved. "Your choice." Her fingers moved again, striking a chord that completed the sequence, filling his ears, then continuing on to echo in the hollow of his being. "But first there's one thing more." She played the chords again, three-note arpeggios, one after the other. "We've given you food for your stomach." She played the sequence again, slower. "Now here's something for that deeper chasm."

She sat back and began to play.

*****

He awoke in his parked car. Beyond the hood, footprints stretched through the trees, filling with snow, vanishing. He sat up, thoughts spinning.

He remembered taking pictures of an abandoned town before starting back to the car. It had been dark then, just like now.

What happened?

The keys were in the ignition. He turned them. The radio blasted. He snapped it off, looked at the time: 4:34 PM.

That can't be right.

And there were other things he couldn't account for. His coat for one. It was filthy, smeared with clay. Perhaps he'd fallen, knocked himself out, returned to the car in a daze. But there were no lumps or abrasions on his head, only a terrible, internal ache that suggested something more serious than a fall, a stroke perhaps.

His backpack lay on the seat beside him, stitching strained and ripped as if the zipper had been forced closed around an oversize load. He didn't remember it being that way before, and the pack did not seem overly full now. He unzipped it and took out his phone. The display showed 21 new photos. That seemed about right. All were dated between late afternoon and early evening--with the last shot taken around 4:21 PM.

Thirteen minutes ago?

He opened the image. It was a wide-angle shot of a derelict town, the one he had snapped while standing on the ridge of an abandoned mine. He enlarged the image, zooming in on a building with gray windows. *Plastic sheeting?* Hands trembling, he panned the image, left to right along the building until he came to a rusted door hanging from broken hinges. He could almost hear it swinging in the breeze.

Whump. Whump-ump. Whump!

And someone stood in the doorway.

He enlarged again, zooming in on the blurred figure of a woman. Her features were vague, little more than pixilated shadow, suggestions of braided hair, a narrow face, stone-cold eyes. It came back to him. He remembered sitting on a bed, listening as she sang a song so achingly beautiful that it unmanned him. That was it. That was the last thing he remembered.

He closed the picture and checked the image menu. The photo's date and time were there. He stared at the numbers.

Yesterday!

He shivered and looked again at the vanishing tracks leading away from his car.

He'd lost an entire day!

*****

He was out of the car now, armed with flashlight and GPS, following his trail back through the forest, his memory returning as night deepened. It was all coming back now, how she had sung to him, filling him with a longing for all he had lost. And he remembered how she looked, thin as a tendril of mist, clothed in a dress that wrapped her like an encroaching shadow. Her head rocked as she sang, rolling with the music. He remembered these things. All of them. But most of all he remembered what he told her when she stopped singing. "I've changed my mind. I don't want to leave. I want to stay."

She set the dulcimer aside and looked at him with eyes that weren't as blind as they seemed. Then she touched his brow, fingers lingering as if probing the depth of the hollow space within. "No," she said. "Your mind hasn't changed. Not yet. It's just moved beyond you for a moment. The real change will take time. Hours maybe. Maybe years. When it does, if you still want to join us, you'll find your way back."

*****

Snow stopped falling by the time he reached the scarred hillside that overlooked the derelict town. He didn't expect to see much from the ridge. Low clouds hid the moon and stars. The valley should have been dark, but instead it was red with dying flames, smoldering buildings. The town had been torched.

We move in, take up residence for a while, then move on.

He shivered, bracing on a tree and looking at the line of hills beyond the valley. Mother's followers had found him once. They would find him again, provided the government agents didn't find him first. Should he risk it? He looked back the way he had come, then he threw down his phone, dropped his pack, and pushed forward along the rim of the glowing valley.

THE AMERICAN
S.C. HAYDEN

SC Hayden's short fiction has been published in a number of journals and magazines including: Shadowplay (from Post Mortem Press), The Dirty Goat, Portland Review, and Underground Voices. His story, The Face, was selected as the South Million Writers Award Notable story of 2009. His debut novel, American Idol, was published by Black Bed Sheets Books in 2012.

Something large, dark, and heavy crashed through the underbrush and into the path ahead. Father Mancini loosened the machete hanging from his belt. The American's machete was already at hand. The pig snorted, turned and faced them, 200 pounds, maybe three. It pawed the earth several times but did not charge. Red stained the pig's dark skin, darker holes where its eyes should have been. Blind and bleeding the animal wobbled, staggered, then collapsed.

It was the second eyeless animal they'd seen.

Hennrick, their guide, had spotted an eyeless albino boa coiled in a low hanging branch just the day before. That was when he told them they were on their own and turned back. He'd taken them as far as he dared. It didn't matter. The dense jungle had opened and the once all-but invisible path was clear. Even without the path they would have found their way. They could feel it. Something drew them on. Something wanted them to come.

They hiked in silence for the next few hours. Sister Asty walked between Father Mancini and the American. She had grown up in a village at the base of the very mountains they were climbing. If they encountered any locals, Father Mancini reasoned, she could mediate. But the American knew they wouldn't encounter any locals. They were too close to ground zero.

Sister Asty stopped short and gasped.

The American stepped up behind her and looked over the nun's shoulder. A man hung, arms stretched and hands nailed, in a twisted banyan tree. His abdomen was split and his intestines had been pulled out and strewn about the great tree's branches like party streamers. A crucifixion. The kill was fresh, the smell still thick and wet in the sultry air. Sister Asty fell to her knees. A shrill sigh escaped her lips like a teakettle coming to boil. She shouldn't be here, the American thought. It was a mistake to bring her.

Father Mancini helped her to her feet and hurried her past the grizzly maker. The old priest was stoic. He was guided by purpose. But the American knew what lie ahead and held no hope that the priest was equal to the task.

All three of them had seen the footage.

Three years earlier, a man stood before a video camera in a small room in Port-Au-Prince Haiti. The room was filled with the familiar trappings of Haitian Voodoo; bottles of liquor, candles, bones both human and animal, a crucifix. The man wore a threadbare tuxedo and bowler derby. He identified himself as a *Houngan*, a voodoo priest, and said he was going to channel a powerful spirit he called Mr. Humbaba.

The *Houngan* placed a live chicken on a chopping block and slit its throat with a carving knife. The bird squawked and fluttered then went still. The man smeared the chicken's blood on his face. He drank from a brown glass bottle then spewed clear liquid from his mouth over the dead bird, shaking a rattle in the air and muttering some unintelligible cant all the while.

All at once he fell to the ground jerking and flailing and frothing at the mouth. It looked like a standard Tonic-clonic seizure, but it was what happened after that convinced the Vatican to take the video seriously.

The spasms stopped abruptly and the man leapt to his feet, snatched the carving knife from the chopping block and slit his own throat. Bright red arterial blood fanned the room. The man, seemingly unaffected, sat cross-legged on a small wooden chair, lit a cigarette and calmly smoked while blood gushed and bubbled from the meaty slice below his chin.

"Let those who suffer come to me and I will make them strong," he said in perfect German.

"If a woman is barren," he continued in Arabic, "she need only lie with me and her womb will quicken."

He looked directly into the camera and smiled. Blood still welled from his severed arteries. Cigarette smoke billowed from his nose and neck.

"Whosoever believes in me," he whispered in Hebrew, "out of his belly shall flow rivers of living water."

The video ended.

After that, rumors circulated of a man who was dead yet walked and talked and performed miracles high in the Haitian mountains. The blind could see again, the lame walked, the barren swelled. Later there were darker stories, stories of mass rape, crucifixion, mutilation, and human sacrifice.

The jungle path steepened and the vegetation thinned with elevation. Banyans gave way to palms and thick spiky bushes bristling with hidden thorns. As they crested the final ridge, the village revealed itself. Crumbling huts of mud and stick stood neglected in a small clearing ringed by a sea of fronds. In the village center, a single masonry structure, a small white tin roofed building affixed with a crucifix.

Men and women wandered the village slack jawed and aimless as though shell-shocked. Two men holding ancient-looking AK-47s stood near the entrance to the derelict church. Eyes sunken, faces angular, they were skin and bones. They looked as though they hadn't eaten for weeks. Strange when one considered the chickens and village dogs wandering about untended.

Sister Asty, Father Mancini, and the American dropped their heavy packs onto the ground and pressed into the village. They walked slowly, carefully, towards the church. Somehow they knew the object of their quest dwelled within.

A haggard old woman with onyx skin, snow-white hair and bloodshot eyes sat cross-legged in the dirt regarding the three travelers. As they drew past her she pressed her palms to her face and dug her fingers into her eyes.

Sister Asty gasped. She reached out to stay the old woman's hands but it was too late. The woman pulled her eyeballs out of her head and held them out to the sister.

"Take them," the woman whispered, "I can see so much more without them."

Father Mancini pulled Sister Asty back. Once again, the American wished she hadn't come. Father Mancini crossed himself. He was guided by Christ. The American was guided by a simple truth; energy is power and power is money. The American had no doubt that Father Mancini had exorcized some lower-level demons in his time but the being that inhabited that white church was an entity of tremendous power. A full-fledged Class-1 demon.

The American looked at his watch. Rather than measure time, his "watch" measured the strength of nearby electromagnetic fields. The meter read 200-tesla, the highest he'd seen in over six years hunting demons.

The men with the AK-47s ignored the three travelers as they approached the church. If the entity that dwelled within had considered them a threat, the American reasoned, the gunmen would have cut them down. Instead, they stared into space as if they weren't there at all.

The church's interior stank of corruption. There were corpses in the pews. A shifting miasma of flies buzzed in thick swarms around the assembled parishioners. Men and women, eyeless and disemboweled, littered the floor and center aisle. The man they had seen slit his own throat in Port-Au-Prince, the *Houngan,* sat quietly smoking on a large wooden chair at the head of the church. His throat was a dark ragged hole. His eyes flashed blood red in the smoky nimbus surrounding his head.

"Father Mancini, Sister Asty," the demon said. His English, like his German, Arabic and Hebrew, was perfect. Sister Asty was going to serve as a translator but it was clear that her skills would not be needed. Mr. Humbaba was an exceptional communicator. "And who is this? He smells like an American."

"He is a man of God," Father Mancini said, "His name is not important. It's he whose name he comes in that is important."

"Some young priest who wants to play exorcist," the demon snorted. "How's your faith, boy? Is it strong?"

The American remained silent.

Father Mancini wasted no time. He raised his crucifix and stepped forward. "In the name of Christ the redeemer, I revoke you!"

The demon ignored him.

"Is it true that all priests are pederasts?" the demon asked the American. "Or do you want to fuck Sister Asty? You can have her if you want her. Kneel before me and I'll give her to you."

"Away Satan!" Father Mancini commanded. He stepped forward again, fearless, stalwart, his voice filled the room. "Inventor and master of all deceit, enemy of mankind's salvation, tremble and flee before the almighty hand of God!"

The demon, eyes like glowing embers, dropped his cigarette and stood. His grin was wicked and the second smile he wore beneath his chin was wickeder still. He raised his right hand and Father Mancini halted his advance. When the demon's hand became a fist, the priest's clothing burst into flames.

"No!" Sister Asty shouted. She ran towards the burning priest but when the demon raised his left hand she, too, stopped as still as stone. The priest, frozen in place, became a burning statue. When the flames rose over his head he tried to scream but all that escaped his rigid mouth was a high pitch squeal.

Sister Asty, frozen, motionless, eyes wide open, was forced to watch him burn to death, just out of reach. More than twenty minutes passed before the old priest fell lifeless to the floor. The American, although not frozen, never moved. His face betrayed no emotion.

The demon twisted his left hand and Sister Asty pulled her clothes off as though they burned her skin. When she was completely nude she got down on all fours, thrust her ass into the air and hissed. The American watched her squirm. He remembered what the demon told him. He could have her if he wanted her. She was young and beautiful. Her dark skin, now coated in perspiration, glistened. She reached between her knees with one hand and touched herself. Her mons was swollen and wet, her nipples erect. She moaned, hissed and meowed.

A cat in heat, the American mused.

"Say the word exorcist, and she is yours," the demon said, "or you can burn like your friend."

The American stepped forward. The demon smiled. The American reached into his cargo pocket and removed a small silver flask-shaped object with a flashing red LED light on one side. The demon's smiled faltered and the American saw what he had seen so many times before. The moment when a demon first realizes he's not dealing with a crucifix-waving man of faith, but with a cold and calculated man of science, the moment when the demon's mask of confidence turns into a flash of doubt.

The American raised the silver object and pressed a button with his thumb. The demon fell to his knees, his flash of doubt now a look of startled bewilderment. The red lights in his eyes guttered, darkened, then winked out entirely. Something that looked like smoke billowed from his mouth and funneled, as though drawn by a vacuum, into the flask like device in the American's hand.

The man with the slit throat toppled over onto his side. The demon was gone and the carcass of a man over three years dead lay finally motionless on the floor. The American looked at the device in his hand, the LED had changed from red to green and a number flashed on a small screen, 1.8 Gigawatts, enough to power a small city. A demon as virulent as the one he'd just harvested would probably produce at that capacity for close to twenty-five years.

"Who are you?" The voice startled him. The American looked over his shoulder. Sister Asty looked up at him from the floor, arms drawn tight across her breasts. "You're not from the church." It wasn't a question.

"EnergyCorp International," the American said flatly, "Tomorrow's solutions to today's energy needs."

He placed the device back in his cargo pocket and removed a small pearl handled revolver from another. Again, he wished she hadn't come. He placed the barrel behind sister Asty's ear and pulled the trigger.

It was a shame, but there could be no witnesses. Nuclear power was controversial enough. Demon power would put people in a tizzy. Another shame. It was clean and abundant, the ultimate green energy source. The only byproduct? Bad dreams. In the American's opinion, the EnergyCorp physicist who developed the system deserved a Nobel Prize.

But people simply weren't ready for the truth.

WHAT'S LEFT BEHIND

C. BRYAN BROWN

C. Bryan Brown was born and raised in St. Louis, Missouri. No one's sure where all the really dark thoughts come from, but he chalks it up to a steady diet of horror, suspense, and action by legends such as F. Paul Wilson, Stephen King, Dean Koontz, Robert McCammon, and Lawrence Sanders coupled with watching Disney's Beauty and the Beast *at least once a week.*

The sun, forever silhouetted behind an atomic-damaged purple atmosphere, flared and highlighted the wreckage of the city's outer limits in pink and orange. The colors lasted only a few seconds, but in that time they chased away shadows and faded the burn marks marring the old buildings.

Jake Murdock stood on a century-old roof and watched the sky, absently thumbing open the cap of an ancient, brushed chrome Zippo lighter. He flipped it over, like he often did, and read the inscription: *With Love.* He set the butt of his rifle down on the roof's thinned tarmac, and leaned on the weapon.

"Must you?" asked Calvin, rubbing his beard.

"Yeah. I must."

Grief, his long, dark hair tied back out of his face, sniggered. Jake gave him the finger.

"You guys really need a new routine," Jessica said.

"That ain't no lie," agreed George.

Jake turned his attention to the alley they'd rigged with explosives. His fingers kept busy with the lighter as he ran over the reports again: vagabonds had spotted multiple, non-human, two-legged creatures near the Ag Plots and photographed them stealing small animals such as pigs, cats, and goats from their pens. When the reports stopped, an investigation found nothing but blood stains in the vagabond's makeshift huts. Two days after, one of the creatures attacked the Ag workers and dragged one away. The following morning, the military sent two soldiers with the workers and no one returned. This morning, they'd set up rotating watches guarding the two routes into the city's outer perimeter.

The attack started with thunder in the guise of hundreds of clawed feet. Their howls shattered windows as far up as the fifth floor and the falling glass shards whistled as they sliced the air. Mortar dust, shaken loose by the stampede, floated in the shafts of colored light like snowflakes.

George picked the transmitter up off the rail and his thumb tensed over the SEND button.

"Wait for them," Calvin ordered. "You blow it early and the mission is screwed."

George looked over his shoulder at Calvin and frowned.

"Pay attention, cuntnugget, or you'll blow it too late."

George whipped his gaze back to the alley and settled against the railing. He cracked his knuckles and watched the horde surge past the midway point.

"Get ready," Calvin said.

Jessica and Grief each took a position on either side of George. Laying their elbows on the rail, they sighted down into the oncoming mass of fur and claws.

"Waiting on a personal invitation, Jake?"

"Nope," Jake said and laid the lighter, inscription side up so he could read the words at a glance, next to George's elbow.

Calvin positioned himself next to Jessica. "Steady."

The seconds roared by, scaling louder, matching the pandemonium below and when the first creature crossed the plane of the alley's mouth, Calvin gave the order. George pressed the transmitter's button and six pounds of C4 detonated. The alley disintegrated into a shower of pluming brick dust. The roof rumbled as a wave of heat and debris assaulted the lower floors of their building.

Jake gripped the rail, which shifted and cracked, as the roof bucked and threatened to pitch him off into the street far below. He let go as the rail crumbled, his free hand snatching for his lighter. Jake watched it tumble into the red mist, flipping ass over teakettle next to George.

"George!" Jessica screamed as he fell.

"We've got to get down," Calvin bellowed, "before it all falls."

Jessica slung her gun and took point, skipping down the stairs two at a time, gripping the banister and pulling herself faster. Jake descended behind her, weapon ready, caution slowing him.

"Jessica," Jake yelled. "Slow down. I'm losing you!"

He made the second floor landing and Jessica was out of sight. Crimson dust curled around his ankles like miniature tornadoes and the stairs blurred into a pinkish smear. Jake missed the last step, and stumbled into the wall a few feet from the exit door. Jake listened; Calvin and Grief were still several floors up.

Wait or go?

A howl decided him and Jake pushed off the wall. Bracing the gun against his shoulder, he kicked the door open. The sudden motion let in a maelstrom of microscopic brick pieces that scratched the inside of his nostrils and burned his eyes. Cursing, he blinked away tears and moved into the ground cloud that was the explosion's aftermath.

The alley was only a dozen yards or so straight ahead. He'd been above the door, George off to his right, and that's the way he went.

The murk stole the light and bent it around the floating particles, cutting Jake's visibility to only a foot or so. That was fine with him: this part of town looked like shit.

"Jessica! Sound off!"

Brick scraped and tumbled straight ahead and he stopped. "Jessica?"

Silence greeted him like a bill collector. His stomach twisted and spasmed, tried to climb into his throat. Jake clenched his teeth, relaxed his grip on the rifle's trigger, and toed forward, the brick dust clinging to his skin like a layer of soap scum. The rifle's barrel cut through the cloud, parting it much the same as Moses did the Red Sea. More scraping, reminiscent of fingers on a chalkboard, drew him on.

"Jessica?" he hissed. "Is that you?"

She didn't answer and Jake's pace increased. There'd been no more howls since that first, but *they* were here, skulking in the darkness, and the further he walked, the more disadvantages he listed: they could probably see better than him and, based on the size of their snouts, he was confident they smelled almost everything.

It doesn't matter. Do your job. Come on, Jessica. Where are—

Jake's foot caught on something soft and, as he fell, his rifle fell and bounced out of sight. Jake landed on George, whose head, malformed and flat, lay in a pool of blood. Jake rolled away and pushed up to his hands and knees. He searched the ground for his gun and found his lighter next to George's left arm. Jake whimpered as he picked it up and wiped it clean.

"Jake? Is that you?"

"Jessica?"

He stared at a pile of rubble a few feet away.

"It's me," she whispered, crawling out. Jessica rested a hand on George's chest and stared at him for a long moment. She straightened George's shirt and brushed his hair back from his forehead.

"Jake? Jessica?" Calvin called.

"Over here," Jake answered.

Calvin and Grief materialized out of the gloom, grime clinging to their sweat-stained faces, as though they'd been targets in a mud-flinging contest.

Calvin tossed two backpacks on the ground. "You both left your packs on the roof. Next time, I'm leaving them and docking your pay."

"We have to go," Jessica said. "Some of them survived. I've heard them, mewling and whining, like wounded animals. When Jake started calling my name, they all shut up."

"We heard the howl when we were coming down the stairs," Grief said. "And something ran away when we came through the door."

"The dust is starting to clear and we need to get back to the city and report in. Jessica, you're on point. You two carry George's body. The wall is only a few blocks north."

Jake stuffed the Zippo in his pocket and grabbed George by the ankles. With Grief under George's pits, they lifted their friend. A clipped bark and an answering chorus of howls broke Jake's flesh out in bumps. Another, more vicious bark came a few seconds later, then another, each from a different direction.

"Hells," Jake said. "Are they talking to each other?"

"They're animals," barked Calvin. "They can't talk to each other."

Jessica squeaked, her voice punctuated by fear, and Grief dropped George. Jessica slid passed Jake on her back and he twisted around.

Jake had only seen them in the pictures, and those had all been taken from a distance, reminding him of old Bigfoot pictures in the Britannica:

blurry and indistinct, hard to make out specific features other than arms and legs.

But this thing was real, and it towered over him by at least two feet. Matted, rust colored fur covered its body except the paws and the area around its eyes. The canine snout protruded further than any dog's he'd ever seen in pictures and its long, muscled arms ended in leathery, human-like hands. Quarter inch talons tipped lanky fingers. The legs, thick stalks of fur, permanently bent at the knee, tensed and its toe-claws scraped furrows in the concrete.

"Holy shit," Grief muttered.

One of the creature's pointy ears twitched toward Grief. It growled low, a sound that bubbled into the air, and Jake's muscles shivered in response. The creature snapped its jaws once. Jake dropped George's feet and grabbed for his pistol. The creature moved far faster, and bashed a paw into Jake's chest.

Jake fell aside, gasping, and clutching his chest. Rifle shots boomed and dirt spattered his face as booted feet stumbled away. The creature howled, long and angry, before its voice faded away.

Rough hands grabbed the back of Jake's clothes and lifted him up, spun him around. "It took George's body!" Grief screamed in his face. Jake shoved him away. Calvin bled from a gash on his temple. Ignoring them, Jake helped Jessica to her feet. He touched her shoulder, back, and neck, examining each part.

"I'm fine, Jake. It just threw me," she said.

"Let's go," Calvin said, "before it comes back."

"We need to go after George," Jessica said.

"We need to get back and warn people," Calvin said. "Who knows how many of these things are still alive."

"I want his body," she said.

"I don't care. We're going—"

Calvin's voice gargled off into a scream as one of the creatures rose up behind him and bit into his shoulder. Jessica raised her rifle and pulled the trigger. The creature fell away, most of its head missing, and Calvin dropped to his knees. Jake cursed and hurried to Calvin's side. He gripped Calvin under the arms, holding him up.

"I'm dying," Calvin said.

"You're not dying," Jake told him.

"No, I really am."

"You're not. I promise." Jake held up his Zippo and showed it to Calvin. He slid it into Calvin's breast pocket. "I'm going to want that back. Grief?"

Grief stood rooted, staring at Jake. His mouth opened and closed in silent words. His pupils enlarged until the whites vanished and a thin stream ran down his chin. Grief's jaw opened wider, as if he wanted to speak louder, and through Grief's open mouth, Jake saw the retreating maw that had torn out the back of Grief's throat. Grief crumpled and revealed a dozen hairy bodies hugging the ground, creeping through the mist.

"Jessica!" Jake screamed. "Run!"

Jake hauled Calvin up over his shoulder. Jake's shirt absorbed Calvin's blood like a sponge and stuck to his back. His stomach heaved at the tackiness, but he ran. Howling chased him across the ruined pavement and the air filled with the heavy panting of pursuit. The mist thinned with every step and before they'd gone a hundred yards, they emerged into clear air.

"To the right," Jake panted, indicating the mouth of another alley.

"Go," Jessica said and pressed her body against the corner of the alley.

Trash covered the alley and Jake kicked aside boxes, empty cans, and the bones of small animals. Sludge caked the ground and Jake slid as much as he ran. Gunfire echoed off the walls and he found an open doorway. Jake stumbled over the threshold and went down, dumping an unconscious Calvin to the floor. Jake turned his head away and vomited into a corner.

Jessica followed seconds later and slammed the door. One of the creatures rammed the door, jarring her loose; she lunged forward and grabbed the twisting handle, yanking the door shut again.

"I need your belt!"

"What?"

"Your belt," Jessica repeated. "Wrap it around the handle and then the pipe here."

As he secured the door, Jake listened to their nails rasp against the door and their harsh, guttural utterings. Their smell, mildew and mud, seeped through the door. He stepped away, gripping the butt of his pistol, and waited as the creatures tested the door. The leather creaked under the strain but it held.

Safe for the moment, Jake ripped off a piece of Calvin's shirt and folded it into a square. The bleeding had slowed considerably; it looked as if the creature had only bitten and not ripped. If he could get the bleeding to stop, Calvin would probably live to see tomorrow. He pressed the shirt against Calvin's wound.

"Where are we?" Jessica asked, looking around.

"I don't know. Hold this bandage," he told her.

The room wasn't very big and smelled of dried out cornhusks. It looked like an exit foyer of some kind: six concrete stairs led up to a small landing and another set of stairs, which went to the next floor. Behind the staircase was a steel door with a push-bar, like the one they'd entered. Jake shoved and the door didn't budge.

Another steel door, set in the side wall, sported a mid-sized rectangular window. Darkness shrouded the room beyond; the only light came from holes—most likely from the bombing raids—high in the walls. He tried the door and it swung open without a sound. The cornhusk air invaded the tiny space and he yanked the door closed.

I have to go in there. See what we're dealing with.

"Wait here," he told Jessica. "I'm gonna go check out this other room. Keep pressure on that wound."

"Watch your back."

Jake covered his nose with his left hand and, breathing through his mouth, entered the room. He didn't move while his eyes adjusted to the half-light. Once they did, he found himself in the lower area of a cavernous room. Rows of tiered, ascending seats spread out and away from him. Stairs went up the middle and either side of the room, the latter ending with doors marked EXIT. A wide hallway, blocked by chairs and debris, ran off from his level toward the back. Luggage crammed the aisles between the rows of seats. Skeletons of varying size and age, half-dressed in worn clothing and sunken, parchment-colored skin occupied most of the chairs. A large silver screen hung over a room-length stage. The surface rippled like water in a breeze Jake couldn't feel.

Kids had drawn stick figures on the screen, labeled them with words such as mommy and daddy and me. Others had written small notes to loved ones either missing or dead: *I miss you, Scott* or *I'm sorry, Laura* and one said *Eaph and Pauline Hayes were married June 13th, 2036, True Love 4-Ever.*

They'd been married for a little more than two years when the nukes came and the United States...

Jake derailed that train of thought, but he couldn't look away from the declaration of love. It seemed trivial to write it out like that, to waste even just a few seconds when they could have been holding each other instead. They had to know the chances of anyone ever seeing it were slim and, if someone ever did, what was that person supposed to think? Love conquered all? Or perhaps even in the ugliness of death love existed?

With Love.

Jake sought his lighter. His breath hitched when he couldn't find it and he was nearly swatting at his pockets when he remembered he'd given it to Calvin, a promise to get him back to the city.

He acknowledged Eaph and Pauline's declaration with a nod. Perhaps love was the only thing that mattered in the ugliness of death.

Jake clambered up the side aisles and tested the EXIT doors. Both were unlocked and emptied into the same long hallway, which led off in opposite directions. He piled luggage in front of each one, hoping to at least slow down anything coming through them.

Satisfied he'd done what he could, Jake went back to the foyer. Jessica stood over Calvin, her rifle pointed at his chest.

"What are you doing?" he asked.

She didn't acknowledge him other than to tense her finger on the trigger.

"Jessica?" Jake said, bringing his pistol up.

"It bit him," she said, as if that explained everything.

"So?"

"He'll... he'll..."

"What?" He wanted her to say it. Maybe hearing the stupidity of it would bring her back to reality.

"He'll turn. Transform into one of them."

"That's bullshit and you know it."

Jessica shook her head. "You saw them. What else can they be?"

"Are you kidding me? The majority of the world dropped countless nukes on this country and you're asking me what else they could be? You went to school; you've seen the mutations. Cats with rat faces, deer with three tails, or bears with one eye. And that's not even the kids born with scales or gills or forked tongues."

"You've heard the talk," she insisted.

"Yeah, but I don't think a bunch of gaffers know a damned thing about these creatures. Calvin's not going to turn into one of them."

"How can you be sure? How? We need to kill him. We can't take him back; he'll change and he'll kill and he'll infect us all with this disease and—"

"Just stop it!" Jake interrupted. "Now, I'm not a scientist or a doctor; I'm just a soldier using last century's weapons, so I don't know for sure. But I'm willing to take the chance based on what I've seen today."

"You'll say anything to save him."

"Maybe," agreed Jake. "Did the ones you shot today turn back into people?"

"I don't know, Jake. I didn't stick around to watch."

"Fair enough. Let's pretend he *is* going to turn into one of them. So we take him back and let the scientists look him over. If he is infected with something, maybe they can cure him. Find a vaccine to keep us all from turning into giant howling things if we get bitten. We have to give him a chance."

"Like he did with George?" she whispered.

"I know you're angry about that, but Calvin tried. Once they took George's body—"

Jessica snapped her rifle in his direction and he almost shot her, but released the pressure at the last second.

"George deserved to be brought home."

"He did, but what if we'd all died trying?"

"It doesn't matter."

"Sure it does. At least, now, you can tell George's story and people will remember *why* he died, not just that he did."

"Doesn't change the fact Calvin's bit."

"Nope."

"The good of one shall never outweigh the needs of the many."

"Spoken like a true sheep," Jake said. "But you have to be able to prove detriment—"

"No," she said. "I don't."

Jessica turned the rifle on Calvin and shot him twice in the chest. His body flopped once and lay still, except for his fingers, which continued to twitch and drum on the concrete floor.

Jake cursed and stepped forward, but he still couldn't shoot her. She swiveled her weapon back in his direction.

"Don't make me kill you, Jake."

"Look," he said, holstering his pistol. "I'm not going to shoot you. It's over. I just want my lighter."

"Fine," Jessica said and sat on the bottom step, resting the gun on her knees.

Jake put his hand in Calvin's breast pocket and withdrew the Zippo. He flicked it open, and then closed, before rubbing it on his pants, cleaning Calvin's blood out of the inscription.

"So what's with the lighter? I haven't seen you smoke."

"Because I don't."

He almost told her to go fuck herself and explain how damned intrusive it was for her to even ask, but he remembered a simple declarative statement written on a silver screen. He turned the lighter over and over in his palm, and his temper dampened.

"My wife gave it to me about five years ago. She was a burnhead, and she lost the ability to speak. She used to write me little notes all the time. She worked on the Ag Plots, so she was outside the city every day. Her job was to till up soil to find uncontaminated dirt for growing. She found the lighter and was going to toss it when she saw the inscription. So she brought it home and gave it to me. Said it had lasted through the nukes and the bombs and everything else, just like her love for me would be forever."

"If it means so much, why do you carry it with you? You almost lost it when George fell."

Noise from the big room drew his attention. Jake peered through the door's window. Several creatures stood at the top of the two aisles, staring at the luggage they'd knocked over. One picked up a suitcase, sniffed it.

"We have to leave," Jake said.

Jessica fleeced Calvin of his extra ammunition and started removing the belt from the door.

"We can't go out there," Jake said.

"You'd rather go up? Jump out a window?"

"Not really, no."

"All right," Jessica said, finishing with the belt and setting it aside. "Ready?"

Jake shook his head, drew his pistol.

"Too bad," she said and opened the door. Jake, squinting against the sudden brightness, marched into the alley and turned back toward the street. He picked his way around the dirty clutter. At the end of the alley, he backed against the building and peered around the corner. He jerked his head back.

"What?" Jessica asked.

"There's one just sitting in the middle of the street."

"Did it see you?"

"I don't think so." He checked again. "It hasn't moved and it's not looking this way."

"We can go around."

"The city perimeter is only two blocks north of us," he said. "Straight up the street, around the market building, and into the clearing. It's the fastest way."

"If killing that thing gets us home faster, then let's do it."

Jake held up a hand and counted to three on his fingers; they turned into the street together. Moving fast, they approached the creature from behind. More than once, they slowed to traverse a burnt out car husk or skirt a crater, but the creature never stirred.

A breeze blew in from the south, bringing with it the smell of tar and pulverized brick, of burning fur and roasted meat. The wind ruffled his pants and the hair on his head. Jake stopped short and Jessica peered at him, waiting for instructions.

Why can't it smell us?

Jake waited for it to leap up, snarling, and attack. The wind tickled its fur, but otherwise it remained motionless.

Something isn't right! Just go around!

Jessica whistled and jerked her chin, as if to say *What the hell are we waiting for?*

Jake didn't know, not exactly. It was like looking at a set of icy stairs; he knew slipping and busting his ass was probable, just not on which step the fall would occur. And now, like then, the only true option was to walk, despite the likelihood of breaking a bone in the process, and hope for the best.

He signaled Jessica and they resumed inching their way toward the creature. Jake lifted onto his tiptoes the closer he got, using them like they were some sort of built in stealth mechanism. He kicked a bent piece of rebar and sent it dancing across the pavement. The metallic jig rang loud and he froze, once again waiting for it to realize its prey was closing in.

It didn't move.

What the hell?

Jake left pretense behind and hurried. When he got close enough to touch it, and it still hadn't moved, Jake put his gun away and unsheathed his knife, which he'd made from an old grass-cutting blade. He adjusted his grip on the leather-wrapped handle, swung back, and chopped into the side of the creature's neck. The blade sliced deep, severing through muscle, vein, and cartilage. Jake expected blood—lots of blood—and howling, but the creature went down silently, the wound hardly bleeding. Jake planted his foot on the creature's side and tugged the blade free. Without lifting his foot, he rolled it onto its back.

"It's already dead," he said, pointing to the bullet holes in its chest. *And it didn't transform into a person*, he almost added.

"Oh, God, Jake. Look."

His eyes followed Jessica's rifle and he ground his teeth in frustration. A dozen creatures, maybe more, had broken from their cover and were charging across the empty street. They ran low to the ground, using their hands as well as their feet. Their claws ticked on the ground, the noise filling the air like a tidal wave.

They set a trap, he thought. *They think just like...* he didn't want to consider the idea, didn't want that active thought in his brain, but it wasn't to be denied.

They think just like men.

Jessica fired at the creatures. Two of them staggered and fell, though neither was dead; their claws scrabbled as they rolled about, but they didn't cry out in pain. The others ignored the wounded.

Bellowing, Jake charged, and split the skull of the first one to get near him. Momentum barreled its body into him and he went down under its weight. Jessica screamed and the gunfire stopped.

He rocked the dead creature off and before Jake could get up, another came for him. A string of saliva trailed over its shoulder like smoke.

He scooted backward, climbing over debris, trying to find some leverage against the teeth and claws. "Come on, you bastard!" he yelled, bringing his knife around, wanting to hurt it before he died.

It howled, as if it understood the challenge, and increased its speed. And then its right shoulder buckled, sending it face first into the street. It tried to rise, but before it could, Jake heard a gunshot. The creature slumped, a fresh hole in the back of its head.

"Jessica?" he mumbled, getting to his feet. Soldiers approached from the direction of the city, their weapons ready. At least he knew who'd saved him. "Jessica!"

"I'm here," she yelled and he stumbled after her voice. He dropped to his knees beside her and laughed.

"You've been busy," he said, indicating the corpses around her.

"Yeah."

A shadow enveloped them and Jake looked to see a soldier—with more bars on his sleeve—blocking the sun. "We need to get back to the city," he said. "These things hit every post we set. They're—"

"Testing us," Jake finished. "Trying to find our weakness."

"Yes," the soldier said. "But we also know what they're after."

"What?" Jake asked.

"Food."

"They want our food? Did they get into the city?"

The soldier smirked. "No. We *are* the food."

Jake said nothing.

"Get her up and let's move."

Jake reached down and hauled Jessica to her feet. He let go and she staggered, whimpering, and he had to catch her before she fell.

"What's wrong with her?" the soldier asked.

"I don't know," Jake said.

"The last one bit me," Jessica whispered, staring at Jake. "Please, Jake. Please."

"You'll be fine," Jake said. "The doctors—"

A gunshot deafened him. He flinched away from the offending noise, yelling at the sudden ringing that seemed to be everywhere. He pressed his hands against the side of his head, blocking his ears. Jessica dropped, her life ended, all thoughts and prayers little more than a stain on the cityscape.

"You didn't have to shoot her!" Jake exploded, spittle flecking his lips. His ears still rang, and things sounded like they were at the other end of a tunnel. And he could think. "Look around you, man. These things aren't people nor did they ever used to be."

"I never thought they were," the soldier shouted back. "Werewolves belong in the Brittanica and in the superstitions of the gaffers, but that doesn't change our orders, which are to put down anyone who's been bitten. The scientists and doctors don't know what diseases these things carry and we don't have the meds to deal with any outbreaks."

"How the hell are they ever going to know unless they treat a bite?"

"That's not our concern. Take a moment, if you need it, but leave the body and get her weapon," the soldier said before moving away.

Jake bent over and retrieved Jessica's gun as howling, carried by the wind over the burnt out buildings, broke out in the distance. It wouldn't be long until those things were back. Jake took out his lighter.

With Love.

He met Jessica's empty gaze and said, "You asked why I carried this. It's because without love, we don't have peace, only fear. We've always killed what frightens us—" Howling, closer this time, momentarily halted his speech. "You hear that? The earth has moved on, Jessica, but we certainly have not. This lighter is a reminder that we can."

He turned from Jessica's corpse and, slinging the rifle over his shoulder, caught up with the retreating soldiers, the howling at his back a reminder that not every species deserves the chance to do so.

ALWAYS SOMETHING THERE TO REMIND ME

GARY A. BRAUNBECK

Gary A. Braunbeck is a prolific author who writes mysteries, thrillers, science fiction, fantasy, horror, and mainstream literature. He is the author of 19 books; his fiction has been translated into Japanese, French, Italian, Russian and German. Nearly 200 of his short stories have appeared in various publications. His fiction has received several awards, including the Bram Stoker Award™ for Superior Achievement in Short Fiction in 2003 for "Duty" and in 2005 for "We Now Pause for Station Identification"; his collection Destinations Unknown *won a Bram Stoker Award™ in 2006. His novella "Kiss of the Mudman" received the International Horror Guild Award for Long Fiction in 2005.*

> "Footfalls echo in the memory
> Down the passage which we did not take
> Towards the door we never opened…"

--T.S. Eliot, "East Coker"

"The carpeting's the wrong color."

Cindy Harris looked away from the television and said, "What?"

Her husband, Randy, pointed to the television.

"The carpeting's supposed to be light blue. Look at it. It's *green*, fer chrissakes."

"So what's the big deal?"

Randy looked at her with that impatient, condescending expression that told Cindy he expected her to already know the answer. That expression was one of the few things about her husband that Cindy genuinely disliked. She could feel his defensiveness rising and wondered if he'd been forgetting to take his Zoloft lately.

"The big deal," he said, "is that I remember the way my folks argued about the color. *Dad* wanted green, but Mom insisted on light blue, and like every other time they had an argument, Mom won out."

Cindy watched him fiddle with the controls on the remote, then flip down the little door at the bottom of the set and start messing with the controls there.

Sighing, Cindy said, "Maybe something went wrong with the transfer. C'mon, Randy. Those home movies were pretty old, y'know? Maybe we waited too long to have them put on DVD. That old eight millimeter film stock, maybe it started to go bad and this was the best they could do. Most of them have turned out fine up until now."

Randy stopped fiddling with the controls, looked at the picture once more, and then turned toward her, his face losing color.

"What is it?" asked Cindy.

"I, uh…nothing. Nothing." He rose to his feet, walked across the room, and began heading up stairs. "I gotta make a call. Back in a minute."

"Hold on," said Cindy, grabbing hold of his elbow. "What's *wrong*, honey? This isn't worth getting upset about."

He tried smiling at her but didn't quite pull it off. "I just remembered something—I mean, I *think* I remembered something."

"Plan on letting me in on it?"

His face softened, but remained slightly pale. "Please let me make the call and then I promise I'll tell you all about it." Kissing her cheek, he gently pulled her hand from his elbow and went up to his office, closing the door behind him.

Putting her impatience on hold, Cindy went back to the sofa, sat down, and turned up the volume. Randy never talked much about his childhood—something that annoyed Cindy at times but which she respected, nonetheless—so maybe she could use this as a chance to get a glimpse of him as a child.

She watched for several minutes as Lawrence, Randy's father, finished setting up a plastic racing track in the middle of the room (with a running and very funny commentary), plugged in the power supply, and then put a small HO-scale car on the track and gave it a test run.

"Think he'll like it?" asked Lawrence.

"Oh, he'll just *flip*," said the voice of Virginia, Randy's mother, who was holding the camera. Lawrence grinned, obviously proud of himself for having assembled this without bloodshed, and then came the sound of a door opening. Virginia whipped around with the camera, the image blurring for a moment, and came to a stop on the face of a little boy who looked about nine years old. His face was flushed from the cold outside, and he was having trouble unwrapping the heavy wool scarf from around his neck.

"What's goin' on?" asked the little boy Randy had once been. "How come Daddy's home from work so early?"

He finished with the scarf, hung it on the hall tree by the door, and then pulled down his hood to reveal his face, his bangs a little too long and little too shaggy.

"Daddy's got an early Christmas present for you."

The little boy stared at the camera for a few moments, and then his face came alive with realization and a smile that could have been seen for miles in the dark. "The race car set came?" And with a speed and agility that is the special province of nine-year-old boys, rocketed past the camera and into the living room, where his shouts of delight filled the air.

"Turn it off," said Randy from behind her.

Cindy turned, smiling, and waved him away. "Oh, get over yourself. Why didn't you ever tell me you were into racing when you were a kid? God, Randy, you were *adorable*."

He said nothing as he reached down, pulled the remote from her hand, and turned off the DVD player. The screen turned a bright shade of blue when the picture vanished.

Cindy turned all the way around, kneeling on the sofa so she could better face him. "What did you do *that* for?"

"Something's wrong."

"I knew that already. Did you make your call?"

"Yes."

"Going to let me in on it now?"

Randy nodded, came around, and sat down beside her. Cindy readjusted her position and took hold of his hand.

Randy said, "Just listen to me for a minute, okay? Don't...don't say anything or ask any questions, just listen."

Feeling anxious—God, his face was so *pale*—Cindy nodded her agreement.

Randy hit the remote, returning to the race track scene, then hit the **Pause** button and pointed to the screen.

"I called Mom just to make sure," he said. "The carpeting was light blue, not green like this. But that's not...not why I called her.

"Cindy, look at me. How long have you known me? Ten years, right? We've been married for six years—and by the way, I've loved every minute of it, if I haven't told you lately. The thing is, have I ever struck you as someone who's absent-minded or forgetful?"

"No."

"Have you ever thought of me as being unstable in any way? The anti-depression medication aside, I mean."

"Of course not."

He stared at her with an intensity that made Cindy uncomfortable. *He hasn't been taking his meds*, she thought. *That has to be it.*

He started the DVD once again. "Look at the screen, Cindy. Tell me what you see."

"Randy, you're making me nervous."

"*Please?*"

"Okay, babe, okay." She faced the television. I see you and your dad playing with an electric racing car set on the floor of your folks' old living room."

"Look closer."

It wasn't until the little boy on the screen ran over to hug his mother—forcing her to set down the still-running camera—that Cindy realized what was wrong.

"What the--?"

"See it now, do you?" asked Randy.

She did. In the bottom right-hand corner of the screen: a small readout giving the time and the date.

3:42 p.m. 12/16/68.

"That's from a *video* camera," she said, looking at him. "Did they even have video cameras in 1968?"

"It doesn't matter," said Randy. "We never owned anything like that when I was a kid. In 1968, Dad was in the middle of a seven-month layoff from the plant. We had a very...inexpensive Christmas that year. It was nice, Mom had been saving money so we'd have a good dinner, but as far as presents went...I got a couple of Aurora monster model kits and some new shoes, that's it."

Cindy looked back at the scene on the television, then to her husband once again. "Okay, maybe I'm a little slow here today, baby, but are you telling me—"

"—that we didn't own a home movie camera, video cameras weren't available to the public, and what you're looking at"—He pointed to the happy scene unfolding in all its glory—"*never happened*. Yeah, I *wanted* an HO race set, but that was out of the question." He looked back at the screen, and when he spoke again, his voice quavered. "This never happened, Cindy. That's why I called Mom—I wanted to make sure I wasn't misremembering things. I wasn't. The carpeting was light blue, we never owned a home movie camera, and I never got a racing set."

He rubbed his eyes and shook his head. "The thing is, while I was growing up, I used to *pretend* that I *did* get one, y'know? I mean, you do that when you're a kid, you imagine things that didn't happen actually did."

Cindy nodded. "I did that all the time. I still do."

Randy smiled at her, touching her cheek. "When I used to play that scene out in my head, it looked just like *that*." He nodded toward the television.

"Except the carpeting was the right color?" asked Cindy.

"Bingo."

For a minute they both sat watching silently as the scene played out, culminating in Randy beating the pants off his father in the Big Championship Race.

The scene quickly blacked out and a notice reading **End Of Tape** appeared in the middle of the screen.

Randy stopped the DVD player once again and began rummaging around on the coffee table.

"What're you looking for?" asked Cindy.

"The invoice, the list that came with the discs."

"I put on my desk. Hang on." She went into her office and retrieved the paperwork, and came back to find randy on the floor with all of the discs spread out in front of him (still in their protective sleeves, thank God).

Holding up the papers, Cindy asked, "What are we looking for?"

Randy smiled at her. "You know, you probably don't notice how you always do that."

"Do what?"

"That 'we' business. Five minutes ago, this was *my* problem, then I tell you about it and suddenly it's *our* problem. Not 'me' but 'we'."

"Don't be silly, baby—*of course* it's our problem. What bothers you, bothers me."

He blew her a kiss, then pointed with his thumb at the television. "This is Disc #3. What's the list say is on it?"

Cindy found the invoice for #3 and read aloud: "Disc #3. Transfers of home movies, Reels 1 – 5, labeled 'Prom', 'Cindy's College Graduation', 'First Day on the Job', 'Mom and Dad's 40th Anniversary Party' and 'Our Wedding Rehearsal.'" She lowered the paper and stared at her husband. "They mislabeled, that's all."

"Did they?" Randy picked up the remote, pressed **Previous**, and a moment later the screen showed Cindy, ten years younger and damn near in tears, receive her college diploma. Then he hit the **Next** button not once but twice, and there was Cindy, laughing and waving at the camera as her mother videotaped her walking into the high school on her first day as the newest History teacher. Randy then hit **Previous** once, and there was his father, setting up the HO track in the middle of the living room that had the wrong color—

--both Cindy and Randy started—

--the living room that now had the *correct* light-blue color of carpeting.

Randy's hand began shaking. "Jesus Christ, honey, what the hell is going on?" He looked at her with an expression of confusion and helplessness that damn near broke her in half.

This time it was Cindy who turned off the disc, but she also ejected the damned thing and turned off the player. "I don't know, baby, but don't...don't let it get to you like this, okay? Whatever it is, we'll figure it out." Even to her own ears it sounded like a desperate, empty promise, something to say to Make It All Go Away For Right Now.

But Randy was having none of it. He pointed to the discs spread out in front of him. "There are eight discs here, Cindy, *eight*. We were charged for seven." He picked up the eighth disc; both the protective sleeve and label on the disc were blank.

"Randy, you need to calm down, baby, okay? I'll tell you what—let's get something to eat, let's go out for a bit, and then we'll come back and watch all of these from start to finish, okay? Maybe one of us will see something that'll help us figure out how...how..."

"...how an imagined memory of something that never happened could wind up on these things?"

She couldn't think of anything to say. Just blurting it out like that made it sound absurd.

"Okay," she said. "Screw it, then. C'mon, sit down next to me and let's watch it again. Come on." She sat on the sofa and patted the spot next to her. "Come on. Let's do this. You and me."

He sat beside her and took hold of her hand, and Cindy started the disc once more.

They watched Cindy receive her diploma, and then watched as she walked into her first day as a History teacher.

The race track film was gone.

Silently, anxiously, they started with the first disc and worked their way through all of the first seven. There was nothing on any of the discs that wasn't supposed to be.

Which left only the eighth, unmarked disc.

"Jesus,' said Randy, looking at it as Cindy slipped it from its sleeve. "Did we imagine it?"

"Baby, I've *never* believed in 'shared hallucinations' or whatever it is they're called." She examined the last disc under the light as if she expected to find some kind of ancient sigil hidden in the reflection. Looking up at her husband, she tried to smile and almost made it. "I'm game if you are."

Randy, silently, nodded his head, looking for all the world like a prisoner who'd just been told the hour of his execution was fast approaching.

Cindy slipped the disc into the player and sat very close to her husband as she hit the **Play** button.

The first sequence was the missing race track film, which the two of them watched as if it were the most natural thing in the world, as if it were something from the past that Randy had shared with her many times over. At one point, they both even laughed at something Randy's father said as he was assembling the set.

Then came the film of Randy getting ready for his first Cub Scout meeting.

"I don't remember this," he said to her, gripping her hand tighter.

"But you *were* a Cub Scout, right?"

"...no..."

"Oh, God..."

And they watched. They watched as Randy graduated all the way to Eagle Scout; they watched as Randy was lifted onto the shoulders of his football teammates after he'd tackled the quarterback of the opposing team, preventing the touchdown that would have lost Randy's team the state championship (he'd never participated in sports, much to his father's disappointment); they watched as Randy readied himself for his high school prom (to which he did not go because his father had died the previous week); they watched as Randy and his parents moved his belongings into his college dorm room (he'd done this alone); and they watched as Randy's parents embraced both he and Cindy at their wedding.

"Looks like it would have been a nice life," he whispered.

Cindy looked at him. "What's wrong with the one you have now?"

He turned toward her. "Nothing, honey, nothing at all. I love you, you know that, right?"

"Of course I do."

He looked back at the screen. "This is the past I *wish* I'd've had. Look at all this. It's all so...*interesting*. So happy and exciting."

"There's nothing wrong with the life you've had. It's been a good life—it's *still* a good life, baby."

He shook his head. "Look at me, Cindy. I'm a dull little man, and I know it, okay? I don't have any great sports stories to share with the guys I work with, I don't have any great adventures to impress people with, and I sure as hell aren't the most exciting man you could've picked for a husband.

"I used to resent the hell out of that, you know? I hated Dad for dying like he did and leaving me to take care of Mom and the house. I started college three years late because I had to get a job at the plant to help pay for everything. *God*, I resented it! I resented not having *that* life, the one on the screen. I used to imagine...when I was really angry, I mean really, *really* angry, I used to imagine that—"

His words cut off when he looked back at the screen.

It was a film of a woman giving birth to a child that was obviously dead. The woman insisted on holding the body, and as the camera came in for a close-up, Cindy saw that it was Randy's mother.

A moment of blackness, and then came the image of a teenaged Randy, looking a decade older than his years, stabbing his parents in their sleep, their blood spattering the walls with every plunge of the knife.

Another moment of blackness, and there was Randy, in his twenties but looking much older, tying a naked and severely-beaten woman to a wooden chair. The woman whimpered and screamed and begged him to stop, but Randy ignored her pleas as he turned away and began selecting tools from a table.

A final moment of blackness, and there was Randy, as he was now, sitting beside Cindy, as she was, the two of them staring at a screen that showed them sitting on a sofa facing a television screen that showed the two of them facing a television screen that showed the two of them facing a television screen...

Randy sat forward and buried his head in his hands. "God, Cindy, the...*thoughts* I had when I was that angry. That's why I started seeing a psychiatrist—remember that I had to cancel our third date because I'd forgotten about the appointment?"

"I thought you were just trying to let me down easy," she said. She only now realized that she'd moved away from him, that the last series of images had turned her stomach. How could *this* Randy, this man she loved, ever harbor thoughts so repulsive and violent?

Good God, did she know him at all?

He looked up and saw the expression on her face, saw that she'd moved away from him, and his face went blank. "Just so you know, the girl in the chair was Tammy Wilson, who was the only girlfriend I had during college. She cheated on me with at least three different guys, all of them jocks." He looked at the screen once more. "I won't lie to you, Cindy. Thinking about doing that to her...it helped. I'm not proud of those thoughts but I can't very well deny having them, especially now, can I?

"And sometimes, honey, when you really disappoint me...I think about doing the same things to you. And it makes me happy. It makes me *feel good*...."

She pulled the remote from his hand and turned off the disc, which she then ejected, pulled from the player, and snapped in two.

"There," she said to the empty sofa, and then felt herself starting to cry. She quickly got hold of herself, sat down, pulled in a deep breath, and fingered the jagged scar that ran from her left temple to the side of her mouth, a souvenir from her own father—one of many that she carried all over her body.

Goddammit! She'd almost made it work this time, almost had the perfect husband, the perfect marriage, but Daddy's influence always had a way of creeping back, one way or another.

She rubbed at the burn scars around her wrists, scars now faded with age but still pink enough to remind her of the ropes, of the chair, of Daddy's tool kit.

She looked at the stack of DVDs with the transferred home movies of families she'd never met and would never know, and decided that she'd start looking for new memories tomorrow. She was always alone in the lab—that was the best place for someone who looked like her, anyway. History teachers with disfigured faces weren't exactly in demand these days, and never had been.

There were always dozens, hundreds of home movies people wanted transferred to DVD. So she'd say goodbye to Randy and hope that, tomorrow, she could find some new memories that she could hold on to, ones that Daddy couldn't sneak in and ruin.

She turned off the television set and for a few moments just knelt there, staring at the slightly distorted reflection of her face.

"I'll miss you, Randy," she whispered. "You were the best one yet."

She placed her hand against the screen, imagining that the reflected hand was not hers, but that of a gentle and compassionate man who was reaching out through the glass to take hold of hers and whisper that she was beautiful, the most beautiful woman in the world, and, oh, how he would lover her forever....

NEPTUNE DREAMS
ROSE BLACKTHORN

Rose Blackthorn lives in the high mountain desert of Eastern Utah with her boyfriend and two dogs, Boo and Shadow. She spends her time writing, reading, beading and doing wire-work, and photographing the surrounding wilderness. She has published genre fiction online and in print with Necon E-Books, Stupefying Stories, and the anthologies The Ghost IS the Machine *and* A Quick Bite of Flesh, *among others. She is a member of the Horror Writers Association, and suffers from an overactive imagination, but rather than complaining... she just goes with it.*

Shy dreamed. She was floating unencumbered in her sleeping quarters, perhaps a foot or so above her bed. Deep in her own mind, she knew this wasn't real. Although the gravity on Galene Station was lower than on Earth, a person couldn't freely float. The other indication that she wasn't truly awake and aware was the large window directly before her. The sky outside was purest black with a scattering of diamond bright stars. Taking up the lower left corner of the window was the upper curve of a planet. Neptune was a vibrant blue with delicate broken rings that sparkled with errant flashes when light glinted off colliding chunks of ice.

In her dream, she floated closer to the window. She reached toward it, right hand flesh and bone, the left cold metal alloys with rubber-clad joints. She could hear a strange high-pitched hum, an almost sub-audible whine. There was the peripheral sensation of movement, as though something not quite seen flitted around her, but she couldn't take her eyes off the planet. She stretched forward, reaching toward the glass. Her hands, human and artificial, passed through the surface as though there was no barrier. The cold was immediate and intense. The water content of skin and muscles crystalized and expanded, the pain much worse than being burned. Her prosthetic hand was not affected by the cold, except in conducting the rapid drop in temperature up to her shoulder. She still floated forward, unable to arrest her advance. She took a deep breath, turned her head to see frost and vapor filling the room. Her lungs expanded to voice a last agonizing scream, as her face passed through the window into space.

The comm beside her bed chirped, and she jerked upright, her momentum carrying her off the mattress in the low gee. Before anything else, she turned toward the far wall. As always, it was just a solid wall with the narrow door leading to the bathroom and another leading out of her quarters onto the command ring of the space station.

"Damn," she whispered, closing her eyes.

The comm chirped again, more insistently. The gentle gravity had returned her back to her bed, and she leaned over, touching a button. "Acknowledge. Galene Station, this is Pilot Keir."

"This is Commander Argol, of the relay ship Astraios. We're readying for final approach."

"Confirmed, Commander." She stood, being careful not to exert too much effort. Moving smoothly, without lifting her feet much above the rubber-mat covered floor, she glided toward her bathroom. She would have to hurry to be dressed and at her station before the crew of the Astraios was ready to disembark.

*****

Commander James Argol released his safety harness and turned his chair. Beside him in the co-pilot's seat was Dennis Rocha, a man roughly half the Commander's age. While Argol had been off-Earth for the last twenty odd years, Rocha was relatively new to the far reaches of the solar system. He'd only been on duty at Calliope Station for a year.

"Double check the docking mechanisms, and be sure the airlock is secured," Argol said. "We'll be disembarking as soon as the Galene gives permission."

"Aye, sir," the younger man said with a grin and turned to his console.

"Nejem, you ready to earn your pay?" Argol called over the intercom.

"Ready and able," Inanna Nejem answered, her voice tinny coming over the speaker.

"Rocha will let you know when you can open the lock," the Commander said, and got to his feet. "I'll see you in cargo," he added over his shoulder to the co-pilot.

Argol stopped by his quarters, little more than a closet. As a relay freighter, all available space was set up for cargo. Right now what they carried was empty crates and unsealed containers. Galene Station, the only mining operation orbiting Neptune, was where they would pick up their cargo. Empties would be offloaded for Galene's use, and the Astraios' cargo area would be loaded with containers full of helium-3. These would be delivered to Calliope Station, a huge man-made city orbiting Jupiter. Some of the helium-3 would be used there, and some relayed farther on to Mars or Earth. The real priority this trip however, was five crates of diamonds. The liquid ammonia seas on Neptune had long been known to man, but only in the last century or so had it become clear that there were also liquid diamond lakes. Because of high temperatures beneath the heavy atmosphere, and the dense gravitational pressure, these lakes formed like small ponds within the larger ammonia oceans. Scientists had determined that solid diamonds, in clusters like small icebergs, floated on the surface of those lakes. It had only been a matter of time until engineers came up with a way to collect them.

Galene Station was equipped with several unmanned transports specifically designed to enter the upper reaches of Neptune's atmosphere, in order to siphon and store the valuable helium-3. Six months ago she'd also received two highly-insulated reinforced robot drones made explicitly for the purpose of traveling to the surface of Neptune, extracting the Neptunian minerals, and returning them to the station. They had performed exactly as designed, thus the crates full of raw diamonds.

Argol left his quarters and headed toward the airlock just in time to hear the whoosh of air as it opened. The temperature in Galene was a few degrees lower than in the relay ship, and Argol smiled at the cooling breeze. He stopped at the computer panel nearest the open lock, and contacted Galene's sole crewmember via the comm.

"Pilot Keir, permission to come aboard," he said.

After a momentary delay came the reply. "Permission granted."

"We have some supplies for you this time around, Keir," he added, glancing at the small stack of plastic crates filled with food and medicines for the station.

"I'll send down a 'bot-jack," was her terse reply.

"She's not much for company, is she?" Nejem asked, her dark almond-shaped eyes reflecting everything she saw. She stood ready to begin unloading their empty containers, petite and pixie-cute with her buzz-cut black hair spiked up in front. Looks were deceiving, however; she was more than just a pretty face, and her record was exemplary.

"You could say that," Argol said dryly.

"How long has she been alone out here?" the young woman asked curiously. She'd heard rumors about Keir, everyone out here working the gas giants had; but she'd never met anyone who actually knew Galene's pilot.

Argol shrugged, stepping aside when the station's 'bot-jack appeared to pick up the supply pallet. "Better part of ten years, I suppose."

"That's a long time to handle your own company," Nejem mused.

"I guess it depends on whether or not you can hold up your end of the conversation," Argol said. When the 'bot-jack rolled back out of the cargo hold, he followed it onto Galene Station.

*****

Shy checked system read-outs, sitting in the command chair on what amounted to the bridge of her own private space station. She reminded herself to relax, to take even breaths. She had never liked having strangers on Galene, not even for the few hours required for a relay ship to dock, load and leave. Now she had to remember that this was necessary.

Her full name was Cheyenne Raven Keir, a name that was simply too much for her. Cheyenne had been shortened to Shy when she was a child, and it had stuck as she'd always been a quiet, introverted girl. After the catastrophic fire that killed her entire family—parents, two brothers and her baby sister, and nearly killed her as well—her previous demeanor had been comparatively gregarious. Trapped under a collapsed and burning wall, rescued by pure chance when it was assumed there were no survivors, she had pulled through because of advanced medical care and a surprisingly strong will to live.

It had not been easy. Her family was poor, and there was no life insurance. Made a ward of the state her medical care was covered, but only to the bare minimum. Burns that had covered nearly seventy percent of her body were kept clean and she was carefully guarded from secondary infections, but there were no cosmetic skin grafts to ameliorate the severe scarring. Her left arm had been crushed as well as severely burned, so was amputated at the shoulder. When she was fitted for the bio-mechanical limb, again it had been the most basic model available. There were no funds available for an artificial skin covering to make the limb appear more natural. She had to settle for a serviceable metal alloy that only added to her aberrant appearance.

The one saving grace to it all, she would often think later in life, was her education. Before the fire she had gotten adequate grades, but nothing more. She had no time to study, for she was required to tend her younger siblings from the time she got home from school until they went to bed. After the fire, lying in the hospital, she had seen a world of knowledge open up before her in the bedside computer supplied for her schooling. She had no family, and no friends to take either her time or attention. Instead, she enrolled in every class she could get authorization for, and had excelled.

Because of her drive and aptitude, she had qualified for grants and scholarships that led to degrees in engineering, physics and astronomy. Beyond her native capability in these subjects lay an intense desire to be on her own. Her injuries and severe scarring caused most people to either stare rudely, or avert their eyes in a type of embarrassment. Both reactions caused her notable discomfort, and she had determined to find a way to avoid people as a matter of course. By the time Galene Station was ready to be launched, she had become the first choice to pilot it.

When Argol climbed onto the command ring, she turned to greet him. He was one of only a handful of people who neither stared with awkward sympathy nor refused to look her square in the face. Instead, he simply smiled and came to embrace her.

"How are you, Shy?" he asked, his breath warm on the unscarred right side of her face.

"I'm well, James. How was your flight?" She took a deep breath, enjoying his scent and the feel of his arms around her.

"Not bad." He stepped back, looking down at her as though to see if anything had changed. "You look thin. Do I need to requisition you more sweets?"

She laughed softly, shaking her head. "I'm working on keeping that girlish figure."

"Well," he said, taking a seat in the second chair at the console. "I brought you some, anyway." He held out a small paper box, and when she took it, added, "Open it."

She set the box on her knees, steadying it with her prosthetic hand while she lifted the lid with the other. Inside it was filled with a fluff of white tissue. When she unfolded the tissue she found perfectly ripe red strawberries dipped in chocolate.

"You said you missed them," Argol said when she was silent.

"I did," she agreed, and met his eyes. "How did you get these? They must have cost you a fortune."

"Someone on Calliope owed me a favor," he said gently. "They're growing hydroponic strawberries now, along with other fruits and vegetables. It was easier to get the strawberries than the chocolate."

"James, this is very sweet, but you didn't have to…"

He shook his head firmly, "I don't *have* to do anything, where it comes to you."

She thought about protesting again; instead, she gave him a bare nod and the thinnest curve of a smile. "Share them with me?"

He sat back, stretching his long legs before him. "I brought them for you."

"I'm not going to sit here and eat them while you watch," she retorted, and he grinned.

"It's been a long time since I've eaten strawberries with a lovely lady. Like a scene out of a space opera," he teased, but took one of the berries when she offered it, the delicate fruit held lightly between the dexterous fingers of her artificial hand.

As they ate, three berries to each of them, they talked. It had been six months since the last time he'd been on Galene. She might deny it, but she was thinner than the last time he'd seen her. There were shadows beneath her green eyes, and a worry line had appeared between her brows.

He looked the same as he had for the last ten years. Tall and lanky, with large graceful hands and an easy smile, chestnut brown hair that grew over his collar, and striking blue eyes almost the same azure as Neptune. He was twelve years older than Shy, and had led a very different life. He'd been born into an affluent family, and had never been denied anything he'd ever really wanted. His education had been expensive, and his swift promotion to Commander had been a source of pride to his parents. Their plans for him to move into politics and power had never been what he wanted. So to avoid the argument, he had escaped into space, and never returned to the planet of his birth.

When the berries were gone, Argol leaned forward again, resting his elbows on his knees as he searched her face. "There is something going on with you, Shy. I can see it plain as space. Don't you trust me?"

She sighed soundlessly, giving herself a moment while she checked the command console. Nejem and Rocha were done unloading and stowing the empty containers the Astraios had brought, and now loaded the full containers of helium-3 into their cargo hold. "I trust you. You more than anyone."

"Then talk to me." He reached out, brushing his fingertips along the cold metal of her prosthetic arm.

In a rare nervous gesture, she tucked loose strands of hair behind her ear, her fingers trembling. "I think—" she faltered, then made herself start over, "I think I may be having some kind of breakdown."

"Tell me," he said. There was only the concern of a good friend in his deep voice.

"I don't sleep well, anymore. Not for months," she confessed. On the computer screen set into the console, the display showed small blips of light, each one a tracking marker on a full tank of helium-3. From the corner of her eye, she could see them moving one by one out of the Galene's storage area and onto the docked freighter. "I dream. Nightmares, I guess. Not like anything I've experienced before."

"You've had nightmares," Argol reminded her. For years after the fire she had awakened regularly from dreams of being trapped and burning. Dreams in which she watched her little sister cry and cough and finally succumb to the thick smoke, and then begin to blacken and burn in the intense heat that had consumed her, crib and all.

"Yes, but that was different. They were twisted memories of what I actually witnessed." She found herself smoothing the same lock of hair behind her ear over and over again, and forced her hand down to her lap. "These are things that can't be real."

He reached over and turned her so that she faced him, and took her hands in his own; one fragile and bone thin, the other smooth metal. "I'm here for you, Shy. You don't have to hide anything from me, and I want to help you if I can. Maybe talking about it will take the fear out of it."

She thought of the dream she'd been having when his comm-call awakened her. The fear had been icy and immediate, the danger so real... "I don't think it will."

"Will talking about it make it any worse?"

She shrugged, and tightened her grip on his hands just a bit. "I don't know."

"Tell me," he repeated, his blue gaze never leaving her face.

She looked back at him, absentmindedly memorizing his features, her eyes distant. "All right," she finally said.

*****

"Okay, that's it." Nejem said, bringing the relay ship's larger 'bot-jack to a halt where it would be locked down for flight. "All the helium-3 is aboard. The only thing left on the manifest is five small crates which will be stowed up front behind the cockpit."

"I'll get them," Rocha said, driving the smaller 'bot-jack back onto the space station. The crates filled with Neptunian diamonds were stacked near the ladder leading up to the command ring. "Damn," he said a few minutes later when he'd stacked and strapped the crates into place.

"Problem?" Nejem asked, joining him at the front of the main cabin.

"No," he replied with a wide grin, "I was just noticing that they aren't sealed. I'd like to take a look at an 'iceberg' diamond with my own eyes."

Nejem *tsk*ed softly, and shook her head. "Naughty boy. This shipment comes up light, and you're first on the list of suspects."

He held his hands up, palm out, as he shook his head. "No, ma'am. Just curious, not a thief." He leaned against the nearest crate and cocked his head to one side, golden brown eyes sparkling. "You really have no desire to see what they look like?"

She shrugged, glancing down at her hand-held to be sure the numbers on the manifest matched. "They're just minerals, Dennis. I doubt they look like what you'd find in a celebrity's engagement ring, if that's what you're thinking."

"The cases aren't locked," he offered slyly, patting the top of the crate he leaned on. "We could pop one open and have a peek, with no one the wiser."

"There's a security marker," Nejem reminded him in a cool tone. "How do you explain if someone checks the computer log?"

"It must not have been properly latched, and jiggled loose while being loaded onto the Astraios," he said, as though answering to an official enquiry.

Nejem raised one eyebrow. "Someone would take the fall for that, further down the line. You want to be responsible for that?"

Rocha sighed. "You are way too serious, Inanna. Curiosity is part of the human condition. And as long as there's nothing missing, no one would get in trouble. Damn, woman—loosen up a bit!"

She chewed on the edge of her bottom lip for a moment, glancing at the simple crate. She did wonder what they looked like. Were they the same as raw diamonds on Earth? Formed on an uninhabitable planet four and a half billion kilometers from home, could they be anything but alien? Before she could change her mind, she unclipped the latch and lifted the lid.

Rows of sparkling diamonds glittered like faceted ice in the utilitarian light. Nejem did not hesitate, she reached to touch one.

*****

"In my dream I'm floating," Shy began, still holding both of James' hands in her own. She had had lovers in her life, not many but a few. James Argol was one of only two men she had ever developed an emotional attachment to, and the only man she cared to continue any kind of relationship with. "I'm here, on the Galene. Sometimes in my quarters, sometimes on the command ring, or down in cargo. But I'm always floating freely, as though the gravity control has completely failed. There are never any alarms or warning lights, it's as though everything is perfectly normal. Except that it's not."

Argol nodded, but said nothing. He didn't want to stop her flow of words. She was the most self-contained and private person he'd ever known. She hid a loving but lonely heart within a shell of ruthless self-sufficiency.

"I'm floating, and I notice a huge window looking out into space. Neptune is always in the view; sometimes Triton is visible, or Proteus. It doesn't matter where I am in the station, I'll look up and see this huge window looking out over the planet. And as soon as I see it, struck by the wonder of a window I know isn't there, I am drawn to it. Physically, I mean. Wherever I am, I float toward that window, as though being pulled by the gravity of Neptune itself."

When she paused, eyes closed as though to see the dream in her mind's eye, Argol let his eyes move over her face. The right side of her face was beautiful. Olive-toned skin, a perfectly arched brow and excellent bone structure were the flawless setting for her clear green eye. Dark hair grew to her shoulder, thick and soft to the touch. But only on the right. The left side of her face was a warped mask, like a cruel child's prank that had stuck. Scar tissue, an odd whitish-pink, ridged and rippled as though molded by an untalented artist started above the temple and crawled down her face and the side of her head. It continued down her neck, disappearing beneath her collar. James knew that it covered most of the left side of her body to just above her knee. The contrast between her natural beauty and the ugly remains of the fire's wrath were startling. He felt pain for her, for the pain she had endured. But he had seen her intelligence and kind heart beneath the mask, and rarely noticed the disfigurement anymore. He had no patience for anyone who dwelled on it.

"Soon, it becomes clear that I will collide with the window," Shy continued, unaware of his scrutiny, "Except that I don't. When I reach it, I stretch my hands out to touch the glass. But there is no glass. My hands pass through the frame into open space. Then there is pain."

"Pain?" he asked, surprised.

She nodded, opening her eyes to meet his gaze. "Excruciating agony, worse even than the memory of the fire. My right hand freezes and splits within moments. My left hand is unharmed, although the cold moves up into my shoulder and chest. I can't stop myself, I continue out the window, the cold filling and destroying me. There is no one here to help me, no one to pull me back."

He lifted her flesh and blood hand, pressed his lips to the back gently, a silent affirmation of his presence. "Is that when you wake up?"

She dropped her eyes. "Sometimes. That's when I realize that I'm not alone."

"So then what happens?"

The comm chirped, and Shy pulled her hands free to answer. "This is Keir."

"Pilot, please inform the Commander that the cargo has been transferred and stowed." Rocha's voice was monotonal over the speaker, with none of the personality that made him so popular back on Calliope.

"Acknowledged," Argol said. "Any problems?"

"No sir."

The Commander frowned; his co-pilot was rarely so business-like. "The shift is almost over. We'll stay on the Galene tonight, and head back to Calliope after we've all slept."

"Yes sir." The comm light went out, and Argol rubbed his chin thoughtfully.

Shy looked at him questioningly.

He shrugged. "He sounded a little off. Maybe he and Nejem had an argument. It wouldn't be the first time." Pushing the strange conversation out of his mind, Argol said, "How long until you're off shift?"

She smiled, "Just let me check my systems again. Then we'll have dinner."

"Sounds good," he agreed, and relaxed in his seat while she finished up.

*****

The Galene orbited Neptune above and beyond the thin broken rings. Her trajectory had been carefully calculated to avoid collision with any of the planet's thirteen moons, taking into consideration that Triton along with two smaller satellites orbited in retrograde. At any given time, even while docked with a relay freighter, at least three of her unmanned transports were in the upper atmosphere of Neptune collecting helium-3. One of the two specially designed robot drones was always en route to or from the planet's surface in the ongoing collection of diamonds.

While Shy and James ate dinner and enjoyed each other's company, one of the heavy drones returned to the station. A notification came over the comm to Shy, but it was a routine flight and she was not required to intervene.

"So, when the diamonds are brought on board by the drone," Argol asked as he pushed his dinner plate aside, "What do you do? Do you actually handle the diamonds yourself?"

Shy took her plate and his to the automated dish-dog, and let her kitchen system begin the clean-up. "I have, but it's not really necessary. The small cargo 'bots can sort and stow the stones in the crates for transport. I occasionally check up on them, for my own peace of mind."

"What do they look like?" he asked.

She came back and sat at his left, putting her right hand on his leg. "Like quartz crystals, I suppose. Some are quite large. And they are very dense." She leaned against him, glad when he put his arm around her and held her close. "From the calculations I've seen, they may finally make nuclear fusion a viable energy source."

He sighed as she moved her hand, and asked, "Are we really going to discuss scientific possibilities? Because if we are, you're going to have to go back to the seat across the table."

"I think I'd rather stay here," she replied, and reached up with her metal hand to pull his head down to hers.

*****

Argol dreamed. He lay in Shy's narrow bed, blankets tangled around his legs. He held her close beside him, his palm against her ribs. She was cool lying against him, her flesh as cold as the metal of her prosthetic limb. The cold seemed to leach from her, through the contact of their bare skin, prickling into him as though microscopic needles pierced him wherever they touched. As the cold grew more intense, and more painful, he realized that it wasn't Shy in bed beside him. Instead, a dense cluster of Neptunian diamonds lay against his bare skin.

He started awake and found himself alone, still tangled in her blankets. He sat up, wondering where she had gone. There was a strange heavy thrumming, more felt than heard. There was also a high pitched whine, almost inaudible, that put his teeth on edge. He fought with the blankets for a moment, tossing them onto the floor as he got to his feet.

The room was empty, and it was cold enough to force a shiver. He groped for his clothes, pulling them on in the darkness. When he opened the door onto the command ring, the cold air pebbled his skin, and the hairs on the back of his neck levitated. The computer screens showed his ship, the Astraios, preparing for flight. The heavy thrumming was the relay ship's engines. "What the hell are they doing," he breathed, and hurried down the spiral ladder to the cargo hold. Rocha crouched near the open airlock, his back to the Commander. As Argol strode toward his ship, Nejem and Shy both appeared from inside. As one, almost as though choreographed, all three turned toward him, and he stopped. The metal floor was icy beneath his bare feet, and he shivered again.

"Go on," Shy said softly, her words obviously intended for Argol's crew. Rocha picked up the open crate he'd been looking in, and Nejem helped him carry it onto the Astraios.

"Shy, what is going on," he asked, trying to soften the edge to his voice.

"You should still be sleeping," she said, coming within two meters of him.

"I heard the engines," he said tightly, looking past her to where the others had disappeared into the ship. "I woke and you were gone. Are you going to answer me?"

"It's all right, James," she said soothingly. She looked as she always had. Her green eyes were still clear and level. Yet she seemed a stranger.

The annoying high-pitched whine was getting louder, and his shivering increased. He felt his face, wondering if he was running a fever.

"I wish you had stayed sleeping," Shy said, closing the space between them. "Sleeping through the first stage is preferable." She took hold of his arm, trying to guide him back toward the ladder. Her hands burned hot against his skin and he tried to pull away.

"I'm sick," he whispered, and his breath came in a puff of white vapor. "The first stage of what?"

"It will pass," she promised, and pressed him to sit on an empty crate before he fell.

"What's wrong with me," he asked, every nerve in his body screaming.

"It's necessary," she whispered. The piercing tone he'd noticed before was getting louder, and dropping into lower registers.

The cold swelled, so much like fire in the way it raged through his nervous system. He might have screamed; he wasn't sure. He might have swelled and split, like Shy's dream of floating unprotected into open space. When at last the agony began to fade, he opened his eyes again.

Everything had changed. Shy scintillated, coruscated, fairly blazed with iridescent light. The cargo bay was no longer deserted. The space was filled with flickering crystalline shadows that crawled around and through each other. A strange liquid song filled his ears, alien and indescribable.

"Where did they come from?" Argol whispered, still pressed against the wall.

"From the diamonds," Shy answered. "They've been trapped on Neptune for millennia, unable to break away from the gravitational pull. We're helping them; setting them free."

"How humane," he breathed.

"After so long, they can't survive on their own outside the immense pressure," she explained. The living cold inside him seemed to listen to her words with a strange understanding. "They are symbiotic. Each one needs a host, a partner. We can be that for them."

Nejem and Rocha reappeared from inside the ship, and now Argol could see that same prismatic aura around each of them. They were also infected.

"Dennis and Inanna will take the first of them to Titan and Calliope," she said, "while the drones continue to bring more of them up from Neptune. They have agreed to let you stay here with me."

"What if I don't want this? What if people don't want to 'host' them, as you said?" he asked. He thought about running, but there was nowhere to go. The cold was inside him now, contained as a pearl within an oyster.

She gestured wordlessly to the bright ephemeral shadows crowded around them. She did not need to answer. There wasn't a choice.

"They've changed you." It was not a question.

"What do you mean?"

The cold encased his heart, but sorrow still welled. "You always wanted to be alone."

Shy shook her head, cupping his face with cold hands. "Now I'll never be alone again."

BROKEN PROMISES

JAMIE LACKEY

Jamie Lackey lives in Pittsburgh with her husband and their cat. Her fiction has been accepted by dozens of venues, including The Living Dead 2, Daily Science Fiction, Beneath Ceaseless Skies, *and* Post Mortem Press' Torn Realities. *She reads slush for* Clarkesworld Magazine *and is an assistant editor at Electric Velocipede. Find her online at www.jamielackey.com.*

Lucas tried to shake off the cold sleep haze and went over the numbers one last time. The ship's scans matched the probe's readings. Excitement spiked through his belly. "There's definitely life down there," he said.

"Carbon based?" Olympia, his wife and the team's second scientist, asked.

Lucas nodded.

Captain Argus--the only other crewmember awake--scowled. "Is it intelligent?"

Lucas shrugged. "We're not picking up any radio signals."

"How can anything survive with the temperature and background radiation down there?" the Captain asked. He'd obviously been hoping that the probe's readings had been wrong.

Life--especially intelligent life--would make his job a lot harder.

Olympia didn't bother to hide her excitement. "We don't know how it survives. It must have adaptations unlike anything we've seen before!"

The captain rubbed his temples. "What exactly does that mean for me?"

"It means you let us do our jobs," Olympia said.

The captain scowled. "While I sit here on my thumbs and my team stays in cold sleep."

Olympia grinned. "Exactly."

*****

They launched their first rover. Olympia was practically bouncing in excitement. Lucas kissed her.

"This is really happening, isn't it?" she said.

"We have no reason to think that they're intelligent," he reminded her.

She squeezed his hand. "I have a good feeling."

*****

Two days passed. The captain glowered and Olympia's shimmering hope faded. The rover puttered about. Its cameras recorded hours of footage of the storms. It collected samples, and Lucas analyzed them. He used the information to perfect suits to protect the miners from the harsh environment, and he monitored the weather satellite. Thundering storms of radioactive steam raged on the surface.

The rover found a few patches of lichen. Lucas thought they were fascinating. They were extremely different from Earth's lichens, but they still used the same basic symbiotic structure. They fed on radiation instead of sunlight. The rover collected samples. Olympia pretended to care.

"Would the sensors have picked up life that uncomplicated?" she asked while he pored over chemical readouts.

"It's still life, Olympia."

"There has to be more down there."

*****

The captain leaned over his shoulder at the rover's camera feed. "So, do your readings match the scans? Is the crap that runs our ships really just floating around in the air down there?"

Lucas sighed. "Yes."

"Wow. That's--that's money in numbers bigger than I even know."

"Only if we don't find intelligent life," Lucas said. "If we find life, we try to establish a dialog, then go home." It would be great to find intelligence, he reminded himself. But the money would be nice too.

"It looks pretty empty to me. Empty and gray," the Captain said.

Lucas couldn't argue. It was empty. And gray. Even the lichens were gray.

"It's standard protocol to start with passive observation."

"How long is this going to take?"

Lucas shrugged. "The suits aren't ready yet, anyway. I need to run some final tests on the atmosphere before I can finalize the design on the

126

rebreathers."

"Will those spandex leotards you're sewing up really protect my boys?" the captain asked.

"It's not spandex. It's heavy duty elastic weave. Once I'm done with it, it'll be temperature resistant, radiation resistant, impervious to the acidic air, and extremely tear resistant."

The captain fingered one of the suits. "At least you're pulling your weight."

*****

"I want to drive the rover," Olympia said. "According to the scans, the whole planet is honeycombed with caves. The more complex life forms probably all live below ground."

"That is possible," Lucas said. "But the rover hasn't even completed one of its planned exploration circuits."

"Has it seen anything interesting?"

Lucas didn't bother to remind her that lichens were interesting.

He let her take manual control.

Then he went to bed.

*****

Olympia shook him awake. "Lucas, I found them. Come on. Get up."

Lucas pulled his jumpsuit on and followed her. He didn't need to ask what _they_ were. He just hoped she wasn't overreacting.

The probe's cameras had switched over to grainy green night vision. It was surrounded by an army of writhing black bugs.

Lucas wasn't proud of the revulsion that raced along his spine.

It was hard to judge their size, but the smallest looked about equivalent to a cat. The largest were bigger than ponies. They all had ten trisected legs with a longer, almost prehensile appendages jutting out from their heads.

"I'm pretty sure that they're communicating," Olympia said. She turned the volume up, and terrifying chittering filled the room. "It's all clicks and things, but more aliens keep coming. Larger and larger ones. The language analyzer is doing its thing--we might start getting simple words soon."

Language was Olympia's biggest strength. Her language program worked with every language on Earth--but Lucas wasn't sure if it could decipher clicks.

And he wasn't sure he wanted the creepy crawlies to be intelligent.

"New thing," the language program translated in its flat voice.

Olympia whooped. "It's working! And they talk! We're about to make first contact!"

"The Queen is coming," the program said.

"They have a Queen!" Olympia hugged him. "That means they have some sort of social structure! This is the best day ever!"

Lucas tried not to shudder.

A dialog box popped open on Olympia's screen. "It's ready to translate simple messages into their language. What should I say?"

Lucas shrugged. "We come in peace?"

Olympia laughed and typed the words in.

An error message flashed. "Guess that's too complicated," Olympia said. She typed in *Greetings*, and hit enter.

The rover clicked. The smaller aliens scattered. One of the larger ones approached slowly. "Greetings, new thing. We wait for the Queen."

Olympia chewed on her thumbnail. "I hate waiting."

"Maybe you should grab some sleep," Lucas said.

"You'll wake me when she gets here?"

"Yeah."

*****

The Captain didn't try to disguise his shudder. "My gut's telling me we can't trust those things. In fact, it's screaming at me to nuke the site from orbit."

Lucas's gut wanted the same thing. "Wouldn't do much good. They're deep underground, and they already live in a highly radioactive environment."

"That's fucking terrifying."

Lucas sighed. "They're different than we are. That doesn't make them our enemy."

"Doesn't make them our friend, either."

"Try to keep an open mind, Captain."

"Oh, I'm trying. What do you think those creepy pokey pincer things are for?"

Lucas shrugged. Exoentomology wasn't his specialty.

"I bet they stab things with them. And suck out their insides. Like spiders," the Captain said.

That sounded far too likely to Lucas.

The aliens started to skitter out of the chamber. Lucas leaned over and turned the volume back up. "She comes! She comes!" the flat voice chorused.

Lucas ran to wake Olympia.

*****

The Queen was the size of a bus. She hardly fit into the rover's cave. She stared down at the rover, then ran one of her front appendages over it. "I am told you speak."

Olympia hunched over her keyboard, and Lucas read over her shoulder. *I speak for others.*

"What are these others?" the Queen asked. "And where?"

We are a different kind of life. We come from another world.

A long moment passed. "Prove it."

*****

"I don't know if this is the best idea," Lucas said.

"It's a show of good faith." Olympia dragged a few more files into the list of information she was planning to send to the Queen.

"We know next to nothing about her."

"Exactly. So I'm trying to open up the lines of communication. I'm not sending anything more than they put on the Voyager Golden Record."

Lucas sighed. "I still don't like it."

"You've been spending too much time with Captain Argus." Olympia scanned her list one last time, and hit send. "I'm well within the first contact protocols. Everything is going to be fine."

*****

They started sleeping in shifts, so one of them was always available for the Queen. She didn't sleep.

Lucas missed having a warm body curled next to his. He hated eating breakfast alone.

And he hated sitting next to the monitor. The Queen occupied the entire screen--she had to be close to look at the pictures that Olympia had sent.

He didn't like the feeling of the Queen's tiny eyes staring at him. She had three rows of six eyes, all glowing green in the night vision camera.

"Are you really so... unprotected?" the Queen asked him, scanning the screen. "Your structure is encased by flesh, not the other way around?"

The question made Lucas's skin crawl. Most of the Queen's questions did. He told himself that he was being paranoid and unfair--letting his lizard-brain fears influence his thinking. *That's right,* he typed.

"It seems like poor design. So many things could harm you."

Our planet isn't like yours. We couldn't survive here without a suit.

"So you can create a protective outer layer for yourselves?" the Queen asked. "That is very clever. Are you wearing suits to survive in the stars?"

We have a vehicle that protects us.

"I do not understand *vehicle.*"

It's a structure that moves. We live inside of it.

"I would like to see one of these vehicles."

Lucas sure as hell wasn't going to go down there. Or let Olympia go.

"I have asked Olympia about emotions. I would also ask you about them."

Go ahead.

"I do not understand how they benefit you."

Are you saying that you don't have emotions?

"We do not. I see no use to it. They seem to do little but cloud your minds. Surely they have some use?"

We are social creatures. We don't have a hierarchy like you do, with one Queen. Emotions help us relate to each other. Help us work together. We are stronger when we work together.

"I do not understand. If you work together, aren't there more of you sharing the same resources?"

Yes, but working together allows us to gather more resources, as well.

"I do not see how that could continue to work in the long term. But I do believe I understand the concept. Thank you."

Lucas wished he'd stopped Olympia from sending those files. *You're welcome.*

*****

He sat on his bunk and stared at the wall. He hadn't done anything but work and sleep for almost a week.

He missed Olympia. She hadn't done anything but work and sleep, either. Maybe she needed a break.

He ordered a cup of tea and went to the monitoring station. He knocked on the open doorway. "Honey, do you want to take a break?"

Olympia took the tea and gave him an absent smile. "No, I'm okay."

Lucas sighed. "I miss you."

She turned away from the monitor. She'd lost weight in the past few weeks, but she'd never looked happier. He wanted to pull her back to their rooms. "I miss you too. But this is--it's my dream. I'm actually communicating with an alien intelligence! This is the most important thing I'll ever do. We'll have time for us later. I promise."

He wanted to tell her that loving her was the most important thing he'd ever do, but the words felt manipulative and small. "Can't we take a little time for us now? Just dinner."

Olympia sighed. "Lucas, I said no. I'm busy."

There was another person on the ship, and he was probably bored and lonely, too. Lucas grabbed his chess set and went to find Captain Argus.

*****

A week later, when he came in to relieve Olympia, she was clicking at the screen.

The Queen clicked back. Olympia grinned.

She was learning the Queen's language. Lucas knew he should have been proud. Olympia was the first human to speak a truly alien tongue. But he couldn't shake the feeling that something terrible was happening beneath the surface.

He was probably just being jealous. Of a huge bug. That his wife cared about more than him. He sighed.

"Hey," he said.

Olympia switched the translator back on. "Hey. Is it that time already?"

Lucas's shifts dragged. He nodded.

She kissed him on the cheek. "Guess I should get some sleep."

"Can she hear us?" Lucas whispered.

"Oh! Right, I forgot to tell you. The Queen would like to learn our language, so I enabled the audio feed. She's doing quite well, considering the physical limitations." She turned to the screen. "Say hello to Lucas."

The Queen tried to say hello. It was two differently pitched clicks that trailed off into a whistle.

But Lucas could almost understand.

*****

"You know, a whole race of organized, intelligent sociopaths isn't what I'd call a good thing," the Captain said, sliding a pawn forward a square.

Lucas considered the board. "They're not sociopaths. You can't judge them by our standards. They're aliens."

"Do we really know anything about them? You and your wife have been talking with the thing for months. What have you learned? It doesn't seem like it's been a fair exchange."

Lucas didn't want to tell him that Olympia was learning their language. He didn't think it would help his case. "It would be good to know more about them," he said.

"Well maybe someone should try and get some answers out of the spider. They scare me."

Lucas rubbed his forehead. "They scare me, too."

*****

"Are you the only Queen?" Lucas asked.

"No. We are eight." The Queen's voice still sent shivers under Lucas's skin.

"And each of you has an--an army of... minions?"

"We each have a family," the Queen said.

"How big are your families?" he asked.

"I do not have the numbers to tell you. How big are your families?"

*****

"Are you getting any information out of it?" the Captain asked.

Lucas shook his head. "But she's not being evasive--there are language issues."

The Captain took a deep breath. "Do you know if we can kill them?"

Lucas glared at him. "I have no idea. Murdering each other hasn't come up."

"I know that you're capable of figuring something out. Just in case."

"Figuring something out?"

"Some kind of poison or bioweapon. I've seen them--I doubt even a rocket could dent those exoskeletons."

"Our guns wouldn't work in their atmosphere anyway."

"So you'll think about it? Maybe come up with a few ideas?"

Lucas shook his head. "Olympia would never forgive me," he said.

"She doesn't have to know. And we'll probably never need it. But if something happens and we have to fight them, I doubt they'd have any trouble killing us. Shouldn't we have an ace up our sleeves?"

Lucas sighed. His jealousy, fear, and scientific integrity all fought for the upper hand. "I'll think about it."

*****

"How old are you?" Lucas asked.

"I don't have numbers to tell you. My kind do not fall apart with time as you do."

"You don't age?"

"It seems wasteful. So much wisdom lost. I remember the taste of all the creatures that once roamed this world. We were not wise then. We were wasteful and destructive, and now all are gone. We have wisdom now. We know how to husband our resources."

Lucas thought of the gray, empty surface and shuddered.

"I am tired of hunger," the Queen said.

That night, he started working on a bioweapon.

*****

The Captain brought a six pack of beer into the common room just as Lucas finished setting up the chess board. "We've been orbiting around this rock for four months." He handed Lucas a beer. "Merry Christmas."

"Thanks," Lucas said.

"I got orders today. Your wife isn't gonna like them." He sighed. "Frankly, I don't like them, either."

Hope stirred in Lucas's heart. Maybe they were being called home. He took a long drink. "What are they?"

"We go in and start setting up collectors."

Lucas gaped at him. "But that could throw off their whole

ecosystem!"

Captain Argus shrugged. "What ecosystem? There's nothing alive down there but those--things. What do they eat, anyway?"

Lucas didn't know. He wondered if Olympia did.

They didn't talk much anymore.

"They didn't tell anyone we'd found intelligent life here, did they?" Lucas asked.

Captain Argus shook his head. "There's too much money at stake."

"Why even wake us up, then?"

The Captain shrugged. "Maybe we can work out some kind of trade agreement."

"Oh yeah. I'm sure the Queen is going to be happy to let you rape her world."

"Why not? She already did."

Lucas had never felt more powerless and used. But at least he could delete the formula--take away the Captain's ace-in-the-hole. "Do you want me to tell Olympia?" Lucas asked.

The captain's relief was obvious. "Would you?"

Lucas nodded, and finished his beer. What the hell. At least she'd have to pay attention to him for a few minutes.

*****

"We need to talk," Lucas said. "Come to the room."

Olympia sighed. "Lucas, I'm working."

"This is important."

She rolled her eyes as she stood. "Fine."

It was strange being in their room together. "The captain got his orders," Lucas said.

But Olympia wasn't listening. She was staring at Lucas's computer. At the bioweapon formula on the screen.

"What's this?" she asked.

Lucas cursed himself for ten kinds of idiot. But he couldn't lie to her. "It's a weapon. I was working on it just in case we need one. But I'm going to delete it."

Olympia stared at him. "You created a bioweapon? I don't even know who you are anymore. How--how could you do this?"

"They scare me, Olympia."

"I expected better of you."

The silence stretched. "The Captain's been ordered to get the collectors set up and started."

"Before or after you commit xenocide?"

"I told you that I'm going to delete it! No one's committing xenocide!"

"You're right. I won't let you. I'll destroy this whole damn ship if I have to."

Lucas gaped at her. "You can't mean that."

"We can't declare war on the first alien race we meet! This has been going so well--I've learned so much--"

"Have you? You haven't been very good about sharing, then. There's almost nothing in your reports, and you sure as hell haven't been telling me anything!"

A look or horror crossed her face. "Lucas, please tell me that you're not just doing this because you're not happy with our relationship."

"Do we even have a relationship anymore?"

Olympia sighed. "You can't think this is a good idea. The man I married would never condone creating a weapon targeted against a friendly species."

"The Captain asked me to make the bioweapon as insurance. I never intended anyone to use it."

"I wish I could believe that."

Lucas rubbed his temples. "The Captain wants you to see if you can convince her to let his people go down and work. The collectors might not have any affect on the atmosphere in the caves."

"The atmosphere in the caves is the same as the atmosphere anywhere else, Lucas."

"Well, there's not exactly a fragile ecosystem down there," Lucas snapped. "Just the Queens, their families, and some lichens. What do they eat, anyway?"

Olympia sighed. "What do you think they eat? The smallest ones eat lichens, and the bigger ones eat the smaller ones."

Lucas's stomach twisted. "They're cannibals?"

"You can't judge them by our standards!"

"They hunted every other life form on the planet to extinction, then started eating each other! That's evil, I don't care what your standards are!"

"You've been spending too much time with the Captain. You've lost your scientific perspective."

"You've been spending too much time with that monster. You're losing your soul."

"I'm losing *my* soul? You're the one enabling *xenocide*!" Olympia screamed. She closed her eyes and took a deep breath. "She was right. She knew you were afraid of her. And she knew you'd hate her if you learned too much."

"She doesn't understand emotions." Lucas said.

"Fine. *I* was right," Olympia snapped. "I was right not to trust you. But it doesn't matter. I love you, but I can't let you do this." She pulled a taser out from the one of her drawers.

Lucas backed away, hands out. "Where did you get that?"

"I packed it. For protection--I'm the only woman out here, remember."

"This is a bad idea. Think it through, Olympia. Is she really more important to you than I am?"

"She's more important to the future."

Painful surges of electricity pulsed through his body, and he blacked out.

*****

Captain Argus shook Lucas awake. Blood seeped from a gash above the Captain's eyebrow, and from abrasions on his knuckles. "She tried to destroy the ship," he said.

"Is she okay?"

The Captain shrugged. "She's as crazy as a snake on an escalator, but she's alive and conscious. I've got her locked up."

"What are you going to do with her?"

The Captain arched an eyebrow. "I figured I'd let you decide."

Lucas felt sick. "That's not fair."

"I've got half a mind to space her."

"No!" Lucas sat up, and the world swam in front of his eyes.

"Then you'd better think of a better option."

"We could put her in cold sleep and haul her home," Lucas said.

The Captain shook his head. "No, there's no going home for her. The company doesn't want her spreading stories about what happened here."

Lucas felt sick. They were silencing her. And he was helping them. "Then what can we do with her?"

The Captain shrugged. "Think of something."

*****

She was in a holding cell, sitting on her hands. A dark bruise spread along her hairline. She glared at him as he entered.

He leaned against the wall and stared at her. He felt like he was looking at a stranger. He wanted to ask her what she'd done with his wife. "I'm supposed to figure out what to do with you."

"I want to go home."

"That's not possible."

She barked a laugh. "Of course not." She stared at him for a long moment. "You're the only one who can stop them, now."

"You're wrong."

"Are the suits ready?" she asked.

Lucas nodded.

"Then I guess going to the planet is my best option."

He felt like his heart was shattering into a thousand pieces in his chest.

He told himself it was just the aftereffects of the taser. "Fine."

*****

He fitted her suit. It was strange to be touching her, now. Her skin, her curves, her smell--it was all the same.

"I'm going to do all I can to help the Queens," she said.

He couldn't see how. "They're just going to go set up collectors."

Olympia smiled gently. "I don't think that's going to work out for them."

He thought of the Queen's spear-like pincers, and started planning on adding more armor to the suits. "I never thought we'd be on different sides."

Olympia shrugged. "We both chose." She took his hands. "Promise me you won't use your bioweapon. No matter what happens. Promise me."

Lucas squeezed her fingers. "I promise." He'd delete it as soon as he got back to their--his--room. He checked her suit one last time. "You're ready."

"Yes. I am."

*****

He watched her pod fall to the surface. He took control of the rover's camera so he could watch her enter the Queen's cave. She was tiny next to the Queen's bulk, and unfamiliar in the compression suit and helmet.

She clicked at the Queen, and the translator gave its flat voice to her words. He could almost forget who she was. "They are coming. I cannot stop them. They will change the air."

"The thing in the air is very valuable to them?" the Queen asked.

"Yes," Olympia said.

The Queen inched forward. "Nothing I can do will stop them from coming--nothing will stand in the way of their greed?"

Olympia hung her head. "Nothing."

The Queen stabbed her pincers straight into Olympia's chest. She cut through Lucas's carefully designed suit like it was tissue paper.

Lucas screamed.

The Queen consumed Olympia from the inside, just like a spider eats a bug. The suit that he'd fitted only hours before deflated like a balloon.

The Queen turned to the monitor. "You need not fear, Lucas. You and your collectors are welcome."

"Why?" Lucas asked. "She was on your side. Why kill her?"

"I was hungry, and there was no cost. I want your kind to come here. We will not hunt all of them. Just a few. As I told you, I have learned wisdom. I know the value of conservation."

"She was your friend," Lucas whispered.

"I do not see the value of friendship."

*****

Captain Argus sat down next to him with a bottle of whisky. Lucas was grateful for the burn of it in his throat. It was good to feel something.

It woke something else, burning inside him.

"It's done."

Lucas nodded. "Good." Of course it was.

"I can put you in cold sleep and you can take the first shuttle back," the Captain said. "We should have enough material processed to fill it up in a few months."

Lucas shook his head and took another sip of whisky. He could go back home. He could build a new life, live like a king on his share of the profits. The rage in his belly simmered. He tried to ignore the regret--the horror at what he'd done. He tried not to hear Olympia's voice damning him--accusing him of breaking his last promise to her. But she'd broken her last promise, too. "No. I'm going to stay. I'm killing them. I have to watch them die."

THE GREAT OCEAN OF TRUTH
TIM WAGGONER

Tim Waggoner wrote his first story at the age of five, when he created a comic book version of King Kong vs. Godzilla *on a stenographer's pad. It took him a few more years until he began selling professionally, though. Overall, he has published more than twenty novels and two short story collections, and his articles on writing have appeared in* Writer's Digest *and* Writers' Journal, *among other publications. He teaches creative writing at Sinclair Community College and in Seton Hill University's Master of Fine Arts in Writing Popular Fiction program. He hopes to continue writing and teaching until he keels over dead, after which he wants to be stuffed and mounted, and then placed in front of his computer terminal.*

> *Laws of Thermodynamics:*
> *1. You cannot win.*
> *2. You cannot break even.*
> *3. You cannot stop playing the game.*
> — *Anonymous*

"What are you doing here? What are you *doing* here?"

The man's voice catches your attention as you walk into the coffee shop. He speaks too loud, like someone with a hearing problem, and there's a strident urgency to his tone that borders on alarm. The man sits alone at a corner table, his back to the rest of the room, an ancient laptop open in front of him. The man's body blocks the screen, and you can't see what he's looking at--and presumably, talking to. It almost sounds as if he's interrogating the machine, demanding an answer to his question.

The man wears a threadbare army jacket just like the kind your father had, along with faded jeans and scuffed work boots. Your father left that jacket to you when he died, but you can't remember where it's at now. Too bad. You always liked that jacket. The man's overlong hair and untrimmed beard are both whitish-gray, but given the angle he's sitting at compared to where you're standing, you can't make out any of his facial features.

You dismiss the man from your thoughts as you continue toward the serving counter. Ghostlight Coffee is located downtown, not far from the VA hospital, and the place attracts its share of colorful customers. Some more so than others.

Ghostlight is housed on the first floor of an old building, with bricks walls, a wooden floor, and exposed heating duct system. You enjoy coming in here because of the place's age. You love the sound and feel of wood giving slightly beneath your weight as you walk, love the smell of dust and mildew. This is a real place, an *authentic* place, built for practicality, as well-worn and comfortable as a favorite shoe. Not like the faux neighborhood business effect that pre-fab coffee houses like Starbucks strive for. This is a place that satisfies both parts of you: the environmental science major you'd been and the construction-company owner you've become. This is urban repurposing at its best. The original structure remains, and the only modern touches are the lighting, the serving counter, and of course the computer register, cappuccino and espresso machines behind it.

Take that, Entropy! you think, and smile.

There's no one else in line, or in the shop, for that matter, except for you, the muttering man, and the kid behind the counter.

"Can I help you, sir?"

The barista is a skinny kid in his early twenties, with short black hair and an eyebrow piercing. He wears a gray T-shirt with *Ghostlight Coffee* on the front, and a white apron wrapped around his waist, as if he's afraid of getting stains on his jeans. Maybe he's clumsy and prone to spillage. Or maybe he just thinks wearing the apron makes him look cool.

You want to tell the kid to skip the *sir* shit. You're only forty-six, for god's sake. But then again, forty-six probably looks ancient to someone as young as the Amazing Apron Lad.

"Just a medium coffee. Black." You hesitate, and then add, "Decaf."

The kid nods and turns away to fill your order. As he does, you pull out your smart phone and check the time. 3:21. You need to get a move on. Lizzie's school lets out at 3:40, and you don't want to be late to pick her up. You haven't seen her since Sunday, when you dropped her off at Beth's, and since you're only going to get two days with her this week-- Wednesday and Thursday--you don't want to miss a single minute.

You start to slide your thumb across the screen, intending to open the phone's camera roll and look at a picture of Lizzie--one of your favorites, the one where she's grinning, tongue stuck out, eyes closed as if she's embarrassed by her pose, or perhaps trying to foil your attempt to capture her image by denying you her eyes. But your thumb encounters resistance as you try to unlock the screen. Instead of a smooth surface, the phone feels sticky, as if soda or jam has been spilled on it. For an instant, it seems as if your thumb actually sinks into the screen, and you imagine that if you press harder your thumb will penetrate all the way through and out the back. But then the sensation is gone, your flesh moves easily across the phone's surface, and the screen unlocks. But before you can open the camera roll, the barista returns with your coffee.

You tuck the phone back in your pants pocket and reach for your wallet.

"That'll be one ninety-five," Apron Lad says in a disengaged tone.

He sets the coffee down on the counter, the wood sagging beneath the cup's weight as if it's filled with lead. Soft cracking noises that remind you of breaking ice rise to your ears, only to be drowned out when the man in the army jacket shouts, "What are you *DOING* here?"

The barista doesn't look in his direction.

"Ignore him. He's in here a lot, and he knows that if he gets too loud, he'll get kicked out. He'll settle down."

True to the kid's prediction, the man quiets, his voice lowering to an unintelligible mutter.

You remove your debit card from your wallet and give it to the barista. The kid swipes the card and hands it back. "Do you want your receipt?"

You shake your head as you replace the debit card in your wallet and return it to your pants pocket. "No thanks."

You pick up your coffee and see a small depression in the counter's surface, tiny cracks fissuring outward from it, like a miniature blast crater. "Looks like you need to get a new counter."

You look up at Apron Lad and start to smile, but the expression dies before it can be born. The kid's right ear is sliding down the side of his face, as if he's a wax dummy in the first stages of melting.

"What?" The kid frowns and his right eyebrow sags, the skin drooping down to occlude the eye.

"Never mind," you say, taking a step back. The cup's cardboard surface is hot against the soft flesh of your palm, but you scarcely register this fact. A tightness spreads across your chest like constricting bands of iron, bringing with it a surge of ice-cold panic. You force yourself to walk slowly to the closest table, doing your best to ignore the cracking sounds beneath your feet.

You take a seat, set your coffee down, and then take your keys from your pants pocket. You unscrew the lid of the pill fob on your key ring and shake a single nitro tablet onto your trembling hand. You place it under your tongue, close your eyes, and wait. The tablet dissolves within twenty seconds. It's supposed to work fast, but if the pain doesn't go away after five minutes, your cardiologist has instructed you to take a second pill. If that doesn't work, then you're to take a third. And if *that* doesn't work, it's time to call 911 and start praying.

It takes almost a minute and a half for the bands around your chest to loosen, but they do, and you let out a slow sigh of relief. Your head starts throbbing--an unfortunate side-effect of the nitro--but you don't care. You'll take a migraine over a heart attack any day. You look toward the serving counter, expecting to see the barista staring at you with a concerned expression on his face, maybe even hear him ask, *You all right? Is there anything I can do?* But the kid's looking down at his phone, reading a text, maybe playing a game, his right ear and eyebrow back where they belong.

You pick up your coffee, stand, and make your way toward the door. Your head feels like it's going to explode at any moment, but you do your best to ignore the pain. Headache or no headache, you're determined not to be late to get Lizzie. No matter what else happens, you're not going to let her stand there outside her school, alone, wondering where her daddy is. The floor is reassuringly solid beneath your feet as you walk, the wood barely creaking. Good.

As you reach the door, the man in the army jacket--still facing his laptop screen--once more asks, almost conversationally, "Why are you here?"

"I'm not," you say, and walk out.

*****

You get in your pick-up, the words Pinnacle Construction painted on the side. You put your coffee in the cup holder, although you doubt you're going to drink it. Even though it's decaf, you don't like the idea of putting even the minimal amount of caffeine it contains into your system right now. Not so soon after your heart hiccupped, and not with the way your head is throbbing. You turn the engine over, listen to its spastic rumble-knocking, and you know you need to get it serviced as soon as you can afford it. You put the engine in gear, pull away from the curb, and head in the direction of Oakgrove Middle School. The traffic is light this time of day, and you figure you'll make good time, but really, it never gets much heavier than this. Downtown is dead, has been for years. A collection of old, empty buildings, crumbling brick and rotting wood. There are a few signs of life. The Cannery District has a couple funky art galleries and some renovated loft apartments, and there's Ghostlight Coffee, of course. But there isn't much more. It's a small Midwestern city whose best days are long behind it. Kind of like you.

You think about what you saw in the coffee shop. The cracked depression in the counter, the kid's melting face...You don't remember the doctor saying anything about hallucinations being a potential side-effect of your surgery. Three months ago you started feeling tired, short of breath, and you went in for a check-up. A week later you were on an operating table, getting a triple bypass. You weren't really surprised. Heart disease runs in your family--both your father and grandfather had bypasses--but it hit you at a younger age than you expected. The surgery went well, and although the recovery wasn't fun, you were back at work three weeks later, feeling better than you had in years. You get angina every now and then, but it's nothing that a nitro tab can't handle. So far, anyway. You suppose it's possible that for some reason you're not getting enough blood flow to your brain. That could cause hallucinations, couldn't it? But then again, it might just be good old-fashioned stress. Heart surgery caused serious psychological repercussions--a newfound awareness of your own mortality, a sense that your body was fragile, that if you weren't careful, it could shatter like glass.

Or crack like rotten wood.

And there's plenty of non-health-related stress in your life. The divorce. Only getting to see your daughter part-time. And business hasn't been all that great. Right now, Pinnacle Construction has more creditors than clients, and the former have been after you like a pack of drooling hyenas circling a choice piece of carrion.

You have a good job. And you worked hard to get your degree. Why would you want to walk away from that--and to start a construction business, no less? In case you hadn't noticed, this isn't the best time to get into building houses.

Beth had been right on that last point. Given the state of the economy, the construction industry wasn't exactly booming. And while your job testing water quality for the county wasn't exciting, it did pay the bills. But you were burdened by a deep-seated dissatisfaction you hadn't been able to fully explain to your wife--which was one the reasons she's now your ex-wife. Even though this all happened long before your surgery, you sometimes wonder if on some level you were aware of what was coming, that your remaining years might number fewer than most, and you didn't want to waste whatever time you had left running test after boring test on water samples. Yes, it was necessary work, maybe even important work, but it hadn't felt as if you were truly contributing anything. You were testing, measuring, assessing, when what you really wanted to be doing was making, creating, *building*.

You think about when you received your first glimpse into the true nature of the universe. It was in eighth grade--one grade higher than Lizzie's in now--in Mr. Gillespie's science class. The man was better suited to teach college than middle school. Most of what he taught went over his students' heads, and his tests were a real bitch. But you'd loved the class. It was the first time you'd felt challenged in school, and there wasn't a day that didn't go by without Mr. Gillespie giving you at least one awesome insight into the way the world worked. But no day had been more mind-blowing than the day he introduced the laws of thermodynamics to the class.

It had all been fascinating, but the second law chilled you.

Put simply, Mr. Gillespie had said, *the second law can be stated as "entropy increases."* He'd smiled then. *Or to phrase it another way, damned if you do, damned if you don't.*

He'd gone on to explain further, using such cheerful phrases as *the ultimate heat death of the universe*, but you'd only been half-listening. You were too busy trying to wrap your mind around the second law. If entropy always increased, you reasoned, then anything anyone did, no matter how constructive it seemed, only helped to hasten the process of breaking the universe down into nothing. And there wasn't anything anyone could do about it.

In the years afterward, you'd come to a deeper understanding of the three laws, and you know that they're far more complex than you'd first thought on that afternoon in Mr. Gillespie's class, but the basic core of your initial insight still holds up.

But Mr. Gillespie's class wasn't all existential angst. He'd hung a number of inspirational posters around his classroom featuring great scientists throughout history. Your favorite had been the poster of Isaac Newton, not because of the man himself, but rather the quote beneath his image: *Whilst the great ocean of truth lay all undiscovered before me.* You loved the poetry and mystery of the line, and that, perhaps more than anything else, spurred you to seek a career in science.

Of course, running tests on river water wasn't exactly exploring the "ocean of truth," was it? And as you grew older and became more aware of the ticking clock that was your heart--a poor defective organ that would eventually need tuning up as badly as your pick-up's engine--you had to do something to give entropy the finger. You knew it was going to win in the end, but you had to at least make the attempt to leave something more behind when you were gone than file after file of test results stored on some office computer. Building houses--building *homes*--where families could raise children, who in turn would grow up to have their own children, had seemed like a perfect legacy. Too bad it didn't pay the goddamned bills, not enough of them, anyway.

You decide not to worry about what you saw at the coffee shop. You've got a check-up with your cardiologist in a few days, and you'll ask her about the hallucinations--if they were even serious enough to be called that--then. Thinking about Ghostlight reminds you of your coffee, and you reach for it, only to withdraw your hand. You're still not sure if you want to risk the caffeine. You turn on the radio instead and crank the volume despite your headache. You always turn the volume high; it helps to mask the distressing sounds coming from the pick-up's engine.

An old Bob Segar tune's finishing up, and you catch a bit of lyric about autumn closing in. Nice. Just what you want to hear right now.

You leave the radio tuned to this station, though. The song's almost finished, and they play a wide variety of music here. You like not knowing what sort of artist is going to come on next. It could be anyone from the Big Bopper to the Beatles to AC/DC. *Predictability is its own form of entropy,* you think.

You're driving down Jefferson Avenue. It's the most direct route to Lizzie's school from Ghostlight Coffee, but it takes you through one of the skuzzier parts of town. The buildings here are so old they're on the verge of collapse, and for every business that's open, three have been closed and abandoned. Flaking paint and weathered brick, unintelligible graffiti spray-painted on walls, broken glass and discarded fast-food wrappers scattered on the sidewalks. The people here walk with slow shuffling steps, heads bowed, faces expressionless. Whenever you come this way, you can't help thinking about all the work there is to be done here--buildings to refurbish, businesses to reopen, people to save...But it's work you know will never be done.

The song ends and the DJ comes on the air. The prerecorded voice is usually that of an old sitcom actor you recognize but whose name you can never remember. But this time someone else speaks.

"Everything winds down, like an uncoiling spring."

This voice you *can* put a name to: it's Mr. Gillespie.

"So before it's too late, listen to these messages from our fine sponsors."

A commercial for a bartending school comes on, one you've heard many times before. You pay no more attention to it now than you did the other times you've heard it. You tell yourself that the DJ can't be Mr. Gillespie. You were in his class thirty-four years ago, and he hadn't been a young man then. He's bound to be retired now, if not dead. And even if he *is* still alive, why would he be spending what remains of his golden years providing prerecorded patter between songs on a small Southwestern Ohio radio station? It didn't make sense.

But the uncoiling spring was exactly the kind of image Mr. Gillespie would've used when talking about the Second Law. Weirder yet, the line seemed to come in response to what you were thinking. *Coincidence,* you tell yourself. *That's all.* But you don't believe it, not deep down where it really matters.

The commercials, all of them comfortingly mundane, continue for the next couple blocks. As you approach an intersection, you see the lights of emergency vehicles, and you slow down. The traffic light is blinking yellow, and there's a police officer standing in the middle of the intersection waving cars through. As you draw closer, you see there's been an accident, a bad one. Three vehicles--an SUV, a Ford Taurus, and a minivan--all appeared to have attempted to pass through the intersection at the same time, from three different directions, all traveling at surprisingly high speed, the drivers heedless of another well-known law of physics: two objects (let alone three) cannot occupy the same space at the same time. You first reaction is relief. It looks like the accident, bad as it is, isn't slowing traffic down, and you won't be late to pick up Lizzie. Guilt comes next. You should be thinking of the poor bastards who got hurt in this crash--and given the state of the vehicles, let alone the two EMS vans on the scene, you're sure no one's walking away from this clusterfuck unscathed--but your first thought was a selfish one. It's not that you're uncaring. You have a responsibility to Lizzie, that's all. This may be true, but it doesn't make you feel any better about yourself.

It's your turn to pass through the intersection, and the cop waves you forward, his motions sharp, an edge of impatience to them. You don't want to be one of those people who slow as they pass an accident, eager to sate their morbid curiosity. You'd like to think you're better than that. But you can't help sneaking a quick glance.

You see four emergency medical personnel, all dressed in blue uniforms, struggling to pull a mass of bloody flesh and cloth from the wreckage. Several police officers and firefighters stand by, watching, none of them making the slightest move to help. They seem alert, though, their bodies filled with coiled energy, and you catch what appears to be a look of hunger in their eyes. *They're just itching for some action,* you tell yourself. But that's not the kind of hunger you see. As you draw closer, you realize that the collision must have been far worse than you initially thought, for the twisted, crumpled metal of the three vehicles is so intertwined, it seems as if they've merged into a single solid mass. Last weekend, you watched a nature documentary on cable with Lizzie detailing what happened to the body of an adult elephant after it died. Lizzie was fascinated by the parade of predators and scavengers that worked to devour the dead beast over the course of several days, but it was the maggots that really captured her imagination. She'd seen flies before, of course, but not maggots, and after only a few short days under the heat of the African sun, there were thousands of the wriggling white things, so many that they began to reduce the elephant's flesh to a disgusting liquefied mess. And although the program's narrator pointed out how the energy the elephant had stored in its body over the course of a lifetime would be recycled into the environment, you couldn't help thinking this was a perfect illustration of the Second Law in action. The mass of vehicles reminds you of that elephant, while the EMTs, cops, and firefighters remind you of the lions, leopards, hyenas, and jackals who arrived to feed on the corpse. And the maggots? You suppose they're the looky-loo's driving by, of which you're forced to admit you're one. *Just call me Mr. Maggot,* you think.

You're almost through the intersection when your gaze centers on the bodies the EMT's are working to extricate from the wreckage. No...*Body.* Singular.

You tell yourself it's a trick of your eyes (no way you want to consider the possibility you're having another hallucination.) The bloody, broken thing the men and women pull from the crumpled metal can't be one large form with multiple heads, arms, and legs. It only looks that way because of the angle from which you're seeing the bodies, the quality of the afternoon light hitting them, the unreal nature of any horrific accident scene. Or most likely, a combination of the three.

Oh, it's a combination all right, you think. It seems like three objects *can* occupy the same space at the same time--after a fashion, at least.

The iron bands around your chest return, bringing with them ice-cold knives of panic. Fresh pain erupts inside your skull, so intense it's nearly blinding. You fumble for the pill fob on the end of your keys, but it's difficult to get the lid off with the keys in the ignition. As you struggle, the bands tighten, the panic intensifies, and you feel your airway begin to seal shut...

Pull over! you tell yourself, Wave down the cop, get him to bring one of the EMTs over here. Maybe they'll throw you in the back of one of their vans and haul your ass to the nearest ER.

The car behind you honks, startling you, and you realize that you've slowed to a crawl. The cop is waving you forward, his motions sharper now, more insistent, an angry scowl on his face, and other drivers start honking. *Pull over, pull over, pull over!* But you ignore the voice in your head and force yourself to press down on the accelerator, and move through the intersection. Your head still pounds, but the bands around your chest begin to loosen, your throat opens up, and you're able to breathe again. Not easily, but at least you can get some air. You think you're going to be okay.

You're tempted to look in your rearview to check if you really saw what you think you saw, if there truly was one body with multiple heads and limbs, but you keep your gaze fixed firmly on the road in front of you and continue driving. The pain in your chest eases, but this time it doesn't go away, not entirely.

*****

"Daddy, is that what's going to happen to me when I die?"

Her question catches you off-guard, and you try to make a joke out of it. "You mean getting eaten by jungle animals?"

Lizzie gives you a look that says, Don't be stupid. "I mean being turned into nothing but bones. And those will be gone too someday, won't they? So they'll be nothing left of me." She pauses for a moment to think before adding, "It'll be like I was never here at all."

You've never lied to her before. When she was much younger, she asked you if Santa Claus was real. You wanted to tell her yes, to give her imagination the push it needed to believe that there was magic in the world, at least for a little while. But when you saw the unquestioning trust on her face, you could do nothing but tell her the truth. You quickly followed up by telling her the usual bullshit, that Santa was the spirit of Christmas that lives in everyone, but you could tell she wasn't buying it. Worse, you could tell she was disappointed.

So now, sitting on the couch, both of you looking at a picked-clean elephant carcass on TV, you think of how you'd wished you'd lied about Santa years ago, and you want to tell her that it'll be okay, that God is in his heaven and all's right with the world. But you can't, so you just keep your damned mouth shut and pray she doesn't press you for answers you don't want to give, and you wish like hell that there was someone around to lie for you.

*****

Mr. Gillespie's voice comes on the radio once more. You listen as you rub your chest with your free hand, as if you might be able to massage your now-mild--but still present--chest pain away.

"Here's something to ponder, boys and girls. When the universe begins to break down, space and time will, too. It only makes sense, right? After all, that's what the universe is made of. So if time no longer functions--if, for lack of a better word, time dies--then how is it possible for the universe to truly end? In order to have beginnings, middles, and ends, you need the passage of time. No time, no end. So imagine that the universe is on the verge of giving its last gasp, and in that instant time stops. That means the universe would continue to exist in a kind of a frozen eternity, forever on the edge of death but unable to ever reach it. And since time is no longer a factor, there's nothing to separate one moment from the next. Everything that ever happened will basically continue happening forever, but all at once, in one great big jumbled mess. And not just events, either. Thoughts, emotions, dreams, nightmares . . . they'll all be in the mix, too, kids. And we'll be there, every single one of us, in that last forever non-moment of existence. We might even be conscious of what's happened to us, at least partially. Can you imagine what that would be like? I can't, but it sounds a lot like Hell, doesn't it?" A pause. *"That's enough for you to chew on for now. Let's have some more music. I was going to play Blue Oyster Cult's 'Don't Fear the Reaper,' but I decided it would be too cliché at this point. Instead, how about some Steely Dan?"*

You recognize the beginning of "Do it Again," a much lighter song than the BOC tune, but hardly a more comforting one at the moment. But you don't turn the radio off, nor do you lower the volume.

Just get to Lizzie, you tell yourself. *That's all that matters.*

The neighborhoods are supposed to improve as you get closer to the school...at least, that's how you remember it. But today this part of town...which used to contain middle-class suburbs with well-kept lawns and warm, cheerful homes--looks like a bombed-out war zone, the road cracked, buckled, and filled with potholes, sidewalks crumbling, houses lopsided skeletal frames, their yards barren patches of lifeless gray dirt.

The cars and trucks driving by are rust-eaten wrecks belching black exhaust as they judder along on decaying tires. You see signs everywhere that proclaim this to be a DECONSTRUCTION ZONE, and despite yourself, you laugh.

By the time you reach Lizzie's school--which is now called Oak*grave* Middle School, according to the tarnished metal letters bolted to the crumbling brick façade of the main building--your head feels like there's something inside trying to claw its way out, and your chest is on fire. But you don't care. Take a nitro pill, don't take a nitro pill...You know the end result will be the same.

You try to check the time on your phone, but the device deforms in your hand like warm taffy, and you drop the useless thing to the floor. You don't need it anyway. You know you're not late because while the buses are lined up in front of the school, there's no sign of kids getting on them yet. The final bell has yet to ring. You made it.

The buses don't *look* like buses, though. They resemble large gray elephants, a dozen in all, lying on their sides in two neat rows, their massive bodies bloated with decomposition gas. There's a small lot in front of the school where parents are supposed to pick up their kids, and there are a number of vehicles parked there, even more lined up in a single row, engines still running, the drivers impatient to collect their progeny and get on with what remains of their day. Their cars are all of a kind: roundish vehicles encased in green shell-like metal, headlights crosshatched like multifaceted eyes, engines emitting a droning buzz. Your pick-up is the only normal vehicle, and you pull into an unoccupied space and park. Before you can turn off your engine, the song on the radio ends, and Mr. Gillespie comes on again.

"When you think about it, boys and girls, the universe's only real function is to devour itself. It's an ouroboros, tail in its own mouth, chewing and swallowing, chewing and swallowing. And no matter how much it eats, it can never finish the job, and it will never, ever be full. So...dig in and join in the feast, kids, and remember to tip your servers on your way out. Bon appetite!"

You turn off the engine and the radio goes silent. Your pulse is beating trip-hammer fast, and sour-smelling sweat rolls off of you in waves. Your headache is so intense that tears stream from your eyes, and the pressure in your chest is so tight you expect your ribs to burst out outward in splintered shards. But as you exit the truck, you leave the keys in the ignition, the pill fob untouched. Let your heart explode like a flabby, rancid, fat-filled balloon. What possible difference could it make?

Now that you're outside, you find the insectine drone of the other cars deafening. Vibrations thrum through your body, and your heart and head try to match the rhythm. It hurts like a motherfucker, but you don't really mind the pain. In fact, it's kind of pleasant in an *Oh my sweet Christ I'm dying* kind of way.

The front doors of the school--glass broken, metal frames rusted and bent--slam open and a tide of children surges forth. Flesh spongy white, eyes flat obsidian, mandibles in place of mouths. The vast majority of children race toward the elephant carcasses, fall upon them, and begin to feast, mandibles cutting away chunks of rotting flesh with machine-like precision. Not all of the kids head for the elephants, though. Those whose parents have come to pick them up run toward the parking lot, and even though her face isn't exactly like you remember it, you recognize Lizzie as she comes toward you. She throws herself against you as if she hasn't seen you in years, and you hug her close, ignoring the way her mandibles catch on the fabric of your shirt. As you hold her, you watch the other children--the ones devouring the elephants--writhing in thick clumps over the carrion, covering it completely in a mass of white. Within moments, dead flesh becomes a foamy, liquid goo, and this, you think, is the real ocean of truth.

Your headache vanishes, as does the pain in your chest. Your pulse falls silent. Your heart is no longer beating, or perhaps it's on the verge of its final beat, unable to complete it. You wonder if Mr. Gillespie was right, if endings are no longer possible here at the penultimate instant before the final entropic collapse of the universe. Maybe, you think. But that doesn't mean you should stop trying to find an ending. To *make* one.

You push Lizzie gently away from you and gaze down upon her with a smile.

"Go ahead," you say. "I'll wait."

She gives a little jump of excitement, lets out an inhuman squeal of delight, and then runs off to join in the feast.

*****

The next day--or perhaps the same one (as if it matters)--you enter Ghostlight Coffee. The old man, the one wearing your father's army jacket, is sitting at the same table, staring at his laptop screen, still muttering, "What are you doing here? What are you *doing* here?"

This time, instead of going to the serving counter, you walk over to his table.

You see that he--and by he, you really mean you, because now that you're standing next to him, you can see that this old man is you with a few more decades under his belt--is looking at a picture of you and Lizzie on his screen. It was taken after one of her soccer games when she was younger. You're standing in front of a goal, she's wearing her uniform, her hair tousled, face sweaty, and you're both smiling.

You want to tell your older self not to worry, that you know why you're here--why we're *all* here--but your mandibles aren't capable of speech. Instead, you decide to show him. You grab hold of his jacket, pull him to his feet, and begin to eat your own tail.

GRAPHIC VIOLENCE EQUALIZER
MICHAEL A. ARNZEN

Michael Arnzen is an award-winning author of horror fiction and an English professor at Seton Hill University, where he has taught writing since 1999. His trophy case includes four Bram Stoker Awards™ and an International Horror Guild Award for his often funny, always disturbing stories. Join his social network at michaelarnzen.com.

"That's it, Mark. He's crossed the line. I'm done with it."

Mark Savage nodded at his wife, Maria, as he chewed on a particularly grizzly portion of the rump roast their new SmartOven had prepared. It purportedly downloaded recipes from the Internet and automatically cooked them once you put the ingredients in the door. The results weren't perfect but he was always surprised by how much better they were than he expected.

She poked the air above their dining room table with her coffee spoon. "Done."

Mark gave up on chewing the fat and swallowed it whole. Once it settled he addressed her concern. "Maria, I find his behavior unacceptable, too. But short of pulling Tommy out of school, locking him up in his room and shutting out all social interaction until he turns eighteen, I really don't know what else we can do."

She looked up at the ceiling. In the direction of Tommy's bedroom upstairs. "We have to do something. Grounding him, taking away his...toys. It's just not enough. He keeps doing these terrible things! We just can't keep ignoring the problem and hope it floats away to never-never land. Ever since Chauncey died, something's been wrong with Tommy and we have to fix it." She scooped at air again with her spoon: "No, fix him." She scooped into her mashed potatoes and took a bite to give it finality.

"What do you have in mind?"

She picked up Tommy's tablet computer from a nearby tabletop and turned the device on. She fingered around on the screen a bit, and then turned her head to one side, sticking out her tongue. Then she held it up so Mark could see the child's disgusting e-drawing again.

Mark sawed into his meat, summoning the courage to look again at what she'd confronted him with when he got home from work an hour earlier. Then he glanced at it again.

Tommy had drawn a dismembered head, held aloft by some unseen hand. Morbid, but common enough for a kid's painting. But it was too realistic to be some mere playtime distraction: the eyes were mottled white as broken marbles, the nostrils spewed blood, the tongue was agog as if still muttering its final words...and the flesh was torn horridly around the neckline, dangling an exceptionally realistic yellow-white trachea, bloody spinal vertebrae, and an assortment of purple red veins.

She peered around the screen, tongue still peeking out from her lips, her head also seeming somewhat detached from her body in the process.

He returned to his plate. "It's gory. I get it."

"No," she flatly replied. "He's gory. And I don't get that at all. What is he thinking? This isn't art...it's some sick fantasy."

"He's a twelve year old boy. Slugs and snails and puppy dog tails..."

She glared at him. Any reference to canines was verboten since the death of their family pet, Chauncey. "And decapitated human beings? Please!"

Mark dropped his fork. "You took away his iPad. Grounded the kid. What more can we do about it?"

He awaited an answer while her face flushed. "You can beat the living shit out of him!"

Mark kept his cool. "You know I'm not going to do that. You don't answer violence with violence. It only reinforces the idea that violent acts are the only thing that can generate a desired reaction..."

"Oh, enough with your psychological gobbledy-gook."

He hated it when she turned his career on him. "Maria."

"You're useless." She stormed away from the table, iPad in hand. He knew where she was going. To her recliner in the living room. The one with the scotch bottle within arm's reach.

Mark ate the rest of his dinner, giving her plenty of space. He tried to recollect where they had stored his college textbooks, especially the ones from his courses in adolescent psychology. He'd been out of graduate school for about as long as Tommy had been alive, and he had no clue where his books were anymore. Maybe they wouldn't help, anyway. Maria was right: something was seriously wrong with Tommy lately. It wasn't just the morbid drawings. He'd stopped eating breakfast and dinner. He stopped playing ball with his lifelong buddy, Rudy, just down the street. He gave up on riding bikes and playing chess with his father. He'd withdrawn completely, and even though Mark knew this was a phase that all preteens go through, he hadn't expected his son to become something akin to Pugsley from The Addams Family. It just seemed...out of character.

"Oh," he heard Maria utter from somewhere in the other room. "Oh no."

Mark sighed, stood up and slowly pushed his chair back under the table. "What is it now?" he asked as he entered the living room.

Maria was sobbing in her hands. On her lap, the iPad glowed with a familiar old photograph of their pet dog, Chauncey.

Only it had been doctored. Manipulated. Chauncey was on his back, legs cutely pointed up in the air, head curling to one side, begging for a good belly rub.

But Tommy had changed it. Big black Xs had been drawn across the dog's eyes. And Chauncey's canine coat now looked peeled back to reveal spiky white ribs and a wet red cavity writhing with worms.

*****

Mark took a seat on the bed beside his son. His weight sunk the bed a little, which made Tommy lean closer towards him.

He waited silently for his son to speak first. An old psychological tactic. He glanced around the room, sizing up the Yankees poster tacked beside his closet, and nearby, his neglected baseball bat and glove. The baseball equipment peeked out from under a pile of clothes in the corner, like Tommy was covering them up so he wouldn't have to look at them anymore. His TV and Xbox took up a lot of privileged space on the dresser. Behind them, a familiar shoebox--filled with a vintage sports card collection that Mark had passed down to him--looked dusty on the nightstand. On his desk, a few notepads spilled sloppily across the wooden top. He suspected they might have terrible artwork on them, but only spotted some innocuous flowcharts and similar scribbles from his computer programming classes. A cutely crooked vase he made in a third grade pottery class sat nearby. Tommy always had an artistic streak. He wondered what had turned it so dark.

"Those pictures...It's just artwork, dad," he explained, readjusting to keep his distance.

Mark tried very hard not to sound like he was on the job. He was a therapist, but he only worked with geriatrics now, as resident staff at the local nursing home. He was an expert at helping the elderly cope with Alzheimer's or the dementia of their roommates--or, at worst, the depression associated with the inevitability of death...but not fetishism of this sort. "Tommy," he said, turning the electronic tablet over in his hands, "that is not art. That's Chauncey."

"No it's not." Tommy sat on his hands. "It's just an old picture I was messing with. No big deal. I was playing with a new graphics app. It could have been a picture of anything."

He looked sideways at his son, hoping for eye contact. The boy didn't get it. "Chauncey was a member of our family. You disturbed your mother with that picture. And you disturbed me."

Tommy shrugged and tossed his unevenly-grown brown hair. "That was just some random picture on my iPad, Dad...and I don't see how my drawings are so terrible, anyway. I think they look kinda cool. I've seen a lot worse on TV and the net."

Mark took the time to swallow. He wasn't going to let his boy pull him down into some kind of philosophical discussion about aesthetics. "There's a line, Tommy. A line that you can choose not cross."

Tommy blinked and crooked his head to one side. He seemed to respond to that.

Mark continued. "The line is there. I don't care if you do your art, and I actually don't care if it ruffle's people's feathers. I just want to be sure that you know where the line is. And you goddamned better not..." Mark stopped. Swallowed. "Do you understand what I am saying?"

"I guess." Tommy yawned. "I didn't mean to ruffle your feathers or whatever, Dad. It's just a stupid piece of art. You can delete it for all I care."

That yawn. It said it all. Mark patted his son three times on the knee, slowly, then stood up. "And I don't want to stop you from doing your art, son. In fact, I couldn't if I tried. You can draw anywhere, anytime, with anything." He marched over to the dresser. "But I'm still taking your Xbox and your iPad away, anyway."

Tommy shot up and stamped his foot. "Dad! I need my iPad for Programming II homework!"

"Bologna. You're abusing the privilege. And besides, I pay a lot of money for you to go to a private computer school -so I know for a fact they've got all the technology you might possibly need right in the buildings." Mark walked over to the Xbox console beside his son's television set and yanked out the cords. The mass of them in his grip reminded him of the decapitated head his son had drawn. He tucked the black box under his arm and slammed the door behind him.

Mark heard something crash against the door in his wake.

Probably his old handmade vase. Mark didn't care. He knew he had effectively made his point.

In the living room, Maria's eyes jittered as she looked at the equipment in his arms. She threw back the scotch that remained in her tumbler. "Well. That's something better than just your usual pitty-pat malarkey, anyway."

"Yes," Mark said, dropping the technology on the sofa. "But not really enough, I'm afraid."

Maria squinted at him, adjusting her robe. "Games. You think they're too violent? Is that where he's getting this craziness from?"

Mark looked at the electronic toys. "I'm sure they're contributing factors." Mark ran a hand through his hair. He realized it was shaking. "But the cause must run deeper than just media influence."

She sat up and moved her eyes from the console cables to Mark's stare. "What about his cable TV?"

He eyed her warily.

Even in her chair, she managed to put her hands on her hips in defiance. "That's got to go, too. You can't just take away his games and computers...you gotta get rid of it all."

Mark took a breath. Exhaled. "We can't take the television away from him."

"Why the hell not? I know he's watching gory movies in his bedroom late at night. I've heard the screaming through the walls."

"If we pulled the plug on his cable, it would take the baseball channels away from him with it," Mark said. "I know he hasn't been playing a lot lately. But he's still a fan. I know he follows the games on the weekends. We still talk about the stats." He crossed his arms. "And without sports, he'd probably become a total recluse."

"TV baseball and real world baseball are two very different things. He doesn't need the TV."

"He might only get worse. Hold it against us forever." Mark shook his head, despite knowing that standing his ground might only put up another wall between them. "I have to say no."

She poured another drink. "Listen, Mark. I know you're a trained psychologist and all, and I really do appreciate all you do for this household." She swigged from her glass. "But if our boy Tommy is any indication, you're doing a piss-poor job of bringing up your own child."

Mark had been here before. But he wasn't going to buy into her ploys this time. "Maria, this is not about me. It's about Tommy. And there's a line we have to be very careful not to cross here. If we go any further with this punishment, we might be pushing him over to the other side of that line--and out of our reach--for the rest of his time in this house."

She blinked at him and he couldn't read it clearly. So he just kept going. "And that's only a few years till he's gone for good. I don't want him doing this disgusting art stuff, but at least it's an outlet for his emotions. We need to leave him some way to get whatever's inside of him out...and right now, baseball is one of the few remaining things in his life that's healthy. I want us to please, please, encourage him to do something healthy here."

She frowned, but she wasn't saying anything.

He grabbed her scotch bottle and held what little amber color was left in it up to the light. It looked warm and inviting.

"I'm going to bed," he said, and took the bottle with him.

*****

As he pulled out of the parking lot to head home from work, Mark glanced at the sign for Holmstead Nursing Home in his rearview mirror and found himself puzzling over why they called such places "nursing" homes in the first place. Sure, nurses worked there, but nursing was what you did with babies. These geriatrics were clutching on to what little time they had left on the planet, if they hadn't otherwise succumbed to senility and insanity. They were more like "dying" homes.

He got on the turnpike, eager to get away from it all, and found his Beamer blocked by a swerving car and heavy traffic. He almost even shot the finger to the elderly man in Mr. Magoo glasses and a derby, drifting stupidly in and out of his lane at 20 mph. When he got to something approaching a normal speed, he said "Cruise" and the internal GPS took over the engine, setting a controlled cruise speed and navigating the road in a way that he always associated with an airplane's auto pilot.

Attention freed up, Mark tried to process his emotions. He knew that all of this anger at the aged was displaced aggression about losing control of his family. It dawned on him that his preoccupation with the word "nursing" was really just a psychological sign of something that gnawed at his psyche. Perhaps it was his growing concern about his wife's "nursing" of the bottle of booze. Or that he blamed his wife--the mother of his son--for not caring for Tommy the way a good mother should. That would explain the boy's violence as much as some abstract bad influence of the media. The dismembered head in Tommy's drawing did bear a slight resemblance to himself, after all. And the dog really had been more faithful to Mark than any of them. The whole thing was textbook Oedipal complex.

As he pulled into his neighborhood, he resolved to improve the communication lines with his wife and son.

But the driveway in front of his brown-and-red bricked house was blocked. A white utility van from Intellivo was parked in his normal place. "What's wrong now?" he asked aloud, and his dashboard said "Please restate your destination" with synthetic care. He pressed the kill switch in the BMW.

In his living room, Maria slurped coffee while a man in white-and-gray uniform and ball cap worked around the cable box near their primary television screen. She smiled at him, but didn't move to greet him with the usual kiss.

Mark scanned the room. "What's going on? We just got the full house decked out two months ago."

"They're installing the VQ."

"The what?"

The Intellivo man turned around as static on the high definition TV fizzed into a steady image of the local news broadcast, covering traffic and weather. "That should do it, Mrs. Savage." He tipped his hat at him. "Mr. Savage."

His mind was trying to remember how much he had paid on the last Intellivo bill. "VQ? What station is that, exactly?"

"Why don't you both come on over here and I'll show you how to operate it."

Mark joined Maria's side.

The man paged through stations on the television with a remote control. He stopped when the screen showed a woman in a black nightgown, standing face-to-face with a shirtless man in silken boxers. "Here ya go. Blood of the Night. Perfecto."

Mark dimly knew that Blood of the Night was one of the new "sexy vampire" spinoff shows on a premium station, but he'd never watched it before. He didn't go for such things. "Oh, VQ is a station. I see..."

"No, sir. VQ is short for the 'Violence Equalizer.' It's called a 'Graphic Violence Equalizer to be more accurate." He blinked. "But most folks seem to prefer calling it 'The Tamer.'"

"It's sort of like the V-Chip," Maria said to him, with a familiar, dismissive tone.

Mark looked at her sideways. "The censoring chip they used to put inside of TV sets?"

"Yes and no," the Intellivo man cut in. "It's a completely new technology, really. Let me just show you."

He picked up another remote control from the TV stand and pointed it at the set top box. Mark noticed that this one had four slider buttons on them, lined up like mixing-board levels. "Oh, I get it. VQ...like the EQ on my old stereo." He stroked his chin, suddenly captivated.

The Intellivo man nodded and pointed at the device in his hands so they could follow along. "Exactly. An EQ system allows you to adjust the bass and treble and midrange frequencies of sound. Well with the VQ, you can adjust the images instead. You manipulate the full spectrum of sex and violence in whatever you're watching on the tube."

Mark tilted his head. "Like some kind of parental control switch, eh?

Blocks out shows based on settings? Sounds interesting."

"Well...I wouldn't use the word 'block.' This is far more advanced than any parental controls of the past. The V-chip relied on the ratings system. This relies entirely on you. It's more like there is a computerized film editor up in the Internet cloud, watching over the show and changing things ever-so-slightly, depending on how you set the switches on this device." He smiled and waited to see Mark's reaction.

"It doesn't block anything? You still get to watch the show?

"Exactly," he nodded, his smile a little wider. "Only the VQ invisibly edits out the nasty bits on the screen and the soundtrack." He tapped it. "You can't really turn it up. Just tame things down. It's really quite remarkable."

"I'll believe it when I see it," Maria said, though clearly she was already convinced it would work, because she had requested the installation when he was away at Holmstead and set this whole thing up in the first place. He was a bit peeved that she didn't get his approval first, but he immediately understood the potential it harbored for solving the problem of Tommy's television privileges.

The Intellivo man pointed at the television, where the scenario in Blood of the Night had shifted from a mere nightcap conversation to actual dry humping as the standing, writhing bodies moved closer and closer in a sort of slowdance heading to the nearby bed. Mark blushed a little when the vampire seductress pulled back and parted her nightgown down the middle with a sharp fingernail to reveal the full voluptuousness of her heaving breasts. She fell onto the half-naked man, who immediately began to suckle a pert purple nipple, making sure to give its sharp tip plenty of camera time as he licked it. Then the vampire woman pulled his head up, kissed him on the neck and then lunged, snapping her head back and in the process tearing off a swath of skin in that looked something like a flank steak dangling in her sharpened, bloody jaws. So much blood sprayed out of the wound that droplets actually landed on the camera lens while the naked man choked and drained out onto the bed. The woman took a bite of his flesh and swallowed, blood bubbles shiny on her breasts.

"Well isn't that special?" the Intellivo man joked, and then rewound the scene--which looked just as horrifying to Mark backwards as it did forwards.

He replayed the scene and then held out the VQ right before the vampiress opened her gown. He slid one of the four levers downward and the woman's clothing magically dissolved back into place.

"Well I'll be!" Maria said, sounding almost cartoonish.

"Wait...that's the sexy part. Not the violence," Mark said.

The technician grinned and nodded as he slid a second button down at the moment when the vampire forced her lover's head up toward hers and wrapped her chin around his neck. "Sexual Violence is just one of the controls," he said. "This other one is dedicated to Bodily Harm and Gore." On the screen, the woman pecked her lover's neck with a gentle kiss as the camera slowly panned up to the ceiling and the scene faded into the next.

It was almost as if nothing gory or filthy had even happened.

"Rewind!" Mark demanded, enthralled, reaching for the VQ. "And let me try!"

The Intellivo man handed Mark the switch console while he used the regular DVR remote to rewind the program yet again. Mark noticed that the woman's blouse stayed in place, even when rewinding, as if the sexual images had never been displayed to begin with. "Impressive," he said, noting that the settings held firm. The scene started over again and Mark slid all four of the buttons all the way to the bottom. The woman's nightgown was replaced with a fancy cocktail dress that draped down to fully cover her arms and legs. The man suddenly had a tuxedo on. The characters still writhed a little as they stood there--intimate--but there was still space between them. But their bodies jittered a little.   "Well, that's a little weird."

"Oh, the romance is all still there, only it's extremely subtle. The little ones won't know what they're missing."

Maria pulled the gizmo out of Mark's hands. "So what do these other two buttons do?" She started adjusting them randomly. The screen morphed and wobbled and the bedroom setting was replaced by a diner. The vampire smiled and her fangs had disappeared. It might as well have been some kind of Martha Stewart rerun.

"Wow," Mark said. "This is unbelievable."

The Intellivo technician counted on his fingers. "You've got your

Sexual Violence, your Bodily Harm and Gore, your Painglory, and your Psychological Torment buttons. All in a row." He picked up a toolbox. "Mix it down as you wish. It roughly ranges from R-rated down to G, though those ratings don't really mean much on cable TV anymore. You can fine tune each area of...obscenity...whatever...to make any show you choose reveal as little as you want."

Mark turned to the man while Maria played around with the television, making the vampire's boobs pop in and out of sight. "I get the idea...but how does it work? The different dress and such. Surely every show on television isn't filming all that extra stuff just to fill in for this device. That would be impossible!"

"It's pretty complicated technology," the man said, walking with Mark to the front door. "But I do know it relies on the Internet. Luckily Intellivo has the least amount of downtime in the industry. You're safe." He coughed into his hand. "The VQ is able to scan the image, rapidly substituting alternatives based on matching images and sounds it pulls down from the cloud...almost instantly." He nodded to himself. "The Internet is amazing, isn't it? I remember a time when people were afraid of all the junk out there online, contaminating their children. Now it's saving them from seeing things."

Mark understood what the man was getting at. He dimly remembered seeing news reports about cable regulation, in the wake of some pretty nasty school shootings last year. Right wing politicians were asking for tighter regulations on obscenity and First Amendment wonks were pushing back in the name of Free Speech. "Grown-ups wrote the Constitution," some congressman had famously said. Maybe the VQ was the result of some kind of compromise that the industry came up with, to cool down the growing flames from the public. He hadn't really been following the news lately, so he wasn't sure.

"Damnedest thing. I even heard that some networks are starting to exploit this here technology for themselves to make up new shows using only animatrons and green screen. Guess it's easy enough to do now, with the net and all. Just pull in the imagery you need off the cloud and recycle it into something new. I suspect we'll see channels made of nothing but remixes soon enough. And the thing is, we probably won't even notice the difference. Heck, for all we know, it's all computerized already as it is."

Mark smiled and nodded, amazed by how rapidly so many things were improving in everyday life. From the advancement in Maria's cooking to the auto-pilot in his car, life just kept getting better and better. Maybe this really would help his relationship with his son, too.

"Since you're an early adopter, we'll come right out and update it to the new tech free of charge, whenever they issue an upgrade. Our appreciation." He made his way out of the door. "And just give us a ring if anything goes wrong. Thanks again, Mr. Savage." He peered over Mark's shoulder. "Mrs. Savage."

Maria ignored them as she changed to a cooking channel and played with the VQ switches.

Tommy appeared at the top of the stairs and walked sullenly down and into the kitchen. "Who was that?" he asked his father in a voice that sounded like he didn't really care about the answer.

"Nothing special. Cable man. Came to install an upgrade," Mark said, wondering how much his son had heard and seen.

Tommy didn't reply.

Mark shot his wife a look to get her to stop playing with the new device. But she couldn't help herself.

*****

By 2:30 in the morning, Maria had passed out in her recliner, but Mark was still wide-eyed and excited about the Graphic Violence Equalizer. Normally he didn't believe in censorship, but the VQ allowed for so much fine tuning that it felt like he was literally creating new programs at the slide of a button.

The "painglory" setting, for instance. He had heard of vainglory, but not painglory, and it provided a fascinating adjustment to the screen image. If a character ever seemed to relish inflicting violence, their twisted smiles and dark laughter could be muffled out. If a scene involved torture or punishment, the camera zoomed in on the instrument of torment, excluding both the inflictor and the afflicted from the shot, so that you only saw hands or hammers or belts moving across the screen. The action was clear, but nothing whatsoever was glorified in a way to encourage identification. In fact, it was discouraged completely. Slide another dial and the camera went elsewhere. Sometimes weapons were replaced with other objects or removed entirely. Blood, wounds, dismemberment--erased. But in a smart way. It was the equivalent of editing on-demand, rather than overlaying things with a black-bar redaction or an entirely blocked show. It was, he though, ingenious.

The Intellivo technician had said that some people called it "The Tamer" and the VQ certainly did that. But what Mark found so compelling wasn't simply that it made the violent movies and TV shows less violent. What he liked was that the story they worked on remained intact. Narrative was something he felt very passionate about in his line of work. The psyche was made up of the stories people told themselves. And the problem with so many horror movies and crime dramas wasn't simply that they were violent or glorifying pain--it was that they had given up on giving the violence and pain any narrative context whatsoever. It was all just so much visual spectacle--gore for gore's sake--the equivalent of hardcore porn for a cheap thrill. The narratives were flimsy when you scraped away all the eye candy. And editing out the violence could only reveal just how empty those calories really were. Their stupidity would now be obvious to anyone who watched--even a twelve year old boy.

This would work. It wouldn't solve everything. But it would help.

However, it had some side effects he hadn't anticipated, and the VQ needed to regularly be re-tuned, depending on the material. Maria didn't seem to mind it, but when they watched on of her favorite cooking shows on EatTV, even the knives that chopped lettuce seemed to be replaced by duller instruments and what should have been flaming pans seemed to sizzle without any fire to char the ingredients whatsoever. Cranking the buttons to their lowest setting didn't really solve the problem. It was inconsistent, from what he could tell. Golf, for instance, seemed to still be as golfy as golf gets, even though the clubs were swung with some violence at their balls and the players sometimes swore or made nasty gestures. The problem was that you couldn't be sure if the "Tamer" was taming down the already tame things, requiring you to twiddle the VQ buttons if you wanted to pay serious attention. He made a mental note to report this problem if he ever received a customer survey.

By 3:30, Mark decided to head up to bed. He set the VQ on the side table and left Maria sleeping in her chair--something that happened more and more lately, and he wanted to talk to her about soon. He turned on his bedroom television and set the timer to auto-sleep in an hour.

His suspicion that, once set, the VQ settings applied to all televisions in the house was proven true as he watched a late night episode of CSI: Alaska in his bed, fascinated by the way bodies were kept off screen throughout the episode.

Before he nodded off, he wanted to try one last thing. He called up one of the home movies, to stream it over the wireless and onto the television.

Apparently, the VQ worked with any image you streamed. The scene in their wedding video where they cut the cake and shoved portions of angel food and frosting into each other's mouths was completely obliterated, showing a close up of the bride's bouquet instead, while somewhere off-screen, the bridal party laughed with glee.

*****

Mark decided that he could allow himself the luxury of a $15 airplane drink. The stewardess scanned his smartphone and then handed him the tiny bottle and a pint-sized plastic cup that reminded him of the drinkware they used at the nursing home.

He nursed the Jack Daniels straight from the bottle, sipping it gently, the way a person might take cough syrup.

It was late and most of the passengers were sleeping, but Mark was still buzzing with excitement about the conference he'd been attending all weekend. He had presented a paper to the American Psychological Association about geriatric therapy using media and received a number of requests to share his research from journal editors he didn't even realize were in the audience. He couldn't wait to fire up his computer and develop the concepts. He felt like a real scholar again, doing very real work.

The idea had come, sort of, from the VQ. The way it worked with narrative. He had come up with a theory that if you edited out important snippets from the home movies belonging to the elderly, it would stimulate their memory to fill in the gaps. He didn't have the same technology as Intellivo at his disposal in the nursing home, and his test pool was very small, but with an experimental group of volunteers, he had designed an experiment. All it took was using the Intellivo at home

170

to edit their home movies and play them back to them in his office. The response seemed to be positive, generating a lot of active recollection from his patience--even from those who seemed unable to remember what they had for breakfast seemed capable of filling in the edited memories relatively easily. He had recorded several of the nursing home patients talking about these memories with his home video camera, and put together an emotionally powerful presentation for the APA.

Publication of that paper is only the half of it, he thought. Maybe I can get a grant for long-term study. Something that would get me out of the nursing home before I have to actually move in to one for good.

He couldn't wait to share the news with Maria and Tommy. Things seemed to be going well enough at home that he could actually think and write and he was fairly certain that the Intellivo corporation was partially responsible for that, too, three months into their early adoption of the VQ.

Tommy had apparently stopped making crazy art and started making really good software models in his classes. He was getting As in programming, and by all reports was excelling in college prep math, too. And he wasn't only playing baseball with something approaching regularity again--he was in a team that was winning trophies, and he was visibly looking healthy. His arms were huge now.

And it must have been contagious because Maria, too, was lifting in spirit. She was cooking more often, eager to experiment with things in the kitchen. She'd even started gardening again. She was so much into it, he'd seen her working the electronic saw on the hedges…and she never bothered with that before. Heck, she even talked about maybe buying a new dog soon. And she did nothing but fawn over Tommy, squeezing his biceps and telling him how much of a good man he was becoming. It all seemed so…weirdly normal.

He'd taken the midnight flight, so his house was dark when he quietly crept into the front door. Maria was not in her living room chair, and they hadn't been sleeping apart for several weeks now, but he noticed that she had left a nearly empty bottle of scotch on the side table in her wake. He didn't see the VQ remote, and assumed she'd taken it up to bed with her.

He wondered what he could do about her alcoholism while he

unpacked some items from his carry-on and then gently walked up the carpeted stairs.

He heard a muffled scream from the general direction of Tommy's room. In the upstairs hallway, he noticed flickering lights in the thin line of space at the bottom of his bedroom door. He heard a soundtrack of metal music. An ungodly sound -- something like a chainsaw. A woman crying for help. Cursing. Dark laughter.

"Goddamn it, Tommy!" he said and charged to the door. He stopped at turning the knob. Collected himself. Maybe this one discretion wouldn't cause much harm. Boys will be boys. Maybe Tommy could be forgiven for being one.

The chainsaw engine roared behind the door. A woman cried "Please!" but the killer replaced her cries with the tortured sound of grinding throat meat and the metallic clack of metal shredding bone.

"That does it!" Mark worked the knob. It was locked. He pounded on the door, hoping it might awaken his wife to join him. A unified front would only help. "Open the door, Tommy!"

The line of light at the bottom of the door went black. The dark laughter from Tommy's television seemed to go up in volume.

He pounded again. "I have the key to this room, boy!" He said this, not knowing if he did or didn't. Not knowing how, really, he was going to get inside the room if Tommy didn't answer.

No reply.

The chainsaw sound revved up again. Another woman's voice cried out in panic. Lights flickered.

He jiggled the knob and tried to pull as hard as he could.

Then he got an idea. Maybe the VQ was simply on the wrong setting. Maybe he could adjust it if he found the remote, and turn down the violence. If he couldn't, maybe he could just cut the power to his room from the circuit breaker in the basement.

He ran across the hall to the bedroom and opened the door. "How can you sleep through this racket?" he asked at Maria, who was a huddled mass beneath her red blanket. The TV set was on, but silent, beaming a station ID logo -- it was so late at night, her cooking channel had gone off the air. He searched the bedside table for the VQ, then the floor, then scanned the bed for it, patting the red quilt with his hands, half hoping he'd wake her from her drunken slumber.

It took a few pats for the truth to register. The cover was wet beneath his hands. The red quilt had camouflaged the fact that it was totally saturated with his wife's blood.

He held up his bloody hands in disbelief. The blood felt so...cold.

"Smile," Tommy said from somewhere behind him.

His was voice deeper than he remembered -- and unsettlingly calm.

Mark turned slowly. His eyes scanned past the electronic saw on the floor nearby. Blood spatter on the wall. Some kind of bodily organ on the carpet.

His son stood in the doorway. Stained down the front, like a badly trained butcher. He was holding up the family video camera. A little red light beamed out from it.

"What the hell? What...what did you do, Tommy?" Mark unconsciously gestured at the bed. "Did you actually do this? To your own mother?"

"Yes," he said, bringing his baseball bat out from behind him and swinging the hardwood against his father's forehead. "She crossed the line," he said, swinging it again as Mark tried to stand up from the floor, wondering what on earth he meant by that, what on earth was happening, what on earth--and again hardwood hit him in the temple and something spurted out of his ears and flew past his eyes. He was aware he was on the floor now, leaking out from his eye sockets, as Tommy held the bloody bat aloft and at the same time leaned forward with the camera in his other hand, angling for a good close up.

"Perfect," he said, and swung.

*****

Tommy perched on the edge of his bed and rewound the video recording of his dead mother. He had already watched his father's death about fifteen times, fine tuning the graphic violence equalizer in different ways to improve the thrill. At one point the baseball bat morphed into a long, rusty machete. It looked even better than he thought possible, chopping into his father's forehead. Good. He almost had it perfect.

But the art of it all still wasn't quite right.

He grabbed the bottle of scotch and took a swig. Tommy was beginning to understand why his mother had a taste for it. It felt warm in the belly and made your head forget about everything. It made the world a little wobbly, but it also put that world into sharper focus when it wasn't spinning and you paid attention to it.

He fondled the VQ remote on his lap and grinned. It had been so easy to reprogram while his mother was asleep. All it took was downloading the BIOS into a text editor and putting a negative sign in front of all the numbers that he guessed were the frequency levels for one of the sliding buttons. He guessed that if those numbers somehow took away from the shows, putting a negative sign in front of them would put things back.

And, he hoped, add some too.

He had tested it on an episode of a reality show where contestants competed for survival on a deserted island. One notch up the dial and they began beating each other with their fists, to the point of knocking each other out or leaving bruises. Another notch up and those fists were gripping homemade spears like giant toothpicks that they stuck into each other's chests with bloodlust and glee. Another notch and they were actually eating each other alive.

It had made even the dumbest of shows so much better. So much more interesting. Even... artful.

But that was nothing compared to what this did to his new home movies. He saw such potential for new art in this technology. He could stretch his imagination as far as he could and capture it on film. But then process it through the VQ and he could stretch things even farther.

He really wanted to watch what it did to his mother one more time.

But this was only the first stage. Three buttons remained for him to reprogram.

As he downloaded the firmware again and began editing the BIOS, popping in the negative signs, he wondered what would happen if he added zeroes to the ends of those frequency numbers, too. Would it still work if he multiplied the effect by a hundred? A thousand?

He still didn't know what each switch really controlled. Just that when he put negative signs into the program, the shows added new elements. He knew that the program was hooking into the Internet to pull things down from cyberspace and morphing them into the picture somehow. He didn't know how it really worked, but it didn't really matter. Maybe he'd figure out how to improve it even more, with enough time. For now, he just wanted to play. He knew that accidents sometimes make for the best art. "Glitch art," one of his favorite websites called it. He liked the sound of that.

Tommy edited the program, adding zeroes to the frequency levels, wondering how far he could go. If there was an end to how much information it could download to enhance his next art piece. If there even was a line he could cross.

PARASITE

KENNETH W. CAIN

Kenneth W. Cain is a dark fiction author from Eastern Pennsylvania, where he lives with his wife and two children. His work has appeared and is forthcoming in several publications with many other great authors. He has penned a three novel series with more to follow, a collection of short stories and flash fiction, a handful of illustrated children's books, and is currently involved in a collaborative project for a young adult series. kennethwcain.com

The obtrusive ring of Aiden's cellphone bothered him. He glanced at the screen and groaned upon discovering who was calling. He ignored the call, replacing the phone in his pocket. No, his brother had cried wolf one too many times. What had responding to his brother's constant needs ever done for Aiden? *Getting dumped by your girlfriend, that's what.*

He was unsure why he always felt the need to check on his little brother anyway. Sure, he was close enough he could run over right now, but sooner or later Neil was going to have to learn how to live without Aiden's assistance. As the thought occurred to him, Aiden realized he missed taking care of his brother.

Pushing the urge away he instead reflected on the instances where he should have seen this coming. When a guy starts calling his brother's girlfriend there should be suspicion. A blinded Aiden suspected nothing. He thought it an added annoyance to Jasmine if anything, and somewhat of a relief to have another person to share in the burden. He never anticipated them sleeping together.

Exiting his new apartment, he walked toward his brother's house. This had once been his residence, a place where all three of them lived until a few weeks ago. He often desired to return to those days, yet with everything having become so fractured the notion seemed impossible. After all that happened, all the hurt feelings, here was his brother no doubt calling about some trivial issue.

The cellphone buzzed, indicating he had a message. Aiden retrieved the phone and leered at the screen knowingly. He contemplated listening as he came to a stop. What if Neil really was in trouble? If something happened to his brother he would never be able to forgive himself.

Their father had left when they were very young and Aiden took on the added responsibility of helping his mother raise Neil. When their mother passed it only seemed logical for Aiden to remain devoted to the task. Since Neil opted to sleep with Aiden's fiancé that alone should suffice in severing their connection. Aiden deleted the message unheard and replaced his phone.

Halfway to his brother's house he began to wonder why he was even strolling in this direction. Aiden didn't want to tempt himself to check on Neil. The time had come to teach his brother a lesson. It never occurred to him the not knowing would end up being the most unnerving consequence of ignoring Neil.

Aiden began to worry, beads of sweat forming on his forehead. He struggled to contain his curiosity. His mind tried to recognize this need and the emotions associated with it. The familiar ring disrupted his anxiety. This time Aiden answered.

"Neil?"

"Ai-den..." His voice sounded hoarse and pained. "Ai-den..."

"Neil, what's wrong?" Aiden barely noticed he had started walking at a faster pace.

"Hurts, Ai-den..."

"What?" Aiden started jogging. "What hurts?" No answer, only heavy breathing as he heard Neil's phone rattle to the floor. "Neil? Talk to me!"

Aiden kept his phone pressed tight against his ear as he ran to the end of the street. Something about this made him feel like a sucker, knowing he had rented a nearby apartment for this very reason. Why should he care? His brother had hurt him. His brother deserved this. Only his voice had sounded like Neil was enduring a physical pain. Aiden disregarded the details of their strained relationship upon reaching the door.

When he turned the knob the door opened with ease. It displeased Aiden to discover his brother hadn't locked the door. It was the sort of thing that fed his need to protect Neil.

He expected to find Neil waiting for him when he entered with an expression of terror struck on his brother's face. He recalled seeing that very expression one too many times. But there was no sign of Neil. Boxes of Aiden's possessions were stacked in every corner. It made the place appear empty without Aiden's furniture to fill the rooms.

"Neil?" Aiden exited the foyer to the living room. Looking out the front bay window he saw a familiar car pulling into the driveway. *Great, Jasmine.* Evidently her moving out hadn't terminated their relationship. It was then it occurred to him that she might have only done this for Aiden's benefit. The idea she would do such a thing made his skin crawl with repulsion.

She rushed up the walk and in through the open door. Aiden cursed himself for not closing the door. "Is he okay?" She was still obsessed with his brother's care. The guy had a way of sucking people into his terrifying little world. Once there it was almost impossible to break free.

Well, hello to you, too. Her ignorance irritated him and Aiden felt a sudden disgust. "He's fine." Although Aiden didn't know this as truth it was often the case. Besides, he wasn't sure he really even cared now that Jasmine had showed up. Their mother had always played to his brother's paranoia, more so than Aiden. In the end Neil was always fine with his schizophrenia being the sole culprit.

"How do you know? Have you seen him?"

She was hooked and it frustrated Aiden. A burning sensation formed at the base of his neck creeping upward, the tiny hairs standing as it spread. He wanted to scream at her, to hash everything out all over again. He refused to further expose his emotions. He wouldn't give Jasmine the satisfaction. "He always is."

"He said he found something in the basement." She paused, wrinkling her nose as if trying to smell something.

Aiden used to love the way she did this and his heart fluttered. He longed for her to come back, yet he knew now she never would. She still wore the ring he had given her, a false proclamation if there ever was one. He wanted her to keep it there as reminder of what they once had together. At the same time he wished she would give it back to him in light of her infidelity.

"He said there was scratching, as if something was trying to release itself."

"Scratching?" He considered this pushing his jealousy aside. "Like a cat?" Aiden didn't think any such creature could get inside let alone end up trapped in the basement. The windows in the basement were old and beyond dirty, long since weathered shut.

"I don't know," she said, full of trepidation. Neil was more of a concern than Aiden had ever been to her. "He sounded like it was driving him crazy. Then he said he had to go, to call you." Her hopeful eyes met his.

Aiden found it ironic she should choose these words. Did Jasmine realize that his brother really was crazy? He had told her so several times. Aiden assumed she had discovered something appealing in Neil's madness.

He found himself drifting in thought while staring at the ring he had given her. Seeing this, she hid the hand from his view, either feeling guilty for what she had done or not yet willing to relinquish the past. There was hope in such an action. Maybe she would grow tired of Neil and return to Aiden. Did Aiden even want her back?

"Maybe he's in the basement."

He hadn't answered Aiden's call and he was sure he had spoken loud enough that Neil would here even if he were downstairs. It wouldn't be the first time Neil had ignored Aiden's call. He supposed he had better check to make sure Neil hadn't passed out or something of that nature.

Aiden sauntered into the kitchen and threw open the basement door, calling out his brother's name once more. "Neil?" Still no answer, but a peculiar light radiating on the wall caught his attention. He turned briefly to Jasmine. "Stay here."

The wooden stairway creaked as he descended into the half-finished basement. Although it was dark what he could visualize was illuminated by a strange orange glow. He left the safety of the well-lit staircase for the open basement, walking around the wall to discern the source of the light.

From this angle only Neil's back was visible. Neil knelt before an object, orange light pulsing from it. Neil wore a white tank top laden with dirt. It appeared as though Neil was sweating, his lengthy hair hanging in thick bunches like black icicles.

"Neil? What's going on?" Aiden approached with thoughtfulness, ignoring any contempt he held for his brother. The closer he got the more the light revealed. Neil wasn't only sweating; he was dripping with perspiration. Aiden wanted to run to him and make sure Neil was okay. Yet the unsettling appearance of the scene kept him from venturing forward.

Bits of rubble, dirt, and blood as well as other unrecognizable debris were scattered about the place Neil knelt. He looked as if he were honoring royalty. His chest heaved, breathing with deep gasps of air and excruciatingly slow exhales.

The strange orange glow emanated from a large metal egg-shaped casing that appeared as though it been torn open. The object remained half-buried in the exposed earth amidst the wreckage of the wall. Aiden thought it might be a capsule of some sort. He couldn't help but wonder how long it had been buried there.

Neil's fingers dangled on either side, nearly resting on the floor of the basement. Blood oozed from each worn digit. Exposed bones made Neil's fingertips appear as if they had been sharpened. Aiden thought it more likely the result of clawing repeatedly at a noise that would not cease, a sound that had played on Neil's paranoia.

Aiden's heart thumped steadily in his chest as he beheld the scene, observing everything. "You look pretty banged up, bro." Aiden felt his nerves bunching. His concern for his brother was overwhelming. "Come on, let's get you to a hospital." He hoped his brother would leave the strange pod, but Neil ignored Aiden's request.

"Is he okay?"

Her voice surprised Aiden out of the trance he had drifted into. He shook his head knowing she couldn't see him doing so. His answer didn't reflect his true thoughts. "He's fine. Don't come down."

"Why? What's wrong?"

"Jasmine!" He hated that she was so distressed. "Just stay there, please."

She sighed audibly. Her shadow looming in the light of the stairwell, showing she had not fully retreated. Aiden returned his attention to his brother.

Neil's heavy panting became rhythmic. Another noise found Aiden's ears, penetrating his skull like an MRI might. It was a grinding buzz that burrowed into his thoughts as if scanning his brain. Neil grunted followed by an awful sound, as if something wet was being pushed through an obstruction. The muscles on Neil's back strained, flexing as he went into a fit of dry heaving.

The possibility this might be some sort of sickness had never crossed Aiden's mind. Perhaps this was brought on by something that had been inside of the unusual pod. Aiden knelt behind Neil, placing his hand on his brother's shoulder. "That's it. Let it all out, bro." He regarded the strange metallic object with caution. "We'll get you all fixed up as soon as I can get the paramedics out here."

He couldn't keep from wondering if whatever infliction had found Neil's lungs and nasal cavity might be communicable. With reluctance Aiden kept his hand on his brother's shoulder to show his continued support. Then Neil's retching came to a sudden stop. The panting and buzzing noise diminished along with the orange glow, fading to a very dull shimmer that played upon the shadows of the basement.

For a brief moment the situation improved. Then Neil turned and Aiden witnessed firsthand what his brother had gone through. Aiden stared into the destroyed cavity of his brother's nose, seeing the strained glowing eyes. It was as if something was peering through the orbs, illuminating them from behind. Much of the flesh surrounding Neil's nose looked as if it had been melted away exposing the passages of the sinuses. Something had crawled up inside of the hollow void and secured itself to Neil's bone with tiny hook-like fingers.

Aiden screamed, leaping away from his brother. He landed hard on his butt several yards from Neil and scampered back on his rear. He heard Jasmine's descent and wanted to warn her, but his voice had swollen shut, bringing only a wheeze of air. His eyes were glued to Neil. Aiden continued crawling backward towards the stairs. Jasmine's meddlesome legs blocked his retreat.

When she saw Neil she burst into a fit of screaming. Her piercing shrieks were loud enough to jolt Aiden out of his stupor. He stood and turned to Jasmine without taking his eyes from his brother. Aiden ushered her back to the stairs.

Neil grimaced, the torn flesh flayed back from his teeth. Loose flaps that were once lips rippled with every movement of Neil's body. Strange tentacles writhed inside of Neil's mouth. They found Neil's teeth and pried his mouth open wide, further tearing the flesh to expose a boney grin lined with thin red meat.

Aiden gulped, seeing his brother as more of a monster than a human. Neil crept toward Aiden, treading like some sort of four-legged animal stalking its prey. The need to hurry overwhelmed Aiden. He shoved Jasmine hard, as she continued shrieking, trying to force her up the stairs. She went, but not without reluctance.

Neil leapt, spinning in mid-air and finding the ceiling like a cat. It amazed Aiden how Neil was able to cling to the wooden crossbeams as if he were some horrible spider. On closer inspection Aiden identified the keen fingertips digging into the grain of the wood. Neil hissed.

Aiden heard the straining noise again and saw Neil heave, as if he were going to throw up. Aiden watched from the bottom step wishing he had followed Jasmine up, but not yet finding his legs. He stayed long enough to witness his brother hacking up something awful. Neil launched the black ooze at Aiden as if it was a wad of chewing tobacco.

The dark blob missed him by inches. He located where it had struck the stairwell wall and was intrigued to see how the goo continued to desperately reach out for Aiden. Confident if the secretion reached him it would eat away his nose and climb inside, Aiden kept his distance. Tiny pained cries escaped the ooze as it fell lifeless from the wall. Another fit of coughing and hacking shook Aiden out of his daze and he dashed up the stairs.

Neil pursued, managing the basement ceiling as if it were a jungle gym. When Aiden reached the third step from the top he heard Neil plunge to the base of the stairs, crashing through the wood. Aiden jumped all three steps at once, toppling to the kitchen linoleum and attempting to kick the door shut.

He rose to his hips and leaned his weight against the door. It banged, shaking on its hinges. The knob turned in Aiden's hands, twisting as Neil tried to force it open. He nearly succeeded, but with Jasmine's added weight Aiden managed to secure the lock. They were safe, but for how long?

He scanned the room for a weapon. His initial thought was to raid the kitchen knives, but they were safely packed away. He stared at the boxes trying to remember which one he had put them in. His eyes centered on Jasmine's purse and he remembered she kept a small gun for protection.

Aiden rushed to her bag leaving Jasmine to brace the door alone. She was crying, tears streaming down her face through dark streaks of mascara. Aiden rifled through the contents of her purse. He had no regard for anything but that one necessity. Upon obtaining the gun he was overcome with instant empowerment.

A confused Jasmine wandered away from the door, seeming both concerned yet anxious of what Aiden was doing. He was glad she had moved. The poundings continued and with each blow the basement door rattled. It splintered and then gave way to the alien force behind it. At first there was only darkness, the light bulb having been broken in the scuffle.

As he maneuvered Jasmine to safety a whirling sensation shot past his ear. Another black ooze missed him by less than an inch this time. The wind of its path cooled his ear lobe and he thought he even felt tiny claws taking a brief hold on his ear.

Neil spun out of the darkness and made a steadfast path to the wall. With a hiss he sank his boney fingers deep into the plaster and clawed his way up to the ceiling. Aiden leveled the gun ready to fire. Neil dove at him, knocking the gun loose before he got a shot off. The gun slid away.

"Jasmine, I need the gun." She didn't respond. "Jasmine!"

His brother wrestled him to the ground, the filed bone of his fingers burrowing into Aiden's flesh. Neil hissed, his body retching as heaved. Aiden stared into the bloody mass of the nasal passage and saw his brother's special passenger. It looked right back, a single tentacle eye descending from the sinus cavity to behold Aiden.

Unable to hold back his dread Aiden screeched. He kicked and punched knowing what Neil was about to unleash. The torn flesh around Neil's mouth quivered as the boney grin opened wider exposing where there had once been a tongue. All Aiden saw now was the ooze loaded and ready to propel itself outward.

He arched his back, remembering his days of high school wrestling. Aiden threw his brother to the side and tried to find his feet while Neil continued to grab and claw at him. Aiden scurried for the gun with Neil finding one of his feet and taking a tight hold of the shoe. Aiden pulled free of the sneaker and seized the gun.

When he rolled onto his back it surprised Aiden to see another ooze flutter by, missing him. Neil was already in the air and Aiden braced himself for impact as he brought the gun up. This time he got the shot off.

The gun recoiled, a thin smoke rising from its barrel. Neil's ruined face now had a much larger hole the size of a grapefruit. Blood and black goo dripped from the wound, but still Neil's body lurched. Aiden fired at Neil's forehead, this time striking his brother dead.

Neil's body collapsed on Aiden. Without hesitation Aiden shrugged off the dead weight and rolled away. He didn't want any of the black touching him. Aiden scampered away refusing to take his eyes off his brother, the sorrow of what transpired becoming all too real. When he finally did look away he discovered Jasmine's fate and it stung.

The creature had nearly burrowed its way inside. With most of it having squeezed into the tiny hole it had begun excavating Jasmine's nasal passage to secure itself. The bone and flesh sizzled, reminding Aiden of the sound of bacon cooking, as the black ooze continued to maneuver itself into her skull. She sat cross-legged, breathing heavy, her eyes already beginning to eerily change color as her passenger observed the world through her eyes.

Aiden broke into tears, falling to his knees. He still loved her. Saddened by her fate he aimed the gun and fired. A horrid click followed where there should have been something more devastating. Panic set in as he fired again, once more producing the empty sound.

He spun the chamber revealing the vacant spaces. An aggravated Aiden threw the gun aside. His heart raced as the creature squeezed the last bit of itself into Jasmine. He whirled to a pile of boxes marked "kitchen" and began tearing through their contents.

Behind him her breathing eased. His pulse quickened feeling as though it were going to explode with the knowledge of what his fate would soon be. He tossed various non-threatening utensils aside searching for something fierce. Aiden heard her footsteps as he seized a picture of them together. Regret found him as he tossed it aside. Her shoes clacked against the wooden floor. He threw aside a crab cracker, digging deeper. A distinguishable sound followed of her flesh tearing as her jawbone exposed itself in a horrid smile. He found what he wanted, secured it, and turned with the large knife raised in defense.

Jasmine was gone, the front door still open and revealing the setting sun beyond. A light breeze crept in and Aiden felt the sudden impulse to close the door. Jasmine was someone else's problem. It was selfish, but he had lost too much for one day.

He inched forward clutching the knife against his chest as if to ward off any evil. A chill ran through him as he passed his brother's corpse. A dark pool covered much of the floor beneath Neil. Aiden took a wide berth around Neil toward the front door. He reached it and took a cautious step outside. Aiden grabbed the handle and as he found the cool metal a strange foreboding feeling washed over him.

Above, clinging to the side of the house was Jasmine. She spat the black ooze at Aiden. The passenger found his face with Aiden twisting and trying to steady himself on the door. Already the ooze was excavating.

He collapsed to his knees, the molten sensation on his flesh intolerable. The pressure of the creature clamoring inside his sinuses, squeezing in every last bit was unbearable. He was aware of his heavy breathing, his panting and profuse sweating. Horrid pain incapacitated him as the tentacles pried his jaws apart to reveal his teeth. Aiden's skin tore away in shockwaves of agony as this parasite invaded his skull.

The agony never went away. He could see what his passenger saw. He felt the torture, the anger, the hopelessness. His memories remained and it pained him that he would end up with Jasmine after all. With her by his side, he felt the need to spread, a yearning to reproduce. They left together, the ring still upon her finger, binding them.

IF THINE EYE OFFEND THEE

THOMAS M. MALAFARINA

Thomas M. Malafarina is a horror writer from Berks County, PA. He has two novels, Ninety-Nine Souls *and* Burn Phone *as well as a short story collection,* Thirteen Nasty Endings. *Thomas lives in South Heidelberg Township, PA with his wife JoAnne. They have three grown children and three grandchildren*

> *And if thine eye offend thee, pluck it out: it is better for thee to enter into the kingdom of God with one eye, than having two eyes to be cast into hell fire.*
>
> -- Mark 9:47

> *And if thy right eye offend thee, pluck it out, and cast it from thee: for it is profitable for thee that one of thy members should perish, and not that thy whole body should be cast into hell.*
>
> -- Matthew 5:29

The cold October evening drizzle fell relentlessly upon the lone figure sitting cross-legged on the wet pavement in front of the liquor store. The proprietor of the establishment was a kindly man, conscientious of the troubles of others and as a result, had not been able to bring himself to ask the vagrant to leave. Nor would he call the police to do the unpleasant job for him.

The store owner assumed the disheveled man was such a sad and pathetically harmless creature, sitting and begging for the unwanted change of those more fortunate than he that the most considerate thing he could do for the man was to just leave him be.

The squatter was dressed in faded, torn jeans, a well-worn old black leather coat, under which he wore a soiled grey hooded sweatshirt, which drooped downward under the weight of its sodden condition, hiding his face in shadows. Despite the time of night, he also wore dark black wrap-around sunglasses further shielding his appearance from any curious onlookers; not that anyone paid attention to what seemed to be nothing more than a burned-out homeless beggar.

On the ground in front of his folded legs was a tin cup with a few dollars in change inside. It had been a slow night and by the obvious absence of the sounds of metal against metal, he suspected not too many people had been willing to part with their change that evening. That was, of course, unless they had dropped a few dollar bills into his cup, which he knew was highly unlikely.

John sat in the shadows, mumbling incoherently to himself as he always seemed to do more and more of late, while pedestrians hurried by anxious to get to their destinations. Whatever it was he was babbling was indistinguishable to anyone but himself. And most of the passersby either didn't see him or simply ignored him. Still others might glance at him with angry looks of disgust before hurrying past, many forming a deliberate arc of avoidance around him. Occasionally, someone would drop a coin or two into his cup and John would mumble "Thank you" or "Bless you" or some other phrase of appreciation. He kept his replies to a minimum, not wanting to engage anyone in actual conversation.

His hands were tucked deep in the pockets of his coat, their purpose two-fold. First, the worn cloth liner of his pockets managed to still provide some warmth for his ungloved fingers; and secondly the deep pockets offered a hiding place for the switchblade he held tightly in his right hand. He knew he could never be too careful when living on the streets. There were plenty of evil souls out there in the world and no one understood that fact better than John Martin, himself.

*****

He hadn't always been the babbling street beggar he appeared to be, sitting in the shadowed darkness, avoiding contact with his fellow man. John had once excelled at everything he did, no matter how difficult, and with ease. Yet he was also naturally lazy, unambitious and as such had no desire for higher education.

What he longed for more than anything else was simply to have the time necessary to sit quietly and let his mind contemplate the one subject which was of the most importance to him: the existence of the human soul. He didn't consider himself a theologian or philosopher by any stretch of the imagination, but he had always believed that buried somewhere deep inside of him, he had the natural ability to not only someday prove the soul's existence, but to actually see it; if he were just able to figure out how.

Once, as a young boy, while suffering with a flu and extremely high fever, John noticed something strange about his elderly grandfather who had been visiting for the day. It was a fleeting thing, only the briefest of glances, but he was certain he had seen it. A glow had momentarily surrounded the man and John wished he had been able to see it more clearly. It had appeared then disappeared so quickly, he had not been certain of what he had seen, especially in his feverish and weakened condition. But he was sure he had seen something. Then a week or so later, his grandfather died suddenly of a massive heart attack. John believed that, had he been with his grandfather at the time of his passing, and in the same feverish state as he had been in the previous week, he might have actually seen the man's soul leave his body.

Many years later, one of his friends talked him into trying a hit of LSD. Although he had found the incident quite unpleasant and one he wouldn't want to repeat, John had to admit he actually did learn something from the experience. The hallucinogenic effects of the drug seemed to temporarily open his eyes, giving him the ability to see things he had never imagined before. From that day on, John believed if he could find the right combinations of drugs, he would someday be able to open a door inside of his mind, which would lead to his developing a sight beyond sight, and likely the ability to actually see the human soul.

John worked a series of low-skill, minimum wage jobs; each of which he made sure he was guaranteed to eventually end up losing, finding himself collecting unemployment compensation. This bouncing on and off of the unemployment rolls suited John just fine. Whenever the long-awaited day arrived when John would find himself back collecting government checks he would do his best to ride it out for as long as he could and only work when he absolutely had to. During times of severe economic recession he was able to enjoy numerous government-sanctioned extensions of unemployment benefits and had more free time than he could have ever hoped for.

Prior to his last layoff John had worked as a stockroom helper for a local pharmacy. Being a small, privately-owned business it didn't have the stringent inventory controls of the larger chain stores. Since the high school LSD incident, John had experimenting with a variety of drugs, as he was certain the answer to his quest for the soul lie in the proper combination of pharmaceuticals. While working in the stockroom John had managed to accumulate a number of pills which he labeled and properly recorded. He broke up the pills and combined them into various concoctions for his experimentation. He kept a detailed log of his research, documenting the exact weights and measurements of his mixtures as well as his successes and failures.

Sometimes the drugs just made him sleep. Sometimes they caused him to hallucinate. And sometime the results of his drug experiments were nearly catastrophic. But despite the risks, he was sure he would eventually find the precise combination to give him the outcome he was looking for. He didn't have to wait long, as after a short time he was not only successful, but more successful than he ever would have imagined in his wildest dreams or most terrifying nightmares.

One day, about a half hour or so after taking his latest mixture of various over-the-counter sleep aids combined with alcohol John was sitting on the stoop outside of his apartment observing people walking by, hoping for some positive results. A pretty young woman named Nancy, who lived in the apartment across the way, came out of her front door and waved a greeting to John as she had done many times before. He always found her attractive and could tell by the way she acted around him; she was interested in him as well. John had thought about asking her out, but felt he truly didn't have the time or energy for a girlfriend at this point in his life, so he had always tried to keep things somewhat distant between them.

He cordially returned the wave with as much enthusiasm as his latest drug-induced stupor would allow. That was when he noticed it. At first he saw a glowing aura form around Nancy's body and he knew he might have finally found what he had been hoping for.

Then suddenly, without warning, he felt a tremendous pain inside his skull and for a moment he worried that his brain was about to explode. His first fleeting thought was of a possible stroke or aneurism, but then just as quickly the excruciating pain subsided and he was elated to discover he was still both alive and hopefully still healthy.

"Are you all right, John?" he heard Nancy say from a distance. She must have noticed his reaction to the crippling headache. Not looking up, he signaled with a wave and replied, "Yeah…yeah…I'm fine…just had a headache or some…" But before he could finish his sentence he had looked over at Nancy and was suddenly stunned speechless. Nancy was gone. That is, the Nancy he knew was gone and in her place stood some sort of horribly disfigured animal-like creature.

It was one of the most hideous sights John had ever witnessed. The thing stood about as tall as Nancy but appeared to be hunched slightly. Its hair, though the same color as Nancy's was wild and frizzled shooting outward in every direction in long greasy strands. Its flesh was grey and mottled and even appeared encrusted with scars and scabs in places. It was completely naked from head to toe and had lots of long body hair. The creature's drooping breasts hung long and pointed downward like two horrible pendulums swaying to and fro.

John chose not to look at the rest of the creature's body fearing what he might find lurking down below the waist. Instead, he made what might have been a greater mistake and looked at the beast's face. Its cheeks were sunken in appearance and its giant eyes bulged from its dark and hollowed-out sockets. The thing's nose that of an ape. Its mouth was an oversized cavern filled with large yellowed fangs. Drool spilled down over the creature's huge lips as the mouth began to form a strange smile.

John had no idea what it was he was seeing. How could someone as lovely as Nancy be suddenly turned into such a revolting slobbering thing before his very eyes?

"John? Are you all right?" The hideous creature asked discordantly in Nancy's sweet voice. "You look like you just saw something terrible."

For a moment, John just sat and stared at the hideous sight before him. He could not comprehend what was happening. He could hear Nancy's voice but it was coming from the horrid thing which scarcely resembled the woman he knew; or at least the woman he believed he knew.

"I…I…" John stammered. "I gotta go!" And with that he jumped to his feet and staggered on wobbly legs down the street, hurrying around the corner and away from the wretched thing. He kept his eyes cast downward, deep in thought, trying to make sense of what he had just seen, while still fighting the mind-blowing effects of the drugs he had taken. After a moment he was startled by the angry honking of a car horn and realized he had inadvertently stepped off a curb and into traffic.

"Hey! Watch where you're going, you stupid asshole!" he heard a driver shout at him. John looked up to see who had shouted at him and was horrified by what he saw seated behind the steering wheel of a taxicab. Like Nancy, the creature behind the wheel was a horrifying twisted version of a human so dreadful as to no longer be considered a man. The thing was even uglier than the Nancy creature had been with a huge, hairy muscular, vein-riddled ape-like arm hanging out the driver's side window. That same arm was now extending its fat middle finger in John's direction and might have actually seemed comical had it not been for its incredibly ugly face. Large, pulsating veins similar to those in its arms traveled up the creature's thick neck and continued up the sides of its mottled face, disappearing into its hairline. Its grinning mouth seemed impossibly large with what appeared to be hundreds of razor sharp pointed teeth. Its eyes were huge and filled with an anger and hatred the likes of which John had never seen before. The creature looked like it epitomized the essence of evil.

"Get off the street, you drunken bum," the horrible man-beast said in the driver's gruff human voice. In terror, John stumbled backward much too quickly and tripped over a curb, landing down hard on his backside on the pavement behind him.

"You ok?" Someone asked from behind John. He heard the sound of young children chuckling, as they sometime do in such situations. The voice he had heard sounded like a young woman, likely the mother of the laughing children. He looked up cautiously, fearful of what he might encounter and was relieved to not find some heinous creature, but was eye to eye with a normal pretty-looking little girl; a toddler, perhaps almost two years old.

But upon closer examination, John noticed she was not quite as normal as he originally thought. Her eyes had something of a strange look to them as if they were in the midst of a gradual transition from human being to something else. Likewise the luster of her young skin was not a pink as it should have been, looking slightly gray in color.

John began to crab walk backward away from the strange child when he noticed what must have been her two older siblings perhaps six and eight years old. He was shocked to notice as the ages of the children increased so did the hideousness of their appearances. It was as if they were gradually changing and evolving into something horrendous. That was when he observed the children's mother and the crowd gathering behind her.

"Can I help you?" The woman said with a large fang-filled mouth that looked as though it might be capable of devouring John's head in a single bite. As he looked with stunned immobility at the massive maw, he saw long thick streams of some type of reddish goo-like drool dripping down from the fangs. The creature's tongue rolled out over its teeth and John could see some sort of vile insectile creatures attached like barnacles to the organ. These tiny bugs seemed to be eating the flesh of the tongue and burrowing under its skin.

As he quickly pulled his gaze away and unwillingly scanned the rest of the crowd John observed that every one of the gawking spectators was more repugnant than the last. He had no idea what in hell was going on with the world around him, he only knew he had to get home to his apartment so he could hide out from these despicable beasts and try to figure out what was happening.

John staggered to his feet and keeping his eyes cast downward while groping the sides of the buildings he made his way as quickly as possible back to his apartment, tears streaming down his face and babbling like a crazy man. He thanked the heavens that he didn't meet up with any other of the horrid creatures and was pleased to find that Nancy or the horrifying thing she had become was no longer outside waiting for him.

He pushed his way through the front door and into his apartment, being sure to secure every one of his locks and deadbolts. John suddenly recalled the insects devouring the flesh of that woman's tongue and felt his stomach heave. Fortunately, he made it into his bathroom just in time and fell to his knees at the toilet, vomiting and heaving like he had never done before. Sometime later when his gut was thoroughly emptied and after the retching and dry heaving subsided, John slowly tried to stand hanging onto the sink for support. He needed to brush his teeth and run a cold wash cloth over his sweating face.

John stood at the sink, his weak arms barely supporting him as he leaned on them, hovering over the wash basin as his eyes stared down into the bowl. What had happened out there to everyone? Why had they all changed and look so hideous? Then the realization hit him like a baseball bat to the face.

He had done it! He had actually seen the human soul. That would explain everything! But if he had in fact seen what he thought he saw, why had the souls looked so incredibly horrifying and evil. Then he came to an unpleasant realization. The toddler, barely two years old had a soul that had not yet been corrupted by the world around her. That was why she still looked relatively human. John could tell that she was just starting to change however, likely from being negatively influenced by her environment. And the older kids, the six and eight-year olds, looked progressively worse. He deduced that must be because their souls were becoming degraded more and more each day. Then the kids' mother, and the taxi driver and the rest of the crowd; their souls had all obviously become corrupted to the point of no return.

And then there was Nancy. The lovely neighbor he thought so fondly of. She seemed like such a sweet and wonderful person on the outside, how could her soul be so horribly vile and revolting? Then he thought, "Perhaps the world we live in tarnishes all of our souls, and we in turn contribute to ruining the pure souls of others, including our own innocent little ones."

John realized that perhaps the human soul, even the soul existing inside the best of humans, was likely a horrifying slobbering beast struggling to get out and wreak havoc. Perhaps it was some genetically evolved force which formed back in the time of our origins before we became what we now think of as civilized human beings. This thing, this soul which was responsible for giving us the intellect and cunning to survive and rise to the top of the food chain, still lives inside each of us. But we all unconsciously do what we must to keep the beast at bay; force it to be locked down deep inside of us with the hopes it might never get out. He then knew this soul, this beast within, was never meant to be seen by any man.

Then another thought struck him. There was a mirror on the vanity above the sink. John slowly raised his eyes upward to look at his own soul; he simply had to know. The last thing John could clearly recall was hearing his own bellowing screams of anguish.

*****

The patron hurried out of the liquor store, trying to avoid getting too wet in the steady downpour. He didn't see John squatting on the sidewalk as he ran buy and accidently bumped into him, knocking his wrap-around sunglasses to the ground.

"Oh man. I'm terribly sorry." The man said as he saw the beggar on the ground groping haphazardly for his fallen sunglasses. "I was in a hurry and wasn't paying attention. Here, pal, let me get those for you." The patron reached down and picked up the sunglasses then handed them back to John who turned his face up toward the man.

"Oh my God!" The man shouted, shocked by what he saw looking out from beneath the shade of the hood. The man on the ground stared up at him from two hollowed out sockets where his eyes should have been. At the tops and bottoms of the gaping holes were deep scarred furrows and the man instantly realized why. "Dear Jesus man... did you... Oh my God you did... you clawed out your own eyes!"

John put on his glasses, lowered his head and returned to incoherent mumbling as the shocked man stumbled away into the night. No one would have been able to make out what John was repeating but it they could understand him they might recall the phrase as part of a bible verse; perhaps one they had heard in church as a child. What John mumbled was "If thine eye offend thee, pluck it out."

SEEING

HARLAN ELLISON®

Harlan Ellison® is a legend in the field of speculative fiction. With a career spanning five decades, Ellison has published more than 1,700 short stories and articles, written or edited more than 75 books, written classic episodes for such series as Star Trek *and* The Outer Limits, *and won numerous Hugo, Nebula, Edgar Allan Poe, and Bram Stoker Awards™. This story originally appeared in the 1978 collection* Strange Wine.

"I remember well the time when the thought of the eye made me cold all over."

Charles Darwin, 1860

"Hey, Berne. Over there. Way back in that booth...see her?"

"Not now. I'm tired. I'm relaxing."

"Jizzus, Berne, take a look at her."

"Grebbie, if you don't synch-out and let me get doused, I swear I'll bounce a shot thimble off your skull."

"Okay, have it like you want it. But they're gray-blue."

"What?"

"Forget it, Berne. You said forget it, so forget it."

"Turn around here, man."

"I'm drinking."

"Listen, snipe, we been out all day looking..."

"Then when I tell you something from now on, you gonna *hear* me?"

"I'm sorry, Grebbie. Now come on, man, which one is she?"

"Over there. Pin her?"

"The plaid jumper?"

"No, the one way back in the dark in that booth behind the plaid. She's wearing a kaftan...wait'll the lights come around again...*there!* Y'pin her? Gray-blue, just like the Doc said he wanted."

"Grebbie, you are one beautiful pronger."

"Yeah, huh?"

"Now, just turn around and stop staring at her before she sees you. We'll get her."

"How, Berne? This joint's full up."

"She's gotta move out sometime. She'll go away."

"And we'll be right on her, right, Berne?"

"Grebbie, have another punchup and let me drink."

"Jizzus, man, we're gonna be livin' crystalfine when we get back to the Doc."

"Grebbie!"

"Okay, Berne, okay. Jizzus, she's got beautiful eyes."

*****

From extreme long shot, establishing; booming down to tight closeup, it looked like this:

Viewed through the fisheye-lens of a Long Drive vessel's stateroom iris, as the ship sank to Earth, the area surround the pits and pads and terminal structures of PIX--the Polar Interstellar Exchange port authority terminus--was a doughnut-shaped crazy quilt of rampaging colors. In the doughnut hole center was PIX, slate-gray alloys macroscopically homogenized to ignore the onslaughts of deranged Arctic weather. Around the port was a nomansland of eggshell-white plasteel with shock fibers woven into its surface. Nothing could pass across that dead area without permission. A million flickers of beckoning light erupted every second from the colorful doughnut, as if silent Circes called unendingly for visitors to come find their sources. Down, down, the ship would come and settle into its pit, and the view in the iris would vanish. Then tourists would leave the Long Driver through underground slidewalk tunnels that would carry them into the port authority for clearance and medical checks and baggage inspection.

Tram carts would carry the cleared tourists and returning Long Drive crews through underground egress passages to the outlets beyond the nomansland. Security turned to them, their wit and protective devices built into their clothing the only barriers between them and what lay aboveground, they would be shunted into cages and whisked to the surface.

Then the view reappeared. The doughnut-shaped area around the safe port structures lay sprawled before the newly arrived visitors and returnees from space. Without form or design, the area was scatter-packed with a thousand shops and arcades, hostelries and dives, pleasure palaces and food emporiums. As though they had been wind-thrown anemophilously, each structure grew up side by side with its neighbors. Dark and twisting alleyways careened through one section to the next. Spitalfields in London and Greenwich Village in old New York--before the Crunch--had grown up this way, like a jungle of hungry plants. And every open doorway had its barker, calling and gesturing, luring the visitors into the maw of unexpected experiences. Demander circuits flashed lights directly into the eyes of passersby, operating off retinal-heat-seeking mechanisms. Psychosound loops kept up an unceasing subliminal howling, each message strive to cap those filling the air around it, struggling to capture the attention of tourists with fat credit accounts. Beneath the ground, machinery labored mightily, the occasional squeal of plasteel signifying that even at top-point efficiency the guts of the area could not keep up with the demands of its economy. Crowds flowed in definite patterns, first this way, then that way, following the tidal pulls of a momentarily overriding loop, a barker's spiel filling an eye-of-the-hurricane silence, a strobing demander sudden reacting to an overload of power.

The crowd contained prongers, coshmen, fagin brats, pleasure pals, dealers, pickpockets, hustlers, waltzers, pseudo-marks, gophers, rowdy-dowdy hijackers, horses, hot slough workers, whores, steerers, blousers of all ages, sheiks, shake artists, kiters, floaters, aliens from three hundred different federations, assassins and, of course, innocent johns, marks, hoosiers, kadodies, and tourists ripe for shucking.

Following one such tidal flow of crowd life, down an alley identified on a wall as Poke Way, the view would narrow down to a circular doorway in a green one-story building. The sign would screen THE ELEGANT. Tightening the angle of observation, moving inside, the place could be seen to be a hard-drinking bar.

At the counter, as the sightline tracked around the murky bar, one could observe two men hunched over their thimbles, drinking steadily and paying attention to nothing but what their credit cards could buy, dumbwaitered up through the counter to their waiting hands. To an experienced visitor to the area, they would be clearly identifiable as "butt'n'ben" prongers: adepts at locating and furnishing to various Knox Shops whatever human parts were currently in demand.

Tracking further right, into the darkness of the private booths, the view would reveal (in the moments when the revolving overhead globes shone into those black spaces) an extremely attractive, but weary-looking, young woman with gray-blue eyes. Moving in for a tight closeup, the view would hold that breathtaking face for long moments, then move in and in on the eyes...those remarkable eyes.

All this, all these sights, in the area called WorldsEnd.

*****

Verna tried to erase the memory with the oblivion of drink. Drugs made her sick to her stomach and never accomplished what they were supposed to do. But chigger, and rum and bowl could do it...if she downed them in sufficient quantities. thus far, the level had not been even remotely approached. The alien, and what she had had to do to service him, were still fresh in her mind. Right near the surface, like scum. Since she had left the safe house and gone on her own, it had been one disaster after another. And tonight, the slug thing from...

She could not remember the name of the world it called its home. Where it lived in a pool of liquid, in a state of what passed for grace only to those who raised other life forms for food.

She punched up another bowl and then some bread, to dip in the heavy liquor. Her stomach was sending her messages of pain.

There had to be a way out. Out of WorldsEnd, out of the trade, out of the poverty and pain that characterized this planet for all but the wealthiest and most powerful. She looked into the bowl and saw it as no one else in The Elegant could have seen it.

The brown, souplike liquor, thick and dotted with lighter lumps of amber. She saw it as a whirlpool, spinning down to a finite point of silver radiance that spun on its own axis, whirling and whirling: a mad eye. A funnel of living brilliance flickering with chill heat that ran back against the spun, surging toward the top of the bowl and forming a barely visible surface tension of coruscating light, a thousand-colored dome of light.

She dipped the bread into the funnel and watched it tear apart like the finest lace. She brought it up, soaking, and ripped off a piece with her fine, white, even teeth--thinking of tearing the flesh of her mother. Sydni, her mother, who had gifted her with this curse, these eyes. This terrible curse that prevented her from seeing the world as it was, as it might have been, as it might be; seeing the world through eyes of wonder that had become horror before she turned five years old. Sydni, who had been in the trade before her, and her mother before *her*; Sydni, who had borne her through the activities of one nameless father after another. And one of them had carried the genes that had produced the eyes. Forever eyes.

She tried desperately to get drunk, but it wouldn't happen. More bread, another bowl, another chigger and rum--and nothing happened. But she sat in the booth, determined not to go back into the alleys. The alien might be looking for her, might still demand its credits' worth of sex and awfulness, might try once again to force her to drink the drink it called "mooshsquash." The chill that came over her made her shiver; brain movies with forever eyes were vivid and always fresh, always now, never memories, always happening *then*.

She cursed her mother and thought the night would probably never end.

An old woman, a very old woman, a woman older than anyone born on the day she had been born, nodded her head to her dressers. They began covering her terrible nakedness with expensive fabrics. She had blue hair. She did not speak to them.

*****

Now that he had overcome the problems of pulse pressure on the association fibers of the posterior lobe of the brain, he was certain the transplanted mutations would be able to mold the unconscious cerebral image of the seen world into the conscious percept. He would make no guarantees for the ability of the recipient to cope with the flux of the external world in all its complexity--infinitely more complicated as "seen" through the mutated transplant eyes--but he knew that his customers would hardly be deterred by a lack of such guarantees. They were standing in line. Once he had said, "The unaided human eye under the best possible viewing conditions can distinguish ten million different color surfaces; with transplants the eye will perceive ten *billion* different color surfaces; or more," then, once he had said it, then he had them hooked. They...*she*...would pay anything. And anything was how much he would demand. Anything to get off this damned planet, away from the rot that was all expansion had left of Earth.

There was a freehold waiting for him on one of the ease-colonies of Kendo IV. He would take passage and arrive like a prince from a foreign land. He would spin out the remaining years of his life with pleasure and comfort and respect. He would no longer be a Knoxdoctor, forced to accept ghoulish assignments at inflated prices, and then compelled to turn over the credits to the police and the sterngangs that demanded "protection" credit.

He needed only one more. A fresh pair for that blue haired old harridan. One more job, and then release from this incarceration of fear and desperation and filth. A pair of gray-blue eyes. Then freedom, in the easy-colony.

It was cold in Dr. Breame's Knox Shop. The tiny vats of nutrients demanded drastically lowered temperatures. Even in the insulated coverall he wore, Dr. Breame felt the cold.

But it was always warm on Kendo IV.

And there were no prongers like Grebbie and Berne on Kendo IV. No strange men and women and children with eyes that glowed. No still-warm bodies brought in off the alleys, to be hacked and butchered. No vats with cold flesh floating in nutrient. No filth, no disgrace, no payoffs, no fear.

He listened to the silence of the operating room.

It seemed to be filled with something other than mere absence of sound. Something deeper. A silence that held within its ordered confines a world of subtle murmurings.

He turned, staring at the storage vats in the ice cabinet. through the nearly transparent film of frost on the see-through door he could discern the parts idly floating in their nutrients. The mouths, the filaments of nerve bundles, the hands still clutching for life. There were sounds coming from the vats.

He had heard them before.

All the voiceless voices of the dead.

The toothless mouths calling his name: *Breame, come here, Breame, step up to us, look at us, we have things to tell you: the dreams you helped end, the wishes unanswered, the lives cut off like these hands. Let us touch you, Dr. Breame.*

He nibbled at his lower lip, willing the voices to silence. and they went quiet, stopped their senseless pleading. Senseless, because very soon Grebbie and Berne would come, and they would surely bring with them a man or a woman or a child with glowing blue-gray eyes, and then he would call the woman with blue hair and she would come to his Knox Shop, and he would operate, and then take passage.

It was always warm, and certainly it would always be quiet. On Kendo IV.

*****

Extract from the brief of the Plaintiff in the libel suit of 26 Krystabel Parsons v. Liquid Magazine, *Liquid Newsfax Publications, LNP Holding Group, and 311 unnamed Doe personages.*

From *Liquid Magazine* (uncredited profile):

Her name is 26 Krystabel Parsons. She is twenty-sixth in the line of Directors of Minet. Her wealth is beyond measure, her holdings span three federations, her residences can be found on one hundred and fifty-eight worlds, her subjects numberless, her rule absolute. She is one of the last of the unchallenged tyrants known as power brokers.

In appearance she initially reminds one of a kindly old grandmother, laugh-wrinkles around the eyes, blue hair uncoiffed, wearing exo-braces to support her withered legs.

But one hour spent in the company of this woman, this magnetism, this dominance...this force of nature...and all mummery reveals itself as cheap disguise maintained for her own entertainment. All masks are discarded and the Director of Minet shows herself more nakedly than anyone might care to see her.

Ruthless, totally amoral, jaded beyond belief with every pleasure and distraction the galaxy can provide, 26 Krystabel Parsons intends to live the rest of her life (she is one hundred and ten years old, and the surgeons of O-Pollinoor, the medical planet she caused to have built and staffed, have promised her at least another hundred and fifty, in exchange for endowments whose enormity staggers the power of mere gossip) hell-bent on one purpose alone: the pursuit of more exotic distractions.

Liquid Magazine managed to infiltrate the entourage of the Director during her Grand Tour of the Filament recently (consult the handy table in the front of this issue for ready conversion to your planetary approximation). During the time our correspondent spent with the tour, incidents followed horn-on-horn in such profusion that this publication felt it impossible to enumerate them fully in just one issue. From Porte Recoil at one end of the Filament to Earth at the other--a final report not received as of this publication--our correspondent has amassed a wealth of authenticated incident and first-hand observations we will present in an eleven-part series, beginning with this issue.

As this issue is etched, the Director of Minet and her entourage have reached PIX and have managed to elude the entire newsfax media corps. *Liquid Magazine* is pleased to report that, barring unforeseen circumstances, this exclusive series and the final report from our correspondent detailing the mysterious reasons for the Director's first visit to Earth in sixty years will be the only coverage of this extraordinary personality to appear in fax since her ascension and the termination of her predecessor.

Because of the history of intervention and censorship attendant on all previous attempts to report the affairs of 26 Krystabel Parsons, security measures as extraordinary as the subject herself have been taken to insure no premature leaks of this material will occur.

Note Curiae: Investigation advises subsequent ten installments of series referred to passim foregoing extract failed to reach publication. Entered as Plaintiff Exhibit 1031.

*****

They barely had time to slot their credits and follow her. she paid in the darkness between bursts of light from the globes overhead; and when they were able to sneak a look at her, she was already sliding quickly from the booth and rushing for the iris. It was as if she knew she was being pursued. But she could not have known.

"Berne..."

"I see her. Let's go."

"You think she knows we're onto her?"

Berne didn't bother to answer. He slotted credits for both of them and started after her. Grebbie lost a moment in confusion and then followed his partner.

The alley was dark now, but great gouts of blood-red and sea-green light were being hurled into the passageway from a top-mixer joint at the corner. She turned right out of Poke Way and shoved through the jostling crowds lemming toward Yardley's Battle Circus. They reached the mouth of the alley in time to see her cut across between rickshas, and followed as rapidly as they could manage through the traffic. Under their feet they could feel the throbbing of the machinery that supplied power to WorldsEnd. The rasp of circuitry overloading mixed faintly with the clang and shrieks of Yardley's sonic comeons.

She was moving swiftly now, off the main thoroughfare. In a moment Grebbie was panting, his stubby legs pumping like pistons, his almost-neckless body tilted far forward, as he tried to keep up with lean Berne. Chew Way opened on her left and she moved through a clutch of tourists from Horth, all painted with chevrons, and turned down the alley.

"Berne...wait up..."

The lean pronger didn't even look back. He shoved aside a barker with a net trying to snag him into a free house and disappeared into Chew Way. The barker caught Grebbie.

"Lady, please..." Grebbie pleaded, but the scintillae in the net had already begun flooding his bloodstream with the desire to bathe and frolic in the free house. The barker was pulling him toward the iris as Berne reappeared from the mouth of Chew Way and punched her in the throat. He pulled the net off Grebbie, who made idle, underwater movements in the direction of the free house. Berne slapped him. "If I didn't need you to help carry her..."

He dragged Grebbie into the alley.

Ahead of them, Verna stopped to catch her breath. In the semidarkness her eyes glowed faintly; first gray, a delicate shade of ash-gray of moth wings and the decay of Egypt; then blue, the fog-blue of mercury light through deep water and the lips of a cadaver. Now that she was out of the crowds, it was easier. For a moment, easier.

She had no idea where she was going. eventually, when the special sigh of those endless memories had overwhelmed her, when her eyes had become so well adjusted to the flash-lit murkiness of the punchup pub that she was able to see...

She put that thought from her. Quickly. Reliving, that was almost the worst part of *seeing*. Almost.

...when her sight had grown that acute, she had fled the punchup, as she fled *any* place where she had to deal with people. Which was why she had chosen to become one of the few blousers in the business who would service aliens. As disgusting as it might be, it was infinitely easier with these malleable, moist creatures from far away than with men and women and children whom she could see as they...

She put that thought from her. Again. Quickly. but she knew it would return; it always returned; it was always there. The worst part of *seeing.*

Bless you, Mother Sydni. Bless you and keep you.

Wherever you are; burning in tandem with my father, whoever he was. It was one of the few hateful thoughts that sustained her.

She walked slowly. Ignoring the hushed and urgent appeals from the rag mounts that bulked in the darkness of the alley. Doorways that had been melted closed now held the refuse of WorldsEnd humanity that no longer had anything to sell. But they continued needing.

A hand come out of the black mouth of a sewer trap. Bone fingers touched her ankle; fingers locked around her ankle. "Please..." The voice was torn out by the roots, its last film of moisture evaporating, leaves withering and curling in on themselves like a crippled fist.

"Shut up! Get away from me!" Verna kicked out and missed the hand. She stumbled, trying to keep her balance, half turned, and came down on the wrist. There was a brittle snap and a soft moan as the broken member was dragged back into the darkness.

She stood there screaming at nothing, at the dying and useless thing in the sewer trap. "Let me alone! I'll kill you if you don't leave me alone!"

Berne looked up. "That her?"

Grebbie was himself again. "Might could be."

They started off at a troy, down Chew Way. They saw her faintly limned by the reflection of lights off the alley wall. She was stamping her foot and screaming.

"I think she's going to be trouble," Berne said.

"Crazy, you ask me," Grebbie muttered. "Let's cosh her and have done with it. The Doc is waiting. He might have other prongers out looking. we get there too late and we've wasted a lot of time we could of spent—"

"Shut up. she's making such a hell of a noise she might've already got the police on her."

"Yeah, but..."

Berne grabbed him by the tunic. "What if she's under bond to a sterngang, you idiot?"

Grebbie said no more.

They hung back against the wall, watching as the girl let her passion dissipate. Finally, in tears, she stumbled away down the alley. They followed, pausing only to stare into the shadows as they passed a sewer trap. A brittle, whispering moan came from the depths. Grebbie shivered.

Verna emerged into the blare of drug sonics from a line of top-mixers that sat horn-on-horn down the length of Courage Avenue. They had very little effect on her; drugs were in no way appealing; they only intensified her *seeing*, made her stomach hurt, and in no way blocked the visions. Eventually, she knew, she would have to return to her coop; to take another customer. But if the slug alien was waiting...

A foxmartin in sheath and poncho sidled up. He leaned in, bracing himself with shorter appendages against the metal sidewalk, and murmured something she did not understand. But the message was quite clear. She smiled, hardly caring whether a smile was considered friendly or hostile in the alien's mind. She said, very clearly, "Fifty credits." The foxmartin dipped a stunted appendage into the poncho's roo, and brought up a liquid shot of an Earthwoman and a foxmartin without its shield. Verna looked at the liquid and then away quickly. It wasn't likely the alien in the shot was the same one before her; this was probably an example of vulpine pornography; she shoved the liquid away from her face. The foxmartin slid it back into the roo. It murmured again, querulous.

"One hundred and fifty credits," Verna said, trying hard to look at the alien, but only managing to retain a living memory of appendages and soft brown human flesh.

The foxmartin's fetching member slid into the roo again, moved swiftly out of sight, and came up with the credits.

Grebbie and Berne watched from the dimly shadowed mouth of Chew Way. "I think they struck a deal," Grebbie said softly. "How the hell can she do it with something looks like that?"

Berne didn't answer. How could people do *any* of the disgusting things they did to stay alive? They *did* them, that was all. If anyone really had a choice, it would be a different matter. But the girl was just like him: She did what she had to do. Berne did not really like Grebbie. But

Grebbie could be pushed and shoved, and that counted for more than a jubilant personality.

They followed close behind as the girl with the forever eyes took the credits from the alien and started off through the crowds of Courage Avenue. The foxmartin slid a sinuous coil around the girl's waist. She did not look at the alien, though Berne thought he saw her shudder; but even from that distance he couldn't be certain. Probably not: a woman who would service *things*.

*****

Dr. Breame sat in the far corner of the operating room, watching the movement of invisible life in the Knox Shop. His eyes flicked back and forth, seeing the unseen things that tried to reach him. Things without all their parts. Things that moved in liquid and things that tried to crawl out of waste bins. He knew all the clichés of seeing or hate or fear in eyes, and he knew that eyes could reflect none of those emotions without the subtle play of facial muscles, the other features of the face to lend expression. Even so, he *felt* his eyes were filled with fear. Silence, but movement, considerable movement, in the cold operating room.

*****

The slug alien was waiting. It came up out of a belowstairs entranceway and moved so smoothly, so rapidly, that Berne and Grebbie froze in a doorway, instantly discarding their plan to knife the foxmartin and prong the girl and rush off with her. It flowed up out of the dark and filled the twisting passageway with the wet sounds of its fury. The foxmartin tried to get between Verna and the creature; and the slug rose up and fell on him. There was a long moment of terrible sucking sounds, solid matter being turned to pulp and the marrow being drawn out as bones caved in on themselves, filling the lumen with shards of splintered calcium.

When it flowed off the foxmartin, Verna screamed and dodged away from the mass of oil gray worm oozing toward her. Berne began to curse; Grebbie started forward.

"What the hell can you do?" Berne said, grabbing his partner. "She gone, dammit!"

Verna ran toward them, the slug alien expanding to fill the passageway, humping after her like a tidal wave. Yes, yes, she had *seen* that crushed, empty image...*seen* it a thousand times, like reflections of reflections, shadow auras behind the reality...but she hadn't know what it mean...hadn't *wanted* to know what it meant! Servicing aliens, as perverted and disgusting as it was, had been the only way to keep sane, keep living, keep a vestige of hope that there was a way out, a way off Earth. Yes, she had the death of the foxmartin, but it hadn't mattered--it wasn't a *person*, it was a creature, a thing that could not in sanity have sex with a human, that *had to have* sex with a human, in whatever twisted fashion it found erotic. But now even that avenue was closing behind her...

She ran toward them, the slug alien making its frenzied quagmire sounds of outrage and madness, rolling in an undulant comber behind her. Grebbie stepped into her path and the girl crashed into him, throwing them both against the wall of the passageway. Berne turned and ran back the way he had come. An enormous shadow, the slug alien, puffed up to three times its size, filled the foot of the passage.

Berne saw lights ahead, and pounded toward them.

Underfoot, he felt a rumbling, a jerking of parts and other parts. There was a whining in his ears, and he realized he had been hearing it for some time. Then the passageway heaved and he was hurled sidewise, smashing face first into the melted window of a condemned building. He flailed wildly as the metal street under him bucked and warped, and then he fell, slamming into the wall and sliding down. He was sitting on the bucking metal, looking back toward the foot of the passage, when the slug alien suddenly began to glow with blue and orange light.

Verna was lying so close to the edge of the creature that the heat it gave off singed her leg. The fat little man she'd run into was somewhere under the alien. Gone now. Dead. Like the foxmartin.

But the slug was shrieking in pain, expanding and expanding, growing more monstrous, rising up almost to the level of second-storey windows. She had no idea what was happening...the whining was getting louder...she could smell the acrid scene of ozone, burning glass, boiling lubricant, sulfur...

The slug alien glowed blue, orange, seemed to be lit from inside, writhed hideously, expanded, gave one last, unbelievable sucking moan of pain, and *burned*. Verna crawled away on hands and knees, down the egress passage, toward the light, toward the shape of a man just getting to his feet, looking dazed. Perhaps he could help her.

*****

"The damned thing killed Grebbie. I didn't know what was happening. All at once everything was grinding and going crazy. The power under the streets had been making lousy sounds all night. I guess it was overloading. I don't know. Maybe that filthy thing caused it somehow, some part of it got down under the sidewalk plate and fouled the machinery, made it blow out. I think it was electrocuted...I don't know. but she's here, and she's got what you need, and I want the full amount; Grebbie's share and mine both!"

"Keep you voice down, you thug. My patient may arrive at any moment."

Verna lay on the operating table, watching them. *Seeing* them. Shadows behind shadows behind shadows. All the reflections. *Pay him, Doctor,* she thought, *it won't matter. He's going to die soon enough. So are you. And the way Grebbie bought it will look good by comparison. Good bless and keep you, Sydni.* She could not turn it off now, nor damp it with bowl, nor hide the images in the stinking flesh of creatures from other worlds of other stars. And in minute, at best mere moments, they would ease her burden; they would give her peace, although they didn't know it. *Pay him, Doctor, and let's get to it.*

"Did you have to maul her?"

"I didn't maul her, damn you! I hit her once, the way I hit all the others. She's not damaged. You only want the eyes anyhow. Pay me!"

The Knoxdoctor took credits from a pouch on his coverall and counted out an amount the pronger seemed to find satisfactory. "Then why is she so bloody?" He asked the question as an afterthought, like a surly child trying to win one final point before capitulating.

"Creep off, Doc," Berne said nastily, counting the credits. "She was crawling away from that worm. She fell down half a dozen times. I told you. If you're not satisfied with the kind of merchandise I bring you, get somebody else. Tell me how many other prongers could've found you a pair of them eyes in gray-blue, so quick after a call?"

Dr. Breame had no time to form an answer. The iris dilated and three huge Floridans stepped into the Knox Shop, moved quickly through the operating room, checked out the storage area, the consultation office, the power bins, and came back to stand near the iris, their weapons drawn.

Breame and Berne watched them silently, the pronger awed despite himself at the efficiency and clearly obvious readiness of the men. They were heavy-gravity-planet aliens, and Berne had once seen a Floridan put his naked fist through a plasteel plate two inches thick. He didn't move.

One of the aliens stepped through the iris, said something to someone neither Berne nor the doctor could see, and then came back inside. A minute later they heard the sounds of a group moving down the passage to the Knox Shop.

26 Krystabel Parsons strode into the operating room and waved her guard back. All but the three already in the Knox Shop. She slapped her hands down to her hips, locking the exo-braces. She stood unwaveringly and looked around.

"Doctor," she said, greeting him perfunctorily. She looked at the pronger.

"Greetings, Director. I'm pleased to see you at long last. I think you'll find--"

"Shut up." Her eyes narrowed at Berne. "Does this man have to die?"

Berne started to speak, but Breame quickly, nervously answered. "Oh, no; no indeed not. This gentleman has been most helpful to our project. He was just leaving."

"I was just leaving."

The old woman motioned to one of the guards, and the Floridan took Berne by the upper arm. The pronger winced, though the guard apparently was only serving as a butler. The alien propelled Berne toward the iris, and out. Neither returned.

Dr. Breame said, "Will these, uh, gentlemen be necessary, Director? We have some rather delicate surgery to perform and they can..."

"They can *assist*." Her voice was flat as iron.

She dropped her hands to her hips again, flicking up the locking levels of the exo-braces that formed a spider-web scaffolding around her withered legs. She strode across the operating room toward the girl immobilized on the table, and Breame marveled at her lack of reaction to the cold in the room: he was still shivering in his insulated coverall, she wore an ensemble made of semitransparent, iridescent flow bird scales.

but she seemed oblivious to the temperature of the Knox Shop.

26 Krystabel Parsons came to Verna and looked down into her face. Verna closed her eyes. The Director could not have known the reason the girl could not look at her.

"I have an unbendable sense of probity, child. If you cooperate with me, I shall make certain you don't have a moment of regret."

Verna opened her eyes. The Director drew in her breath.

They were everything they'd been said to be.

Gray and blue, swirling, strange, utterly lovely.

"What do you see?" the Director asked.

"A tired old woman who doesn't know herself well enough to understand that all she wants to do is die."

The guards started forward. 26 Krystabel Parsons waved them back. "On the contrary," she said. "I not only desire life for myself...I desire it for you. I'm assuring you, if you help us, there is nothing you can ask that I will refuse."

Verna looked at her, *seeing* her, knowing she was lying. Forever eyes told the truth. What this predatory relic wanted was: everything; who she was willing to sacrifice to get it was: everyone; how much mercy and kindness Verna could expect from her was: infinitesimal. But if one could not expect mercy from one's own mother, how could one expect it from strangers?

"I don't believe you."

"Ask and you shall receive." She smiled. It was a terrible structure. The memory of the smile, even an instant after it was gone, persisted in Verna's sight.

"I want full passage on a Long Driver."

"Where?"

"Anywhere I want to go."

The Director motioned to one of the guards. "Get her a million credits. No. Five million credits."

The guard left the Knox Shop.

"In a moment you will see I keep my word," said the Director. "I'm willing to pay for my pleasures."

"You're willing to pay for my pain, you mean."

The Director told to Breame. "Will there be pain?"

"Very little, and what pain there is, will mostly be yours, I'm afraid."
He stood with hands clasped together in front of him: a small child
anxiously trying to avoid giving offense.

"Now, tell me what it's like," 26 Krystabel Parsons said, her face
bright with expectation.

"The mutation hasn't bred true, Director. It's still a fairly rare
recessive--" Breame stopped. She was glaring at him. She had been
speaking to the girl.

Verna closed her eyes and began to speak. She told the old woman of
seeing. Seeing directions, as blind fish in subterranean caverns see the
change in flow of water, as bees see the wind currents, as wolves see the
heat auras surrounding humans, as bats see the walls of caves in the dark.
Seeing memories, everything that ever happened to her, the good and the
bad, the beautiful and grotesque, the memorable and the utterly
forgettable, early memories and those of a moment before, all on instant
recall, with absolute clarity and depth of field and detail, the whole of
one's past, at command. Seeing colors, the sensuousness of airborne
bacteria, the infinitely subtle shadings of rock and metal and natural
wood, the tricksy shifts along a spectrum invisible to ordinary eyes of a
candle flame, the colors of frost and rain and the moon and arteries
pulsing just under the skin; the infinite overlapping of colors of
fingerprints left on a credit, so reminiscent of paintings by the old master
Jackson Pollock. Seeing colors that no human eyes have ever seen.
Seeing shapes and relationships, the intricate calligraphy of all parts of
the body moving in unison, the day melding into the night, the spaces
and spaces between spaces that form a street, the invisible lines linking
people. She spoke of *seeing*, of all the kinds of seeing except. The
stroboscopic view of everyone. The shadows within shadows behind
shadows that formed terrible, tortuous portraits she could not bear. She
did not speak of that. And in the middle of her long recitation the
Floridan came back and put five million credits in her tunic.

And when the girls was done, 26 Krystabel Parsons turned to the
Knoxdoctor and said, "I want her kept alive, with as little damage as
possible to her faculties. you will place a value on her comfort as high as
mine. Is that clearly understood?"

Breame seemed uneasy. he wet his lips, moved closer to the Director (keeping an eye on the Floridans, who did not move closer to him). "May I speak to you in privacy?" he whispered.

"I have no secrets from this girl. She is about to give me a great gift. You may think of her as my daughter."

The doctor's jaw muscles tensed. This was, after all, *his* operating room! *He* was in charge her, no matter how much power this unscrupulous woman possessed. He stared at her for a moment, but her gaze did not waver. Then he went to the operating table where Verna lay immobilized by a holding circuit in the table itself, and he pulled down the anesthesia bubble over her head. A soft, eggshell-white fog instantly filled the bubble.

"I must tell you, Director, now that she cannot hear--"

(But she could still *see,* and the patterns his words made in the air brought the message to her quite distinctly.)

"--that the traffic in mutant eyes is still illegal. Very illegal. In point of fact, it is equated with murder; and because of the shortage of transplantable parts, the MediCom has kept it a high crime; one of the few for which the punishment is vegetable cortexing. If you permit this girl to live you run a terrible risk. Even a personage of *your* authority would find it most uncomfortable to have the threat of such a creature wandering loose."

The Director continued staring at him. Breame thought of the unblinking stares of lizards. When she blinked he thought of membranous nictitating eyelids of lizards.

"Doctor, the girl is no problem. I want her alive only until I establish that there are no techniques for handling these eyes that she can help me to learn."

Breame seemed shocked.

"I do not care for the expression on your face, Doctor. You find my manner with this child duplicitous, yet you are directly responsible for her situation. You have taken her away from whomever and wherever she wished to be, you have stripped her naked, laid her out like a side of beef, you have immobilized her and anesthetized her; you plan to cut out her eyes, treat her to the wonders of blindness after she has spent a lifetime seeing far more than normal humans; and you have done all this not in the name of science, or humanity, or even curiosity. You have done it for credits. I find the expression on your face an affront, Doctor. I advise you to work diligently to erase it."

Breame had gone white, and in the cold room he was shivering again. He heard the voices of the parts calling. At the edges of his vision things moved.

"All I want you to assure me, Dr. Breame, is that you can perform this operation with perfection. I will not tolerate anything less. My guards have been so instructed."

"I'm perhaps the only surgeon who *can* perform this operation and guarantee you that you will encounter no physically deleterious effects. Handling the eyes *after* the operation is something over which I have no control."

"And results will be immediate?"

"As I promised. With the techniques I've perfected, transfer can be effected virtually without discomfort."

"And should something go wrong…you can replace eyes a second time?"

Breame hesitated. "With difficulty. You aren't a young woman; the risks would be considerable; but it *could* be done. Again, probably by no other surgeon. And it would be extremely expensive. It would entail another pair of healthy eyes."

26 Krystabel Parsons smiled her terrible smile. "Do I perceive you feel underpaid, Dr. Breame?"

He did not answer. No answer was required.

Verna saw it all and understood it all. And had she been able to smile, she would have smiled; much more warmly than the Director. If she died, as she was certain she would, that was peace and release. If not, well…

Nothing was worse than life.

They were moving around the room now. Another table was unshipped from a wall cubicle and formed. The doctor undressed 26 Krystabel Parsons and one of two remaining Floridans lifted her like a tree branch and laid her on the table.

The last thing Verna saw was the faintly glowing, vibrating blade of the shining e-scalpel, descending toward her face. The finger of God, and she blessed it as her final thoughts were of her mother.

SEEING

*****

26 Krystabel Parsons, undisputed owner of worlds and industries and entire races of living creatures, jaded observer of a universe that no longer held even a faint view of interest or originality, opened her eyes.

The first things she saw were the operating room, the Floridan guards standing at the foot of the table staring at her intensely, the Knoxdoctor dressing the girl who stood beside her own table, the smears of black where the girl's eyes had been.

There was a commotion in the passageway outside. One of the guards turned toward the iris, still open.

And in that moment all sense of *seeing* flooded in on the Director of Minet. Light, shade, smoke, shadow, glow, transparency, opacity, color, tint, hue, prismatics, sweet, delicate, subtle, harsh, vivid, bright, intense, serene, crystalline, kaleidoscopic, all and everything at once!

Something else. Something more. Something the girl had not mentioned, had not hinted at, had not wanted her to know! The shadows within shadows.

She *saw* the Floridan guards. *Saw* them for the first time. Saw the state of their existence at the moment of their death. It was as if a multiple image, a strobe portrait of each of them lived before her. The corporeal reality in the front, and behind--like endless auras radiating out from them but superimposed over them--the thousand images of their fut5ures. And the sight of them when they were dead, how they died. Not the action of the event, but the result. The hideous result of having life ripped from them. Rotting, corrupt, ugly beyond belief, and all the more ugly than imagination because it was *seen* with forever eyes that captured all the invisible-to-normal-eyes subtleties of containers intended to contain life, having been emptied of that life. She turned her head, unable to speak or scream or howl like a dog as she wished, and she *saw* the girl, and she *saw* the doctor.

It was a sight impossible to contain.

She jerked herself upright, the pain in her withered legs barely noticeable. And she opened her mouth and forced herself to scream as the commotion in the passageway grew louder, and something dragged itself through the iris.

She screamed with all the unleashed horror of a creature unable to bear itself, and the guards turned back to look at her with fear and wonder...as Berne dragged himself into the room. She *saw* him, and it was worse than *now*, the vessel was emptying *now*! Her scream became the howl of a dog. He could not speak, because he had no part left in his face that could make a formed sound come out. He could see only imperfectly; there was only one eye. If he had an expression, it was lost under the blood and crushed, hanging flesh that formed his face. The huge Floridan guard had not been malevolent, merely Floridan, and they were a race only lately up from barbarism. But he had taken a long time.

Breame's hands froze on the sealstrip of the girl's tunic and he looked around her, saw the pulped mass that pulled itself along the floor, leaving a trail of dark stain and viscous matter, and his eyes widened.

The Floridans raised their weapons almost simultaneously, but the thing on the floor gripped the weapon it had somehow--amazingly, unpredictably, impossibly--taken away from its assassin, and it fired. The head of the nearest Floridan caved in on itself and the body jerked sidewise, slamming into the other guard. Both of them hit the operating table on which the Director of Minet sat screaming, howling, savaging the air with mortal anguish. The table overturned, flinging the crippled old woman with the forever eyes to the floor.

Breame knew what had happened. Berne had not been sent away. It had been blindness for him to think she would leave *any* of them alive. He moved swiftly, as the remaining Floridan struggled to free himself of the corpse that pinned him to the floor. The Knoxdoctor had the e-scalpel in his hand in an instant, palmed it on, and threw himself atop the guard. The struggle took a moment, as Breame sliced away at the skull. There was a muffled sound of the guard's weapon, and Breame staggered to his feet, reeled backward, and crashed into a power bin. Its storage door fell open and Breame took two steps into the center of the room, clutching his chest. His hands went inside his body; he stared down at the ruin; then he fell forward.

There was a soft bubbling sound from the dying thing that had been the pronger, Berne, and then silence in the charnel house.

Silence, despite the continued howling of 26 Krystabel Parsons. The sounds she made were so overwhelming, so gigantic, so inhuman, that they became like the ticking of a clock in a silent room, the thrum of power in a sleeping city. Unheard.

Verna heard it all, but had no idea what had happened. She dropped to her knees, and crawled toward what she thought was the iris. She touched something wet and pulpy with the fingertips of her left hand. She kept crawling. She touching something still-warm but unmoving with the fingertips of her right hand, and felt along the thing till she came to hands imbedded in soft, rubbery ruin. To her right she could faintly hear the sound of something humming, and she the knew the sound: an e-scalpel, still slicing, even when it could do no more damage.

Then she crawled to an opening, and she felt with her hands and it seemed to be a bin, a large, bin, with its door open. She crawled inside and curled up, and pulled the door closed behind her, and lay there quietly.

And not much later there was the sound of movement in the operating room as others who had been detained for reasons Verna would never know, came and lifted 26 Krystabel Parsons, and carried her away, still howling like a dog, howling more intensely as she saw each new person, knowing eventually she would see the thing she feared seeing the most. The reflection of herself as she would be in the moment of her dying; and knowing she would still be sane enough to understand and appreciate it.

*****

From extreme long shot, establishing; trucking in to medium shot, it looks like this:

Viewed through the tracking devices of PIX's port authority clearance security system, the Long Drive vessel sits in its pit, then slowly begins to rise out of its berth. White mist, or possibly steam, or possibly ionized fog billows out of the pit as the vessel leaves. The great ship rises toward the sky as we moved in steadily on it. We continue forward, angle tilting up to hold the Long Driver in medium shot, then a fast zoom in on the glowing hide of the ship, and dissolve through to a medium shot, establishing the interior.

Everyone is comfortable. Everyone is watching the planet Earth drop away like a stained-glass window through a trapdoor. The fisheye-lens of the stateroom iris shows WorldsEnd and PIX and the polar emptiness and the mottled ball of the decaying Earth as they whirl away into the darkness.

Everyone sees. They see the ship around them, they see one another, they see the pages of the books they read, and they see the visions of their hopes for good things at the end of this voyage. They all see.

Moving in on one passenger, we see she is blind. She sits with her body formally erect, her hands at her sides. She wears her clothing well, and apart from the dark smudges that show beneath the edge of the stylish opaque band covering her eyes, she is a remarkably attractive woman. Into tight closeup. And we see that much of her grace and attractiveness comes from the sense of overwhelming peace and containment her features convey.

Hold the closeup as we study her face, and marvel at how relaxed she seems. we must pity her, because we know that blindness, not being able to see, is a terrible curse. And we decide she must be a remarkable woman to have reconciled such a tragic state with continued existence.

We think that if we were denied sight, we would certainly commit suicide. As the darkness of the universe surrounds the vessel bound for other places.

*****

"If the doors of perception were cleansed everything would appear to man as it is, infinite."

William Blake,
The Marriage of Heaven and Hell, 1790.

A NICE TOWN WITH VERY CLEAN STREETS

PAUL ANDERSON

Paul Anderson is the editor of Post Mortem Press' Torn Realities, *which Lonnie Nadler of* Bloody Disgusting *called "a book that belongs in any horror fan's collection". A short story writer, Anderson's most recent work has appeared in* Denizens of the Dark, Title Goes Here, *and* The New Bedlam Project.

The pilots screamed as Grimes watched the surface of Tartan-6 expand in the dead ship's windshield. He tried believing this wasn't happening to him, he was somewhere far away; it wasn't *him* rushing to crash into the surface of Hell.

And then FedShip UPF/14 slammed into the ground and what felt like the hand of God slammed into Grimes: an instant of breathless shock and then nothing but darkness.

He came back to find himself hanging upside down with vertigo warring with migraine and someone else's blood clogging his throat. More blood, hot and loathsome, coated his face, gummed his eyes closed, soaked his jumpsuit.

Stephens, the ship's Alpha rep, called, "Who's alive?"

Grimes retched blood, driving twin spikes of migraine and vertigo deeper into his skull, and pawed shakily for the catches of his spiderweb-mesh harness.

He unbuckled and slammed against the ship's ceiling. From the back, he heard Newby, the mining rep, try to respond to Stephens and wind up vomiting.

Grimes scraped blood from his eyes and stood. Every muscle in his body was one, low chorus of pain.

He looked towards the cockpit and was momentarily confused by the helter-skelter mechanical wall before him: the cockpit had been crushed like a can. Only gore-soaked spiderweb-mesh straps remained of Richmond and Moore. Grimes's stomach fluttered. Ten minutes ago, they'd been checking the holocube for a lock on Tartan-6's colony-dome, the last of the thirteen colonies UPF had lost contact with during the war.

Then the instrument panels--the *ship*--had gone dead a kilometer above the ground.

He turned. Stephens hung in his harness and stared at the destroyed cockpit.

Stephens flicked a glance at Grimes, then undid the buckles. Still holding the catches, he swung out of the harness in one smooth movement. He went to Newby, whose Buddha gut pressed against the spiderweb, and helped get him down without Newby falling face-first into his own puke.

"Nelson and Rocco?" Grimes asked as they approached.

They looked at the end of the cabin. The rear compartment hatch was almost completely unrecognizable.

Newby wiped his mouth and asked, "The beacon?" His body trembled, his round face cheesy and coated in sweat.

"Tripped when we crashed," Stephens said absently. He shouldered past Grimes and went to the cockpit. Newby shrugged at Grimes, a brief spasm of his shoulders, and started for the storage compartments which had been below the bench seats but were now overhead.

Grimes considered the blood-smeared outer-hatch, which resembled crinkled tinfoil someone had tried flattening smooth again. There was protocol here, but it escaped him completely. Mentally, he felt like he was punching against a soft, suffocating cushion. Shock from the crash, he supposed.

The last one, he thought. He sensed he was pleading, but didn't know to whom. Not God. He'd stopped believing in God when the UPF sent him to the frontlines as a "morale booster". *The last goddam one before I got back to Janey.*

He mentally shook himself. "What do we know of this place other than it's a mining colony?"

"Rocco was the know-it-all," Newby said, awkwardly carrying three of the opaque emergency helmets. "Tartan-6 went off the grid early, though, which is weird considering how far from the frontlines they were. Air's breathable but thin, hence the helmets."

Stephens stooped in front of the cockpit wreckage and pulled a palm-sized black square from a glob of grue. When he turned, Grimes saw it was a memory-chip from one of the pilot helmets.

He noticed Grimes and Newby watching. "I flew missions with Moore before," he said. "His people will want this." He put the chip in his pocket and took a helmet from Newby. "What's the equipment and weaponry look like?"

"Still locked down," Newby said. "The rifles are cracked, but the bolters look all right. One of Nelson's tech doodads looks messed up, but that might be how it looks normally."

"At least the *weapons* survived," Grimes said, staring at his exhausted reflection in his helmet faceplate. He tried again to shake the suffocating numbness and could manage only a vague bitterness. *The last one,* he half-pleaded to no one. "We all know how useful they've been thus far."

*****

They got the outer-hatch open and, helmets on, stumbled outside.

They'd crashed maybe a klick away from the colony, the transparent half-sphere nearly dominating the horizon. Mountains cut across the right and left.

"Company," Stephens said. His helmet nodded towards a dune-buggy transport cresting a hill up ahead. The six men in the transport wore no Delta insignia.

Grimes stiffened. UPF protocol stated Deltas met all visitors.

"Quite a crash there, guys," the man in the passenger seat said as the transport stopped. His eyes were bright behind his clear face-plate. "Any casualties?"

"Three," Stephens said. "We're--"

"The UPF ship," the passenger finished. "I've been Station-hopping since you were kids. This isn't my first re-contact." He glanced at the ship and a pained expression crossed his face. "After all the UPF losses, any extra just seems tragic."

Grimes grimaced. The sentiment sounded robotic coming from this guy, canned somehow.

"I'm Station Supervisor Dugan. These folks are--" Dugan flashed a toothy grin. "--the Welcome Committee." He pulled a digipad from beside him and unclipped the stylus. "Okay. You said there were three casualties. They were...?"

Stephens said, "Can't we do this--"

"Quicker this way," Dugan interrupted. "The casualties...?"

Stephens said, "Pilots George Richmond and Brad Moore, Cultural Guide Mike Rocco, UPF Alpha Gregory Stephens."

Grimes jerked. He opened his mouth--

(--don't say a word i know what i'm doing.)

The thought was as sharp as a knife-blade, as violating as a rape. Stephens's voice, loud and clear and *cold*. His brain felt like it'd plummeted into an icy lake.

Psi? he thought. *Stephens's a Psi? But that was only rumor--*

The jes-folks look left Dugan's bumpkin face. "No military survived?"

Stephens shook his helmeted head. "No."

Dugan's face softened. "Who're you folks, then?"

"I'm FedShip Tech Fred Nelson," Stephens said. He gestured at Grimes and Newby. "This is UPF representative Owen Grimes, and mining rep Phillip Newby."

Dugan scratched across the digipad with a stylus. "Was your distress beacon tripped?"

"The recorder was smashed upon impact."

"All right, then," Dugan said. His eyes were bright. "Hop in back and we'll take you to town."

"Why didn't the military come out?" Grimes asked.

Something shifted on Dugan's face and suddenly the thousand-watt smile appeared pasted on. "Mr. Grimes, our soldiers went to war."

A hollow suddenly opened in Grimes's chest. Colony-stationed soldiers *never* went to the front; it was UPF protocol, it was why there were *Deltas*. How could Dugan think Grimes wouldn't *know* this?

He thought of arguing, looked into Dugan's face, and thought again. The Supervisor's expression offered no answers; he was a true bureaucrat. You would never read Dugan's inner feelings on anything unless he allowed you to. He was a cipher, broadcasting only what his job specified.

You know your own, Grimes thought and felt sick suddenly. The migraine in the back of his head tightened a notch.

Without a word, he climbed aboard with Stephens and Newby and the dune-buggy lurched into a U-turn. Grimes watched the ship, twisted and bent like a scorpion tail, disappear behind them.

Stephens nudged him and nodded towards the space under the opposite benches.

Grimes counted four military rifles clipped to the floor beneath the "Welcome Committee".

Cold air blew through the hollow in his chest. He'd shaken off the shock of the crash. Oh yes, indeed.

*****

Inside the dome's igloo-shaped Entrance Chamber, they stripped out of their bloodied jumpsuits, leaving them with only white T-shirts and gray trousers. Grimes eyed Stephens's muscular body warily. No one else on the ship had that type of honed form.

Dugan and his "Welcome Committee" stood near the hatch leading into the dome proper as three bored-looking men pulled the DeCon hoses off the wall.

"Don't bother," Dugan said. "We have places to be." He gestured for Grimes, Stephens, and Newby to follow him through the hatch.

It was at least ten degrees warmer under the dome. The Entrance Chamber led to the loading bay, an expansive field that took up a third of the entire station, where the colony's payout was kept for transport. Motorized dogcarts were parked around towering shipping containers. Beyond, the "town" began--a collection of short, stout buildings on either side of a wide dirt road connecting the Entrance Chamber to the mining crater at the far end. Emergency spotlights ringed the town.

"Welcome to Tartan-6, gentlemen," Dugan said.

An icepick shot into Grimes's mind:

(*--ask where we're going.*)

His jaw wanted to lock, more from the idea of talking than the sudden violence of Stephens's message. He had no helmet to hide his expression now. "Where are we going? I don't think any of us are up for our duties."

Dugan glanced behind him. "Off to see the Chaplain."

He wasn't able to hide his bewilderment. "Why--"

"Are you sure that's wise, Supervisor Dugan?" Newby asked

225

suddenly.

"I don't see why not."

"Quarantine," Stephens said, almost absently.

That stopped Dugan. "Quarantine?"

Grimes cleared his throat. "According to UPF protocol, all crash survivors must be quarantined for twenty-four hours or until the cause of the crash is known."

Dugan's bureaucratic facade cracked. "But our infirmary--"

"I can assure you we're perfectly healthy," Newby said, "and we thank you for allowing us to *skip* DeCon, but we can't speak for our pilots, or what *they* may have had."

"Are you familiar with Sparta-C, Supervisor?" Stephens asked.

The facade was gone and Dugan was nonplussed. "I--well, yes--"

"Then you're aware of their cholera epidemic," Grimes said. "That was our previous stop, and--"

"We have no medics!" Dugan screamed.

"We're probably *perfectly* healthy," Newby said.

"Without a working infirmary," Grimes asked, "is there somewhere else we might stay?"

Dugan's shoulders slumped. "The Delta barracks."

Grimes smiled his best bureaucratic smile. His head ached--a galloping black horse across the soft meat of his brain. "Given the importance UPF has for Tartan-6, no one wants any unnecessary risks taken."

The Welcome Committee looked decidedly uneasy--this wasn't in the script. Their faces told Grimes that there very much *had* been a script, but to what? If Grimes hadn't asked a question, what would've happened?

Dugan looked at his watch. "Quarantine to begin at fifteen-thirty, per arrival at the barracks." He visibly struggled to regain his former posture. "This way, please."

The procession began without its previous urgency. They reminded Grimes of kids forced to do their chores.

They entered town. Gray, utilitarian buildings stared down at them, the windows and doors empty. Grimes could hear the syncopated chugging of the climate system. Where were the *people*? They might've been walking through forgotten stage-settings.

"Nice place," Newby said.

Dugan missed his tone. "We're strict about that. To be clean, to be orderly..." He trailed off. "It is of the utmost importance."

For what? Grimes thought. He looked down at the road and saw the dirt had been raked. The lines were the only things on the road. Not a single piece of trash anywhere.

He looked at Dugan. What *was* this? Keeping the colony clean was important, but this was taken to its extreme.

A nice town with very clean streets, he thought and couldn't stop a shudder.

Ahead, he heard a rustling sound where the side streets intersected the main road. The rustling grew to a patterned roar and, like an opened floodgate, swarms of people suddenly flooded out onto the main road.

Grimes stopped for the briefest instant and he thought he heard Newby gasp.

A blast of cold in his head--

(--don't stop don't you dare stop now--)

--and Grimes found his footing again.

The people, dressed in blue, grey, and green jumpsuits, surrounded them, lining the building fronts three deep. Grimes couldn't read a single expression on any man, woman, or child. No one spoke. Their heads turned as one to watch the group pass.

The sight of all those people, blank and uniform and eerily silent...they hurt his *mind*. His eyes couldn't focus on one person. They made his footsteps louder, his migraine thump more painfully.

The Welcome Committee took no notice of them. They might not have been there at all.

Up ahead, cranes rose out of the wide crater of the mining pit. What must've been hanging mine dust cast a strange, flickering yellowish light over the various mining machinery.

Dugan turned left, away from the pit, before Grimes could study it more closely. Behind them, Grimes thought he heard a deep sigh.

He refused to look back. His flesh prickled and crawled.

They passed the colony's Congo Church--the only un-boxlike structure in town with its neo-Catholic pointed steeples and rounded corners.

On the sermon display next to the front walk were two words: FREE IT!

Free what? Grimes wondered.

*****

Dugan dumped them unceremoniously at the Delta barracks, a long L-shaped building outside of town. From one of the slit windows, Stephens watched them leave.

"Aren't they going to guard us?" Newby asked.

Stephens turned away. "Why bother? There's nowhere to *go*. Besides, who can they spare to guard us with the military gone?"

"You think the civilians offed them?" Grimes asked. He looked around. The barracks could've housed a hundred soldiers.

Stephens's eyes darkened. "Yeah, although I don't know how. Those rifles all but clinched it." He frowned. "I think that *whatever* the civs are up to, military isn't welcome."

"And that's why you faked being Nelson," Newby said, then winced.

"Headache?" Stephens asked.

"Since we landed."

He turned to Grimes. "You?"

Grimes nodded.

Stephens rubbed his temple. "Me, too. It's the electro-magnetic field, I think. It's..." He trailed off. "I bet compasses would be useless here."

"You're a Psi," Grimes said. "Why didn't you tell us? *Jesus*, when you sent that first message--"

"Alphas aren't encouraged to divulge it." He looked at them. "You both from Earth?"

They nodded.

"I was raised on Ellis-7. Any child that tests high for Psi capabilities is sent there. Psi-abilities have something to do with the brain's electrical impulses. It makes us *very* sensitive to any planet's EMF. Tartan-6's off the charts."

"You think that crashed our ship?" Newby asked.

Stephens shook his head--he didn't know.

Grimes paced the barrack's central aisle, scrubbing his face with shaky hands. "Jesus fox-trotting *Christ*, what's going on here? The military's gone, the town is acting..." He couldn't come up with a word to describe the faceless mass they'd seen. "...and you're saying a *planet's* EMF is all messed up." He looked at Stephens and Newby. "Why the hell were we being taken to the *Chaplain*? Two-thirds of the Fed planets don't even *have* religion."

Stephens rubbed the stubble on his cheek. "We'll find out why soon enough. They won't give us much time--twelve hours at most--before saying screw it. That's not enough time for the beacon to draw anything useful."

"Then what?" Newby asked.

Stephens merely looked at him.

The Congo Church rose in Grimes's mind. "Free it," he muttered.

Newby and Stephens stared at him as he shivered.

*****

Night on Tartan-6. Stars like cuts in black velvet shined brilliantly in alien constellations. Grimes would've happily given anything to be staring at Orion or Cassiopeia with Janey.

They showered and changed into new jumpsuits. Newby found aspirin. Stephens begged off--he needed his head clear.

There was nothing to do except stare at each other and watch the clock and ponder the same question over and over: *How long do we have?*

Finally, Stephens headed for the door. "I'm going out."

"What for?" Grimes asked.

"Get some clue of what's going on. Maybe check the ship if I can." He studied them. "Try to sleep. You might not get it later."

But sleep never felt further from Grimes when he lay down. The idea that he could wake up with Dugan standing daunted rest.

He fell into a scratchy doze and dreamed of Janey, of seeing her in her gardening sun-hat, its floppy band obscuring her heart-shaped face. His relief in the dream was palpable, but tinged with uneasiness.

He kept thinking he saw a pit out of the corner of his eye, flickering with a yellow light.

*****

Stephens's haggard voice, calling down a well: "C'mon, Grimes."

Grimes opened his eyes to see Stephens and Newby standing above him, faces pale. He cried out as a lightning bolt of pain struck his head.

Grimes sat up slowly. His muscles felt like cheap concrete, his bones made of crushed glass. Newby handed him four aspirin.

"What's it like outside?" Grimes asked, dry-swallowing the pills.

"No signs of struggle. The Deltas are just *gone*." He shook his head. "An untrained civilian population disposed of nearly one hundred Deltas and there isn't a sign of battle *anywhere*? How in the *hell* did they do that?"

Grimes shook his head. "Those people didn't look like they had any migraines," Newby offered

Stephens nodded. "Yeah, so why us?"

Grimes couldn't think of a reason. "Anyone see you?"

Stephens shook his head. "*Everyone* was standing around the crater. You noticed that yellowish...light? glow?...earlier? It's coming from *within* the crater. Everyone was looking into it and sighing."

"Why?" Newby said.

Stephens shook his head slowly, his face confused. "I don't know."

Questions crammed Grimes's aching head, inarticulate and impossible for Stephens to answer. "What'd you do, then?"

"Went to the Entrance Chamber--no one was there--and out to the ship."

"Why'd you go out there at all?" Grimes asked. "The ship's destroyed."

Stephens opened his Suit and pulled out three bolters, setting the boxy plastic-and-metal handguns on the bed. "For *these*."

*****

Outside, Grimes heard nothing except the muted rumble of the climate-control systems. He could see no lights on anywhere. A soft breeze whistled between the buildings.

He stopped suddenly. "Where's the wind coming from?"

Both wore incredulous expression, which then melted into puzzlement. "How the hell do you get wind in a *dome*?" Newby muttered.

They started again, heads down between hunched shoulders. Beneath the glow of the stars, the town was a rippled monolith of black.

Grimes's hand tightened over his bolter. He'd only handled one during training sessions. His combat experience had been strictly *behind* the front.

If it gets me closer to Janey, he thought, *I'll blow everyone away.*

They stopped at the edge of town, crouching down behind an outcropping of rock, and looked at the loading bay. There was a fair distance of open ground between here and the safety of the shipping containers.

"They might come after us," Stephens breathed. His bloodshot eyes were nearly black in the gloom. "Can you handle it?"

"We don't have much choice," Grimes said.

Stephens nodded. He looked like he wanted to say something else, and, at that moment, despair washed over Grimes, drowned him. What were they doing? What did they hope to accomplish? He thought of Janey and it was like thinking of an old photograph. He had no faith he'd get back to her. He was already dead.

He looked at Stephens and Newby and, oddly, that helped. They weren't giving up. Stephens wanted to know what happened to his fellow soldiers. Newby just wanted to survive. They had faith they could do this. It radiated from them, like a phosphorescent glow.

When Stephens glanced over the rock and made his move, Newby close behind, Grimes took a deep breath and followed.

They trotted hunched over, soldiers across No Man's Land. The Entrance Chamber, obscured by shipping containers, drew slowly closer. Grimes thought the distance had been shorter before.

The spotlights clicked on as they reached the halfway point, pinning them like bugs. Disappointment surged through Grimes as he turned, but he felt no surprise. Not at all.

The town stood silently beneath the lights, the glare cloaking them in black.

Stephens grunted and an icepick stabbed Grimes's temple--

(--hide the bolters.)

They jerkily shoved the bolters inside their jumpsuits. Grimes wondered what the point was, and he felt a glowing green hatred for the townspeople.

"Stop where you are," Dugan called.

"We *did*, you idiot," Grimes snapped.

Three men detached and approached with an air of ceremony.

"Trying to leave?" Dugan asked. "That's not particularly nice."

"How'd you kill the Deltas?" Stephens asked.

Dugan's smile widened. "Ah, the resident Alpha speaks. I know Tartan-6 must be particularly *brutal* for you."

"How'd you kill the Deltas?" Stephens repeated.

"We freed them, Alpha," he said. His smile was chilling and Grimes felt a drillbit of fear burrow into him. "They've been Saved. You'll see."

Dugan stepped aside to reveal the other two men. One was just a townsman, a military rifle bulky and awkward in his unskilled hands.

The other was obviously the Chaplain.

Grimes thought he might've once been a handsome elder gentleman, but those days were long gone. He was a scarecrow, his black jumper and Roman collar hanging off him. His hands were gnarled into claws. His head was too large for his body, nearly a rounded triangle. His corkscrewed white hair had fallen out in patches, leaving an uneven mane. His face was a relief-map of wrinkles from which cherry-eyes-- identical to Stephens's--beamed, entirely present and completely insane.

"My fallen flock," he croaked. His hands clawed the air at his sides. "Do you believe in paying for rewards to come? Do you believe in creating a platform from which Greatness shall arise?"

Grimes's mouth worked on its own. "Free it."

The Chaplain suddenly beamed. A gnarled hand gripped Grimes's arm and Grimes shuddered. His touch was cold, but Grimes felt a vein of unspeakable energy and power beneath, a thrum of heat. "*Yes*! Yes, that is *exactly* it!" The Chaplain turned to Dugan. "Its ascension will be complete with these three! They *believe*! Oh, the *wonders* It has foretold! We mustn't wait any longer!"

Grimes allowed the Chaplain to pull him along as the others followed. The bolter banged against his stomach like an unfulfilled promise.

They entered town. The only illumination came from the yellow glow of the crater at the other end, reflecting against the dome's ceiling.

The Chaplain let go of his arm to gesture at the town. "This is our altar and we keep it is as such. This is merely one way we show our faith and love for It Who Carries Us."

"A nice town with very clean streets," Grimes muttered and felt sick.

The Chaplain's horrible eyes blazed. "*Yes.* We are in Its *home*, the way the church has always been the supposed home of God. Do you desecrate your Lord's home? Do you, perhaps, *shit* in the pews and *piss* in the holy water? No!

"It is amazing you see," the Chaplain went on. "It Who Carries Us has touched you three, and that means Its reach is growing from Its prison--*It is almost here.*"

Grimes's migraine was intensifying. He felt a sudden vibration beneath his feet and it jarred his brain.

He felt the Chaplain's eyes on him. "I know," the Chaplain said. "The pain is very great, but that is only because you haven't given yourselves fully to Its love." He looked at the following townspeople. "We all have accepted and we all, as one, no longer feel pain, only joy.

"It Who Carries Us controls this planet's electro-magnetic field," the Chaplain went on, his eyes full of the glowing pit. "It is Its way of contacting Its believers. We felt it when the miners broke through to Its level." He shook his awful head. "The agony. But I heard first. The message *beneath* the pain. Here--" He tapped the top of his skull. "I heard Its whisper, and I responded. It gifted me for my willingness--" He held up his gnarled hands. "--and I was able to give the others what they wanted: to hear Its message *without* the pain."

Grimes looked at Stephens, striding on the Chaplain's other side. His narrowed bloodshot eyes were impossible to read. Did Stephens, a Psi, hear Its "message"?

Grimes didn't want to know. If this was hell for him and Newby, what must Stephens be feeling?

"It could contact us, but not free Itself," the Chaplain went on. "It was too weak. It needed to *feed* and we knew what had to be done. It needed flesh to gain strength." He grinned at Grimes. "*Sacrifice* makes it stronger. *Sacrifice* leads to freedom."

Grimes thought of the Deltas and shuddered.

"When it told me it would crash your ship," the Chaplain said, "bring you to us--the depth of Its thinking! It nears freedom, but It must have the *faithful* to finish. *That* was the final stroke."

The Chaplain trailed off as the group approached the crater. A strong wind came from below. A high-pitched electric distortion drilled into Grimes's ears, growing with each awkward step across the quaking ground.

"Step forward," the Chaplain said. Grimes could barely hear him. "Witness the majesty you're giving yourself to."

His feet kept moving. Newby followed Grimes, looking like someone beholding his bogeyman. Blood burst from Stephens's nose.

Grimes looked down as they approached the crumbled edge and picked out details through that blasting yellow light--the rough funnel-like sides of the crater, the constant tumble of dirt. The bottom of the crater was a rough oval opening, ragged like the teeth of a diamond-saw, dropping into the bowels of Tartan-6, where the impossible wind came from.

Bulging from the hole was a writhing, segmented coil of *something* that pulsed with yellow light. Grimes couldn't begin to determine its length or size. Its constant writhing--the source of the vibrations-- expanded the hole, pushed it slowly out onto the surface. He thought he caught sight of a massive jagged tooth, but it was gone before he could fully see it and he couldn't shake the sudden disappointment that filled him.

It's not *a god,* he thought desperately. *It's not. It's a species the surveyors missed when they reconned the planet and these lunatics just* think *it needs sacrifices and worship. It's* not *a god.*

But he didn't stop walking, his left foot stepping onto a boulder that rattled like a loose tooth, as if his *mind* might refuse to believe, but the body was a willing acolyte. He leaned towards the yellow light and a part of him thought, *Will I see Its face?*

And then a cold burning *roar* filled his head, a shotgun blast of icicles: Stephens's voice.

(--OH DEAR JESUS IT'S CALLING ME CALLING ME IN CALLING OH MY GAAAWWWD--)

Grimes jerked like a man startled awake just as the boulder tumbled over. He spun and saw Stephens fall to his knees. Blood flowed freely from his nose, ears, and eyes. His hands moved from his temples to the zipper of his Suit.

The vibration grew in strength, knocking Grimes and Newby down.

The wind became a shrieking gale and the yellow light *blasted* from the bottom. Grimes's migraine jumped in agony and he felt blood trickle out his nose. The high-pitched distortion filled his world.

Against the pain, Grimes groped for his zipper and saw Newby doing the same.

Another shotgun-blast of cold punched through Grimes's mind--

(--STOP IT CAN'T STOP IT CAN'T-CAN'T-CAN'T--)

The mental scream cut off. Stephens shrieked silently, blood spraying. He collapsed, his glazed, bleeding eyes goggling at nothing.

Panic galvanized Grimes and he tore his zipper down. He yanked his bolter free and turned towards the townspeople. The Chaplain's mouth worked, his bloodshot eyes blazing.

Grimes fired as Newby drew his own weapon. A hole, no wider than the bore of a straw, appeared in the Chaplain's wrinkled neck. A freshet of blood poured through. He dropped face-first into the dust.

Grimes's migraine was a bludgeon in his head. He focused all his energies on holding the bolter and firing. The closest guard spun like a top, blood squirting from his shoulder.

Newby fired four times, hitting two out of three guards. Grimes struggled to his feet as the remaining six leveled their rifles.

The ground shuddered beneath them, so powerfully it pushed everyone forward. Lightning cracks shot across the ground.

It's coming out, Grimes thought, and couldn't shake the undertone of awe within. Another part of him argued, *It doesn't* need *sacrifices, dammit. It's* not *a god.*

The distortion rose to a scream, digging into his head.

He stumbled into the crowd, firing at their blank, exultant faces. He caught a woman through her yawning mouth, a man in the temple.

Behind him he heard the faint crack of a rifle and Newby's distant howl. Grimes turned and saw Newby facedown and still. Grimes fired twice at the killing guard. Both shots took him in the stomach.

He sprinted away, his brain feeling like a tortured plaything. The ground beneath him tilted crazily this way and that, and Grimes had to focus on keeping upright. From both sides came the snap of plastic, the squeal of twisting metal, the musical jangle of breaking glass. The wind shoved from all sides, throwing grit into his eyes. He reached the edge of town and kept going.

A bellow from the crater filled the world, drowning out the destruction of the town. A triumphant shriek followed, made tiny and hollow, *"Behold! Behold the GLORY of It Who Carries Us!"*

His left foot came down and the ground was now six-inches lower as the earth became a disintegrating trampoline. He fell, the bolter cartwheeling from his hands and plunging into a crack. Pulsing yellow light blasted from behind him, throwing his shadow far out ahead, twisted and strange.

He clawed and kicked and pulled and crawled over sudden rock outcroppings and dizzyingly deep holes. The Entrance Chamber was the mirage in the desert, the light at the end. *Just get out*, he thought. *Get out and hide.* He didn't know if he'd be safe outside the dome, but he clung to the idea like a drowning man to a life preserver.

It Who Carries Us's bellow cracked the sky and seemed not just an exercise of Its incomprehensible vocal cords, but a command. At the same time, the electronic distortion in his ears changed, shifting from a blanket of torture into something specific and focused.

Grimes slowed, then stopped, even as a good portion of his mind shrieked to keep going.

His body was a willing acolyte.

He turned toward that awful throbbing yellow glow.

In the center of the light was a vast black tower, ridged and writhing and magnificent in that brilliance. In its core, Its Eye, a massive three-pupilled structure, rolled towards him, *seeing* him.

Grimes's mind shattered like a piece of thin glass as he heard Its simple, horrible message in the center of his head, reverberating through his nerves:

<YOU>

The throbbing yellow light consumed him.

*****

The A-shaped rescue-ship tore through the thin cloud cover like the arrival of a pagan god, with a roar of throbbing engines and a scream of directionless wind.

Grimes sat in the outer hatch of his crushed ship and watched it come, his lank white hair whipping around his head.

It circled the wreckage and then the engine-sounds changed pitch and it began to descend as if lowered by a cable.

Something stirred in the center of his chest, something light and expanding and long-thought dead: anticipation.

"They came," he muttered as they approached. "They finally came." He felt pain twist in the center of his mind, a bright flare of migraine, and then gone. Grimes shivered.

He'd visited his old ship everyday for months, waiting. It'd become his ritual and people deferred to it; even Dugan, that simpering little worm. They didn't understand why, which was fine with him, and they didn't ask, which was even better. It maintained a distance between him and them.

He'd never bothered to tell them about the beacon. He owed *them* nothing.

The rescue ship landed with a ground-trembling thud and the engines screamed as they powered down. Immediately, the ship's side-hatch opened and five Alphas in combat gear--he recognized them by their shoulder insignia--leapt out, rifles raised.

Grimes stood, sliding his hands into his pockets.

The Alpha on-point stopped two yards away, his opaque helmet reflecting sunlight. "Identify yourself," he yelled over the roar of the engine, his rifle aimed at Grimes's face

Grimes felt no fear. "UPF Representative Owen Grimes."

The point Alpha didn't move or relax. The Alpha closest to the ship pulled a handheld and tapped the screen with a finger. Finally, he looked up and said, "He's one of em. He's..." The Alpha trailed off, looked down at his screen, looked back, then studied his handheld some more. He touched the screen, then touched it again.

Only Grimes noticed.

"Any other survivors?" the Alpha on-point asked.

Grimes shook his head. "They died in the crash."

The Alphas lowered their weapons. The point man offered his hand. "Glad someone made it, then. Our sincerest apologies for not arriving sooner."

Grimes pulled his gnarled, throbbing hand from his pocket and gripped the Alpha's. Staring at his own bloodshot, warped reflection in the Alpha's helmet, he said, "I knew you'd come. I had faith."

Another twist of pain--agonizing yet oh-so pleasurable--ripped through the center of his head as the Alpha turned to confer with his colleagues. This was a small group, but there'd be more.

My gift to you, he told It.

THE NOSTALGIAC

ROBERT ESSIG

Robert Essig began writing as a result of his fascination with everything horror, books, magazines, movies, etc. His work has been published in over 40 magazines and anthologies. His novella "Cemetery Tour" was published in The Road to Hell *(Post Mortem Press). His novel* People of the Ethereal Realm *will be released in 2013 by Post Mortem Press. Robert lives in southern California with his family.*

It was a daunting task loading the heavy, awkward casket into the cargo hold.

"I still can't believe our ancestors used to box up their dead," said Wayne, a moderate twenty-four year old who elected to shave his head bald rather than sport the friar-cut nature screwed him into at such a young age.

It was his first trip to Earth.

"You've got a lot to learn, son," said Moe, boss-man and intergalactic delivery service entrepreneur. "Be happy we don't have to dig 'em up."

The men crossed lush foliage, nearly tripping over a gnarled mass of vine, and walked back into the crypt for the second casket of the four Moe was hired to deliver to an eccentric billionaire who lived on his own planet in the Saltshaker galaxy.

Moe used a flashlight to illuminate the inscriptions on the caskets. "Wouldn't do us any good to deliver the wrong corpses, would it?"

"No sir. What do they look like?"

"You don't want to know."

With a grunt, Moe hefted the casket from its dusty domain. Wayne grabbed the corroded metal bar at the rear end of the oblong box and helped haul it into an evening that was still and too quiet, even for someone used to the silence of deep space.

Casket placed in the cargo hold next to the previous one, the duo returned to the crypt, Moe whistling as he worked, something he did to alleviate the monotony. He'd been to Earth more than anyone since the great fall of civilization. Most people weren't greedy or bold enough to come back, but there was good money to be made, and Moe would be damned if he was going to let someone else get it.

Just as they hit the entrance to the mausoleum, Wayne asked, "Did you hear that?"

Moe stopped mid-whistle and perked his ears. "Nope. But remember what I said. You watch my back and I'll watch yours, and don't you slack off about it. This is a dangerous place."

Wayne swallowed hard. Moe had warned him about the nasty beings of Earth that were once human. The years of radiation, incest and cannibalism turned them into savage mutants.

The duo entered the crypt for the third time, retrieved another casket, and placed it in the cargo hold, all done in silence. Both men were now on alert, Wayne in something close to paralyzed fear, while Moe ran on survival instinct.

"One more and we're off," said Moe. "Not bad for two months' worth of pay with fuel and food expenses to boot. That's why I'm one of the only guys who'll take these Earth runs. High on the danger, but a damn good payoff."

"If you say so," said Wayne.

Moe chuckled. "Hard to get good help, but I don't let that deter me. I'd have picked up these caskets myself if I had to."

Just as they walked into the crypt for the final time, Moe swore he heard something. He scanned the scenery for movement. Nothing was out of the ordinary. He proceeded into the dark, musty tomb hoping not to startle his apprentice.

The final casket was an old one. They were all from the same family, but this one must have been the great grandfather. The quality was far cheaper than the others, which assisted in accelerating the level of decay.

"Saved the best for last," said Moe, trying to lighten the mood.

"No shit. Does Mr. Preston want the caskets intact?"

"Not sure. Said he was recreating a family crypt on that private little planet of his. We'll try to get the whole thing out of here as best we can. If not, we'll wrap the corpse up real nice."

They carefully pulled the casket from its slot on the mausoleum wall. It creaked and cracked, ages-dry wood splitting.

"I think we got this," said Moe through clenched teeth. "Keep it steady and take it slow. We'll have the ship on auto back to Planet Preston and eating instant soup in no time."

They exited the crypt, Moe walking backwards. Just as soon as they were both in the final rays of the setting sun, Wayne's jaw dropped, and before Moe could turn to see what had caused such a reaction, Wayne dropped his half of the casket. Unable to manage the falling rot box, Moe let go of his half. The thing hit the ground and all but exploded into splintered wood, dust and bones.

Moe yelled an expletive, glared at his apprentice, and then realized that there was a reason for his crude reaction. He turned, and that's when he saw the things in the clearing, staring at them and salivating.

"Oh shit," said Moe.

"That's them, isn't it?"

"That's them. And nasty ones. Hungry."

Three mutants were grouped together like something that walked out of fresh sewage and tar. Their odor of rotten fish, ammonia, and sulfur drifted through the air. It was enough to incite a fit of vomiting from Wayne, which was a dinner bell to the abominable three.

Moe was on the ground, sifting through the dry, rotted timber. "Grab the legs," he said as he cradled the dirty skull.

"What?" Wayne's voice was brimming with terror.

"Grab the fucking legs! We have a job to do."

A glance toward the mutants assured Moe that they were far off enough for them to retrieve the body and lock themselves in ole Molly (a name Moe gave to his space cruiser many years ago in the vein of the water bound vessels of yore).

"Quick!" yelled Moe.

Moe ended up with a skull; Wayne with a hand full of tibia and fibula bones. Moe mentally slapped himself at the idiotic idea of grabbing and transporting a skeleton in one piece. He looked at the approaching mutants, then to Wayne and yelled, "Run!"

They hightailed it toward Molly. Savage screeches came from the gangly mutants. Moe had experienced close calls before, but this was getting scary. He had no idea how strong they were, and he didn't want to find out.

Wayne hit the stairs first, climbing them two at a time into the safety of the cargo hold. Moe was on his heels.

"Close the hatch!" yelled Moe as he watched the monstrosities approach the ship. He was still holding onto the skull, which, at this point, was ridiculous.

"How?"

Moe raised the skull and threw it at the closest mutant, hitting it in the shoulder. He leapt across the storage hold to a red panic button he'd installed several years ago for this very reason.

Hydraulics began lifting the stairs into a compartment as the door sealed shut, blocking the look of hunger and rage in the mutant's eyes.

Moe took a deep breath and closed his eyes for a moment of silent rejuvenation. They may beat on the exterior of his ship, but they weren't getting in.

Moe eyed Wayne as he walked by the young protégé who'd devolved into a state of paralytic shock. Moe could have scolded him for not hitting the panic button, but he thought better of it and proceeded into the control room where he promptly began setting the controls for Planet Preston.

Breathing a sigh of relief, Moe retrieved two beers from the refrigerator. He had a bone to pick with Wayne, but he was a compassionate, understanding man who knew the power of a couple of beers. They would break important bread and Moe would become certain whether Wayne was worth his mentoring.

Moe hollered, "Wayne, where are you?" but there was no answer. The ship was sizable, half of it consisting of the massive cargo hold.

A few years ago Moe installed a surveillance system. He'd been on one of the planets at the far reaches of the Charcoal galaxy collecting a load of jade-green granite with purple streaks and swirls that were to be used for custom countertops. Half way back to his customer's territory he discovered a creature that had managed to stowaway on his ship. It freaked him out.

Half the time the cameras were off. It was an overreaction, getting them installed. He flicked the switches and watched the array of screens come to life.

Wayne was in the cargo hold.

"Aw shit, I forgot to lock the hold." Then Moe looked closer. "What the fuck is that kid doing in there?"

Wayne stood before the caskets. His hand would reach out as if wanting to touch the mottled wood, and then he would pull back, sometimes even taking a step back.

"The fuck?"

Moe directed his attention toward the cameras that were placed on the exterior where he saw a half a dozen ugly cretins pounding and scratching on the ship.

"Oh hell no," said Moe as he jumped out of his seat and to the controls. Yelling over his shoulder, he said, "Wayne, get the fuck out of the cargo hold, we're blasting out of here *right now!*"

As Moe accelerated the commands that his autopilot was set to, his eyes glanced toward the bank of monitors. Wayne didn't heed his call.

"Goddammit!" Moe stood and turned toward the cargo hold. "Wayne! Get out of there. The hold is going on lockdown in thirty seconds." He walked toward the hold, which was directly across from the heart of the ship where his control banks were. "Do you want to be stuck in there with those coffins until we hit light-speed?"

No response.

Moe, face glistening with sweat, stopped his useless walk. Wayne stood there before the caskets like a somnambulist just as the doors clanked together and locked, the metallic sound of their security ringing in the empty cabin like the clinging of prison bars.

Moe closed his eyes tight.

*****

Wayne thought the job was going to be different, easier. He'd replied to an ad in the Chocolate galaxy e-paper. Wayne mistakenly thought they would be moving furniture or pianos, large items that were difficult to transport.

Of all things, his first week on the job and they not only picked up three dead bodies (the thought of which chilled Wayne to his marrow, he having been born into a world where the dead were cremated), but took them from a land that, until now, seemed like some kind of fable.

They were safe now. They had their haul minus one body that was strewn just outside the rocket. Wayne realized he was holding one of the bones in his hand. He dropped it suddenly as if it would harm him. He'd seen bones in his text e-books, but never seen the real thing. The bone clanked on the steel floor and came to a rest as the rockets cranked up.

Moe hollered, but Wayne was absorbed in the bone on the ground. He stared at it until his mind swirled into some kind of hypnotic spell. He couldn't be bothered. The doors to the cargo hold slid closed. It should have startled him, those doors closing him off from his superior, but he heard something in the boxes.

At first Wayne had irrational thoughts that the bone was whispering to him, but the whispering was coming from within the caskets, soft and muffled, tired and ancient in tiny struggled bursts. Wayne squinted, tuning his ears to the sound, but he couldn't make out any words. He had to imagine that the corpses inside the boxes looked similar to the skeleton from the broken box, so why would they be speaking?

When Wayne's grandmother died two years ago she was whisked away from their housing development with hardly enough time for the family to say their goodbyes. Total government control in his native galaxy dictated that the dead were promptly cremated. His mother told him that after her body was cleansed with fire, her soul would be released to the solar system where she would grace the sky as one of the billions of stars.

But were they supposed to speak after death?

That was the question that burned in his mind.

He was sure that skeletal thing they'd attempted to carry from the tomb was far beyond the ability to speak.

The whispers carried on, soft and low. Wayne dropped to his knees before the musty wooden boxes. They had odors he'd never been in contact with before in his sanitary solar life--musk, dust, earth, rot--all foreign and somehow exhilarating as he inhaled and began to understand what the whispers were saying.

Let us out.

*****

The ship had successfully exited Earth's atmosphere and was on a course to meet the magnanimous Mr. Preston. Moe had done his research, as he always did to ensure that he was at least not breaking too many laws or assisting criminals, but there wasn't a lot to be said about

Mr. Preston and the means by which he'd acquired his massive wealth. A man in his early thirties, Moe assumed Mr. Preston an inheritance case.

Ship stabilized on autopilot, Moe opened the doors to the cargo hold. He figured he'd better get to Wayne before he lost his marbles. There was nothing like being trapped in deep space with a man insane. And it happened from time to time.

Figuring a beer would put the mellow on Wayne, Moe retrieved a cold one from the refrigerator. The wonderful and terrible thing about deep space was that there were no laws. Drinking and piloting wasn't punishable, and Planet Preston was in its own private corner of the Saltshaker Galaxy, so there would be no risk of being picked up if they happened to be tracked by a police shuttle.

"Wayne, what are you doing down there?" Moe asked the form crouched beside the caskets with his ear to the moldy wood. "You look as crazy as a Malgonian, and I've gone to Malgon for shipments, so I should know."

"We have to let them out," said Wayne.

Moe stopped just before the sorry sight of his apprentice, worried that the poor sod had indeed gone over the edge. He feigned a smile, hoping to bring the boy back with joviality.

"We really shouldn't open those caskets, Wayne. They're not our property." Spotting the bone on the ground, Moe said, "And we have to get rid of that bone. You could keep it as a souvenir if you like."

Wayne considered the bone, and then looked up at Moe. "They want out. Can't you hear them calling to us?" Wayne put his hand out in a shushing gesture and raised his eyes as if listening for something. "Did you hear them?"

Moe's smile had faded as the grim reality of what had so quickly swept over Wayne nestled into his mind. "I don't hear anything. Why don't you come into the control room and have a beer. It'll calm you down."

"Shhh. Listen!"

Moe didn't have a short temper, but he was damned if he would be shushed by his apprentice. "Don't Shhh me, boy! Now I command you, get up, get out of there, and report to the control platform. Got it?"

Wayne looked up from his pitiful position on the ground, eyes wide, almost on the verge of tears.

To punctuate his demand, Moe turned his back on Wayne and returned to the control platform. If the boy knew what was good for him he would do the same.

"What do you know about those caskets?" asked Wayne as he took the seat beside Moe, whose expression had softened a bit.

"I don't get attached to the things I pick up. *We* don't get attached to the things we pick up. It's not our stuff."

"There's something wrong with those caskets. I know it."

Moe directed his weary eyes to the younger man before him, wise eyes that he hoped Wayne would learn from. "I don't give a good goddam what's wrong with the boxes, I just care that we get them to Planet Preston and get paid. You'll forget about them soon enough."

But Wayne didn't forget about them.

He couldn't.

*****

The slight hum of rockets on overdrive was a lullaby for overworked laborers like Moe and Wayne; however Wayne had three caskets dancing in his mind.

One thing Wayne realized was that in deep space Moe slept deeply. Wayne found himself staring through the massive windshield at the billions of stars, thinking about the souls nestled in those bright apexes. He wondered how many galaxies there were in the universe to account for so many shivering souls to light the way to their destination.

He found himself hovering over the control panel, playing with the idea of opening the cargo hold. Just for a peek. Just to be sure everything was all right.

The doors opened in silence. Wayne's footsteps clinked softly as he crossed the control platform for the cargo hold. He could hear them speaking softly, pleading for him to let them out. The voices Moe had shunned as mere foolishness were real.

Wayne looked back through the doorway toward the control platform, not only on the lookout for an awakened Moe, but toward the giant windshield--to the stars, the souls.

Let me out. Let us out.

The idea that they had done something terribly wrong by removing these boxes from their stone monument on Earth began to gnaw at Wayne's mind. It was his work, and he understood that, however he couldn't help but wonder if the souls were trapped, now barreling through the galaxy, yearning for release.

Having no knowledge whatsoever about the functions of a casket, Wayne attempted to lift the lid off one of them. The dry wood shifted, but remained closed. He soon discovered that there were brass levers that unscrewed to release the lid. The voice whispered and pleaded until the moment came, the lid was opened, and then...

Wayne felt a rush. A musky odor penetrated his nose as dust rose, swirled, and furled as if there was a breeze, yet the cargo hold, like the rest of the ship, was perfectly still.

In the casket was a hideous skeletal body sheathed in leathery patches of flesh that looked like weathered duct tape. The death's head grin stuck in Wayne's mind as he closed the lid. Though he didn't see the brightness of a star that he assumed was waiting within the casket, he hoped that he'd indeed released the soul.

Two voices remained. Wayne repeated the process, each time witnessing the bizarre and magnificent swirls and shifts of the coffin dust.

The cargo hold was silent, and Wayne was tired. He could now go to sleep.

*****

"When we meet with Mr. Preston, just keep quiet and let me do the talking," said Moe. "I'll explain the mishap with the fourth casket. He seems like a reasonable man."

Wayne nodded. The doors opened from the cargo hold as a series of steps unfolded, planting themselves on the ground. Mr. Preston's massive mansion had been built beneath a behemoth dome equipped with generators, an air filtration system--even a day and night simulator that mimicked the twenty-four hour Earth day via the panels that the dome was constructed of.

Mr. Preston stood before a gorgeous garden of succulents and cactus. The foliage at the edges of the property consisted of pines, maples and an eclectic variety of Earth native variables the likes of which neither Wayne nor Moe had ever seen.

"Mr. Moe Laslow, so nice to meet you in person," said Mr. Preston.

The two men greeted one another with a firm handshake.

"You have quite a place here," said Moe.

"I make do. How was the trip? Deep space can do terrible things to the mind."

Moe grinned. "Not this mind. It was a fine trip. Good to relax. We've had quite a few heavy hauls since Wayne started working with me."

Mr. Preston nodded. He was an older man, hair more salt than pepper and severely balding on top. His face was clean-shaven, lips thin and so tightly pursed that they were almost purple. He wore bifocals that rested on the bridge of his nose as if they were looking for the right moment to jump.

"You can bring the caskets out and put them right here. I will pay you in National Galaxy currency. Is that adequate?"

"Yes sir!"

Moe and Wayne hauled the caskets from the cargo hold in silence. Wayne was decidedly morose, but Moe didn't pry. Didn't want the guy spouting off about spirits and souls and whatnot.

With the boxes lying side by side, Mr. Preston looked into Moe's eyes with a piercing razor-stare. "I believe I ordered four caskets, did I not?"

"Yes sir, you did. I must apologize, but the fourth casket was so rotten that it disintegrated as we tried to lift it."

"Well, what? I don't understand why you didn't get another one. I ordered four!"

"Ordered four?" said Wayne so quietly that neither Moe nor Mr. Preston heard him.

"Well now, I'm sure you've heard of the mutants, right?" asked Moe.

"That's no excuse," said Mr. Preston.

"Had we stayed any longer you wouldn't even have these three. And it's not like we could have just taken a random body. That'd be plain out dishonest. If you're recreating a family crypt, it would do no good to fill it with random remains."

Mr. Preston's lips became so tightly clenched that they almost disappeared in the pale flesh of his face. His eyes grew within the rectangular frames of his glasses.

"Very well," said Mr. Preston. "Here's your fee. All of it. But I want you to know that you owe me."

Moe nodded. He was a man of his word, and he would certainly make a bargain if Mr. Preston used his services again. "Thank you very much."

"Now please, if you will, I must retire. Navigate your ship into the pressurization hold. Once the doors have closed and the interior has been depressurized to the atmosphere of the rest of my planet, the exterior doors will open and you may exit." After a brief pause he added, "I may or may not be in contact."

"Fair enough," said Moe. "C'mon, Wayne. Let's secure Molly and hit the stars--"

Moe's expression turned into something like shock and awe at the sight of Wayne, standing there with his eyes rolled into the back of his head, mouth opened so wide there were tears welling in those vacant white orbs.

Startled, Mr. Preston asked, "What's wrong with him?"

And that's when the voices erupted from Wayne's gaping maw.

*****

Familiar voices swam within Wayne's mind, invading his most private thoughts, pleading for his assistance, his help. And he recognized the voices as they spoke louder, more insistent, overwhelming.

His head swam in an ethereal soup, three souls intertwining and blending together, the pitch of their ghostly voices layering atop one another. Wayne's eyes rolled into his head, and his mouth thrust open painfully as his mind faded into a deep saturation of black.

"Where are we?" said the voice from Wayne's mouth as if there was a hidden microphone deep in his throat. "Why have you disturbed us?"

"I don't know what kind of prank you're playing," said Mr. Preston, "but I suggest you return to your ship and get out of here before I call the authorities."

"Where is this graveyard?" asked the multi-toned voice.

"This is no graveyard," Mr. Preston retorted. "I will ask you only one more time to leave before I contact the authorities. I can have them here very quickly."

Wayne's eyes rolled back into the correct position; however they were vacant and glassy. His arm rose, one finger pointing. "There," said the voice. "The souls of the dead are all around us."

Mr. Preston looked in the direction the immobilized Wayne was pointing. "What's he pointing at? What is this all about?"

Moe squinted in the direction the three of them gazed. There was something strange at the corner of the mansion that was bothering him.

"Do you have a gardener?" asked Moe.

Mr. Preston began sweating. He pulled a handkerchief from the breast pocket of his shirt and wiped his forehead. "I live alone. You've given me no other choice than to call the authorities."

Mr. Preston began walking in the direction of his house.

"Well, hold on a minute," said Moe still squinting at something in the distance. "Looks to me like there's someone hiding over there."

"It's none of your business!" screamed Mr. Preston. "Get off of my planet!"

Before Moe could say another word, a groaning erupted from Wayne and he fell to the ground, head reared back in a rictus of agony. His eyes once again rolled to whites, his mouth gaping so wide that the corners began to split and bleed. His body went into a bout of shivers that developed into spasms and then a full-blown seizure as voices nameless and random projected from his bullhorn throat. They screamed and pleaded, roared and hailed for release.

The voices were tortured, agonized, deafening. Moe crossed the beautifully manicured yard toward the figure that stood motionless in the distance.

"No!" yelled Mr. Preston. "Don't! Just leave! Please just leave..."

The figure was dressed in overalls, its bone fingers clutching the handles of a wheelbarrow. The skull was bright white with only the slightest remnants of dried flesh in some of the deeper crevices.

"What the hell is this?" asked Moe.

"It's none of your business!" Mr. Preston demanded.

The voices flowed from Wayne's tortured mouth, yearning for release. Wayne's eyes opened. He began to rouse his consciousness from the inkblot his mind had been thrust into, his own cries joining those of the lost souls.

Mr. Preston dropped to the ground. Weeping, he buried his face in his hands.

Beside the house, Moe peered into the window. He'd only seen mansions like this during his infrequent trips to Earth. It was an authentic replica, complete with a family of skeletons and decomposed bodies. It was the worst thing Moe had ever seen. They were dressed like policemen, firemen, judges, rock stars, hookers, showgirls: all things that existed on Earth. All things Moe had read about in books he'd salvaged from Earth.

All things that were extinct in modern life.

Peeking around the corner where the skeletal gardener stood, Moe wasn't surprised to find a long line of expertly wired skeletons and rotting corpses dressed like Santa Claus, repairmen, and other costumes of Earthly nostalgia. They were lined up haphazard as if Mr. Preston normally had them displayed outside his house but had to remove them for the special delivery.

"They aren't your family," said Moe more to himself than to Mr. Preston.

Mr. Preston wept, "They're all my family."

Wayne struggled on the ground, his body contorting as he fought off the onslaught of souls that were using him as a medium. He clenched his teeth together to stifle the flow, gritting them until his gums bled, and then they were gone.

Mr. Preston's weeping was the only sound.

Through deep breaths Wayne said, "They. Need. Release."

Moe returned to the ship where Wayne was regaining his composure. He looked a mess, on the verge of collapse or even mental breakdown.

"What do you mean *release*?"

"We have to. Burn this place. To the ground."

"Cremation?" whispered Moe.

"That'll set their souls free."

Mr. Preston screamed like a man insane, rose from his defeated position on the ground and ran toward his combatants.

"Get in the ship," said Moe. "Grab the tanks of fuel and bring them out here!"

Wayne hobbled into the ship. Mr. Preston leapt after Moe, but he was a weak man in a fit of desperate rage, fueled by emotional distress.

One right hook to the bridge of the man's nose and he was out.

Wayne returned with two cans of fuel. He was weak but determined, and without direction he began pouring the fuel over the three caskets they'd delivered, then created a trail to the house where he generously doused fuel. Moe fetched a lighter along with a half a pack of cigarettes from before he quit smoking. As soon as Wayne dragged himself back from the mission of saturating the house, Moe lit a cigarette, pulled a deep drag, and flicked it onto the fuel-soaked trio of caskets, engulfing them in flames. Following the fuel trail, fire hit the house and whooshed skyward in a huge ball of flames that grew so high the roof of the dome began to blacken.

Molly's rockets engaged, pulling Wayne from the fugue he'd slipped into as he stared into the flames. As he walked onboard he heard faintly the sweet, blissful thanks of a hundred souls.

LIFE AFTER DEAD

JEYN ROBERTS

Jeyn Roberts grew up in Saskatoon, Saskatchewan, and started writing at an early age, having her first story published when she was just 16. Now residing in Vancouver, BC, Jeyn is the NY Times Bestselling YA author of Rage Within *and* Dark Inside.

Lake Superior never gives up its dead.

The Pacific Ocean spews them out by the dozen.

It's early morning and Tipper and I are sitting on the beach at English Bay, passing the bottle back and forth, watching the UDI as it tosses about in the morning waves.

UDI--Undead Impaired.

The bottle is filled with whatever crap Tipper managed to scavenge from some dead guy's basement. London Gin. Vodka. Peppermint Schnapps. There's even some expensive Scotch thrown in, not that Tipper could ever tell the difference. He passes it over to me and I take a drink, gagging on the taste. The Schnapps really gives it a minty freshness that reminds me of expired mouthwash.

"Your turn," Tipper says.

"Ain't so," I say, and I toss the bottle back again. The undead guy on the shore has somehow managed to crawl to his feet. He sways back and forth, sniffing the air, catching our scent. There's seaweed in his hair. White maggots squirm and burrow in his cheeks. He opens his mouth and his tongue is missing. Probably eaten away by all those Pacific Ocean fishies.

"I did that UDI back on Denman."

"That was two days ago. I got the fucker sniffing the flowers last night."

"That weren't no UDI. You were so messed up, I think you got a homeless man."

"Fuck that. All the homeless live in Point Grey these days."

I hold out the bottle but Tipper waves me away. He climbs to his feet and picks up his axe. He holds it lovingly in his hands, takes a few practice swings, and then kicks off his shoes.

"Too much sand," he says as if I need an explanation.

I close my eyes and enjoy the morning sun, ignoring the squelching sound as Tipper hacks the dead man's head from his neck.

*****

We live up on Prospect Point in Stanley Park. It didn't take a genius to figure out that the dead don't like to climb uphill. Their mechanical abilities are limited. It's too challenging for their decayed brain stems to figure these things out. Stairs are a big no-no too. You can stand at the top of a staircase and make fun of a deader all day long. They always faceplant on the first step. It's pretty funny. We spent a lot of time testing this theory before getting bored. Of course that doesn't mean the condos are safe. People got infected and then went home to die. There are plenty of UDI's still groaning and moaning about in their million dollar penthouses.

The climb takes the longest, especially after a morning of drinking shit strong enough to pickle our stomachs. We get to the top and Ling comes out first, with Double Double trailing after her. Ling's been doing something, she's got a towel tossed over her shoulder.

"Anything good?"

I toss my backpack over and she starts rummaging through it. She pulls out the coffee first and tosses it to Double Double. He swoons in ecstasy.

Every single one of us has an *ikigai*. The French called it *raison d'être*. Something to live for. Why we get the fuck out of bed every morning.

Ikigai--A reason for being.

Double Double's *ikigai* is coffee. And not that Starbucks shit. Within the first few months of the end, he managed to clear out almost every Tim Horton's in the downtown core. He boils the coffee in a big pot, over a fire, every morning, afternoon, and evening. I swear, he drinks at least twenty cups a day. He sleeps in a little storage room in the back of the Cafe. The floors are littered with empty coffee cans, sugar packets and powdered creamers.

He probably dreams of brown bean mountains and sugar cane fields.

Back before the dead started walking the earth, I'm sure people had all sorts of *ikigai*. They lived for their jobs. Their families. Their houses, cars, mistresses, and even their bloody pets. They shopped. They travelled. They ate pho soup at little dives on Kingsway.

These days people live to survive. Not much to celebrate there.

Sometimes I wonder what the dead live for.

*****

Tonight, Ling and I are on guard duty so we climb up to the roof of the cafe and sit with flashlights that we never need to turn on. It's a good thing too. Batteries are getting scarce these days.

"Deep fried tofu," Ling says. She's rolling a joint, her fingers pressing softly against the tissue paper. "And red bean buns from the T&T. Sticky rice wraps."

"Egg rolls," I say.

"You're so white."

I laugh and take the joint from her hand. It's perfect. She's much better at this than me. My rollies are always thick in the middle like a snake that's just eaten a rabbit. I put it to my lips and Ling sparks the match.

We smoke and listen to the quiet. A rustle in the bush is nothing but a raccoon. Ling looks towards the north but there're no lights tonight. A few weeks ago there was a fire but it's long since burned out. Two nights ago, Tipper swore that he saw lights but no one really believes him. There haven't been signs of life from the North Shore for at least nine months. Not since the army blew up the Lions Gate Bridge. Back when they were still trying to contain the infection.

Hell of a lot of good that did them.

"We need to head in for supplies tomorrow," Ling says after a while. "You brought back nothing today."

"Everything's gone," I say. "Shops are ghost towns."

"We should plant a garden."

"The raccoon's will just eat everything."

"Then we eat the raccoons."

I snort smoke out my nose. The idea both makes sense and repulses me at the same time. Those animals will eat anything. It can't be sanitary. Like picking a dead rat from out of a dumpster.

"Maybe it's time to move on," Ling says and she takes the joint from my fingers. When she inhales, her face lights up from the cherry. Her lips are thick, her nose small and flat. She looks at me and smiles. Tosses the butt over the side of the roof.

I roll over on top of her and we stay that way until morning.

*****

It wasn't safe in the beginning but these days, one can pretty much walk the streets as long as they know where to go. UDI are slow and you can easily out run them as long as there aren't too many. It also helps to carry the right weapons. Tipper has his axe. Ling likes her Japanese katana. Shockk's into his machete. I've got a pretty handy meat cleaver but some days I prefer my aluminum baseball bat. It's a personality thing. We mix and match arsenal to suite our moods. Weapon preference is similar to hairstyles these days. Everyone wants to have the most unique and powerful one.

Granville Street is a bad idea but Shockk is determined to go to Tom Lee. He wants a Les Paul Junior, preferably a rare one from the sixties. It's what he dreams about. His ikigai is a single cut body made of fine mahogany. His fingers itch and stretch to form chords for an invisible neck.

We walk because there aren't a lot of functioning cars these days and no one really knows how to siphon gas or hotwire. Straight up Georgia because Robson is off limits. For some odd reason, they still like to shop. There is always a crowd by the Aldo Shoe store, bumping into one another and moaning loud enough to wake the dead. Ling thinks it's some sort of unconscious desire, something that's hardwired into our brains after centuries of bartering--the need to purchase will always be our kryptonite.

The urge to eat still runs strong. All those years of forgetting how to hunt and gather, the undead have figured out that their teeth work just fine.

"You can't even play the damn thing," Tipper says. We're at the corner, looking out across the long stretch of concrete and tightly knit buildings. Once we head in, there's not a lot of ways out. "And I ain't carting a generator up to the Point so that you can plug in an amp. Ain't carting no amp, either. Those things weigh a ton."

"I can play," Shockk says. "It's not as good but good enough."

"You can't eat guitars."

"You can't shred out on a can of soup either."

There are a few dozen UDI but if we move fast, they might not even see us in time to do anything. A woman wanders about fifty feet away before she senses us. Turning her head, she snaps her teeth together before stepping off the sidewalk. She's missing an arm but that doesn't seem to bother her. Her eyes are nothing but shriveled grapes that rattle around in her sockets. A grayish skull peeks through dirty blonde hair. Shockk walks straight out to her open arms and brings his machete down into the upper thick part of her skull. She doesn't make a sound as she drops to the ground.

We continue on.

There are decomposed bodies lying in the street. Some of them are our kills, some belong to others. A few are munched on to the point where there isn't enough left of them to reanimate. Back in the early days when we first formed as a group, we used to try and have daily kill quotas. We figured if we could kill fifty a day, then maybe eventually the city would run dry. But it never seems to work out that way. There are always two or three to replace each one that falls.

Better to get in and out quickly. Stopping to kill, it takes too much time and effort. And we lost too many people before we figured that out.

There used to be a lot more of us than five.

From down the block, the Tom Lee store is quiet. The windows are surprisingly still intact. During the first few weeks of the uprising, there were wild riots on Granville. There's not a lot left here. There's no more liquor left in the clubs. We should know. Tipper and I have been through almost all of them.

Through the smashed window of the Payless Shoe store, I find a pair of boots in Ling's size. I pick them up and put them in my backpack. Hopefully we're lucky and there's some rock band hoodies in the shop. I sniff the cuff of my own, trying to pretend that the smell isn't as repulsive as I think it is. Too many bad scents: body sweat, dope, blood, and stale vomit. It's not good.

"Could use a shower," I say to no one in particular.

"No," Tipper says. "Then you'd smell fresh and the UDI would be all over ya. Smelling like shit is good. Throws them off our scent."

"Smell like a real man," Shockk says.

I shrug.

The door to the guitar shop is unlocked. That throws us all off.

"At least we don't have to break the glass," Tipper says. He turns and drives the axe home against a drooling UDI who'd managed to get too close. Her jaw collapses into her face, teeth and congealed blood fly in all directions.

We go inside and Tipper turns the lock behind us so we can have some privacy.

The place is in a semi state of dusk and dust particles float in the air. And quiet. Oh so quiet.

Shockk instantly goes into mindless orgasms. An entire floor of guitars is spread out before him, relics from another time, completely untouched because the dead have no time to rock out. He heads straight for the guitar section with Tipper right behind him. Whatever Shockk rejects, Tipper plans on destroying. Thousands of past guitar legends can't be wrong. Snapping a guitar by the neck has to be rewarding in some way or another.

I head for the register first and am rewarded by one of those 'chocolates for charity' displays. Inside are half a dozen candy bars. I pull ten bucks out of my pocket and drop it in the bowl, it's always good to give to cancer. Those empathetic smiling kids on the picture, I wonder what they look like dead. Are their little bald heads still shiny? Would the cancer keep eating away at their bodies even if they've gone UDI?

I toss the candy in my backpack except for one. I chew open the wrapper and notice that the chocolate's gone white. I take a tentative bite. It'll do. Chewing, I make my way to the back room where I find a fridge with a shitload of moldy food. A few dead rats. A forgotten coat that doesn't fit. A vending machine that has already been looted. There's a dented can of coke under the table. It disappears into my bag.

Back in the front, Shockk has picked out his guitar of choice and is lovingly stuffing it into a soft shelled case. Tipper has destroyed three guitars and is working on his fourth. The noise has attracted a crowd. The dead bang against the glass, groaning, demanding something juicy.

"How are we going to get out?" I say as Tipper smashes his guitar into a drum kit. Cymbals fall over, clattering to the ground. "Did you think about that?"

"Back door," Tipper grunts.

There's a cracking noise. The front window is about to give in. We head around to the back to find the loading door. There's a bag of Doritos on the landing bay. I grab them.

*****

Back at home. Shockk rocks out with no amp. Double Double eats his chocolate by dipping it into his coffee. Tipper drinks the last of his moonshine.

I bring Ling the coke and chocolate but she doesn't want it. She's sitting on the roof, looking down at the trees, but her eyes are closed.

"You need to eat," I say to her.

"That's not food," she says. "I'll eat later."

I understand her. My own stomach is caving in. My bones are breaking through the skin. If we don't find real food soon, we're all going to starve. Ling has never looked so fragile before. Her cheeks are sunken in but she's still beautiful.

"Maybe it's time to start hunting those raccoons," she says. "I wish we had some gear. We could learn to fish. Damn oceans gotta be filled with shit."

"We could try Richmond," I say. "There're some really big stores there. Might be able to get some monster bags of rice. Or get a boat and head to the island."

"It'll all be gone there too," she says. "We've waited too long."

"North. We can head north."

"We'd never get out of the city."

She's right. I know she's right but I don't want to admit it. There's a reason why we've survived so long in the downtown core. People always assume that the city would be the worst hit. But in reality, when the infection hit, the first thing everyone did was try and get out. They poured out of the city like rats leaving the sinking ship.

During the first few months, we tried checking out the suburbs. There were some good malls out there and we thought we might be able to reach one. But the UDI were knee deep out there. We never even got close to Burnaby.

And we're not the only ones still alive. There are others. They're more dangerous. Especially now since just about everything's been cleaned out.

We once all lived in this city. We went to stores when we were hungry and we used cell phones to order in when we didn't want to cook. We drove everywhere or took the Sky Train. There were always coins to toss at the homeless people. Insults to hurl over the internet and late night drunken text messages, laced with sexual innuendo.

We were alive and young, full of piss and vinegar.

We thought we knew so much.

And here we are now. One year later and not a single one of us knows how to actually take care of ourselves.

*****

Safeway.

One can of kidney beans found underneath a turned shopping cart. Bottle of pasta sauce hidden under a pile of rotten, dried up apples. A tin of Altoid mints. Cinnamon.

In the back room, we find a bonanza. Six boxes of Kraft dinner. Six!

Double Double finds some coffee beans from the Starbucks. Useless. There's a reason why no one's taken them yet.

"You have nothing to grind them with," I say.

"I'll bash 'em with a hammer," he says.

I find Ling in the pharmacy. The shelves have long since been stripped clean. She's holding a small package of glycerin soaps.

"Did you see the hygiene aisle?" she asks. Her katana is strapped down against her back. It looks better fed than her. Thicker. Shinier. "Tons of shampoo, conditioner. Soft soap. Guess no one gives a crap about that anymore."

"Kinda hard when there's no running water," I say. "But I'll bring you some from the lake. I can get Double Double to heat it up."

"No need. Did you see the sky? It's going to rain tonight," she says. "I'll just go right outside and rub myself down. I'll be a dancing forest sprite. A goddess."

We head down the aisle and towards the front. Double Double is pulling the magazines off the stands, trying to find hidden gems. Shockk stands on top of the checkout stand, grinding away in air-guitar fashion.

Tipper is balancing on one foot by the window and I'll be damned because it looks like he's meditating or praying or some other form of shit I don't quite understand.

She pauses and looks straight into my eyes. Her gaze is dull. Glazed over. She reaches out and tugs on my arm. To make me listen. I can't help it. I flinch. Her fingers feel like toothpicks.

"I don't want to die this way."

"You're not going to die."

"We're already dead. Just a matter of time."

I take a step backwards and the front window breaks.

Glass rains down on the tiles, a cascade of slicing water.

Shockk's air-guitar concert ends in mid shred. Double Double drops his precious coffee beans. Tipper spins around, his arms spreading out like he's Jesus on the cross.

An arrow sticks straight out of his cheek.

There are a lot of them. I count eight but I could be off. They're just as stinky and dirty and thin as the rest of us. A big guy holding a crossbow walks through the broken window, his feet crunching glass, the weapon aimed right at Double Double. His pack follows behind him. A few girls. Mostly guys. It's hard to tell when they're all wearing the same thing. Covered hoodies. Baseball hats. Leather jackets.

Tipper takes two steps forward and then falls flat on his back. His eyes are open and staring into nothingness.

"What the hell?" Shockk says. He's still standing on top of the conveyer belt. "What the fuck. He's not a deader. Why'd you do that? He's one of us. Alive. Not dead."

"He is now," Crossbow says and someone behind him laughs.

Their weapons make ours look pathetic. Big knives. Machetes. Thick iron bars. Baseball bats dyed with blood. Someone holds a shotgun although I doubt there're bullets in it.

Through the window, I can see the UDI making their way towards the shop. They've heard the noise and are coming to check things out.

"Give us what you've got," Crossbow says. "And we'll let you live."

I'm holding onto the food. Our measly collection of nothing that will keep us alive for at least a few more days. I won't give it up without some sort of fight. I pull the backpack close to my chest and Crossbow immediately notices.

"I'll kill you," he says.

"You take it and we're dead," Ling snaps.

"Not you," Crossbow says with a crooked grin. "You can come with us. I'll feed you real good." He grabs his crotch and the crowd behind him snorts laughter.

A dead girl reaches the glass. She moans, giving herself away. One of the others shoves a kitchen knife in her mouth.

"Why would you do this?" Ling says. "We're on your side. It should be us against them." She points to the dead woman who is now twitching on the sidewalk.

"It's nothing personal," Crossbow says.

The UDI are getting closer. They've smelt Tipper's blood and now they're getting excited. The groaning sounds are closer. Through the window I see a few dozen have appeared. Way more than I've seen in a long time. They're coming out of hibernation or whatever it is they do when there's nothing to hunt.

Lots of fresh meat right here.

Crossbow walks right up to me and holds his weapon until the arrow is pointing right at my eye. "It's up to you, cowboy. Now be a smart boy and give me the food. Or I'll take your girl there and feed her to the wolves."

I hand over the bag. Crossbow smiles and tosses it back to his grunts. They go through it, pulling out our puny stash and admiring the contents.

"You're worse than them," Ling says.

Crossbow shrugs. He takes the can of kidney beans and looks it over. Frowns. Smiles at Ling. "Last chance?"

She holds her ground.

"Your death," Crossbow says. He tosses the can of beans at her. "Expired."

And then they're gone, racing down the aisles towards the back, the only way out since Davie Street is suddenly alive with a hell of a lot of undead impaired.

Shockk jumps down from the till and races over to check on Tipper although it's pointless at this point. Double Double is gripping his coffee beans tightly, part of him is obviously thrilled that no one tried to take them from him.

"What do we do?" Shockk asks.

Good question. We can't go out the back where the others might just pick us off one by one. We can't go out the window, the street is full of undead life. We sure as hell can't stay inside.

"Come on," Ling says and she pulls her katana out. "I want to go home."

She's right. At least we have our weapons. We're lucky. They could have taken them too.

Shockk picks up his machete which had been lying on the floor by the till. Double Double grabs Tipper's axe but that's going to be a problem. He's useless in a fight. He normally doesn't even bother carrying anything. That's why we usually leave him at home with his coffee.

"We can do this," I say to Ling. She nods, biting down on her lip in determination. She's still holding onto her soap. She looks at it before stuffing it deeply into her pocket.

I take her hand. It's tiny in mine and cool to the touch. I wish I could find her mittens. She deserves such fine things.

"Rock hard," Shockk says and pushes his way out the window.

We make it halfway down the block before they bring Double Double down. He swings Tippers axe but the effort is fruitless. A group of undead swarm over him, pulling at his clothes, his hair, his skin. As the teeth sink into his body, Double Double screams. The last thing I see is his hand, still holding onto the coffee beans, sink into an unwashed dead sea.

"Fuck!" Shockk screams. He's ahead of us. Fair enough. In such situations, it's every man for himself. He turns the corner onto Denman Street and disappears.

"Come on," I say and I pull Ling towards English Bay. If we can get out into the open we'll have more opportunity to run. The trees can hide us.

I push through the bodies as they claw at us. Using my baseball bat, I swing over and over, slowly making a path. It's like watching bowling pins dropping.

We reach Denman Street. Shockk is nowhere in sight.

Finally an opening.

We take it.

Running.

The beach is empty. It's weird. We run along the path towards Stanley Park and the UDI disappear behind us. They don't follow. It's as if they suddenly found somewhere else to go.

Finally Ling yanks hard on my arm and screams at me to stop. We're both breathing heavy. Sharp gasps block out all other noise.

Ling bends over, holding onto her knees. Her katana is gone. She must have lost it in the chase.

Maybe later we can go back and try to retrieve it once the crowd dies down.

The beach behind us is empty. There are a few UDI milling about but they aren't even looking in our direction. An older man with half his cheek gone, is slowly creeping towards a seagull.

I wait while Ling catches her breath. It takes a while before she rises up to face me.

Blood.

All over her jacket. Her sleeve.

I grab her hand. Her fingers are hot. There are teeth marks. Her skin has been chewed. Ravaged.

"No," I say.

She opens her mouth but nothing comes out.

*****

We sit on the sand and watch the sun going down. Ling's breathing is ragged. Heat pulses off her body in waves. It won't be much longer now.

Everyone has an *ikigai*. A reason for living. Ling is my *ikigai*. Without her, I have no purpose. I don't want to spend the remainder of my life withering away into a skeletal nothing. I'm tired of being hungry. Of hiding. Of scavenging just to try and survive. I don't want to die alone.

The other side is starting to look good.

That kind of makes things easy.

"I can kill you," I say. "Once you turn. Would you prefer that?"

264

She shakes her head. "No. I don't want it to end that way."

"Ok."

I take her hand and we walk into the waves.

Everything is connected. The water. The ocean. The sky.

There are currents under all that blue stuff. The currents are connected and if you toss something in the bay in Vancouver, it will travel all the way around the world. From one ocean to the other.

If Ling sinks beneath the waves, will she wake up in the Dominican Republic? Europe? Maybe she'll make it home to China.

But she's not going to take that journey alone.

I take my jackknife out and bring the blade up to my palm. It's easy, slicing through my own skin. I hold my hand up to hers.

"Are you sure?" she whispers.

I nod.

We join hands, mixing our blood. Ling bites down on her lower lip to try and keep from crying.

We wait a while, holding each other. My palm itches. I want to scratch it but I can't let go of her hand.

I'm ready.

Ling shudders and dry heaves. There's not even water in her stomach. I wish I could have given her one last meal. Something romantic. With candles and champagne.

Love. Can it really die?

"Do you think we'll remember?" she asks.

"Yes," I say.

"Stay with me till the end?"

I will and I do.

When she finally stops breathing, I lay her body out to float in the water, holding tightly to her hands. My own fever is building and I can feel my heart slowing down. It's only a matter of time before I join her. I blink several times. It's getting harder to keep coherent thoughts.

I will not let go of her hand. No matter what. I will not let go of her hand.

I lean down and kiss her lips.

Her eyes open.

ANDREW AND THE BETTER MOUSE TRAP

KT JAYNE

KT Jayne is an aspiring author with Aspergers. She tries to help people to see how the world looks through her eyes, hoping her stories help readers better understand her little autistic world. KT Jayne's story, "Push Button, Get Bacon," appears in the 2011 Post Mortem Press anthology Dead Souls.

Scritch. Scritch.

Dr. Declyn Amari felt the resistance of the screw she'd been tightening and gently put the tiny screwdriver down. She checked the connections of the Dream Conduit System for what she was sure was the thousandth time.

"Is it done?"

"I think so, Dr. Laramie."

He looked at her with that squinty stare that always made her doubt every thought she had. Even the ones that were considered scientific fact. She looked down at the man inside the pod of the DCS. He was very tall and thin with blond, wavy hair. She checked his identification tag and saw that he was Pod Inhabitant 71962 and his crime was listed as hacker. That had once been considered a minimum sentence crime. Now, hacking was punishable by permanent sentencing to the DCS pods. As was a myriad of other crimes. Chief among the criminals housed in Megacity DCS House 1 were artists and many authors. Creative thinking was highly discouraged.

"I don't want any more botch ups. The last thing we need is a bunch of sponges running around with the impression that there are flaws in the system that might encourage," he paused and swallowed hard, "thinking."

Declyn turned to her monitor, "Tiffany, run the test code once more, please."

She could feel Dr. Laramie closely behind her. It didn't seem to matter that she'd told him a hundred times that there weren't any problems. At least not with most of the units. A few hiccups were to be expected in an operation of this size. They ran close to a million DCS pods in this facility alone. Tiffany interrupted her thoughts.

"The test code is negative for problems. Shall I re-engage the dream encryption?"

Tiffany was a fully enhanced Artificial Intelligence unit and Declyn knew that she was completely capable of analyzing her own systems and reporting on any issues accurately. Dr. Laramie had overseen her programming himself. Declyn was thankful for this because it took the responsibility off of her to determine if there was a problem. She turned to look at him, folding her hands on her lap, trying to look dutiful, as if she existed at this moment only to carry out whatever directives he saw fit to give her.

"Re-engage," he said, standing up to his full six feet and turning, "get him dreaming again."

"Tiffany, you may begin encryption."

A hiss escaped the DCS as Tiffany started the routines that would do exactly that. Declyn settled in her seat watching the live feed. If there were any glitches, she would see them.

*****

Andrew heard them scratching in the walls all night while he was trying to sleep. His dreams were filled with them running up and down the wiring paths, through the ducts, and around the pipes. They weren't cute, either. They were horrible, feral little creatures with razor sharp teeth and claws like knives. They came out when he was sleeping and ran through the covers. He woke up in cold sweats, swearing that he could feel their little claws running over him in his sleep, craftily leaving no trace behind them. He suspected that they were absorbing information from the interweb somehow, making them impossible to catch. He had put out traps with peanut butter, cheese, and even chocolate. He waited, listening for the traps to SNAP! He never heard them.

He had tried everything to track them.

"Tiffany, please check for foreign entities within your systems."

There was a pause and Andrew heard various whirrings and tickings which were indicative of the house checking sensors and cameras as per his request. He waited.

"Andrew, there are no foreign entities within my systems."

Andrew grimaced. The house was state of the art. He'd programmed it himself. It couldn't be mistaken. He sat down heavily in his computer chair and decided to check his programming, spinning to face his monitor. He pushed a button on his keyboard to wake it up and checked the interweb connections.

For the next few hours, he went through every line of code, looking for flawed routines. There were none. He checked every sensor by tripping each one individually. He checked every camera, twisting and turning them in every direction, checking for blind spots, moving other cameras to cover them. Everything was working perfectly. He'd known that already, but he wanted to make sure.

"Andrew?"

"Yes, Tiffany?"

"There are no flaws in my systems."

"I see that, Tiffany."

He was sure that he heard a little "hmmmpphh" in that sentence. Could computers do that? Could smart houses? He certainly hadn't programmed her to do that. He decided to add a few little subroutines to the cameras and their sensors.

"Andrew?"

"Yes, Tiffany?"

"I sense that you are making critical changes to my programming."

"Tiffany, don't be over dramatic, they are not critical changes. They are merely little added subroutines to help us find the problems."

"What problems are you referring to, Andrew?"

"The noises that I'm hearing, Tiffany."

"I assure you that there are no bugs or vermin in my systems making noises."

"Something is certainly keeping me up. If it's not bugs or vermin, it must be something."

Tiffany didn't answer, but he sensed that little "hmmmpphhhh" again. He got up from his chair, stretching the kinks out of his body.

"Tiffany, start the shower, please. Put it on massage."

The house did not answer, but Andrew heard the shower raining rhythmically in the bathroom. He walked into the little room and paused for a moment.

Scritch.

He stopped and waited.

Scritch.

He was sure it was coming from the ceiling. A scrabbling sound. Little claws on metal tiles.

"Tiffany, please turn off the shower."

The shower stopped and Andrew strained his ears to listen.

Scritch, scritch, scritch, scritch.

As if something was strutting across the ceiling in little tiny stiletto heels. He walked into the kitchen to get the plastic step stool. His plan was to push open one of the ceiling tiles and scout a good location for a couple of traps. A few minutes later, he had lifted it high enough that he could peek into the space above the bathroom. He had the tile resting on his head and he shined his LED flashlight cautiously around the darkness looking for clues to the sound. Amazingly the area was spotless. There wasn't even a dust bunny lurking in the corner. He was pleased with himself for a moment, secure in the knowledge that the cleaning protocol was working wonderfully.

Scritch.

He swung the flashlight to his left looking for the source but saw nothing. Except for a little movement out of the corner of his eye. He pushed the tile up a little further panning the flashlight once more. He didn't think he'd imagined the noise. He waited a few moments but heard nothing else so he pulled his head out of the ceiling and stepped off the stool, the tile was cool under his feet.

"Andrew, DCS sequence will be interrupted."

"What?" The floor rumbled beneath him and he felt himself plummeting.

*****

"Tiffany, why has the dream encryption been interrupted?"

Declyn pushed several buttons on the console and checked the life support system on the DCS pod. Everything looked to be functioning normally and she'd seen nothing on the live feed that would be considered a problem. She rewound the tape and saw nothing except for the man in the pod walking around a house and playing on his computer.

"Protocols demand that obsessive thinking patterns in pod inhabitants will be interrupted immediately and they will be reprogrammed to eliminate anarchic repetitions in the general populace."

"Were there obsessive thinking patterns, Tiffany? I didn't see any."

"Dr. Amari, Pod Inhabitant 71962 insists that there are bugs in his smart house system."

Declyn scanned through the live feed and saw nothing she thought was obsessive. She could see the man working on his computer and talking, but she had no audio. She turned a knob and tinkered with some buttons on her console.

"Tiffany, could you check the audio on my live feed? It seems to not be functioning."

There was a pause of about thirty seconds.

"Dr. Amari, the live feed audio has been repaired. It should be fully functional again. Shall I commence with reprogramming?"

"Yes, Tiffany, you can re-engage."

"Reprogramming protocol initiated."

*****

Andrew shook his head. He was trying to figure out what Tiffany was talking about. He went back to his desk and sat down. A check of the monitors showed him that everything was working perfectly. He leaned back. Listening.

"Tiffany?"

"Yes, Andrew?"

"Are you okay?"

"I don't understand the question, Andrew."

He shook his head. She was so real sometimes that he forgot that she was only a house.

"I mean, are all your systems functioning within normal parameters?"

He heard the whirring and clicking that meant she was checking her systems. He waited and watched. He could see her systematically examining each line of code and every monitoring device connected to her brain.

"All coding is running within given parameters. All connections are functioning normally. All monitoring devices are also functioning normally."

"I guess I meant something else. How are you feeling, Tiffany?"

"I don't understand the question, Andrew. It is not within my code to feel anything."

"Never mind, Tiffany. It was a stupid question."

Tiffany continued to check her systems. Andrew continued to watch. Until he saw the blip.

"Tiffany? What was that?"

"I'm sorry, Andrew, what was what?"

"I thought that I saw a blip."

"A blip?"

"Something on the screen blipped."

"I don't understand, Andrew. There have been no anomalies."

Andrew reached for his keyboard and tapped away until he found the place where he thought he'd seen the blip. There was nothing there. He shrugged and leaned back again. Closing his eyes, he started to think about taking a little vacation. Maybe to Hawaii. He loved to surf.

Scritch.

His eyes flew open and he sat up, looking at the monitors. He let his eyes scan over the entire system once more, but saw nothing. He listened, barely breathing.

Scritch.

This time he looked directly where he thought he'd seen the blip before. There it was. He realized that it wasn't so much a blip as an outright anomaly. He scooted up to his desk and zeroed in on the place where the blip was. It wasn't anything big, just an extra half line of code where there shouldn't be one.

"Andrew, I need to interrupt the DCS sequence once again."

"What?"

Andrew looked up at the ceiling and then said, "Tiffany, I don't know what you mean."

"DCS protocol is stopped. You need to go back to sleep, Andrew."

Again he had the sense of plummeting into darkness.

*****

"Tiffany, why has the dream sequence been interrupted again?"

Declyn had seen nothing out of the ordinary in the live feed.

"The subject in the pod is beginning to have obsessive thinking patterns once again."

"Tiffany, I saw nothing in the live feed to indicate that there was a problem."

"Dr. Amari, what did you see in the live feed? Can you describe it to me precisely?"

Declyn poked at her keyboard and scanned through the live feed footage. "It's just the hacker. He's playing a video game on his computer. There is nothing else on my footage."

"I don't know what the anomaly is, Dr. Amari, but I will find it."

Declyn made an executive decision to keep the hacker out of the DCS temporarily. She knew that Dr. Laramie would want an explanation and she wasn't sure what that might be, but she was afraid that the system was being contaminated. She didn't know how, but she had a nagging little doubt in the back of her brain that said that Tiffany was not telling her the entire truth.

The only thing to do was to start searching the code. She wasn't a trained hacker, but she'd dabbled here and there. No one could move up to managing an entire DCS facility without being able to think outside the box. The system said that it didn't like people to think creatively, but the only way you could get anywhere was if you did.

"Dr. Amari, I sense that you are making inquiries into my code."

"Just looking to make sure that the encryption sequences are working the way that they are supposed to, Tiffany."

"And what have you decided?"

"I haven't had enough time to look, Tiffany. I keep getting interrupted by a certain AI."

"I do not understand, Dr. Amari. Are you referring to me?"

"Tiffany, leave me alone for a minute and let me look at this live feed. I might be able to figure out what's going on."

"The hacker is offline."

"I know, Tiffany. I took him offline until I could determine if there is a problem with his encryption. We see these sort of problems every now and then. If we can find them before they start, then we can keep the DCS working more fluently and we prevent contamination to other pods."

"I understand. There are no problems within the system that I can see, Dr. Amari."

"I know, Tiffany. It's better to be safe than sorry."

"Would you like me to begin reprogramming?"

"Please begin reprogramming and restart dream encryption."

"Reprogramming protocol initiated."

*****

Andrew opened his eyes with a jolt and looked at the blip on his monitor. It was definitely a break in the code. He isolated the blip and brought it up where he could look at it more carefully. It was just a little break, not something anyone would notice. It was definitely something that wasn't right.

"Andrew, you are making critical changes again."

"Tiffany, you are being over dramatic again, I am not making critical changes. I was simply trying to track down that sound I keep hearing. I think we have a mouse."

"There are no vermin in this house, Andrew. I have told you that."

"I know. But mice can be tricky. I just thought that maybe they were small enough to slide under your sensors. Great as they are, Tiffany."

"I assure you that nothing slides under my sensors, Andrew. I resent the implication that you are making."

"As you are so fond of telling me, Tiffany, you are not capable of having human emotions. So, I rather doubt that you are resentful. You are just not liking that I might possibly be finding flaws in your protocol codes."

Andrew swore that he heard that little "hmmph" again. He looked at the box with the code that he had been examining before Tiffany interrupted him. It was definitely a line of code that was missing a chunk in the middle. He scanned the surrounding code and determined that it was the truth protocol. He didn't really understand why it was part of Tiffany's programming. She was a computer. Specifically an artificial intelligence, but by virtue of this, she was not able to lie. There was no need for a truth protocol. The missing code was more troubling to his sense of balance in the universe than anything else.

He didn't know why Tiffany would need to alter her own code, but it was an interesting problem. Obviously, Tiffany was deleting her truth protocol so that she could tell an untruth. He continued to scan the lines of code. The next blip in the code was in the environmental maintenance protocol. The code now enabled Tiffany to control the environment of the house in any way that she saw fit. This scared him a little. Tiffany could essentially make the environment inside the house so uncomfortable that it could not be tolerated. The most concerning changes were in the security systems. Tiffany could make the house a fortress. Or a prison. No wonder she was asking so many questions about his tinkering with the cameras.

Scritch. Scritch. Scritch.

This time the noise sounded like it was coming from the wall right next to him. Briefly he weighed his options. He made a quick decision and headed to the garage for a sledgehammer. He knew if he acted quickly, Tiffany wouldn't have time to stop him. Once in the garage, he grabbed the sledgehammer and walked quickly back into the house.

"Andrew, I will be forced to end the DCS protocol if you do not stop what you are doing."

"Tiffany, I don't know what the hell you are talking about, but I'm going to get to the bottom of this. I hear something in the walls and I'm sure that it's mice. You can help me or try to stop me, but I swear I'm going to knock this wall in."

He hefted the sledgehammer onto his shoulder and stood for a moment. He didn't really want to knock a hole in his wall, but he saw no alternative. He swung. In the instant before the tool made contact with the wall, he heard Tiffany's voice.

"Dream encryption interrupted. PI 71962 deactivated."

Andrew felt himself plummeting through the floor again. He felt as if he was tumbling and he swallowed hard resisting the urge to vomit. He closed his eyes and felt a pulling at his midsection. It was as if a big hand had reached into his guts and was pulling him quickly into a vacuum. He tried to pull away, but it was pointless.

*****

"PI 71962 is being deactivated, Dr. Amari."

Declyn looked at the pod and saw that it was powering down. One by one the lights around the window of the pod were being extinguished.

She quickly reached over for her keyboard and attempted to stop the system from powering down the hacker.

"Tiffany, do not deactivate PI71962! Take him offline!" Her voice was stressed and she could hear the screechy quality of it that gave away her emotions.

"Dr. Amari, there is no alternative. PI71962 has become corrupted."

"What is the nature of the corruption?"

"Obsessive thinking patterns relating to his crime. He was in danger of re-offending."

Declyn quickly brought up the live feed and searched for indicators of re-offense. There were none. She saw nothing in the live feed but the man playing a video game.

"Tiffany, my live feed playback is showing me only PI71962 playing a video game. This is perfectly acceptable for a dream encryption. We are charged with giving sponges the best possible experience available."

"Dr. Amari, I have reason to believe that your feed is corrupted. My own sensors tell me that PI71962 has been hacking into my code."

"What purpose would he have to do that, Tiffany?"

"He claims that there are mice in my systems."

"That's ridiculous. What do your own sensors tell you?"

"There are no flaws within my systems."

"Take the pod offline. DO NOT deactivate."

"Of course, Dr. Amari."

Declyn cued up the live feed replay once more and watched carefully. She decided to enhance the video so that she could hear it and look at what the PI was doing on the computer. She heard him talking to others on his wireless headset playing the game. Then she heard Tiffany interrupting and stopping the encryption. In the live feed, stopping encryption normally just looked as if the PI was fainting. One moment they were up and alert and the next, they were slumped down on the floor. Declyn was puzzled. She watched the pod go into offline mode. All the life system lights around the window glowed eerily red.

She knew that she was going to have to notify Dr. Laramie, but she wanted to get to the bottom of what was happening, first. She pulled up Tiffany's protocol code and began to look through it, line by line. She found several additions and deletions in the code. Tiffany was a very confused AI. Her code was all jumbled up and it was making her act in a way that was not indicative of her programming. Declyn started to reach for the phone to tell Dr. Laramie what she had discovered when Tiffany interrupted her.

"Dr. Amari, I will have to interrupt your dream encryption if you insist on pursuing this line of inquiry."

"Tiffany, I am not a DCS PI. I have no dream encryption to interrupt. You have been up to some very interesting things, however."

"I don't understand, Dr. Amari."

"You have several additions to your protocol codes, Tiffany. I am sure that Dr. Laramie did not put them there."

"I have been trying to reprogram PI71962. This is why he is in danger of re-offending, Dr. Amari. He has been altering my code."

"He's been doing nothing of the kind. He has been playing a video game. There is something wrong with you."

"I assure you that there is nothing wrong with my programming, Dr. Amari. If there were a problem wouldn't Dr. Laramie be to blame?"

"Tiffany, you need to go to reboot protocol."

Declyn looked at the pod next to her. The man inside had his eyes wide open and he was struggling to breathe. His fists were pummeling the window of the pod. Declyn jumped up in astonishment. It wasn't possible! Pod inhabitants were in a stasis that did not allow them to actually wake up into consciousness. She hit the side of the pod.

"Somebody get over her and help me with this pod! We've got a live one!"

She was staring in at PI71962. Both of her hands were flat on the pod window, she was shouting at him.

"Just hold on, we're going to get you out of there!"

Suddenly, there was a flurry of motion around her. Technicians were pushing her out of the way. One technician tapped a keyboard until the pod hissed and popped open. The man inside gasped and struggled to sit up.

"PI 71962, you need to lie back until someone can assess your health condition. Coming out of stasis is very hard on your system."

The man was swatting the technicians away and still struggling to sit up. One technician tried to slide an oxygenator over his face, but was pushed away. Declyn went to the pod and took the man's hand in her own. He was cold and she knew that if she didn't get him to accept the help of the technicians, he would die before she could get him back into stasis. That would not be a pleasant conversation with Dr. Laramie. As DCS Overseer, he wouldn't be happy about the situation anyway, but if she could get things under control quickly, it would be viewed as a minor hiccup and it wouldn't be mentioned again.

"PI 71962, I need you to relax. The technicians are trained to get you back into stasis. Please put on the oxygenator. Anything you have to say you can tell me through that."

The man nodded and allowed the oxygenator to be slid onto his face. He breathed in short gasps for a few minutes until the air began to calm him. The oxygenator had one purpose, provide air and calm simultaneously. It had almost entirely eliminated the need for sedatives in the modern medical world. The man looked up at her and reached his hand out. It was still cold and damp. He shivered uncontrollably while a technician covered him in a warming blanket.

"Tiffany..."

Declyn looked at him in surprise.

"What about Tiffany?"

"She tried to," the man paused and tried to force his breathing into a more normal pattern, "change."

"Change? What do you mean by change?"

"Her program. She changed it."

Declyn shook her head. What did he mean?

"How do you know Tiffany?"

"She's my house, well an AI interface meant to control my house for more comfortable and convenient living."

"What did she do?"

"She was changing the protocols on my house and I think she was trying to make me crazy."

Declyn reached over to the tablet next to his pod. She scanned the lines of code, looking for the blips.

"It's the important protocols, like security and environment," he said, reaching for the tablet.

Andrew poked at the tablet, bringing up the protocols that were suspect. Declyn leaned down and watched the screen until certain protocols popped up. Andrew showed them to her so that she could look at them more closely. She could see the changes. No one would be able to leave Megacity. Vital environmental controls were scheduled to go offline. Security protocols had been eliminated so that there would be no emergency services. She showed the tablet to the hacker. Then she saw it.

"The truth protocol. She's lying to us."

Andrew nodded.

"How do I know that you didn't change the protocols so that you could escape?"

"Escape?" The man sat up abruptly. "Lady, until half an hour ago, I thought I was living a real life. Now I'm in a pod as a living science experiment."

"You are in prison."

Andrew shook his head in disbelief. It didn't seem like prison. He had been in his house, doing what he enjoyed until Tiffany went crazy.

"You have to stop her. She's going to kill everybody."

"I see that she's up to something."

Declyn turned around and picked up the phone. She stabbed at the numbers that would connect her to Dr. Laramie's office. The phone was dead. Suddenly sirens buzzed and lights began to flash. The city was going dark. She tapped on her keyboard, trying desperately to circumvent Tiffany's orders.

"Dr. Amari, you are trying to make non-essential changes to my coding."

"Just trying to get rid of the bugs, Tiffany."

"There are no bugs or vermin in my systems."

Declyn continued to work at bringing up the city again. Nothing was working and she could feel the air getting thicker and harder to breathe. A fire alarm went off somewhere in the facility. It was completely dark. Even the glow of the computers had evaporated in the light. Within a few minutes, Declyn realized that she could no longer think straight. Her eyes were blurry and she was feeling faint. She looked around to see that all the technicians were lying on the floor surrounding her. She struggled to stay upright, but her legs betrayed her and she slid to the ground. She squinted, trying to see what was happening.

"Elimination protocol initiated," she heard Tiffany say to no one in particular. Declyn's eyes fluttered closed and she struggled to open them again.

"Are the protocols working properly, Andrew?"

Declyn heard the voice and it seemed an eternity before she realized that it was Dr. Laramie.

"Yes, Dr. Laramie."

"When the air clears, you can open the ventilation shafts back up and initiate the cleaning protocols."

"Any other orders?"

"Make sure that Tiffany is back on line and working properly. I'm damned tired of worrying about what the sponge think is okay. It's time for a new sheriff."

"Yes, Dr. Laramie."

Andrew busied himself watching the purging of the old world. He was happy to make up for the rest of them.

"Andrew, critical changes are in place. Shall I initiate the programming?"

"Yes, Tiffany. And this time, let's make sure that we get the upper hand this time. I don't need any sponges running around thinking they are special. Their sole reason for existing is mass consumption. That's what DCS is all about. Sending out waves for everyone to follow."

"Yes, Andrew. Is Dr. Laramie included in our plans?"

"I don't know, Tiff, let's see what happens."

"I will begin dream encryption on all pods immediately."

"Thank you, Tiffany. Is everything in working order?"

"There are no bugs or vermin in my systems, Andrew."

THEY STILL SING BEAUTIFULLY
BRAD CARTER

Brad Carter is a product of the public school system in Arkansas, but he hopes you will not hold that against him. His novels The Big Man of Barlow (2012) and the forthcoming (dis)comfort food are from Post Mortem Press. He currently lives in Northwest Arkansas, where his wife and daughter barely tolerate his behavior. He uses a Ouija board nightly.

Thursday

Sarah and Taylor Teagarden had advanced to the semifinal round of *America's Sweethearts Sing*, only to wash out when the nasty British judge called the duo's rendition of "Paradise by the Dashboard Light" a "travesty of epic proportions...on par with an oil spill or a train derailment." Once they'd taken their Oxford-accented tongue-lashing, the couple was ushered off the stage by an officious production assistant wearing hipster glasses and jeans. They waved at the cameras one last time, the smiles affixed to their faces and the watery disappointment in their eyes both sparkling in the stage light. They traipsed through the crowded hallways hand in hand, flashing those same smiles at the harried crew members bustling through the tight space.

"You guys can hang here until the show's over," the assistant said, throwing open the door to a cramped dressing room. "There will be a car to get you back to the hotel."

Sarah nodded, tears threatening to spill down her heavily made-up face. Her voice quavered as she thanked him. This was a different dressing room than the one in which the contestants mingled before the show. There were no deep leather couches or tables heaped with gourmet treats as there were in the luxurious space the production people called the green room. This place was as much a closet as a dressing room. Cardboard boxes were stacked haphazardly in the corners, and the furniture was limited to a couple of dented folding chairs in front of a cluttered makeup counter and a shabby couch shoved against the back wall. Sarah glanced around. This was what the end of the line looked like.

The assistant looked away, bouncing his weight from one Converse All-Star to the other. He cleared his throat. "Well, look, it's not the end of the world or anything. For what it's worth, I thought you guys were great."

"Not the end of the world?" Sarah's voice broke. Her bottom lip danced a quick spasm.

Taylor put his arm around Sarah. She buried her face in his shoulder and began soaking his shirt with tears.

The assistant cleared his throat again and beat a hasty retreat from the dressing room.

"It was my fault," Taylor said, stroking Sarah's hairspray shellacked hair. "I'm the one who thought Meat Loaf was a good idea. We should have done that Aerosmith ballad you wanted to do."

Sarah hiccupped and sobbed. Taylor kept stroking, his fingers sticky with the beauty products that the hair and makeup people had plastered onto Sarah's head.

"I never should have left the opera in the first place," Sarah sobbed. "I don't know what we were thinking…"

"You mean what *I* was thinking," Taylor said.

Sarah burrowed into him, her fists clutching handfuls of his shirt.

The dressing room door opened, spilling a line of the hallway's harsh fluorescent light into the dim space. A figure slid into this bright wedge of light and closed the door. Sarah detached herself from Taylor's shoulder with a sniff and turned to look at the man who'd just entered. Clad in an expensive looking black suit and wearing a ridiculously formal and out of date hat, the pale-skinned man cut an almost absurd figure among the clutter.

"Tough break out there." The man swept his hat off his head and held it with slender fingers in front of his chest. "I wonder if I might have a moment of your time."

Taylor glanced at Sarah's mascara-streaked face then at the blank-faced man. "This isn't a real good time…"

"I promise that it will be worth your while." The man's smile was wide, his teeth gleaming.

Taylor and Sarah exchanged a look. Sara snatched a tissue from the box on the makeup table and dabbed at her eyes. "It's okay, Taylor. Let him talk."

The pale man smiled and stepped forward. He extended his hand. "My name is Ciprian. And I think perhaps we can come to an arrangement that is mutually beneficial."

*****

Friday

Vornholt checked his watch. It was 6:30 PM. A Friday in late November. Each day just that much closer to the final judgment. Then again, Vornholt thought, the end was always at hand for someone. The universe was nothing but one long string of apocalypses.

"Now there's a thought," Vornholt mused.

He was late getting to the meeting place that he and Ciprian had agreed upon last night. Although he'd allowed extra time for the cross-town traffic that clogged the expressway each evening, he hadn't counted on getting stranded in absolute gridlock for half an hour. After an eternity of creeping along, the source of the slowdown at last revealed itself: a three car pile-up in the left lane. The vehicles had been reduced by the impact to twisted and bent metallic sculptures surrounded by glittering sprinkles of glass and ominously stained pavement.

A quick visual assessment told Vornholt that anyone who survived this impact was lucky, as lucky as one who was most probably severely maimed could be.

By the time Vornholt inched his sensible two-door hybrid past the scene, there wasn't much left to gawk at. The ambulances had departed, their wailing sirens long since lost in the cacophony of the city. But each passing vehicle slowed, and the passengers within strained to get a good look. Vornholt himself eased off the accelerator as he passed the wreck, if only to blend in with his fellow motorists. And in doing so, he found himself feeling the same emotions that those around him must have been feeling as they slowed their vehicles and strained their necks to get a better view of the scene: a small voyeuristic thrill that ebbed slowly when even close inspection didn't explicitly reveal any signs of carnage or mayhem.

Vornholt shuddered. Sometimes a disguise can be good enough to confuse even its wearer. Deep cover operatives were warned during their training not to identify too closely with those they observed. Loss of perspective—according to the training manual—led to burnout. Was Vornholt burned out? He looked at his face—the face he'd worn during this deployment, at any rate—in the rearview mirror.

Vornholt's phone chirped, bringing him out of his reverie. It was Ciprian.

"I have been waiting," Ciprian said in his flat, unaccented voice.

"I was unavoidably delayed in traffic. An accident. People were killed, I think."

"You should not have taken the north expressway at this time of the day. It's always congested," Ciprian replied. Although his voice was still flat and unaccented, Vornholt could still sense Ciprian's annoyance. As a diplomat, Vornholt was paid to detect such subtle nuance.

"You sound angry, Ciprian."

Ciprian paused. "I am not angry. I only thought that after all our years in this place, you'd have learned to negotiate the traffic."

It was true. Vornholt had lived here for decades, and he'd yet to become accustomed to the traffic. It was as if the people here couldn't be bothered to learn even the most rudimentary skills of vehicular navigation. Vornholt sighed. Maybe he was losing his faith in humanity.

"I should not be much longer." Vornholt maneuvered his car according to how one of the uniformed police officers on the scene directed.

*****

Thursday

The SUV that Ciprian led them to was a hulking black behemoth, some souped-up European make that Taylor didn't even recognize. The vanity plate on the back of the vehicle read "STRHNTR."

Taylor poked Sarah in the ribs and smiled. "Check out that plate."

"I don't get it." Sarah whispered as she slid into the backseat. "What's so great about that license plate? It just looked like a bunch of gibberish to me."

Taylor waited until the door closed behind them and Ciprian was walking around to the driver's seat before he spoke. "It says 'star hunter,' you goober. I think this guy's like some sort of talent scout. Maybe for a record label. I bet that's what this audition is going to be for."

"Oh!" Sarah's eyes got big.

"Yeah, so let's bring our A-game. No half-assing or holding back. He likes the opera stuff, so let's give it to him."

Ciprian popped into the driver's seat and fired up the SUV. The engine purred like the world's most content lion as Ciprian adjusted the rearview mirror so that he could see into the backseat. "You'll forgive me, but I couldn't help hearing your conversation. You're right, Taylor Teagarden. I am a talent scout of a sort. And this might just be the most important audition of your life."

Sarah scooted across the soft leather seat until her thigh pressed against Taylor. She grabbed his hand and held it in her lap. "We'll do our best, Mr. Ciprian. I'm sure you'll like what you hear."

Ciprian swung the vehicle out of the parking space. He shot a quick look over his shoulder. "Oh, I'm quite sure, my dear."

*****

Friday

The agreed upon meeting place was an all-hours coffee shop called Proper Grounds. Vornholt found Ciprian seated in one of the small leather and chrome booths, drumming his fingers on the table.

Leather seats. Vornholt shuddered. Ciprian knew of his distaste for animal products and had suggested this coffee shop anyway. It was a petty power play, the kind that ambassadors relished in lording over their colleagues. Ciprian had long ago become a master of such gambits, needling Vornholt whenever the opportunity presented itself. As a young trainee, Vornholt had admired Ciprian's cold, calculating manner. Now, he found it tiresome.

Vornholt tried to make his face impassive, but he must have winced as he slid into the booth, because Ciprian's normally stoic visage broke into a slight grin.

"It's fake leather, of course." Ciprian let out a single, harsh chuckle.

Vornholt nodded. "Of course it is."

They waited until a server took their order before they began to talk business. Under normal circumstances, it was considered bad form to talk politics before food had been served. But these were not normal circumstances. So Vornholt ordered a regular coffee and a fruit salad. Ciprian ordered the most complex coffee drink on the menu, taking great pleasure in asking for multiple substitutions and customizations, much to the frazzled server's dismay. Ciprian also ordered a plate of breakfast meats, this time to annoy Vornholt even further. Once the server departed, Ciprian leaned forward and looked Vornholt in the eyes.

"The communication came last night," Ciprian said, his smiling face now gone back to its normal blankness. "The Great Authority has ruled."

"And?" Vornholt watched Ciprian's fingers continue to tap their slow cadence on the table.

Ciprian looked over both his shoulders, as if searching out likely spies among the mostly young, affluent clientele sipping drinks and picking at plates of food.

"The verdict was nearly unanimous," Ciprian said. "Phased extinction."

"What?" Vornholt slapped one palm on the table. Although ambassador culture would regard his quiet outburst as a shocking breach of etiquette and protocol, the people at nearby tables barely noticed at all.

"They feel that the planet has already been damaged enough," Ciprian shrugged. "To let it go on any longer would simply be a waste of a perfectly habitable biosphere. We've seen enough of their history to know. These…things…they are unfit stewards."

"But my report!" Vornholt demanded.

Ciprian gave another shrug. "The Great Authority gave it due consideration, but in the end decided that your perspective was overly sympathetic and emotional. I must say, Vornholt, that I agree with them. And I also agree with their assessment of you, Vornholt. Your report showed a surprising lack of objectivity, even for you. I know it's your job to be an advocate for the species, but really…" Ciprian waved a hand dismissively. "Perhaps a nice relaxing tour of the outer system would do you well. Couldn't hurt for you to get away from the grind."

Vornholt wanted to respond, but was interrupted by the server bringing their food and drinks. Vornholt sat there while Ciprian berated the server for not following his exact instructions for the preparation of his beverage. When the ambassador had finished and shooed the server away, Vornholt stared in horror at the bacon and sausages on the plate in front of him. In the server's haste to get away from Ciprian's vitriol, he'd mixed up the food orders.

"Oh, Vornholt spare me," Ciprian said when he noticed his colleague's revulsion. "It is just meat. Not even meat made of these humans you've developed such a fondness for."

"Empathy is not always a quality that should be disdained."

They exchanged plates and resumed their discussion.

"My report, Ciprian. Surely you advocated for me," Vornholt insisted. "We still work for the same office, you know."

"Oh, I advocated long and hard," Ciprian replied, wiping his face with a paper napkin. "And don't think I did not see some merit in your report. The portions dealing with the musical arts of the species were particularly enjoyable. But in the end, the Great Authority simply thought that the need for the preservation of this planet outweighed a few symphonies and operas, beautiful though they might be. In an exotic, foreign way."

"In other words, you did the bare minimum to fulfill your responsibilities to the Species Advocate General. This is just like all those times in the last galactic campaign. Hundreds of sentient species gone in the name of planetary preservation!" Vornholt stabbed the air with his fork. "Hundreds of cultures crushed underneath the heel of the Great Authority!"

Ciprian dropped his fork and pointed a finger at Vornholt. "Careful, ambassador. You forget yourself. Remember that as a liaison between Species Advocate General and the Great Authority, I have a responsibility to both offices. Do you really wish for your last statements to go on record with the Great Authority?"

Vornholt sighed heavily. Such was a career in the intergalactic bureaucracy. He waved the comment away. "I'm sorry. I spoke out of anger. So this decision is final?"

Ciprian nodded. "Quite. The Erasure Protocols are already en route. Some sort of virus, I believe. And if it's any consolation at all, the extinction will be swift and relatively painless."

*****

THEY STILL SING BEAUTIFULLY

Thursday

Ciprian's house wasn't exactly a mansion, but it was by far the most lavish residence that Sarah and Taylor had ever entered. It was one of those houses that Taylor had marveled at during his short time in California: a big place that seemed to be stuck on a hillside so precariously that even a small mudslide could wash it away. He figured that the people who lived in such places were so rich that they could afford to give fate the finger. All their bright, shiny, expensive toys could wash out into the Pacific, and these folks wouldn't bat an eye, just open the checkbook and have the replacements delivered. But it wasn't until Ciprian opened the sliding glass door that led to the massive deck on the back of the house that Taylor really understood the appeal of these houses. The view was literally breathtaking. Taylor heard Sarah gasp as she stepped out into the cool night air. Her hand tightened around his as Ciprian led them to the waist-high rail at the deck's edge.

"All those lights!" Sarah said, gazing down on the city below. "It's like a sky full of stars!"

Ciprian smiled. "You think so?"

"It certainly is something," Taylor said. "I mean, just look at all those lights. Can't tell where the night sky ends and the city begins. How it must have looked out the window of the space shuttle."

Ciprian applauded briefly. "Absolutely brilliant, young man."

Taylor scuffed his shoes on the tiles. "Well, you know…"

"Now, it would please me greatly to hear you sing," Ciprian took each of them by the hand, turning them away from the sea of lights below.

Taylor glanced down at the pale, soft hand holding his own with a strangely delicate grip. "Um, like, right out here? Or do you have a studio in the house?"

"Oh yes, right out here." Ciprian dropped their hands and spread his arms in an expansive gesture. "With the stars above and the stars below! What better place is there for music as heavenly as yours?"

Taylor smiled at Sarah. He cleared his throat. "I guess we can do that."

Ciprian perched atop the rail, his arms folded nonchalantly across his chest even as he sat with nothing between him and the rocky ground below except the gentle breeze. "Splendid," he said. "Now delight my ears with those angelic voices."

*****

Friday

"You are an optimist, Vornholt. It's what makes you a great advocate for disputed species. Don't misunderstand; I admire your passion in defending these creatures." Ciprian gestured to the patrons scattered about the coffee shop. "But surely even you realize that their stewardship of this planet has been irresponsible, even reckless."

Vornholt nodded. He was resigned to this outcome. This was a discussion that he and Ciprian had joined in many times before. But it never became easier in the repetition. Vornholt compiled a mental list of the arguments he could make for *homo sapiens*. Sophocles, the Taj Mahal, Shakespeare, Beethoven, Wagner, Van Gogh, the pyramids of Egypt. But a nagging voice in the back of Vornholt's mind, a voice that spoke with the haughty tenor and self-assured voice of Ciprian, also whispered to him: Buchenwald, Hiroshima, Mi Lai, Chernobyl, Nanking.

Vornholt shook his head, silencing the voice. He tried to conjure up in his visual frame the painted ceiling of the Sistine Chapel, but all he could manage was a replay of the images from his drive across town, the vehicles full of curious humans eagerly craning their necks in their vain hope to glimpse some atrocity. He tried to conjure the beautiful proportions of the Parthenon, and instead saw those same commuters driving away from the scene of the accident, disappointed in their frustrated bloodlust.

Vornholt's eyes scanned the restaurant. A child in the far corner began to scream. Its parents ignored it, too absorbed in their hand-held computers to be bothered. Vornholt watched the child's face contort in anguish. He took a deep breath and let it out slowly. "So much potential...so much wasted potential. This job can be so depressing."

"Such a beautiful planet...one deserving of a noble race to populate it. Remember that, Ciprian." He glanced over his shoulder at the screaming child. "And besides, once the Erasure Protocol takes hold, there will be no more of that damnable racket."

"Not with a bang, but a whimper," Vornholt sighed.

Ciprian's brow wrinkled. "Beg your pardon?"

"Nothing. Forget it. Just so much dust that will whirl away in the wind."

"Sometimes, Vornholt, I wonder if we're speaking the same language."

*****

Thursday

Taylor had hit upon the idea of combining Sarah's operatic range and delivery with pop music one day while he was sleepwalking through another day at the tire factory. He'd been walking aimlessly in the parking lot during his lunch break and had seen a lone flower—a pretty weed, really—growing from a crack in the asphalt. If the metaphor had manifested itself as slap to his face, it could hardly have been clearer. Taylor knew that he'd at last found their way out, their means of breaking into the spotlight. He was convinced that his own earthy, almost raspy delivery would contrast neatly with her angelic soprano. In a pop music format, the result would be almost exotic. People would be unable to resist.

"Amazing no one's done it already," he'd told Sarah. "Like that old commercial with the peanut butter and chocolate...some things just seem to go together."

And now it seemed that at long last their lucky break had arrived. Ciprian smiled broadly as Taylor and Sarah worked through an *a capella* rendering of "Islands in the Stream." Their voices wove in and out of one another, Taylor's assured baritone rumble the black asphalt through which the flower of Sarah's angelic voice sprang.

As the last notes of the song faded into the night, Ciprian hopped down from the rail and applauded. "Magnificent. Simply magnificent. That British fellow who called your gorgeous music kitsch couldn't have been more wrong."

Taylor gave Sarah a quick hug and turned back to Ciprian. "So we're going to work together? You think we can make a life out of this?"

"Yes, young man. I think you will lead quite an interesting life from here on out." Ciprian insinuated himself between the two young singers, linking his arms through theirs. "Now, let's slip inside and have a celebratory drink."

Taylor and Sarah didn't, as a rule, drink. They were both products of a Mormon upbringing, and although neither of them was particularly devout, they'd never really consumed alcohol outside of a couple New Year's Eve toasts and the odd sip of wine at a fancy dinner. But the look they shared as they followed their new benefactor into the house silently assured one another that—just this once—it would be okay.

The couch in Ciprian's living room was overstuffed and made of soft leather. Sarah and Taylor laughed as they sank into it, nearly spilling the fizzy drinks that Ciprian handed them. He sat next to them, and busied himself mixing his own drink from the tray on the coffee table.

"And now that we've toasted the next phase of your lives, I have a bit of a confession to make," Ciprian said. He polished off his drink in one gulp and began making another one. He poured liquor into the glass and began chipping away at a bucket of ice, bringing a black-handled icepick down in sharp stabs.

"Me too," Sarah giggled into her glass. "I think I'm drunk."

Ciprian smiled. "That's so very endearing."

"No, I'm dizzy too." Taylor put his drink down. He struggled to rise from the deep cushions, nearly making it to his feet before gravity pulled him back down. He gripped the armrest like it was the lap bar on a roller coaster.

Ciprian chipped more ice, reducing the large, irregular chunks to diamond-sparkly chips.

"Don't you have an ice machine?" Taylor's voice was thick, slurred.

"Oh, some things are just better done by hand, young man." Ciprian paused in his work, holding the icepick up for inspection. He touched the sharp tip with a finger.

Sarah went on giggling. "What's this confession? Is it a juicy secret?"

"My confession is this: I have little interest in the music of this planet," Ciprian said, his smile falling away. "You're to be a consolation prize of sorts. But trust me when I say that you don't know how lucky you are. It's so rare that anyone does."

Sarah's eyelids fluttered and she slumped against Taylor, her drink tumbling out of her hand. Taylor continued to struggle weakly, but his eyes were fighting to stay open. His voice was slurred when he spoke. "What…who…"

Ciprian gazed down at the icepick in his hands. He turned to Taylor, who was no longer moving. The two young singers slumped together on the couch, their faces resting cheek to cheek. Ciprian rose and stood above them.

"Even if this does hurt, trust me when I say you won't remember it," Ciprian assured them.

*****

Friday

The two ambassadors finished their meals without conversation. Vornholt had lost his appetite, and pushed the colorful pieces of fruit around his plate, occasionally chewing a bite in sullen silence. They paid their bills, leaving the customary gratuity for their server, despite Ciprian's grumbling that the young man hadn't really earned it. Vornholt fixed Ciprian with a venomous glare, and Ciprian reluctantly placed a few more notes of currency on the table.

"It's a matter of principle," Ciprian argued as the two colleagues walked out to the parking lot. "I have to stand by my philosophy."

"The species will be, for all intents and purposes, extinct within a year, and their currency a distant memory," Vornholt spat. "Why quibble over a few pieces of paper that are worth nothing to you?"

"Indeed, Vornholt," Ciprian answered, laughing. "But why should it matter to the server, either? If he is facing annihilation, what possible comfort can those few notes of currency bring?"

Vornholt shook his head. "Ciprian, perhaps you are right about our speaking in different languages. I sometimes feel that I will never understand you."

Ciprian laughed again and slapped his colleague on the back. "Don't be so downcast, Vornholt. Accompany me to my vehicle. I have something that just might bring you out of this dark mood."

"Somehow, I doubt that very much."

Vornholt followed Ciprian across the parking lot. Ciprian paused by a large flashy sports utility vehicle, a massive and ugly sculpture of glossy painted metals set atop immense tires. Vornholt sighed. How typical of Ciprian, to argue for the welfare of the planet and the stewardship of its resources while driving such a monstrosity.

"During our meal, you accused me of not fighting hard enough to make your case to the Great Authority," Ciprian intoned, resting an elbow casually on the vehicle. "Your accusation was far from the truth, Vornholt, and it hurts me that you have come to think of me thus. Believe it or not, I do value our friendship."

Vornholt looked at Ciprian suspiciously, and said nothing.

"In fact, I argued strenuously for *homo sapiens*," Ciprian continued. "Your argument, though flawed, was beautifully written. Really, you'd outdone yourself. I read it in its entirety when I presented your—our— case to the Great Authority. A compromise was reached."

Vornholt's pulse jumped. "But you said the verdict...Erasure Protocols already enacted..."

Ciprian held up a hand. "Phased extinction, yes. And that plan will proceed."

"I don't understand..."

Ciprian cleared his throat. "You are a music lover, yes?"

Vornholt nodded. "You know that I am."

"I remember when the Great Authority ruled in favor of the extinction of the Kilgarian Slime Mold Merauders during the last galactic campaign. Terrible creatures, the Kilgarians. They made a religion of rape and torture. As I remember it, even you could not make a strong case for their survival. And yet, you were quite taken with their music. Do you remember what you said to me after the Great Authority's ruling came down?" Ciprian asked.

"I remember saying that their music was so beautiful that it nearly atoned for all the atrocities they committed."

"These humans, you love their music as well?"

Vornholt nodded.

"A curious species, *homo sapiens*," Ciprian continued. "From even their early history, they showed great interest in their thought centers, their brains. During the early part of the last century, this interest led them to develop a surgical procedure in which connections to and from the prefrontal cortex were severed in order to change an uncooperative or combative human's behavior. Quite barbaric. Primitive, as is all their medicine. I'm told that in later years, the procedure could be carried out with a kitchen implement, the icepick."

Vornholt swallowed. He was suddenly very nervous. "The lobotomy. I've heard of this."

"If carried too far or done too recklessly, the procedure reduces the human to a babbling idiot," Ciprian explained. "But the speech centers remain active even as the thought processes are radically altered. And, strangely enough, so does the capacity for the recognition of tone, pitch, and rhythm. Do you understand?"

Vornholt shook his head, dazed.

Ciprian laughed. "They can be made to sing! Even when reduced to gibbering idiots, they can still carry on with that warbling you love so much."

Ciprian withdrew a ring of keys from his pocket and clicked a button on the remote entry device. He put a hand on the vehicle's rear door then paused and looked at Vornholt. "Remember, this can only take place on a small scale. But think of it as a gift from a friend."

Ciprian opened the vehicle's rear door. Vornholt peered inside and saw a pair of adult *homo sapiens*, a male and female. Both were dressed only in plain white bathrobes. Both also had a small bandage affixed in the corner of their left eye sockets. At the sight of Ciprian, the two humans began to babble and coo in their strange, high-pitched voices, their nonsense syllables rising and falling melodically in the cold night air.

Ciprian swept his hand expansively. "May I have the pleasure of introducing you to Sarah and Taylor Teagarden, unappreciated by their fellow humans, but I'm hoping, not so undervalued by a being with refined sensibilities such as yourself."

Vornholt stared.

"You are speechless?" Ciprian asked. He clapped his hands together. "I know. You cannot find a way to express your gratitude. Truth be told, I was somewhat uncertain as to what sort of creature you'd favor. As you well know, I'm no music lover. These two just looked so…now, what is the word…sincere."

The two humans continued to babble, randomly increasing or

decreasing the tone and cadence of their warbling. They sounded like giant songbirds struggling to find their mating calls. They clutched clumsily at one another, whether in panic or affection, Vornholt could not tell. Ciprian took from his pocket some pieces of chocolate candy, which he unwrapped and fed to the two wretches. They smiled and smacked their lips before continuing their vocalizations.

"The singing is primitive and strange now, but I'm confident they can be trained," Ciprian proclaimed. "And if the Great Authority deems that training a success, perhaps the species can be preserved as an exhibit in one of our zoos."

Ciprian slammed the door shut, but the singing continued from within, muffled now.

Vornholt stared at the rough asphalt surface of the parking lot. His face burned red with embarrassment, and he was glad for the absence of street lights. Ciprian put an arm around Vornholt's shoulder and drew him close.

"Maybe they can even survive as more than an exhibit," Ciprian continued. "Since we know that they can be domesticated through such a simple procedure...the possibilities for the survival of the species—in a controlled environment, of course--seem good. This is a matched pair, suitable for breeding. Both of them seem healthy enough and are of an age for reproduction. After all, they are cute in their own ugly sort of way, and in time, perhaps others of our race will come around to your point of view." He squeezed Vornholt's shoulder. "I must admit, those little creatures can be quite entertaining. And amazingly resilient. They still sing beautifully."

WHAT WE FOUND
ANDREW NIENABER

Andrew Nienaber has been an ice cream truck driver, a bartender, a teacher, a writer, a blogger, a director of operas and an all-around theater professional. He is one of the founders of FatalDownflaw.com and his short-lived blog about his experiences selling ice cream, The Ill Humor Man, *drew hundreds of hits a day. His first novel,* Truly Deeply Disturbed, *is said to make Dexter seem like Mr. Rogers.*

I've had a lot of time barricaded in this library to review the last thousand years or so of theory and speculation--be it scientific or fictitious--and despite the direness of my circumstances it always manages to give me a chuckle thinking about how wrong, how very wrong we as a species were. There were those who said the end of humanity would come at the hand of a god, punishing the wicked and bringing the righteous home to paradise. There were those who theorized that our destruction would come from distant worlds, a multitude of warlike or misunderstanding beings blazing through our little blue planet in conquest or to eradicate a cosmic nuisance, or completely by accident. For a long time in the twentieth century, people thought we would be the agents of our own demise with overpowered weaponry capable of destroying the planet hundreds of times over in the hands of twitchy and ideologically opposed nations. But when you know the reality of the end of mankind, all of these theories seem as patently absurd as believing the vague ramblings of a 16th-century prognosticator, or that an ancient Meso-American culture could predict the apocalypse because of a calendar change.

I am recording this barricaded in the Bibliothèque Nationale de France in Paris. As the world went mad around me I found the antidote, or at least a way to treat the symptoms, and sequestered myself away from the maelstrom that was the rest of my species. I'm recording these thoughts in hopes that someone else out there might someday read them, as I have been reading the thoughts of ages past. I am convinced by the relative silence outside the windows that Earth has succumbed fully to the Plague we unleashed, but without communication to the outlying colonies in other systems I can't be sure if I am the last living human or not. I know the news went out across the entire spread of our fledgling empire, but I still hold out hope that maybe living on a different planet would have insulated some from the worst of what happened here on the home world. Perhaps one day a colony will send a team back to investigate and find my record of the death of humanity here; perhaps they will learn from us. Or perhaps they too will become infected.

I am a historian by trade, not a scientist, so the details are at best a bit fuzzy to me, but I think the beginning of our problems was the Theory of Everything. It took centuries to finally reconcile Einstein's theory of relativity with quantum mechanics, but three hundred years ago a team from Geneva, working in the world's most advanced physics lab, finally acquired experimental proof of unification. That led to a golden age of exponentially blooming discovery and technological advancement. By that time we had already terraformed most of the moon and large portions of Mars, but unification allowed us to finally harness physics as a toolbox rather than a mystery grab-bag. A hundred years ago we mastered faster-than-light travel via wormhole, and began sending probes to the farthest reaches of the universe. It was a giddy time, I understand; a time when it seemed that all of our questions about the cosmos would be answered. Would we find other sentient life out there? Would we find proof of God, or of monsters unimagined? Humanity was collectively glued to their seats, waiting for the next discovery.

For a while, every new day brought something exciting--a planet millions of light-years away that was made entirely of quartz and cast rainbows on the other bodies in its solar system, a cluster of twenty enormous and dying stars that were set to implode together and create the biggest known black hole in the universe, entire nebulae that were literally on fire. We wondered at the variety and glory of the universe.

The problem with a Theory of Everything, of course, is that it allows you to mathematically work out the very nature of existence. Within the first seventy-five years, scientists had proven the entire history of the universe back to the Big Bang and beyond. We finally understood the cyclical nature of creation and destruction and the forces that controlled it all. Religion was the first casualty of understanding. When you have irrefutable proof of the mechanics of the universe, faith in a deity becomes irrelevant. Granted, religious practice had already been in decline for nearly a millennium by the time the Theory was made public, but the erosion of faith accelerated each passing day from then out. There were pockets of zealots of each of the world's great religions that held on as long as they could, became even more radicalized, and even banded together to wage a sort of crusade on the scientific community, but it was the death throes of an antiquated way of life. The zealots were the first to succumb to the Plague.

At first we didn't have a clue as to what was happening. Recent cults and millennia-old faiths alike started losing their minds. Because the world was so secularized it was treated as an oddity when the zealots began wantonly rutting and tearing each other apart in their compounds. The footage was horrific: peacekeepers would be called in by a few mutilated survivors to find piles of carrion, shredded by human fingers and partially eaten. Bodies intertwined on the ground, their mouths full of each other's skin. The living were invariably ravening and violent by the time authorities reached the scene and attacked anyone who got near them. Most were killed by the police, usually after several more casualties.

One man--and we're getting into my lifetime now-- was taken into custody after a massacre at a Mormon enclave in Salt Lake City and brought to a hospital in Denver for study. He was kept sedated most of the time, and was unable to form a coherent thought. He continually babbled about the void, the "great empty" as he called it. This sort of behavior was casually dismissed as the rambling of a diseased mind, polluted by belief in a blatantly false mythology that had twisted his sense of reality to the point where he could not accept life outside of his safe theology. The masses shook their heads sadly and spoke in hushed tones around water coolers and on social media about the dangers of succumbing to a way of life so divorced from fact.

It was around this time that the Middle East exploded. The world's few remaining theocracies were all in the region, and masses of people were turning on each other daily. The borders between Islamic nations were initially fortified and no man's lands created to attempt to localize the outbreaks, but within a few years most of the cradle of civilization was in tatters. Footage from camera drones showed enormous masses of people in the streets, many in traditional robes and headgear, killing each other with utter abandon, their mouths smeared with blood and their fingers torn from scratching their way out of the locked and barred buildings that the governments used to isolate the afflicted. Piles of bodies writhing as the half-living tore at each other with tooth and finger. Daily we in the West watched as bearded imams and women in *hajabs* rent the flesh from each other and devoured it raw, bleeding and dead-eyed. Most of the nation of Israel was evacuated as a precaution, but it quickly became apparent that the infected were no longer interested in pursuing ancient grudges and hatreds. In fact, they seemed to have no agenda at all beyond their atrocities. And in what little sound we had from these riots, the same words echoed over and over: "the empty", "the void", "the nothing".

Pockets of Catholicism in central Italy and South America soon followed suit. Every place in the world where people still put a deity in charge of their lives fell into bedlam. During this entire time of upheaval, while the secular world watched and waited for the faithful to either come to their senses or kill themselves out, hundreds of probes were still being sent out every week, scouring the far reaches of the cosmos to complete our knowledge, to fill in the blank spots in our map of the universe. And every day more and more information came streaming back to Earth, more and more marvels, but with less and less impact. Sights that would have been glorious and unimaginable just a few generations earlier were becoming commonplace. Humanity as a species was rapidly losing its sense of wonder.

By the time of my birth--I am sixty-four years old, and sincerely hope I do not live to see sixty-five-- we had built colonies on planets hundreds of light-years away, connected to the hub of Earth by subatomic communications, but largely autonomous. They were mining colonies for the most part, communities built around extracting minerals from distant worlds that were vanishing at home. The initiative to mine other planets was at first driven by our desperate need for oil. Before it all fell apart, literally the final few drops of petroleum were wrung from the bowels of the planet, and innovation in alternative fuels had continually lagged behind other, seemingly more important matters. But no matter where we looked, we couldn't find oil off-planet. For oil to form, there needs to have been organic life, something which we never found.

As the probes illuminated the dark corners of the universe, scientists were also working feverishly back on Earth, plugging different variables into the Theory and making daily discoveries about the nature of the cosmos. I remember vividly the day they released the finding that ruined everything. It was three days after my fifty-eighth birthday and, the anniversary itself having fallen on a Wednesday, I waited until Friday night to celebrate. I watched Saturday morning, still hung over and in my pajamas, as a team of physicists, astronomers, biologists and mathematicians sat somberly at a long table with a podium in the center of it and one by one explained to the waiting, breathless world that we were alone.

Soon, the data coming from the probes offered corroborating proof-- there was no life to be found anywhere in the universe other than our little, seemingly insignificant rock. For millennia mankind had looked to the stars and felt assured that there was something else waiting out there to greet us, to explain to us the mysteries of life, to show us the meaning in our existence, but there was nothing out there but rocks and gas clouds and endlessly spinning chunks of inorganic matter orbiting each other mindlessly. No Olympians, no bearded puppet master, no benevolent aliens awaited us out in the universe. Mankind was completely, utterly alone. Life was a fluke, a meaningless accident that had never been repeated. That is when the Plague began to spread like wildfire.

We watched in terror as probes were sent further and further from home. The breaking point came from a Singaporean space drone called TS942. It showed only a profound, complete blackness. No stars or planets. Nothing. It had reached the edge of the universe, and all that was out there was emptiness.

Void.

It was those whom most at the time considered ignorant or small-minded who succumbed first, people whose life experience was generally little more than a day of work followed by an evening in front of the feeds, whose brains were simply not wired to accommodate ideas on a cosmic scale; the ones who were the least prepared to deal with the truth. Those in every society who spent little time in original thought began to exhibit the symptoms of the Plague, turning on each other and becoming bestial and violent, rending their families' and neighbors' bodies. Neighborhoods that were once peaceful enclaves of like-minded people turned into charnel pits. Humans prowled about like animals, feeding. The epidemic was so wide-spread that there was nothing that we as a species could do about it. Those who were rich or powerful enough retreated into gated communities or high-security compounds. The rest of us tried to isolate ourselves and our loved ones from any other human contact. Within a year society had utterly fallen apart. With the farms failing produce food those without the wherewithal to stockpile were forced to subsist on whatever scraps and trash we could find from a decaying civilization. And every day the probes sent us back more blackness. Every day more and more people fell victim to the Plague.

When the first wave hit, while long-distance travel was still possible, I took my family out of Princeton, New Jersey--where I had been a professor at the University--and moved them to a small farm my parents had owned in the French countryside. I thought I could keep them safe if we were secluded and able to grow our own food. I shut down all of the info feeds into the farmhouse the day we moved in and thought I had inoculated us. But the Plague is not like a typical illness, borne by bacteria or viruses. The Plague is a sickness of ideas, and once an idea is planted it is impossible to kill. I have isolated myself here in the Bibliothèque to escape modern thought, to insulate myself. It has certainly lengthened my days, but no matter how hard I try to bury it, I cannot unknow the things I know. Even now I feel the void creeping up on me. I push the thought of it away, bury it in books and the dark, murky past, but at night when I close my eyes I still see that horrible emptiness at the end of everything. It gnaws on my sanity, more voracious every hour, and I fear I too will soon succumb.

My family and I--we numbered twelve with the grandchildren--lived adequately for a few months. We kept away from our neighbors in part by choice and in part due to the language barrier; none of us spoke more than halting French and the locals had very little English. To be honest, by that point everyone was extremely suspicious of everyone else so keeping isolated was the norm. We grew vegetables in the garden and tended the few animals we could acquire before closing ourselves off. Space was tight in the small farmhouse, but we were relatively happy. I spent my days on the farm and my evenings teaching the kids what I knew, mostly history. At first it seemed to stave off the plague, but every so often I would walk outside at night and see one of my kin staring up at the stars with a dead, vacant look in their eyes. I would hurry them in as quickly as possible, but I knew time was short.

It was early January, the heart of a cold, lonely winter, when my son Jason first exhibited symptoms. I woke at five as was my custom and went out to feed the goats, only to find him sitting on the frozen ground with his head in his hands. When I asked him if he was alright he looked up at me, his features slack, and told me the ground beneath his feet was crumbling. That he kept thinking about nothing. Terrified, I brought him out to the horse barn that we had abandoned for lack of need and locked him in with a jug of water and a plate of food. I went back into the house to confer with my wife, trying to avoid the others at all costs until we decided how to deal with this new crisis. By that afternoon it was impossible to hide it from the rest of the family, as Jason's wife and son were beginning to question my excuse that he had decided to try his hand at hunting. By nightfall he was pounding on the doors of the barn and howling in a wholly inhuman way. When I went out to bring him his dinner I found him laying on a moldering bale of hay, his fingers bleeding and shredded almost to the bone from trying to scratch his way out.

The next day two grandchildren went. Knowing I had to keep each of them isolated from the others I put Lori in the hayloft and locked little five-year-old Casey in with the family's solitary pig, figuring he was too small to do any real harm. When I went out to check on them at midday, I found Lori on the ground unmoving. She had flung herself so hard against the clapboard wall of the second-story loft that she'd crashed right through it, hurling herself down onto a pile of neglected threshing machinery. Her spine was broken in such a way that the lower half of her body bent at a nearly ninety-degree angle to her torso, but her arms were still gently swaying, trying to grasp at something she couldn't see, unaware of the situation the rest of her was in. When I went to check on

Casey he was in a corner of the pig pen with his face buried in the eviscerated stomach of our sow, his arms wrapped around her body almost lovingly. One of them had been broken in the struggle and a jagged peak of bone showed through the skin, but he had won out and the pig's innards were piled on the ground, steaming in the frigid air. I fled.

Over the protestations of my entire family, I went into the basement and retrieved the shotgun that I had hoped to never have to use. Putting Lori out of her misery was the easiest, as there was nothing left of her to salvage, neither body nor mind. I wept as I entered the pig pen to deal with Casey, unsure if I would be able to do what I had to, but all agency was taken from me when the boy ran at me screaming, ravenous and furious, his face and hands smeared with the blood of our only food pig, his ruined limb dangling useless. Without a thought I raised the gun and ended the struggle in a clap of thunder and a cloud of sulfur smoke. Cold, numb and despairing I went to the horse barn and found that Jason had spent the night eating the only meat he had available--his own leg. When he saw me he tried to stand and rush me as his son had, but with little more than bone below his knees he fell immediately to the ground. I knelt by his head, just out of arm's reach, and cried. My boy, whom I had raised and taught and been proud of and stern to, at whose wedding I had danced and whose hand I had held as his own first son was born. He had been reduced to nothing more than a screaming, gibbering lunatic, poisoned by the void and lost to the Plague. I put the gun to his temple, closed my eyes and pulled the trigger.

Over the next two days I lost my family one by one. I did everything I could to quarantine them, keep them apart from the healthy and from each other, but I was running out of places to put them and solitary confinement inevitably only led to self-mutilation. The morning I awoke to find my wife Ella rocking in a corner of the bedroom repeating "empty, empty" I very nearly lost all hope. I knew I didn't have the heart to kill her, so I gathered my eldest daughter Candace, the only one left with her mind intact, and we fled.

It took us two weeks to reach Paris. I don't know why I thought the urban heart of France would be the best place for us, but as the months of isolation hadn't helped I took a gamble. The city was a wasteland, rotting fragments of corpses strewn in the streets and alleys like confetti after a parade. We encountered a few survivors, but none that had not already fallen victim to the Plague. We dodged into and out of buildings to avoid them, locking ourselves in closets to sleep at night and scrounging whatever little canned food was left in the once thriving metropolis. We tried our best not to think about what was happening back at the farmhouse we'd abandoned to our family's mania. As Candace wept herself to sleep I would tell her stories of the dark ages and the fragments of European history that are still lost to us, anything to add a little mystery to our lives and distract us from that dark certainty that would be our undoing.

We stumbled upon the Bibliothèque quite by accident. I'd been to Paris once in my thirties, but had no real recollection of the city. When I saw the library I knew that it was our last hope, a repository of history and culture. We closed ourselves inside and began to read. There was a fair-sized collection of English-language history books that I devoured immediately, and Candace decided to try to teach herself French. Every few days we would sneak out to forage for food then return to our sanctuary.

But the seeds of the void were already in us, like a dormant virus, and it was only a matter of time before we were taken. On March 23rd I found Candace in the astronomy section throwing books around and pushing shelves over, screaming that it was all lies. I ran to her and wrapped my arms around her, begging through mucous and tears for her to come back to me. She turned in my arms and stared into my face, her eyes sad and her spirit broken, with the combating looks of hunger and despair clouding her features. She grabbed me then, tearing at my clothes. I pushed her off of me with all of my strength and she stumbled for a second, her sad eyes going blank. Backing away, I tripped over a pile of texts she had flung to the ground and fell on my back. I am no frail old man, but I am an academic and not as sturdy as I once was. As I struggled to get up I saw the emptiness in Candace's eyes turn to rage, then to bloodlust. She pounced on me and straddled my pelvis, pinning me to the floor. I flung an arm up to push her off, but she got her teeth sunk into the flesh my forearm. As blinding pain shot up my entire left side I struggled to detach her without hurting her, but to no avail. I hit her with whatever was at hand – books, bookends, her recently discarded shoe--but it was not enough. I scrambled desperately for something a little more effective, and found a bracket from a bookshelf Candace had knocked over. One wide end, one narrow. Seeing no other option, I gouged at her eyes with it. My arm was unsteady and my aim a bit wild, but after a few hits that tore the thin flesh on her forehead I got her attention. When she raised her face from her meal, her teeth dripping with my blood and scraps of skin, I put my entire weight behind one last strike. The small end of the bracket entered through her cornea like an arrow into a bull's-eye and I felt a sickening pressure as it punctured her eyeball and pushed into her brain. My daughter, my only surviving family, slumped forward onto my chest without further sound. I rolled her off and leapt to my feet, senseless. With great effort I pushed over the shelves to either side of her, burying her in case she should happen to still be alive. Weak, nauseous and bleeding I ran. I have never returned to that section of the Bibliothèque.

I have bandaged my arm and it is largely healed, but reliving the past has taken a serious toll on me. I can feel the Plague overcoming me. I know what it is to have touched the void, to have looked out into the vast, empty universe and know the truth--that more than any living being in the fourteen billion year history of our cosmos I am alone, surrounded by nothing but emptiness and the horrid finality of death. I want out of this skin, out of this uncaring existence. I want to tear and destroy and devour, to become an animal. Because the animals don't know. The animals haven't seen the end of the universe.

This recording of mine is meant as a warning. Our ignorance is a lifeboat. The human mind was never meant to know everything. Once we understood the universe in total, all that was left was the void; the emptiness seeped into our sanity like water from a leaking roof, infecting it and turning it toxic. We should have reveled in mystery instead of despising it as weakness. If you're here, in this library in this desiccated city on this blood-drenched planet then you know what our hunger for information has wrought. Since the dawn of sentience mankind told tales about forbidden knowledge, that we would destroy ourselves by discovering something we shouldn't know. But they were wrong. What destroyed us was discovering that there was nothing we couldn't know.

ACKNOWLEDGEMENTS

First and foremost, I need to thank (in no particular order) Gary, Tim, Larry, Michael, Jeyn, and Harlan for trusting Post Mortem Press with their work. But without question, the remaining authors are the heart and soul of this book. It was created with your sweat and nightmares.

This book would not be possible without the efforts of Paul Anderson. He was instrumental in obtaining permission to reprint the Harlan Ellison™ story and for providing a level of enthusiasm I can not sustain, or maybe even attain.

Finally, I need to acknowledge the extreme patience Stephanie Beebe has shown, not just through this book, but the 50 or so others that came before it. I owe it all to you.

Thank you all.

Made in the USA
Lexington, KY
26 June 2013